Uncle Tom's Clinic

Or The Liberated Choice

Jay Mikes

Jay Mikes

Writers Club Press
San Jose New York Lincoln Shanghai

Uncle Tom's Clinic
Or The Liberated Choice

All Rights Reserved © 2000 by Jay Mikes

No part of this book may be reproduced or transmitted in any form or by any means, graphic, electronic, or mechanical, including photocopying, recording, taping, or by any information storage or retrieval system, without the permission in writing from the publisher.

Writers Club Press
an imprint of iUniverse.com, Inc.

For information address:
iUniverse.com, Inc.
5220 S 16th, Ste. 200
Lincoln, NE 68512
www.iuniverse.com

Scripture taken from the HOLY BIBLE, NEW INTERNATIONAL VERSION. Copyright © 1973, 1978, 1984 International Bible Society. Used by permission of Zondervan Bible Publishers.

ISBN:0-595-09959-9

Printed in the United States of America

*To Emily and Joshua, the joy of my life;
and to their birthmothers, Jeanne Marie and Carla,
who chose life, the truly liberated choice;
and to my wife, Karen, whom I love,
who is blessed with a mother's heart.*

Preface

The title of this story is obviously a play on the epic novel, *Uncle Tom's Cabin*, by Harriet Beecher Stowe. Although the author is the first to admit that he lacks the genius of the woman who challenged the nation to take a hard look at itself and the issue of slavery, he makes no apologies for using the fame of that momentous catalyst of change in creating this fictional account. Indeed, if she were alive today, Mrs. Stowe may well have written this book, too, for she was a woman who lived in a time of great suffering and evil and was committed to doing her part to make this a better world. Hence, the author feels a smile of approval shining down from heaven.

It is difficult for us to imagine in this day and age that such an abhorrent evil as the enslavement of an entire race could ever have been possible in a nation such as ours. Yet, it happened. Man is a sinner; self-interest is inherent. Greed is one manifestation of man's nature. This being true, it is possible to understand how a large region of the country not only employed the system of slavery as a means to economic prosperity, but it did so without a disturbed conscience. In fact, politicians and clergy alike improvised scores of rationalizations to defend slavery. Incredible as it seems, some tried to draw support for slavery out of the Bible! And just as incredible, so many good people did nothing to abolish it; that is, until *Uncle Tom's Cabin* created such a moral embarrassment for its generation of Americans, both nationally and internationally, that the issue could no longer be swept under the rug. Slavery had to be addressed, ultimately through civil war.

Abortion, like slavery, is evil. It is the triumph of selfishness and self-deceit over the sanctity of human life. One day this fact will be as clear to Americans as we now unanimously admit that slavery was unjustifiable in its day. The parallels between these two evils are striking, and, to men and women of conscience, haunting.

The reason abortion has become acceptable in our society is because individuals and factions have turned this moral issue into a political issue. Put simply, the pro-abortion faction has obfuscated the morality of abortion with clever rhetoric and rationalization. The real issue, pro-abortionists say, is not the sanctity of human life, but the right of a woman to control what happens within her own body. According to pro-abortionists, there is no conflict between the child's right to life and the woman's choice to end the child's life because the fetus is less than human and thus has no rights. In addition, pro-abortionists claim that a woman not only has a "right to terminate" the child's life, but she also has a right to privacy about the matter. Hence, abortion is not about right and wrong; the issue is power.

Historically, a similar argument was made in support of slavery before the Civil War. Was it right for one man to own another? As today, the moral question was turned into a political issue. The issue, Southerners said, was not about the morality of slavery; it was about "States' rights." They sidestepped the ethical aspect of slavery by constantly pointing to the "right" of a state to determine what happens within its own jurisdiction. When the issue of slavery arose in the developing western territories, Stephen Douglas, the notorious political rival of Abraham Lincoln, proposed an insidious twist to the concept of States' rights. Douglas insisted that the matter of slavery be determined by "popular sovereignty." In other words, Douglas wanted the people in a territory to **choose** whether or not they would have slaves. Using contemporary rhetoric, Senator Douglas was "pro-choice" on the issue of slavery. Finally, let us not forget that Southerners also made the argument that Africans were less than human; hence, they did not have any rights. Blacks were property, not people. In the final analysis then, slavery was not about right and wrong. The issue was power.

It is not surprising then that today's pro-life movement is strikingly similar to the abolitionist movement of last century. The present battle against abortion is being led primarily by national and state pro-life organizations, local pro-life crisis pregnancy counseling centers, pro-life newspapers, and pro-life activists, most of whom are Christians. These organizations and individuals are clearly the New England Anti-Slavery Society, Underground Railroad, *Liberator*, and William Lloyd Garrisons of today. Unfortunately, however, the pro-life crusade today also has a radical element, albeit a minuscule minority. These extremists and terrorists that commit violence for the sake of righteousness, do so as modern day John Browns. Tragically, they only complicate the situation by perpetrating their own evils under the belief that the end justifies the means. They neither understand the Gospel nor realize how counterproductive they are by doing God's work through Satan's methods.

On the one hand, it was a momentous misfortune that the issue of slavery could only be resolved by civil war. On the other hand, the war was such that the enemy could be easily targeted and force brought to bear to put an end to the enslavement of Africans. Today, unfortunately, the battle is not so simple as North versus South. The distinctions that separate pro-life and pro-abortion camps are not geographical, or based on gender, race, socioeconomic status, or religious or political affiliation. The difference between camps is solely in the heart and conscience of every American. Thus, the only real hope for the unborn is to change the hearts of men and women. We were once a nation that believed in "life, liberty, and the pursuit of happiness." Now, as evidenced by our politics, news media, and entertainment industry, we cherish only liberty and the pursuit of happiness. Sadly, these too may only be euphemisms for licentiousness and hedonism. What happened to the sanctity and value of life?

And last, beyond the political, philosophical, moral, and scientific debates surrounding abortion, there is God's view on the matter, which comes out very clearly as He speaks to us through His word. In the Old Testament, in Psalm 106:37-40, Leviticus 18:21, and in numerous places in Ezekiel (16:20, 16:36, 20:25, 20:31, 22:3, 23:37) and Jeremiah (7:31,

19:3-6, 32:35), God is unequivocal when He says that He abhors child sacrifice and will bring judgment upon the perpetrators.

To understand these passages of scripture requires a little background on the pagan worship of Baal, or Molech, the fertility god. In Phoenicia and Carthage, and later in Canaan, followers of this false god offered living children, their first-born sons or daughters, in hope of greater fertility of soil and womb. The manner of this sacrifice was abhorrent, though not any more so than our shredding of fetuses today. In ancient practice, infant children were placed in the lap of a statue representing Molech. In the lap of this false god, fires burned ferociously and consumed the flesh of newborns whose cries of pain were drowned out by the blaring of trumpets and the piping of flutes. The question is what kind of civilization could allow such a thing to happen? And what kind of parents could do such a thing to their own flesh and blood? The thought of such a detestable practice is so grotesque it is almost impossible to imagine; that is, until we remind ourselves of what is happening in our own nation today. Four thousand times a day, every twenty seconds, an equally gruesome sacrifice is allowed to happen. What "enlightenment" of heart, mind, and soul would lead anyone to think that abortion, the poisoning and/or mutilating of life in the womb, is any different than the live burning of an infant on a pagan altar? The times may have changed and the methods may have changed, but the sin is the same.

In Jeremiah 32:35 the Lord declares:

> "They built high places for Baal in the Valley of Ben Hinnon to sacrifice their sons and daughters to Molech, though I never commanded, nor did it enter my mind, that they should do such a detestable thing and so make Judah sin."

Meanwhile, Psalm 106:37-40 makes it absolutely clear what God thinks of infanticide and abortion and those who allow it to happen. He who has an ear let him hear:

> "They sacrificed their sons
> and their daughters to demons.
> They shed innocent blood,
> the blood of their sons and daughters,
> whom they sacrificed to the idols of Canaan,
> and the land was desecrated by their blood.
> They defiled themselves by what they did;
> by their deeds they prostituted themselves.
> Therefore the Lord was angry with his people
> and abhorred his inheritance."

And so, having said all this, it is the prayer of this author that the reader's moral vision concerning abortion is brought back into focus by the ensuing sketches. Their purpose is simply to awaken sympathy and compassion, not only for the unborn and the women who are confronted with an unwanted pregnancy, but also for those couples who so dearly want to have children but cannot.

The scenes of this story hope to show that there is an alternative to abortion. It is a choice founded on love and self-sacrifice, not power and self-interest. It is the narrow road less traveled. It is adoption.

Those readers who hope for the day when righteousness will prevail may find comfort in the words that close the preface of *Uncle Tom's Cabin*:

> "For, while politicians contend, and men are swerved this way
> and that by conflicting tides of interest and passion, the great
> cause of human liberty is in the hands of one, of whom it is said:
>
> "He shall not fail nor be discouraged
> Till He have set judgment in the earth."
> "He shall deliver the needy when he crieth,
> The poor, and him that hath no helper."
> "He shall redeem their soul from deceit and violence
> And precious shall their blood be in His sight."

Contents

Preface v

Chapter 1. A Victim of the Lust for Power 1

Chapter 2. It's Not Fair! 11

Chapter 3. Test Results 17

Chapter 4. Kara's Confession 29

Chapter 5. Faith Confides in Hope 37

Chapter 6. The Parable of the Poker Game 43

Chapter 7. A Mother's Heart 53

Chapter 8. A Proper Burial 59

Chapter 9. A Morning at the Clinic 69

Chapter 10. Protest 81

Chapter 11. Discussions Over Dinner 93

Chapter 12. Faith's Desire 105

Chapter 13. Conspirators..113

Chapter 14. The Writing on the Wall.......................................121

Chapter 15. An Open Window 131

Chapter 16. Vivian's Stand 137

Chapter 17. The Innocent Condemned 145

Chapter 18. The Truth Comes Out 155

Chapter 19. Faith's Choice...173

Chapter 20. Gray Skies 187

Chapter 21. The Wisdom of Solomon..201

Chapter 22. An Emotional Roller Coaster 211

Chapter 23. Moonlight in the Darkness 225

Chapter 24. A Match Made in Heaven 241

Chapter 25. Election Day!..255

Chapter 26. Haman's Gallows 263

Chapter 27. Esther's Choice 279

Chapter 28. The Hope of Heaven 289

Chapter 29. Vengeance! *299*

Chapter 30. True Tests of Faith *307*

Chapter 31. Faith's Gift *323*

Chapter 32. Results *339*

Chapter 33. The Liberated *349*

A Victim of the Lust for Power

Faith Brandon staggered into the lobby of the Gulfshore Condominiums. The security guard's eyes followed the slender figure as she slipped past his desk toward the elevator. He could not help but notice her disheveled hair, teary eyes, and mascara-stained cheeks.

"Are you all right, Miss?" he asked.

Faith ignored him, keeping her shocked gaze affixed to the floor.

"Pardon me, child, but you look like you've just seen some trouble," the chunky black man said insistently. "Is there anything I can do?"

Faith passed silently into the elevator and pushed the button for the eighth floor. The warm, humid, late March breeze did little to prevent the chill running up and down her body. Her damp, wrinkled T-shirt and torn, mud-stained shorts offered less. She felt the nakedness of guilt and shame.

When the door opened at the eighth floor, two gray-haired women were waiting in the hallway. Faith stepped quickly from the elevator avoiding their eyes.

One of the ladies said to the other, "I wonder what happened to her? She looks awful!"

"I wonder where her friend is?" the other replied.

Faint and weak, Faith focused her eyes on the door at the end of the long, narrow hallway. She was consumed by an overwhelming sense of urgency to be alone, hidden from the world. Halfway down the corridor

1

she swooned but steadied herself by reaching out to the walls on the right. Staggering hand over hand, Faith slowly made her way down the passage. When she finally reached the apartment, she fumbled in her purse.

"Where are they?" she shouted inwardly. At last she heard the rattle of keys and felt their jagged edges on her fingertips. Her right hand quivered as she tried to put the key into the lock.

"Oh!" she whined as she failed to find the keyhole. Finally, she steadied her right hand with her left and inserted the key. The key refused to turn. Faith pounded on the door in frustration.

"Please, God," she cried and then collapsed leaning against the door. She slid into a pile on the hallway floor and sobbed.

•••

The evening began innocently enough. Faith and her best friend, Hope Stuart, met an attractive young man at the pool earlier in the afternoon. Hope was invited to a party that evening and Faith was asked to join them. Before getting ready for the party, Faith made her obligatory call home "just to check in."

Hope's mother, Vivian, usually chaperoned the two girls on their annual trip to Florida over spring break. But this year, in the midst of a tight race, her first venture into politics, Vivian could not take time off to be with the girls. She was back home in the Midwest campaigning in the primary election for the spot on the Democratic ticket in the race for Congress. After much pleading on the girls' part, Hope's mother and Faith's parents allowed the girls to take the trip by themselves.

"Hope, I'm not sure about this party," Faith said as the two girls were in the bathroom getting ready for the affair.

"Why?"

"I don't know."

"You worry too much! Besides, the guy at the pool was really cute!"

"I know. But I just don't feel comfortable about it," Faith said.

Just then the phone rang. Hope answered.

"Hi, Hope. Is Faith there?"

"Just a minute," Hope said. "It's for you," she said as she handed the phone to Faith. "It's Chris."

Chris had been Faith's boyfriend for almost a year.

"Hi, Chris!" Faith said.

"Hi. Have you had enough sun? Are you ready to come home?"

"I never get enough sun. But I'm ready to come home. I miss you!"

"I miss you, too."

There was a short silence. Then Chris asked, "What are you doing tonight? Any big plans your last night away from home?"

"Nothing big. We're invited to a party. We're going to check it out."

"Don't get too wild!" Chris said in mocking admonition.

"You never know. I just may have the time of my life!"

"Without me? That will be the day!" he said with a laugh.

"Well, I guess you'll never know since you're there and I'm here."

"I guess not," he said. "I'll see you tomorrow at the airport."

"Okay. I love you."

"I love you, too."

Faith hung up the phone in the kitchen and returned to the bathroom.

"That was short," Hope said.

"Yeah. He's not real big on talking on the phone."

Hope was standing next to Faith in front of the bathroom mirror, first holding a red halter top to her chest and then a black tank top. She continued alternating between the two, holding up one and then the other.

"Which top looks sexier?" Hope asked.

"Why? Are you advertising?"

"Maybe," Hope said smiling.

Hope was a replica of her mother. She was an attractive, short, petite blonde, with deep blue eyes, a narrow nose, and high cheeks. Her attitudes were a reflection of Vivian as well and created in Faith reason for concern.

"You really ought to be more careful about sex, Hope."

"Oh, don't be silly," Hope said. "There's nothing wrong with sex if you're careful. I always make the guy wear a condom."

"But you know they don't always work," Faith said. "Aren't you worried about AIDS or getting pregnant?"

"You worry too much, Faith. You've got to learn to live a little. Loosen up!"

"I can't," Faith replied. "My parents would kill me if they found out I was having sex."

"So who's going to tell them?"

"No one. But I would still feel guilty," she said, blushing.

Hope looked at her friend in the mirror and shook her head slightly as if with compassion. She said, "I like your parents, Faith, but I think they're too old-fashioned. I'm glad my mother treats me like an adult. She knows I'm going to experiment. She just tells me to be careful."

"I wish I could be like that."

"Well, tonight's your chance," Hope said.

"Yeah, right! I can't do that!"

"Why not?"

"Well, because of Chris and because of my parents."

"Oh, come on! For tonight, just let your instincts be your guide."

"That will be the day!" Faith said. "Ever since I can remember my father has said to me, 'Guilt is everything. If there's something you're doing that doesn't seem right then you're better off not doing it.'"

"Nobody can live like that. Not nowadays."

"You're telling me?" Faith said as she began brushing her long brown hair. "I know you don't believe in God, but I do. And I really admire my parents and their values. But there are times when I feel like I'm missing out on life. It's hard always trying to do what's right!"

Faith brushed a few more strokes and then confessed, "Sometimes I wish I could do something as innocent as drink a beer and not have to feel guilty about it."

"Tonight's your chance," Hope said as she left the bathroom.

Faith put down her brush. She stared at herself in the mirror and said, "Maybe she's right."

The girls arrived at the party in progress just as the sun was setting over the gulf.

"You made it!" said the young man with the blue eyes and cute smile who charmed Hope earlier in the day and invited the girls to the party.

"Of course, we did!" Hope said with a smile. Then she excused herself and walked over to the keg at the far end of the long balcony overlooking the water. She drew two beers and returned to the others.

Faith blushed as Hope handed her a beer. She sampled it and said quietly to Hope, "This stuff is terrible!"

"It'll get better after you have a few."

"I'd rather have a Diet Coke."

A young black man, known only to the others as "Jimmy," soon joined the discussion on the balcony. No one really knew who he was or where he was from, but someone had remarked that they thought he played football at some university in the South. In any case, he was an imposing physical presence, tall and solid, with most of his might on display. Tight sweat shorts and a skimpy T-shirt revealed a thin waist and a hairy, barrel chest and massive pectorals. Large veins protruded from his huge biceps and forearms. His enormous thighs tapered down to finely sculpted calves and suggested a powerful sprinter. He was a figure lifted from a muscle magazine.

His personality exhibited muscle and strength as well. He was glib, quick-witted, and had a stinging sense of humor. Nearly everyone in the group found themselves at some point to be the recipient of a playful invective. Although uncomfortable with his crass humor, Faith was impressed with the way Jimmy held court. Not only did he hold his audience spellbound with tale after humorous tale of spring break mischief, but the enormity of his laugh conveyed the degree of approbation to be appropriated to the tales of others.

As the evening progressed, Hope grew increasingly attracted to the young man she met at the pool and she was in the mood for romance.

When he asked her to go for a walk along the beach, she knew exactly what that would entail and looked forward to it. They slipped out quietly into the darkness.

It was not long before Faith realized that Hope had abandoned her. Without her companion and feeling the effect of two beers, she grew uncomfortable in the strange setting and decided to return to the condo. As she was heading for the door, Jimmy intercepted her.

"Leaving so soon?" he asked.

"Yeah. I'm kind of tired and my flight leaves in the morning. I thought I'd go home and get packed."

"That's cool. But it might not be safe going alone. I'll give you a ride."

"That's all right. Our condo is just down the street. I'll walk. It'll be okay."

"No, I insist," Jimmy said with a smile.

Faith hesitated. "Okay," she said finally.

When their elevator reached the lobby, Jimmy asked, "Why don't we walk along the beach?"

"I'd prefer the sidewalk. It would be safer," Faith said.

"Come on, where's your sense of adventure? You're not afraid of *me*, are you?" he said with a smile.

"No. Of course, not!" she said, wary, but not wishing to offend him.

"Then that settles it. Let's go!"

His smile was so disarming and he was so persistent that she hesitantly nodded her head and soon found herself walking through the white sand with the gulf waves lapping up on the shore and licking her feet. They were alone on the beach.

The sky was now overcast and only a pale glow from the nearby condominiums illuminated the beach. The breeze off the gulf was warm but it was not enough to overcome the chilling sense of danger Faith felt in the presence of her escort. As they walked, Faith nervously fidgeted with a white seashell she had picked out of the sand. The serendipitous article was whole and pristine, without a flaw.

"Put it in your pocket," he said.

"What?"

"Save it. It'll make a nice souvenir."

Faith smiled as she put the shell in the pocket of her shorts.

"There. How's that?"

"Good."

After passing a short row of high-rise condominiums, they came to an empty lot where an excavation had been dug for another high-rise. The project had been abandoned for months as the developer had hit on hard times and filed for bankruptcy. The lot was now sitting idle, waiting to be sold. In front of the excavation stood several tall mounds of sandy soil.

"That was the first time I ever drank beer," Faith confessed.

"I could tell."

"You could? How?"

"You winced every time you took a sip," he said with a laugh.

Faith blushed as she looked down at the water slipping in around her ankles and nibbling at her toes before receding back into gulf. Then she raised her eyes to meet his, hoping for a look, or word, or gesture of grace. Instead, her eyes picked up the glimmer of a shiny object in his hand.

"Oh, my God!" she screamed.

Her escort suddenly became her assailant. He held in his hand a long switchblade. His free hand grabbed her wrist while the knife was put to her throat. Though his physical strength held her in check, it was terror that paralyzed her. Faith's heart pounded as the overwhelming fear of death seized her. Her terror had made her powerless. She was completely at his mercy.

"Move!" he commanded as he shoved her to the ground between two large dirt piles.

"No!" she screamed hysterically.

"Scream all you want. No one will hear you!" he said with a fiendish laugh.

It was true. The beach was deserted and the waves lapping up on shore muffled her cries. It was as though her screams were silent.

"No! Don't!" she cried out again as the truth only made her scream louder.

She tried to get up and run but he pushed her back to the ground with his foot. Then he pounced on her, his knees straddling her at the waist. He grabbed her by the hair and once again put the knife to her throat. He looked down on her with a self-satisfying smile.

"Don't kill me!" she pleaded between frantic gasps.

"I won't…if you cooperate," he said with an evil grin.

"What do you want?" she asked, still gasping for breath.

"I want you," he said with lusting eyes.

"Please, no!" she cried and began kicking wildly.

He struck her face with the back of his hand. It jarred her and she almost fainted.

"Don't fight me!" he shouted angrily.

"Stop! Stop!" she whined.

"Shut up!" he said, slapping her hard across the face again.

Faith broke into a hysterical sob, shaking her head frantically. Jimmy grabbed her head with both hands and made her look into his eyes through the tears in her own.

"You're mine to do with as I please!" he said angrily. Her fervent, unspoken prayer was only to survive the moment, although she half wished for death, too. In the back of her mind she knew that even if she survived, she had now lost all sense of dignity.

When the violation was complete, Faith felt the suffocating crush of his body, as it remained momentarily motionless on top of her. Finally, as he struggled clumsily to his feet, his crushing weight pressed on her one last time as if squeezing the last ounce of self-respect from her soul. She felt like a shriveled tube of ointment being exacted for one last application. Standing over her, he adjusted his bright red sweat shorts, and dusted the sand from his arms and legs with most of it falling on his victim. He left without a word, uttering only a loud, sinister laugh as he walked away.

Faith remained still except for her breathing. Her chest expanded and contracted violently with each sob. Then she realized that he might come back for more or that someone might see her pitiful condition. She hurried back into her shorts and felt a sharp edge scrape her leg. She reached into her pocket and realized that in the attack the pristine seashell she had found on the beach had been broken. It was no longer a flawless work of nature. It had been forever changed.

Faith was in a daze. She stumbled and fell several times as she made her way around the excavation to the street. Having reached the sidewalk, she suddenly felt sick to her stomach. She bent over to vomit but produced only a dry heave. "I'll die if anyone sees me like this!" she thought. Fortunately, the street was empty except for a few parked cars. She realized she was only half a block from her building. She walked hurriedly along the sidewalk, wiping the steady flow of tears from her eyes. Although the assault had left her in a state of shock, she still had enough presence of mind to know she had to shut out the raging emotions inside and focus on getting back to the security of the apartment unseen.

•••

Faith was nearly unconscious as she lay momentarily on the hallway floor, but the urgency to hide her shame gave her the strength to try the key once more. This time the door opened and she disappeared into the privacy of the apartment.

She went immediately to the bathroom and locked the door behind her, sealing herself from any human contact. She stepped into the hot shower and spent the next hour soaping and rinsing, trying to wash away the feeling of being soiled irrevocably. In some strange way she felt responsible for the heinous crime committed against her. The haunting question, "Why did I walk with him?" kept spinning around in her mind. She had decided that she would never tell anyone of her experience—not the police, not her family, not Chris, and not even Hope. It would be her secret that she would hide away forever.

When she finally emerged from the shower, she went directly to the bedroom and put on a sweatshirt and a pair of sweat pants. Then she threw an extra blanket on the bed, and once again, locked the door behind her. She climbed into bed and pulled the covers tightly around her and over her head. Having thus woven a cocoon of insulation, she cried herself to sleep. Like the seashell, Faith was no longer whole, but rather a broken remnant of what she once had been.

It's Not Fair!

The afternoon skies were cloudy and the mid-April winds were whistling when Robert and Kara Ellison pulled into the parking lot of the medical office complex. The two story colonial brick building sat on high ground overlooking the parking lot and a small man-made pond below that. A flock of geese had claimed squatter's rights on the pond and the low grassy knolls surrounding it. On the near bank at the crest of the knoll walked a goose and a string of goslings behind her.

"Oh, Robert! Look at the baby geese!" exclaimed Kara as they were getting out of the car. "Aren't they adorable!"

"Yes, they're cute," Robert replied smiling. "But you can't take them home. A puppy, maybe, but not goslings."

"If the news is bad, I might take you up on that," Kara said.

"Don't be discouraged. We don't know what he's going to say."

"I know. But I have a feeling that we weren't meant to have children."

Robert smiled sympathetically. He said, "Let's just leave it up to the Lord, okay."

"Okay," Kara said, forcing a smile.

Two pregnant women in their mid-twenties were chatting in the waiting room of Dr. Feinstein's office when Robert and Kara entered the suite. The protruding abdomen of the first woman, a petite blonde, clearly gave away her condition. Attached to her leg were two small children, blonde girls with broomsticks for limbs. The other woman was large and round with dark brown hair and a deep voice. The conversation paused momentarily as the pregnant pair scrutinized the Ellisons as they approached the receptionist's window.

"Kara Ellison to see Dr. Feinstein," Kara said.

"Thank you. You may have a seat," the elderly receptionist said with a quizzical glance. "The doctor is a little behind schedule today."

Robert and Kara were accustomed to the second glances. Robert was a stocky, dark-skinned, black man with thinning hair and a thick mustache. Kara was Scotch-Irish and German with shoulder length red hair and sparkling green eyes. She had a trim figure and was nearly as tall as her husband.

They were in their early thirties and had been married for six years. For four years they had tried to get pregnant but without success. They finally decided to try a medical solution to their problem.

It was now a week since Dr. Feinstein had performed a laproscopy on Kara. The procedure was intended to remove scar tissue from around her fallopian tubes, the result of a severe case of endometriosis. A minute video camera on the point of a probing instrument provided a clear picture of the damage to Kara's organs.

Robert and Kara took seats in the waiting room along the wall opposite the two pregnant women. Robert picked up a magazine and began leafing through it. Kara sat quietly and prayed inwardly for a moment but her attention was drawn to the two women.

"Are these your only children?" the heavy woman asked.

"Yes. So far."

"They must keep you busy."

"Too busy! Do you have any kids?"

"No. This will be our first."

"I bet you're excited!"

"We are. We're making plans for the baby's room. We're shopping for all the things we need. There's so much to do! But we're enjoying it," the heavy woman said with a smile, her face glowing.

"Are you hoping for a girl or a boy?"

"Oh, it doesn't matter to me. Either one would be wonderful. But my husband definitely wants a boy. He says he doesn't care, but I know he would really like a boy."

"Have you picked out any names yet?"

"If it's a boy, we might go with Derek James. If it's a girl, we might name her Emma Mae."

"Emma Mae. That sounds lovely!" the petite woman said.

A nurse entered the waiting area and called for the heavy woman. Taxed by both her obesity and pregnancy, the woman struggled to her feet.

"I'll be glad when this pregnant part is over," she said.

"You're not the only one."

With the heavy woman's exit, the petite woman's two children began asserting themselves. Kara watched with envy at the way they clung to their mother and asked a myriad of questions. The mother answered the queries patiently at first. Then, as fatigue set in, she tried to distract them.

"Here," she said as she handed each of the girls a magazine. "Why don't we look at the baby pictures?"

The scheme backfired. The magazines only served to generate more questions. The mother, needing just a few minutes to sit and relax, tried to ignore the girls by pretending she was immersed in her reading. But, since there is nothing more persevering than children who are being ignored, she was forced to take serious measures.

"That's enough!" she scolded. "Can't you see I'm trying to read! Just sit in your chairs and be quiet!"

She was embarrassed by the outburst and gave a quick glance at the Ellisons out of the corner of her eye. Kara, who had been observing for quite some time, and Robert, whose attention was piqued with the scolding, instinctively tucked their noses back into their magazines. Shortly, the nurse appeared again and called for the mother of the two children.

"Now you just sit here and behave yourselves. Mom will be back in just a few minutes," she said.

Kara tried to develop an interest in her magazine but her mind wandered restlessly and she began to imagine what it would be like to have two precious little girls like the ones giggling in front of her. Then she realized the danger of the exercise and immediately turned back to her magazine.

When Kara's turn came the Ellisons were ushered into a small, square, sterile office decorated with gray wallpaper, gray carpeting, white ceiling tile, and florescent lighting. There were no windows. A large white desk with silver chrome legs bisected the room. In front of the desk were two chairs, also white with silver chrome legs. The wall behind the desk was lined with shelves stocked with medical journals and textbooks. On the opposite wall hung a collage of degrees and plaques certifying the doctor's educational, professional, and civic accomplishments.

"Hello, Kara, Robert," Dr. Feinstein said as he stepped into the office. Robert rose to shake hands but was not fast enough to catch the doctor who had quickly taken his own seat behind the desk and opened their file. "Sorry I'm late," he said. "I had a procedure this morning that had all sorts of complications and the operation took much longer than I had anticipated. I'm just now catching up. Just give me a moment to review my notes."

Robert reached for Kara's hand. They gave each other a quick glance. Then their eyes became riveted to the doctor, a small, wiry, Jewish man in his early forties.

"Well," he said finally, "the laproscopy corroborated my diagnosis. The scar tissue from your endometriosis is, in effect, clamping down on your tubes and causing the blockage so that your eggs cannot pass to the uterus. But there was so much scar tissue around your tubes that I didn't want to risk using the laser too much to vaporize it. You have to be very careful with this new laser technology. One bad aim and a major artery could be ruptured. I didn't think it was worth the risk to try removing all the scar tissue."

"We understand," Robert said. Kara nodded in agreement.

"Good," said the doctor. After a pregnant pause he delivered the bad news. "Without proceeding further with another method of fertilization, your chances of getting pregnant are maybe ten percent."

Kara's eyes grew misty. Robert gently squeezed her hand. "What other method are you referring to?" Robert asked.

"*In vitro* fertilization. Are you familiar with it?"

"I've heard of it," Kara said.

"You'd better clue me in," Robert said.

"*In vitro* simply means 'external,'" Dr. Feinstein said, looking directly at Robert. "Eggs are surgically removed from Kara's ovary and united with your sperm in a Petri dish. Since the fertilization is done externally, it is called '*in vitro*.' The fertilized eggs are then implanted in Kara's uterus. But the implantation is not guaranteed to take. Its rate of success is not real high and it often leads to multiple births. It would be a gamble. But it's your decision."

"How expensive is it?" Robert asked.

"It's very expensive. But the state now mandates that insurance companies cover the cost of the procedure."

The couple said little as they began their drive home. Kara had a forlorn look in her eye as she stared out the side window. The shock of the doctor's disclosure was wearing off and the harsh reality was sinking in.

"Ever since I was a little girl, I had dreamed of being a mother. And now it will never happen. I'm sorry, Robert. It's all my fault," she said with tears welling up in her eyes. She could not bear to look at him.

Robert pulled the car over to the curb of the residential street. They were parked in front of a row of early sixties ranch houses, just a few blocks from their home.

"It's not your fault," Robert said as he reached over and drew his wife close for a comforting hug. "You can't control what's happening inside you."

"But I've let you down!" she said and then began to cry heavily on his shoulder.

"It's not your fault," he said again.

The couple shared their grief for a long moment with tears also escaping Robert's eyes. Nothing was said. There was only the sound of soft sobs and sniffles.

"Something will happen and things will work out," Robert finally said.

"How?" Kara asked, the frustration evident in her tone.

"Maybe we should try the *in vitro* fertilization."

"I don't feel right about it. It's like playing God," Kara replied. "Besides, what if we ended up having triplets or quadruplets?"

"The odds of that happening are not real high."

"And neither are the odds of getting pregnant. I don't want to go through all the medical hoops only to be let down again in the end. It just seems hopeless!"

"I know it does. But they say when the Lord closes a door, He opens a window."

"But why did He have to close *this* door? It's not fair! Why do I have to be infertile? It's just not fair, Robert!"

"You're right. It doesn't seem fair. We'll just have to trust in the Lord. He may have plans for us that we just don't know about."

Test Results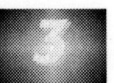

Faith held her hand to her mouth as she suddenly burst into the second floor bathroom.

"Hey!" Ryan shouted as she stormed past him on her way to the toilet. He was standing at the vanity combing his hair getting ready for his morning classes.

Ryan was a tall, lanky lad, with many of his father's features, only leaner, with dark brown hair and blue eyes. His salient feature, however, was the nervous energy inherited from his mother.

Just as he was about to say, "Don't you think you ought to knock?" Faith vomited into the toilet. He edited his remark to, "Oh, sick!"

As Faith hovered over the toilet bowl in her pajamas, Ryan asked in jest, "Morning sickness?" He had no idea that the question was a valid one.

"I think I have a touch of the flu," Faith responded deceitfully, her heart pounding. "Does he know? Is it obvious?" she wondered.

Faith sensed Ryan peering down on her from behind as though his eyes were tickling the back of her neck.

"Do you mind? Can I have some privacy?"

"No problem. I'm out of here."

For a couple of weeks now she had spells of nausea, mostly in the morning. At first, she honestly thought it was the flu; but now, she knew better. There were other disturbing symptoms: a long overdue period, constant fatigue, tender breasts. From the outset she tried to dismiss the facts. "It's probably just stress from *that night*." The explanation was plausible enough. Besides, everyday she had experienced cramping and the feeling that her period was coming. "Just wait till tomorrow," she would tell herself, holding out hope. She knew enough about feminine physiology to suspect a pregnancy, yet she felt so ignorant.

Faith gingerly pulled herself up off the floor and moved to the basin to wash up. She ran the cold water, tested it, and splashed her face. With her eyes closed, she reached for a towel and patted herself dry. Then lifting her face from the towel, she looked into the mirror and said, "I have to find out!"

•••

Ryan yawned as he trudged down the stairs. He heard his father's deep voice echoing throughout the main floor.

"What a bunch of hypocrites!"

"Who's that? About what?" Ryan asked as he entered the kitchen.

Joan and Ryle Brandon were sitting at the breakfast table drinking coffee, reading the paper, and watching the morning news on television. Joan, a small, energetic woman with short brown hair was still in her bathrobe. Ryle was dressed in his gray business suit ready for a full day of meetings on campus.

"The TV news just reported a story about a newborn baby left in a trash bin," Joan said.

"Oh, yeah. That was on the news last night," Ryan said as he was rummaging through the cabinet for a box of cereal. "Did they find the mother yet?"

"Yes. And she's facing murder charges. She may possibly get the death penalty," Joan said.

"Why are you so upset, Dad? She deserves it, doesn't she?"

"That's not the point."

Dr. Brandon was a tall, robust figure with dark brown hair graying around the temples, blue eyes, and a deep voice. As President of Justin

College, he had an outstanding reputation as a Christian educator, author, and speaker.

"What *is* the point?" Ryan asked.

"The point is, we have a double standard about murder," his father said. "This woman is going to be punished for killing her child. But every day in this country we have over four thousand women kill children in the womb. And we justify it by saying they're 'exercising their rights.' What's the difference if the child is killed in the womb or shortly after leaving it? Why is one considered a right and the other a felony?"

"Sounds like a good subject for your next book," Ryan said, pouring milk onto his bowl of raisin bran.

"It's not a novel idea," his father said.

"Who said anything about a novel? Write another self-help book. You can call it, *Timing is Everything*. Then subtitle it, *Kill Your Kid While You Still Have the Chance*," Ryan said, a sparkle in his eye, as he joined his parents at the table.

"Very funny," his father said dryly.

"No, really!" Ryan persisted. "Write it tongue-in-cheek."

"It's not a subject to make light of, Dear," his mother said. "Abortion and child abuse are serious sins."

"Okay, okay! Just a thought, that's all," Ryan said with an embarrassed smile.

"Actually, a book might not be a bad idea," Dr. Brandon said. "We have to expose the lies."

"What lies?" Ryan asked.

"Mostly euphemisms. A euphemism is when you use nondescript language to make a terrible act sound better than it is. An example would be Hitler's Nazis referring to the mass murder of the Jews as 'the final solution.'"

"I know what a euphemism is," Ryan said. "'Termination of pregnancy' is another one."

"That's right," his father said. "It's a nice, clean, nondescript way of referring to the poisoning, shredding, or mutilating of babies in the womb. It doesn't conjure up vivid mental pictures of the gruesome reality of abortion."

"No, I guess not," Ryan said. "Although I did see a pro-choice bumper sticker the other day that said, 'Have you shredded your kid today?'"

"Ryan!"

"Sorry, Mom. I couldn't resist."

Joan shook her head and said, "I've got another example. Babies are referred to as 'tissue.'"

"Yes, that is a good example," Dr. Brandon said. "Referring to a child as 'mere tissue' makes it easy to deny that abortion is murder."

"Well, to be fair, a fetus is 'just tissue,' isn't it?" Ryan remarked. "I mean, after all, it's just starting to develop. So, it's kind of sub-human, isn't it?"

"What do you mean by sub-human?" his father asked.

"I mean it really can't do anything. It can't walk. It can't talk. It can't think. It's just not a fully developed person," Ryan said.

"So, you're saying humanity depends on the extent of a person's development."

"Yeah, I guess."

"Well, if that's the case, tell me, where do you draw the line?"

"What do you mean?"

"I mean, where do you draw the line?"

Ryan could see the fire in his father's eyes. It meant that a full lecture was underway.

"Does humanity begin when a child can walk? If so, why don't we give parents the right to do away with their children anytime before they take their first step. Or, does humanity begin when a child can talk? If so, why don't we let parents kill their children anytime before they say their first word. Or, does humanity begin when a child can read and write? Surely, a person is not fully developed before he's literate. Or, does humanity begin when a person can think and reason logically? If so, we can abort a few judges and politicians."

"That's enough, Ryle," Joan said.

"I'm sorry," he said. "It's just that too many people think you can draw the line of humanity at one place or another beyond conception. But the truth is, humanity begins at conception. From that point on, we're constantly developing or deteriorating—physically, mentally, and spiritually. You just can't draw a line on humanity except at conception and death. And even in death, the soul lives on."

There was a short silence. Then Ryan asked, "What do you think about protesting in front of clinics? Do you think it does any good?"

"Why do you ask?"

"Well, I have a friend in my philosophy class, Jason Warner, who keeps asking me to go on a 'rescue' with him. He's very passionate about abortion. He had a lot to say about it in class last week."

"If you want to rescue, that's fine. You should stand up for what you believe," Joan said.

"Just be careful," his father warned.

"About what?"

"That you don't get mixed up with the extremists. I think it's fine to demonstrate and picket, but I wouldn't go beyond that."

"Like doing what?"

"Breaking the law. Like vandalism, or arson. That's inexcusable."

"I know that."

"Good," his father said with a smile. "I'm glad to see that you're discussing these issues in class. Who's your professor?"

"Dr. Bennett. He's a good instructor. He makes you think," Ryan said. After pausing a moment he added, "Today we get our test results on the euthanasia exam. I'm kind of nervous about it. I don't think I did that well on it."

"I'm sure you did fine, Dear," his mother said. "Besides, there are more important things to worry about than test results."

•••

By the time Faith made it down to breakfast her father and brother had left for college. Her mother was still sitting at the table reading the newspaper.

"You're late," Joan said.

"I know. I'm kind of slow this morning. I feel tired."

"Well, have some breakfast and you'll feel better."

"I'm not that hungry. Besides, Hope will be here in just a minute."

"You should eat *something*, Dear."

"I'll be all right."

"Well, don't forget your lunch."

"Oh, yeah."

Faith grabbed it from the refrigerator.

"Mom, you don't have to make me such a big lunch."

"Big lunch? You have a sandwich, an apple, and some chips. That's a big lunch?"

"Yeah. Kind of—half a sandwich would be enough."

"You're eating like a bird lately, Faith. What are you trying to do, lose weight?"

Before she could reply, Hope pulled into the driveway in her new red Mazda Miata, an early graduation present from her mother.

"Hope's here! Gotta go!" she said with a kiss to her mother's cheek.

"Hi!" Hope said excitedly as Faith climbed into the car. "How's it going?"

"Don't ask!"

"Why?"

"Oh, nothing."

"Guess what?" Hope asked.

"What?"

"It's official. Chad and I broke up for good."

"Really? How come?"

"I just don't want any commitments or anyone tying me down."

"That's nice," Faith said, her mind still focused on the possibility of pregnancy.

"Nice! Is that all you can say? I'm going through this traumatic experience and all you can say is, 'that's nice?'"

"I thought you said you wanted to break up," Faith said.

"I do."

"Then what's the problem?"

"I'm taking a risk here. I don't have a date for prom," Hope said.

"But you told me last week that three guys had already asked you to prom when they heard you and Chad were breaking up."

"Yeah, but they're not guys I really want to go to prom with."

"Yeah, you're right. You have big problems," Faith said with a smirk.

Faith struggled through her first period class. Her notes were sketchy with doodles filling in the gaps. During her second period study hall, she went to the library. She wasn't sure where to begin. An encyclopedia seemed like a logical place to start. When she came to the reference stacks, she thought, "What a mess!" The encyclopedias were in complete disarray on the shelf, out of order, and piled on top of one another. "Why can't anything be easy!" she said in a soft voice. She eventually found the displaced volume "P" and her fingers trembled as she looked up "pregnancy."

"See **Childbirth**," it said.

"This is so annoying!"

She tossed the book back onto the pile and picked up volume "C." She scanned the library. Satisfied that she was safe in her private research, she skimmed the article on childbirth. The subtitle, "**Signs and Symptoms of Pregnancy**," immediately drew her attention. Her heart began to beat rapidly as she started to read:

"In most cases, women are able to detect many signs and symptoms early in their pregnancy...For a woman who is usually regular, a missed period is a strong indicator of pregnancy...Fatigue is also common as is morning sickness."

She felt queasy and sat down at the empty table next to the stack. Her eyes continued to scan the article. Under "**Diagnosis of Pregnancy**," she read:

"Today, home pregnancy tests are inexpensive and accurate and can be performed quickly. The test kits are available at many drugstores...Since the results may not be as accurate as standard pregnancy tests, they should be viewed with caution."

Faith sat back in her chair and stared across the room. She thought, "What are Mom and Dad going to say when they find out?" Her eyes blurred with tears. She needed comfort but there was no one to comfort her. She wrapped her arms around herself and gently stroked her triceps.

Suddenly, she heard Hope whisper loudly, "There you are! I was looking for you in the cafeteria but you weren't there."

Faith quickly closed the encyclopedia and wiped her eyes before Hope took a seat next to her at the table.

"What are you up to?"

"Oh, nothing! Just sitting here thinking," Faith said, feeling self-conscious about her evasiveness.

"What are you reading?"

"Nothing. The book was just on the table here when I sat down."

"Do you want to go to the mall after school? I have to find a graduation dress."

"No, I don't think so. Not today. I don't feel well," Faith said.

"Really? What's wrong?"

"My stomach's upset. I was wondering if you wouldn't mind stopping at the drug store after school on the way home? I think I might pick up some Pepto Bismol or something."

"Don't you have any at home?"

"Uh, no. I checked this morning."

Hope shrugged and said, "No, I don't mind."

•••

Faith met Hope in the parking lot after school.

"Are you sure you don't want to go shopping?" Hope asked.

"No. Sorry, I'm still not feeling well. I just want to stop at the drugstore for some medicine and go home," Faith said.

As they pulled into the parking slip at the large food and drug, Faith said, "You can wait here. I'll just be a minute."

"That's okay, I'll come in with you. I want to get some gum."

"You don't have to. I'll get it for you!"

"No, that's all right. I want to come in."

Faith rolled her eyes. "Nothing's easy!" she thought. "How am I going to pull this off?"

Once inside, Faith scanned the overhead signs and spotted the pharmacy in the far corner of the store. The girls began walking in that direction. Suddenly, Faith stopped in the magazine aisle.

"Look!" Faith said. "There's that article in *People* about Oprah that I wanted to read!"

"Oh, yeah. I wanted to read that, too," Hope said.

"Well, why don't you stay here and look it over and I'll go get my medicine? I'll be back in a minute."

Without giving Hope a chance to respond, Faith was off, keeping an eye out for anyone she knew. She spotted the home pregnancy tests in front of the pharmacy counter. She picked up the smallest box on display and quickly read the label. "This should work," she thought.

"Do you need some help?" asked the pharmacist.

Faith was startled, then embarrassed. "No," she said as she looked up at the woman behind the counter. She immediately turned and walked away. She was looking up and down the aisle for stomach medicine when she was startled again.

"There you are!" Hope nearly shouted. "What's taking so long?"

"Oh, you scared me!" Faith said with her back toward Hope. Her heart was pounding. She discreetly buried the pregnancy test kit in her purse and scrambled for an excuse. "Oh, I'm comparing prices. I think I'm going to get this," she said as she grabbed a small generic box of stomach medicine off the shelf.

"Price shopping!" Hope said, shaking her head in mock disapproval. "You're so much like your mother, Faith!"

"I'm ready. Let's go," Faith said.

As the girls approached the checkout counter, Faith said, "Why don't you get the car while I pay for this?"

"What's your rush?" Hope asked.

"No rush. I just thought it would save time."

"Really, Faith. You're too much like your mother," Hope repeated. But she acquiesced.

Faith discreetly removed the pregnancy test from her purse and placed her two items on the belt. The cashier, a young woman not much older than Faith, picked up the pregnancy test package, read the label, and then ran it across the scanner. As she did the same for the generic stomach medicine, she looked Faith in the eye, smiled, and said in a smart tone, "You better hope your test comes out negative, or you're gonna need more than this stuff!"

Faith turned red as she surveyed the customers waiting in line behind her.

"The test isn't for me. It's for my girlfriend."

The cashier smiled. Then she spotted her supervisor approaching and politely said, "That'll be twelve twenty-three, please."

Embarrassed, Faith walked briskly to the exit.

"Hey, you forgot your receipt!" the cashier yelled as Faith was half out the door. The cashier shook her head and said to herself, "Give it to your boyfriend. He ought to reimburse you."

Hope was waiting in front of the exit when Faith emerged from the store. Red-faced, Faith slipped into the car and slammed the door.

"What's wrong?"

"Nothing. The cashier was just very rude, that's all."

Faith arrived home to find the house empty. A note on the kitchen table read, "Faith—gone to the grocery store. Will be back soon. Love, Mom."

Faith quickly ran upstairs to the bathroom. She nervously pulled the merchandise from the small plastic bag.

"I can't believe this is happening to me!" she said. With the trembling hands of an old woman, she opened the pregnancy test and pulled out the contents. The directions read:

- Add urine to test vial. Wait one minute.
- Add Kwiktest teststrip to test vial for five minutes.
- Rinse Kwiktest teststrip and place in developer solution.
- The results are positive if the result pad turns blue after 3 minutes.
- The results are negative if there is no change within 7 minutes.

Faith religiously followed the instructions. She prayed, "Please God, I can't be pregnant! I just can't!"

Her eyes were riveted to the teststrip for nearly a minute. Then she heard the garage door open.

"Oh, God, please!" she prayed again.

Then she heard the laundry room door open below. In a moment her mother called up the stairs, "Faith, are you home?"

"I'm in the bathroom!"

"Can you help me bring in the groceries?"

"In a minute!"

As her mother returned to the garage, Faith stared again at the teststrip.

"Oh, my God!" she gasped as she detected a hint of blue. For two agonizing minutes, the strip corroborated her worst fears.

"I don't believe this is happening!" Faith muttered as she hid the test kit in her top dresser drawer. Then she hurried down the stairs to help her mother. By the time Faith reached the kitchen Joan had all the groceries sitting on the counter ready to be put away.

"Faith, you look pale!" her mother said. "Are you okay?"

"Not really. I feel kind of sick," she said truthfully.

"I think you'd better lie down. I'll take care of the groceries."

"Thanks," Faith said. She returned to her room and flopped down on the bed. Teary-eyed and exhausted, she soon fell asleep.

•••

Faith awakened her from her nap a few minutes before six. She went to the bathroom and looked in the mirror.

"I look terrible," she thought. She rinsed her face and tried on a cheerful countenance. "I can't let them know," she thought. "Maybe the test was wrong. Don't say anything until you're sure!"

Faith was the last one to sit down to dinner. The others were already eating.

"We already prayed," her mother said. "And why didn't you tell me you were sick this morning? Your brother tells me you threw up in the bathroom. You should have stayed home from school!"

Faith looked across the table at Ryan. "Traitor," she thought. She said, "I didn't feel that bad. Really! Besides, I didn't want to miss the review for my government test on Monday."

"Well, it's not worth being miserable all day, Dear. Next time I want you to stay home," Joan said.

"If you say so."

Faith stared down at her dinner and picked at the salad.

Joan turned to Ryan and asked, "How did your test results come out, Dear?"

Faith dropped her fork. Her heart sank to her stomach. "Oh God! She knows!"

"I got a B-plus," Ryan said. "I was so relieved when I saw the grade on the top of the paper. I really thought I failed."

Faith was relieved, too. Her secret was still safe.

Kara's Confession   4

Kara was having a restless sleep when a thunderclap suddenly exploded outside the bedroom window. She bolted up in bed, looked at the clock, and squinted to read the blue digital figures. It was 1:15. She rolled over on to her side and looked at her husband sleeping soundly, unaware of the raging storm. It was a Friday night in mid-May, four weeks since they had the bad news confirmed by Dr. Feinstein.

"I'm so sorry, Robert," she whispered.

Silent tears dripped onto her pillow. She rolled onto her back and stared at the ceiling. Vivid visual images resurrected from the past played in her mind. When she closed her eyes and tried to go back to sleep again, it was futile. The pictures, haunting and accusing, refused to go away. Sudden, sharp cramps from her endometriosis added to the psychological torment, and reminded her of the pain suffered in that troubled time thirteen years ago. Now it was all coming back—the pain, the sorrow, the regret, and the guilt. She looked at the clock again. It was 2:53. She rolled back onto her side. "Make it go away!" she prayed silently until, at long last, out of utter exhaustion, her body and mind succumbed to sleep. But the dark secret Kara kept hidden away in her heart would not keep still. After years of absence, the recurring nightmare which had once haunted her nights had returned; except now, it had changed in one important detail.

Kara was driving on the residential street in front of her parents' house. A twelve-year-old boy stood in the middle of the street, waving his arms, signaling for Kara to stop. She slammed on the brakes but they didn't respond. She tried swerving left or right but the car wouldn't turn. As she drew closer to the child, the dream shifted into slow motion. Nearly on top of him, she could read his lips as he screamed, "Mom, no!" But there was no sound. The scream was a silent scream. "Move! I can't stop!" she yelled back. But the boy didn't and it was too late. "No!" she shrieked as the car made impact.

"Wake up! Wake up!" Robert said, gently shaking his wife.

Kara sat up, panting and sweating. "What?" she said in a breathless, sleepy stupor. As the mental haze faded, she realized it had only been a bad dream. For a short moment she felt relieved. Then vivid memories rushed to her consciousness. "Oh, no! It's back!" she said and fell sobbing into Robert's arms.

"What's wrong?"

"It's back," she sobbed.

"What is?"

"The dream."

"Tell me about it."

"No. Just hold me."

Robert held Kara close and tried putting the pieces of the puzzle together—the infertility, the depression, and now the nightmare. He knew she was hiding something terrible. "Be patient," he thought. "In her own time, she'll tell you."

•••

Robert rose early the next morning and immediately went to work in the backyard of their modest split-level home. A soft, warm, spring breeze slipped in from the south and with it came a sense of peace and joy as he tended to his gardening. Others weren't so content. A bright red cardinal and his female mate were anxiously building their nest in the towering blue spruce that stood in the back corner of the lot. A hefty, black crow, perched high above at the top of the spruce was cawing like a political candidate running for office, obviously upset with the local state of affairs. Two yards over, a large, black, frustrated Doberman barked incessantly in her quest to be liberated as she ran back and forth along the fence that hemmed her in. But Robert was oblivious to it all as he patiently planted his marigolds in the beds surrounding the cement patio. He had been busy for a couple of hours before Kara showered and made it down to the kitchen in her bathrobe.

Kara poured herself a cup of coffee and sat down at the breakfast table in front of the sliding glass door overlooking the patio. She slowly stirred two packs of artificial sweetener into her cup, looked out the patio door at Robert, and smiled. He was singing softly as he pulled the marigolds from the plastic tray and plugged them into the holes dug into the bed. "I'm so lucky to have such a good husband," she thought. And the more she thought of how she did not deserve him, the more she felt compelled to walk out onto the patio and confess the sin that had haunted her conscience for so many years. But the thought of confession was terrifying. Surely he would reject her if he knew what she had done, and she could not bear the thought of having to live without him. But she knew she could not go on living the lie, letting him think she was something that she was not. She would tell him the whole thing, every disgusting, self-deprecating detail. And if he left her, then that would be her penance and it would be just.

Kara opened the sliding glass door and stepped out onto the patio.

"Good morning, Love," Robert said smiling. "Isn't it a beautiful day!"

Kara managed a polite smile.

"About last night, Robert," she said, "I have something to tell you."

Robert put down his little spade and sat back on his heels.

"What is it?"

He looked so intently into her eyes that she felt him peering into her soul. Her resolve wavered as a tear rolled down her cheek.

Robert held out his hand and took her hand in his. Kara sat down on one of the plastic chairs and gathered her thoughts. She shifted back and forth looking for comfort where there was none to be had. Then she took out a tissue from her bathrobe pocket and wiped away her tears. With one final shift in her chair, she let out a big sigh and started in with her confession.

"When I was a sophomore in college and dating Warren," she began nervously, "he and I were sleeping together pretty regularly. I was on the pill but I wasn't very careful. I got pregnant. It happened sometime around Thanksgiving. I realized I was pregnant around Christmas but I went through a period of denial. I was so stressed! I didn't know what to do. I couldn't talk to my parents. They were so authoritarian. We didn't communicate on anything, certainly on anything like this. If my dad had found out I was pregnant, he would have gone through the roof. I wanted to get married and have the baby but Warren didn't. He said he was too young to be tied down. He had big plans. He told me that if I didn't have an abortion, then we were through."

Robert knew what was coming. It made him sad for the child and for his wife. He also felt guilty that she never felt comfortable enough to tell him. He gently squeezed her hand.

"I didn't know what to do," she said. "I felt abortion was wrong and I was beginning to feel so much love for the child, but I wasn't very assertive. I wanted the baby but I knew I needed Warren. I just didn't have much self-esteem. I thought that if I lost him, my life would be over. I delayed as much as I could. I was hoping that Warren would change his mind but he didn't. All he could think of was himself. Finally, when I was about sixteen weeks pregnant, I knew I had to do something. Warren would hardly talk to me and the clock was ticking. I finally gave in and had the abortion."

Kara's eyes were downcast. She did not dare to look into Robert's eyes. Her stomach was in knots. There was a long silence.

Finally, Robert said, "It's okay, Love. You don't have to say any more."

"No. I have to tell you about it! Don't you see? If I don't tell you everything, I know you won't understand what I'm feeling."

Robert looked compassionately at his wife.

"Okay," he said. "Then tell me."

Kara felt an enormous burden lifted from her heart. She now looked directly into Robert's eyes.

"Being sixteen weeks pregnant, I ended up having a saline abortion," she said. "At the time, I didn't know that much about pregnancy and birth, but they told me they were going to inject some fluid into my uterus that would cause me to miscarry."

"Where did this happen? At a clinic?"

"No, at a hospital," she said. "It was spring break. I told my parents that I was going with Warren and some other kids to Colorado to go skiing."

"So your parents never found out?"

"No. They still don't know. And I don't think I'll ever be able to tell them."

"Go on."

"Well, there were several women having the same procedure that day. We were going in one after another. The doctor was an older man and said it wasn't going to be that bad, but it was horrible! It was the most painful experience of my life. After they put the saline solution in, they put me in a room with several other women. The pain was almost unbearable and I was scared. I didn't know what was happening to me. I just lay there in pain, cramping horribly. We were all crying it seems, not only because of the pain but also because of the feeling of being alone."

"Was Warren there with you?"

"No," Kara said with a sad and far away look in her eyes. "He actually went skiing with some of his friends. He said he needed the break from school and that there wasn't anything he could do for me anyway."

Robert shook his head in disbelief. Kara's eyes returned to her husband.

"I know. I was dumb," Kara admitted with an embarrassed smile. "But I was so infatuated with him that I overlooked a lot."

"Yes, an *awful* lot."

Kara nodded gently. She continued, "I had this terrible bloated feeling. I felt like I had a gallon jug of milk in my uterus. I was afraid to stand up. I thought if I did, my whole insides would fall out. But they encouraged us to get up and walk around. They said it would come out sooner if we did. I got up to walk but it was horrible because I was on the same floor as labor and delivery. As I walked up and down the hall, I would pass the nursery filled with beautiful little babies. I would touch my stomach and start to cry knowing what was happening to my baby. I felt so awful! I was killing my baby! I hated Warren. I was bitter. I kept thinking, "How could he make me do this? This is such a selfish thing for him to do!"

"I received the saline injection in the morning and by the following morning, I started to miscarry. I knew what was happening. I knew I had expelled the fetus. I felt it come out and I could feel it lying there between my legs on the bed. I wanted to look at it, but I was too scared. I called the nurse, but she wouldn't do anything. She said they had to wait until the placenta came out. I waited forty or fifty minutes, crying the whole time. Finally, another doctor came in and did a D and C."

"A what?"

"Dilation and curettage," Kara said. Her tone was now almost clinical. "The doctor scrapes the inside of the uterus with kind of a spoon. It hurt so badly because they didn't give me an anesthetic. I thought I was going to die. When they carried the fetus away, I overheard one nurse say to the other, 'It was a boy.' That hurt the worst."

"Then what happened?"

"I went back to school and stayed in the dorm the rest of vacation. The doctor had written me a prescription for a painkiller. That helped because I had severe cramping. But it didn't do anything for my emotional pain. I was a wreck. When Warren came back from skiing, he didn't even ask me how everything went. I guess he just assumed everything would be a breeze."

"I'm sorry."

Kara dropped her eyes again and shook her head.

"That's not the worst part," she said.

"It's not? What happened?"

"We weren't together more than five minutes when he started to talk about how he didn't think we were right for each other. I knew right away what was coming. I asked him if there was someone else and at first, he denied it. But I told him he wasn't fooling anyone and that he might as well admit it and not act so foolish. Then he finally confessed to me that he had met another girl on the trip. I was furious. I felt so used and abused. I hated him. I hated all men for a long time."

"I'm sorry you had to go through all that," Robert said. He started to get up to give Kara a hug, but she quickly held up her hand motioning him to stay.

"Wait," she said. "Let me finish."

Kara took a tissue out of her bathrobe pocket. It was already soaked with tears, but she used it again anyway to wipe her eyes.

"After a few months I started having anxiety attacks, two or three a week. I would shake and cry and feel out of control. It was scary. I also had a recurring nightmare like the one I had last night. I would be driving and all of a sudden, there would be a baby boy lying in the middle of the road. I would try to swerve to miss him or put on the brakes but the wheel and brakes wouldn't respond. I would hear and feel the thud as the car rolled over the baby, and I would always wake up at that point. Finally, I went to a counselor at the university. We talked about the dream and my abortion. He said I was suffering from a guilt complex and there really wasn't any need for it. He tried to convince me that this was not really a child at that point and that I was just deceiving myself and getting worked up over nothing. He said an unwanted child was better off not being born. He said I had actually done it a favor. I listened politely but I knew deep down that it wasn't the truth. It was only time that helped me get over it. Of course, I guess it's obvious I'm not altogether over it. Eventually, the nightmares stopped; that is, until last night. The only difference is that this time the boy in the dream looked like he was twelve or thirteen, the age that my child would be now if I hadn't aborted him. I can't help but feel that my infertility is God's way of punishing me. I'm so sorry you're being punished along with me."

Robert and Kara sat silently for a moment. Kara was utterly depleted of strength and emotion. She was willing to accept Robert's reaction, whatever that may be. Even if he didn't feel he could love her anymore and wanted to leave her, she would accept that as her punishment. She felt she certainly deserved that much and probably much worse.

Robert finally replied, "God's not punishing you with infertility. He doesn't work that way. The Lord tells us that, *'though your sins may be scarlet, they shall be white as snow.'* He has forgiven you and He still loves you. And so do I."

Faith Confides in Hope

"Some graduation party, huh?" Hope said with a laugh.

"It's all right," Faith said.

"Yeah, but when I asked to have a graduation party, I was thinking more like a beer bash around the pool, not a house full of Mom's friends. This is more like a political fund raiser than a graduation party."

"I wouldn't mind a party like this if my mom bought me a Miata for graduation."

"I shouldn't complain, should I?" Hope said.

"No."

In the backyard garden of the Stuart estate, Faith and Hope were walking down the winding brick path that wove through neatly groomed shrubs and flower beds. A soft, spring breeze was no longer warmed by the setting sun and left a chill in the air.

"Oh, guess what!" Hope said, her eyes sparkling.

"What?"

"One of the receptionists at my uncle's clinic is taking a leave for a couple months and he wanted to know if I would fill in. I said, 'Yes.' What do you think?"

"Why do you want to work if you don't have to?"

"I don't know. I thought it would be good experience."

"Do they still do abortions there?"

"Yeah. Why?"

Faith shrugged, struggling to find the words to share her burden. But her heart was too heavy, the burden too great. What she could not begin to express in words, she finally released through tears.

"Oh, my God, Faith! What's wrong?" Hope asked as she stopped and turned toward Faith, now crying in heavy sobs.

"Come and sit down," Hope said. She led Faith to a white wrought iron bench that sat beside the path at the back end of the lot where the garden bordered the woods.

"Faith, what's wrong? Tell me!"

Faith's head was downcast as she choked back tears. At last, she collected herself.

"I'm pregnant," she said.

"What? You're kidding? You can't be!"

"But I am," Faith said faintheartedly, drawing a deep breath. "And I don't know what to do."

"Are you sure?"

"Of course, I'm sure. I wouldn't make something like this up."

"But how did it happen? I mean I know how *it* happens, but how did it happen to you? Did Chris pressure you into it?"

Faith dropped her head and shook it as though she could not believe the story herself.

"You know the last night in Florida when we went to the party?"

Hope nodded.

"Jimmy, the guy who told all those stories?"

"Yeah."

"Well," Faith said, wiping the tears away, "he offered to escort me home and I really didn't want him to but he insisted."

"And?"

Faith was sniveling throughout as she told her story, pausing in a staccato fashion to catch her breath and summon fragments of courage. "And we were walking along the beach…and we were talking and I was looking at this shell I found…and I looked up…and he had a knife…and he pushed me down…and—"

"Oh, my God! He raped you?"

Faith nodded and fell weeping into Hope's arms.

"Oh, my God!" Hope repeated. "I'm so sorry, Faith. I shouldn't have left you alone. It's all my fault!"

The two girls cried together on the bench as if mourning the death of a friend. After several minutes, Faith said, "It's not your fault, Hope. I was the stupid one. I don't know why I trusted him. I just did."

"You're not stupid, Faith. How were you to know the guy was a rapist?"

"I don't know. I'm so angry! He just used me and left laughing. And there was nothing I could do. I've never hated anyone so much in my whole life!"

Hope looked compassionately at her friend and sighed. She asked, "Why didn't you tell me when I got back to the condo? We could have gone to the police."

"I didn't want anyone to know. I was too ashamed." Faith's head remained bowed and her hands busy with a tissue wiping tears from her eyes. "Besides, the police would have called my parents. After all I said about how I could take care of myself, I couldn't let them know."

"But I hate to see him get away with this."

Faith drew a deep breath and exhaled loudly. She said, "I know. But I just can't deal with that now." Then she looked down at her stomach and rubbed it gently saying, "I have other things to worry about."

"Oh, yeah. That's right," Hope said. "Does anybody else know about this? Does Chris know?"

Faith dropped her hands on her lap and stared up into the evening sky. She sighed deeply once again and said, "No, nobody knows."

"What are you going to do?"

"I don't know. I've thought about adoption, but sooner or later, my parents would find out. I even fantasized about running away and keeping the baby. But I wouldn't know what I'd do to survive. I don't think I could take care of myself, let alone a baby."

"Faith, your parents are wonderful. They love you. They would understand if you told them what happened."

"Yes, I know. But the whole thing would be so embarrassing for my father. Imagine the President of Justin College with a daughter who's an unwed mother. That would go over real well! I just couldn't do it to him."

"I think I know what you're going to say, but have you considered an abortion?"

Faith hung her head. "Yes," she said. "That would definitely be the easy way out. And I've thought of every excuse for doing it. But then I realize there's a life growing inside of me, and I don't think I'd be able to live with the fact that I took the life of this child. Besides, I've had these dreams lately."

"Dreams about what?"

"Well, they're more like nightmares, actually," Faith said. "They start out on the beach where I was raped. And the whole scene comes back to me. I dream about kicking and screaming, trying to fight off Jimmy. Then, all of a sudden, the dream changes, and it's not Jimmy I'm fighting. It's a doctor! He's grabbing my legs and starts pulling hard, real hard, like he's trying to tear them off. And it's really painful and I'm screaming the whole time but no one hears me. Then I realize that I'm not on a beach. I'm inside my mother's womb. And what I'm going through is not a rape after all, but an abortion. Fortunately, the dream is so horrible that I always wake up before the doctor is done."

"What do you think it means?"

"I'm not sure," Faith said. "All I know is, the more I think about it, the more it strikes me how similar the two things are."

"What two things?"

"Rape and abortion. After having been raped, I can't see myself doing a similar thing to someone else."

Hope nodded and said, "Yeah, I guess I can see that."

The two girls were quiet for a long time. Finally, Faith confessed in a whisper, "But I've prayed for a miscarriage." She paused, shaking her head gently in self-condemnation. "If I had a miscarriage, then the problem would be solved and it wouldn't be my fault. I'm so ashamed! I can't believe I actually prayed for that!"

The girls sat silently for another moment. Suddenly, Hope said, "Faith, you have too much to live for to have this *accident* ruin your life. You didn't want to be pregnant. You never even risked sex because you thought you might get pregnant. It's not your fault that this happened to you. You have a right to an abortion. You have a right to control your own destiny. I'll get my Uncle Tom to help so that your parents won't have to know about it. Faith, think of your future!"

"I know, Hope! I've thought about my future a lot! I can't help but think about it! And the more I think about it, the more I feel that I don't have a future. Every option has a down side! If I have an abortion, I'd have to live with that for the rest of my life. If I have the baby, it'll ruin my plans for college. If I keep the baby, there's so much responsibility! If I give her up for adoption, she'll wonder why her mother gave her away. It's just tearing me up inside."

Hope gave Faith another hug. She asked, "How do you know it's a girl?"

Faith cracked a tiny smile.

"I don't know. It's just that every time I think of the baby, I think of a girl, a biracial girl. I wonder whether she'll look white or black or both. And I wonder whether anyone will want to adopt her because she isn't all white or she isn't all black. There is so much prejudice in this world!"

"Well, that *is* another thing to consider," said Hope. "Do you really want to bring an unwanted child into this world?"

"I've thought about that a lot, too," Faith said. "And the answer seems obvious when I think about it from my own point of view. But when I begin to think about what she would want, it's a different story. How could I really believe that she wouldn't want to experience the beauty of a purple iris or the warmth of the sun on a hot summer day? Or that she wouldn't want to share her innermost secrets with a best friend? Or dream of the future and of raising a family? Even though this is a real difficult situation, I am so glad that I'm alive! And if the situation were reversed and she was pregnant with me, what would I want her to choose?"

"Oh, this is so messy! There's no easy answer, is there?" Hope said with a sigh.

The girls sat silently watching the last rays of sunlight flicker through the trees. A robin landed at their feet, picked up a twig, and flew back to its nest overlooking the garden. To their left, in the woods, they heard the rustle of dead oak leaves on the ground as a squirrel scampered about in search of food. To their right, on a small grassy knoll, a chipmunk raised himself on his back end, conducted a cursory examination of the intruders in his garden, and satisfied that they apparently meant no harm, scurried off. No words passed between the girls as they observed the life around them. Yet, they were thinking the same thought. Life can be beautiful, even in the worst of circumstances.

The Parable of the Poker Game

"So how's our schedule look for tomorrow?" Vivian asked Jack Ruland as she escorted him to the door.

Jack was considered a heavyweight among campaign consultants. Typically, his clients were senatorial or gubernatorial candidates. But Vivian made him a handsome offer, enough to convince him to take on her campaign. With Jack's help, she had won an easy victory in the Democratic primary in the spring. Now they were after bigger game in William "Wild Bill" Johnson, the staunchly conservative Republican incumbent.

"It's pretty full," Jack said. "We have a women's breakfast at Bethany Baptist in Riverdale. Tread lightly there. We're trying to get the women's vote without upsetting the pro-lifers. Focus your remarks on the need for a woman in office. But if someone raises the abortion issue, stick to the line about abortion being a private matter between a woman and her doctor and clergyman."

"Oh, I hate those church engagements," Vivian complained. "Those holier-than-thou women drive me crazy."

"Regardless of how you feel, you can't come across that way."

"Don't worry. I'll wear my smile. Are you sure you don't want to stay for the party, Jack?"

"Sorry, I've got a few more calls to make. There's a lot of work to do."

"Well, I'm willing to do whatever it takes to win this election. You know that."

"Good. See you in the morning," Jack said as he passed James Ashton on his way out the door.

"Hello, James," Vivian said as he was about to ring the bell. "I'm so glad you could make it!"

"I told you I'd be here," he said.

James was divorced less than a year. He met Vivian during his separation and they had been seeing each other ever since.

James came from generations of wealth. His grandfather was the founder of the *Journal*, the city's leading newspaper. He had passed on the publishing responsibilities to his son who, in turn, had passed them on to James.

James grew up along the exclusive North Shore, attended private schools, went on to undergraduate school at Princeton, followed by law school at Duke before assuming duties as a Vice President of the *Journal*. Now, in his late forties, he was President of the paper.

Vivian, on the other hand, was self-made from middle class stock. At eighteen, she was pregnant with Hope and married Hope's father in what she knew was going to be a bad marriage. After a year of constant quarreling, Bill left home. When the divorce was finalized, he dropped out of sight, moving to the West Coast.

With no alimony or child support, Vivian began to baby sit full-time to pay the bills. As she took on more children and began making a decent income, she started to visualize the business potential of child-care. With her parents' financial assistance, she moved her day care out of her rented house to a storefront in a small strip mall. Within a few years, she expanded to several sites and began to franchise her "Wee-Care" day care centers. Now, in her mid-thirties, the striking blonde owned a chain of day care centers nationwide. Having conquered the business world, Vivian turned her talents and energy to the political arena and entered the race for Congress.

"Well, let's get you a drink and I'll start introducing you to some guests," Vivian said. She escorted James by the arm to the dining room where Faith's parents were standing near the punch bowl and hors d'oeuvres. "I want you to meet the dearest and most interesting man I know!"

"Joan and Ryle," Vivian said as she arrived with her escort, "I'd like you to meet James Ashton. James is the publisher of the *Journal*. And James, this is Dr. Ryle Brandon and his wife, Joan. Ryle is the President of Justin College *and* he writes books."

"You're looking for trouble, aren't you?" James asked, smiling.

"How is that?" Vivian asked.

"Drawing together the liberal press and the religious right without giving either side a warning," he replied jokingly.

"So you know about Ryle's work then?"

"Of course. What puzzles me is how you know each other?" James said, looking back and forth at Ryle and Vivian. "Liberal politicians and conservative critics generally avoid each other like the plague."

"Our daughters have been best friends for years," Joan interjected. "We got to like Vivian before we knew she was a closet liberal. But we try to love the sinner and hate the sin."

The remark drew a laugh from the group. Then James asked, "So Dr. Brandon, what's your current project?"

"I'm afraid it's a book that wouldn't get very good reviews in the *Journal*."

"Give us a clue anyway," James said.

"Well, I'm expounding on an analogy I've been making recently on the lecture circuit," Ryle began. "It's an analogy I make between American society and a poker game. I call it the 'Parable of the Poker Game.'"

"Sounds like an interesting premise," James said.

"Before you start," Joan interrupted, "you'll have to excuse me. I've heard this all before. I'll go mingle with a few of the other guests. It was nice meeting you, James."

"I'll come, too," said Vivian. "You fill me in later, James."

Dr. Brandon began his parable.

"One summer not long ago, four 12-year-old boys began playing poker in the basement of one of their homes. They started playing five-card draw, but kept adding 'wild' cards as the game went on. At first, they had deuces wild, then sevens, and then one-eyed jacks. Pretty soon every face card was wild. Foolishly, they believed that adding wild cards would enhance their chances to win. They didn't understand that poker was basically a game of psychology, not chance.

"Well, it wasn't too long before they discovered their folly. They began to realize that drawing more cards and having more wild cards did not make them any more successful. In fact, it just made the game ridiculous. By trying to increase their power with wild cards they actually ended up with less control. None of them had any more success than they did with a normal deck of cards."

"I think I know where you're going with this," James said with a sincere sparkle of intellectual interest in his eye. "But go on. Tell me how this parallels society."

"Well, just as a poker game begins with an understanding among the players about the value of each card, society begins with an understanding of the value of its rules, morals, and obligations. These we can think of as the 'regular' cards in society's deck. But society also begins with an understanding of the liberties it will allow, some of which might be more appropriately referred to as vices. These liberties and vices we can think of as the 'wild' cards.

"When our country first started out, in fact, even only a generation ago, we were playing with only a few 'wild' cards. Most people accepted the limits and restrictions which church and government placed on individuals to maintain an orderly, just, and righteous society. But over the years, particularly in this past generation, people have shunned the wisdom of the traditional rules and guidelines which earlier generations had upheld as necessary and prudent. They began to demand the use of more 'wild' cards, that is, more liberties and vices.

"At first, we had our traditional vices like alcohol and prostitution. Then in recent decades, the divorce wild card was added to the deck. About the same time, drugs became socially, if not legally, acceptable. During this same period, in the name of 'freedom of speech and press,' we added pornography, not to mention, explicit sex and violence on the screen. Then abortion was made legal, leading to greater sexual freedom, another wild card. And of course, we now have gays and lesbians demanding not just acceptance, but special status. More recently, those who desire great riches without working for it have been dealt a gambling wild card. Now we have state lotteries and casinos everywhere. And since we're on the topic of money, let's not forget deficit spending. And I could go on."

"That's okay. I get your point," James said.

"But I haven't made my point yet. My point is this. The new rules do not enrich life as they had promised. All these new freedoms were supposed to lead to greater happiness. Unfortunately, we've discovered the opposite is true. And the sooner we, as a nation, admit this, the better off we'll be."

James took a sip of his cocktail, smiled, and said, "If you don't mind, I'd like to play the Devil's advocate."

"Sure," said Ryle. He carefully set down his punch cup, folded his arms in front of him, and leaned against the large mahogany dining table.

"Who is it that decides which rules, or cards, are 'wild' and which ones are the 'regular' cards?" asked James.

"You raise a critical issue I was about to get to," Ryle replied. "Our problem is a changing world view. At one time there was no question that this was a Christian nation. We knew exactly where to go to get our rules. We went to the Bible. We had a few minor differences of opinion on what the rules meant; but at least, we had the ultimate Authority making the rules."

"But, of course, some would question the Bible's validity," James said. "Some, like myself, are agnostic, or even atheists. Isn't it possible to have a good set of moral principles based on a humanistic, philosophical foundation?"

"No! That's the problem!" Ryle exclaimed. "As a nation we've come to embrace moral relativism. But as recent history bears out, relativism doesn't work. We have seen our society crumbling all around us. Our new 'liberties' have left a painful trail of broken homes, victims of crime, drug abuse, gambling addiction, and teenage pregnancies."

"Some of what you say is true. Liberties can be abused," said James. "However, I don't see what's wrong with adding liberties if it means the potential for a better life, especially if it's not hurting anyone? Some would say that abortion, for instance, helps to improve the quality of life for women."

"I can't see how a woman's quality of life can be improved by living with the guilt of having killed her own child. And what about the child?"

James smiled and said sardonically, "You mean the fetus?"

"Is there a difference? Life is life."

"Some very intelligent people believe a fetus is just a blob of tissue," James responded. "And if it's only tissue, what's wrong with cutting it out like you would a cancerous tumor?"

"That's a good question," Ryle said. "Let me try to answer it with another story."

"Several years ago a young woman was starting out in a career and because of her promiscuity had become pregnant. Unfortunately, because the timing was poor and the relationship was not a serious one, the woman decided to have an abortion. 'After all,' she thought, 'it was *only* tissue, not a real child. Besides, don't I have a right to determine what happens within my own body?'

"A few years passed and the young woman met the man of her dreams. After a torrid romance, the couple married and settled down. At first, they were satisfied to pursue their careers. But after a while, they decided their marriage was incomplete without children. For the next few years, they tried to get pregnant but without success. For some reason that an army of doctors and specialists could not explain, they were infertile. They began to realize how precious life really is. When the doctors explained that they could offer them little hope, they began to mourn the child they could not have.

"Then, one day, much to their surprise, the woman discovered she was pregnant. Once again the doctors could not tell her what had finally enabled them to conceive. They could only tell her that the fetus was at approximately the sixth or seventh week of development.

"The parents-to-be were so excited they began calling their friends and family to tell them the good news. They began making plans for the baby's room and discussing possible names. All this, even though the birth was more than seven months away.

"Then the worst of all possible fates occurred. The woman had a miscarriage! Once again the joy disappeared and their lives came under the darkness of grief. And for what? Over the expulsion of mere 'tissue' from the woman's body? Or was it more than that?"

As Joan and Vivian returned from their rounds, James said, "That's a very touching story and perhaps it makes a point, I think. But it's based on sentiment, not science. With an emotional issue like abortion, I think you have to stick to the medical facts."

"Well, James, has my husband converted you to a conservative viewpoint?" Joan asked with a smile.

James laughed. "Not quite. But he's trying. It seems our discussion has turned into a debate on abortion."

"It can't be much of a debate," Vivian quipped. "A woman's right to control her own body is an open and shut case."

"Not as open and shut as you think," Ryle said.

"How can you even suggest that, Ryle?" Vivian asked. "Of course a woman has the right to decide what happens within her own body!"

"On the surface, one might think so," he said. "The problem is there's a conflict of rights at stake. There is the right of the woman versus the right of the unborn child."

"What Ryle was about to explain," James interjected, "was how a fetus could be considered anything more than a blob of tissue in a woman's body. That seems to be the critical question. But I've asked him to stick to the medical facts."

"Let me answer that one," Joan said anxiously. "I've done my research."

"Go ahead, Honey," Ryle said.

Joan smiled. "Well, let me see," she said. "By the end of the first month of pregnancy, the blob of tissue you are referring to is already forming its brain, eyes, ears, and nose. It also has a heart that is beating regularly and pumping blood cells through its own system. And, by the way, the child's blood type may be different from that of the mother. That, in itself, suggests that there are two separate human beings involved."

Joan took a second to look James and Vivian in the eye to see if they registered the point. They both nodded and she continued her case.

"The developing fetus has a nervous system, skeleton, and musculature that is separate from its mother. Most importantly, the child *is genetically different* from the mother or any other human being that has ever existed. It has an entirely separate set of genes dictating its development. If it were *just tissue,* it would have the same genetic code as its mother, but it doesn't. Therefore, one has to conclude that the fetus, or child, is a separate human being."

"So even if you don't accept Biblical precepts about the soul of the individual, or the emotional reaction of a woman who has miscarried," Dr. Brandon added, looking James in the eye, "you still have to deal with scientific fact."

"Maybe that's true," Vivian said, "but I think it's still important to keep abortion legal to keep it safe. We have to eliminate the back alley. After all, women have always had abortions and always will. Making abortions illegal isn't going to prevent women from having them."

Ryle replied, "What you're suggesting, first of all, Vivian, is that we should abolish laws simply because they're broken. Now think about that. Should we legalize murder just because so many are committed? Should we legalize theft, just because it happens all the time? Imagine what our society would be like if there weren't laws against murder and theft. So, I'll ask you, how is abortion any different? The answer is, it's not! But because we've made it legal, nearly forty million people have died from abortions in the United States since *Roe v. Wade*."

"Making abortions legal does not necessarily make them safe," Joan added. "Besides all sorts of possible complications like hemorrhaging, cervical tears, perforated uteruses, and you name it—many women die each year from *legal* abortions. Wouldn't you be at least a little bit worried if Hope had an abortion?"

"Not if it were done by a qualified physician," Vivian said.

"Qualified or not, I'd still be worried about Faith," Joan said. "Accidents happen more than you think."

"Well, I don't think you have to be paranoid about abortions," Vivian said. "Sure, accidents happen. But they happen in any kind of surgical procedure. We just have to make sure we reduce the risks through proper monitoring."

"And let's not forget that overriding all of this is individual freedom," James said. "Even though I appreciated your parable about the poker game, Ryle, I think we have to protect individual liberties, including a woman's right to choose. Besides, in reality, this is a *political* issue. Abortion rights will always be determined by nine justices in Washington who, whether you like it or not, are influenced by public opinion. And probably one day, we'll have an amendment that guarantees abortion rights. It will be passed because of public pressure and interest groups."

"But what if *the people* are wrong? What if they're misguided? Public opinion is not, and never has been the basis of truth," Ryle replied.

"Perhaps not. But that's not the point," James said. "The point is that even if the public is wrong, the public is right, because power makes it so."

"So you're saying that might makes right, is that it?" Ryle asked.

"It sounds uncivilized the way you put it," James said. "But the *might* I'm talking about is the *might* of the people. It's democracy in action."

"You call it democracy but I call it 'tyranny of the majority.' I think in your own heart you know you're just playing with words to cover up the truth.

"Well, why don't we just agree to disagree? You have your views and I have mine," James said.

"I'm sorry. But we can't let you off the hook that easy," said Ryle.

"What do you mean?"

"The *status quo* is that abortion is legal even though it's wrong. If we just agree to disagree, nothing changes and abortion is still legal. I'm afraid we have to keep hounding liberals with the truth."

"You keep talking about truth," James replied. "But what is truth? Like I said before, what is true to you may not be true to me."

"Wasn't that Pilate's question?" Ryle mused out loud. But the comment was lost on James and Vivian. "I guess we're back to square one again," he said.

A Mother's Heart   7

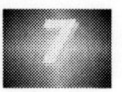

School was almost over for the year and Kara was spending the last half-hour sharing a good-bye hug with each student. Her eyes were misty by the time she got around to the last student, Shawn Benson. When she stepped up to Shawn with her arms opened wide he said, "That's okay, Mrs. Ellison, I don't need a hug. I'll be seeing you around school next year."

"Well, how about a 'good-bye for the summer hug' then?" Kara asked.

"Oh, okay, if it'll make you feel better," Shawn said with feigned indifference.

Kara wrapped her arms around him and ordered, "Take care of yourself. Stay out of mischief!"

Shawn blushed.

"Who me? No sweat!"

Kara was joking, of course. She often spoke of Shawn as "her little gentleman" and had a special place for him in her heart knowing that his mother had died in an automobile accident when he was an infant. At the final bell, Kara led her troop to the front door for the last time.

"Good-bye! Have a nice summer!" she said.

The cue was like the starting bell in a horse race. When she opened the door her students bolted out like thoroughbreds from the starting gate. Kara stood just outside the door and waved as they disappeared onto the busses and into the neighborhood. It was a good feeling to be through for the year; yet, as always, she was sad to see the children leave. They were hers for a season but now they were gone.

Sharon Huxtable, a tall, dark-haired woman in her late thirties, was also standing at the door waving good-bye to her class.

"I'm going to miss those kids, especially Shawn," Kara confessed as she wiped her eyes with a tissue.

"Teach sixth grade, then you won't miss them," Sharon said.

Kara smiled but quickly admitted, "It's a relief to be done, but saying good-bye is still tough."

"You need kids of your own, Kara," Sharon said.

The comment was like a bee sting to her heart—unexpected and sharply painful. "It's not by choice," Kara felt like saying, but held her tongue.

Sharon sensed her pain through the profoundly despondent look in Kara's eyes. She felt contrite and immediately attempted to salve the wound.

"Why don't you come down to my room for a minute? There's something I want to share with you."

"Okay," Kara said, still taken aback by the comment, but nonetheless feeling obliged to accept the invitation.

The two women walked side-by-side down the long, vacated hallway to Sharon's room at the far end of the building. "About a month ago," Sharon began, "I overheard you talking to Sandy about your infertility. I just want you to know that I know how you feel. I have the same problem."

"You do? But how can that be? I've heard you talk about your kids."

"I do have kids," Sharon said as they entered her barren classroom.

Only four days before Sharon's classroom was gaily decorated and buzzing with students. Now there was hardly a sign of life. The students were gone, the walls were bare, and the chairs and desks were stacked neatly in one corner of the room. Sharon pulled out two student desks from the stack and the two women sat on the desks facing each other.

"I don't understand," Kara said.

"My kids are adopted."

"I didn't know that."

"Oh, yes," Sharon said. "I have a little boy, Kirk, who was adopted at birth and is now ten. He's white. And I have two little girls, Christine and Colleen, sisters from Korea, who are now seven and eight, but we adopted them when they were one and two."

"That's wonderful! Robert and I have been talking about adoption, but my gynecologist suggested that we try *in vitro* fertilization. We don't know what we're going to do."

"I heard you talking about *in vitro* at lunch. I wanted to say something then, but I didn't want to be too forward," Sharon said.

"What did you want to say?"

"I have a friend who's also infertile. She just recently went through her second attempt at *in vitro* fertilization. Both attempts failed."

"Oh, really? Are they still trying?"

"Well, I don't know if they've decided yet. Besides the hassle and low success rate, it's a real emotional roller coaster."

"I can imagine!"

Sharon nodded. She said, "I'm not saying this to discourage you, Kara. But, I just thought you should know the pitfalls before you got your hopes up."

"Oh, Sharon!" Kara sighed. "I don't know what to do! I *want* children so badly! But I just can't get pregnant. It's not fair! It's not right!"

Tears rolled down Kara's cheeks. Sharon walked to her desk and pulled out some tissue from her purse that she kept in the drawer. "Here," she said as she handed the tissue to Kara. "I'm sorry. I really didn't mean to upset you."

"No, I'm sorry. I shouldn't be such a baby."

"Believe me! I understand! I went through the exact same thing," Sharon said and then gave Kara a hug. "It's okay. Just let it out."

The emotion dammed inside for so long, now poured out in gentle sobs until Kara was drained of emotion. Wiping her eyes with a tissue, she said, "I'm sorry! I'm usually not like this."

"You have nothing to be sorry about," Sharon said. "God designed women to be mothers, physically and emotionally. When things get messed up physically for a woman so she can't have children, then naturally she's going to be affected emotionally as well. In your case, you might not be able to bear children, but you certainly have a mother's heart!"

"But what good does that do me?"

"Plenty, if you're able to adopt. You'll make a great mother!"

"Well, that's what I want, but this whole infertility business is so frustrating!"

"I know! I went through it myself. But you know what they say, ' When God closes a door, he opens a window.' Let adoption be your window."

Kara sighed. After a short pause, she asked, "Can I ask you a personal question?"

"Sure."

"I've thought about adoption a lot. But I've always wondered if it would really be the same. Do you think Robert and I would be able to love an adopted child?"

Sharon reached out and took Kara's hands in hers.

"I worried about that, too," Sharon said. "But do you know what I realized? You can love any child if you want to. That's because love is a choice, not an emotion. Just because a child is yours biologically doesn't guarantee that you'll love the child. Look at all the women who abort their babies or abuse their children. But, a woman who chooses to adopt *chooses* to love a child. She makes a sacrifice in order to give to another. If you're a *giver* and not a *taker*, you won't have any trouble loving an adopted child as if it were your own biological child. There really isn't any difference."

"Do you mean that?"

"I certainly do!" Sharon said. "I can't imagine loving any child more than I love my three kids."

"Thanks. That's reassuring to hear, Sharon."

"Well, that's just my opinion. I feel that a child is a child, adopted or not."

Kara nodded and then asked, "Would you mind if I asked you why you decided to adopt Korean children?"

"It just came down to cost and availability," Sharon said. "John and I wanted more children but we didn't want to wait. Some couples have to wait more than five years in order to adopt a white infant. And the cost of adopting a white baby can be anywhere from ten to thirty thousand dollars."

"Oh, my!" Kara said, her heart sinking. "Why is it so difficult?"

"It's supply and demand. There are more people who want to adopt infants than there are infants," Sharon said. "And the short supply drives the price up. But some people are willing and able to pay a lot of money for a baby."

"I didn't realize it was so difficult, or expensive," Kara said. "I'm not sure Robert and I can afford to wait that long or to spend that kind of money."

"It can be discouraging. Our first adoption took almost three years and I was on an emotional roller coaster the whole time."

Kara shook her head sadly and said, "Here I am, desperately wanting a child, and it seems like there's a conspiracy not to let me have one. Why is that?"

"I don't know," Sharon said. "But I know what you're going through."

A short time later, Kara walked out to her car and found Shawn sitting on the curb next to it.

"Shawn! What are you doing here?"

Shawn shrugged and said, "I just wanted to say thanks for being my teacher this year."

"Well, thank you, Shawn. That's nice of you to say."

"Yeah, well, having you for a teacher was kind of like having a mom. It was neat."

"Oh, Shawn—" Kara said while holding back the tears. "Well, I want you to know that if I ever have a boy of my own, I want him to be just like you."

"Thanks," he said with a smile. Then he jumped up and gave Kara a hug.

"Have a nice summer, Mrs. Ellison," he shouted as he turned toward home.

"See you in the fall, Shawn," Kara said with a wave as she watched Shawn disappear down the sidewalk.

"If…" she said to herself, "if ever I am so blessed…"

A Proper Burial 8

Elston was an aging industrial town that grew up along the banks of the Wolf River, forty miles west of the city. At the turn of the last century, it was a thriving center of industry and commerce. But like many small cities born in the industrial age, Elston failed to adapt to the times. Slowly, over the years following World War II, plants closed and businesses moved out of downtown, leaving the core of the city a mere silhouette of its prime. Meanwhile, Elston's neighborhoods had undergone a metamorphosis of their own. The once proud Victorian mansions of the white upper class professionals and industrialists had been converted into three and four flat apartment houses mostly inhabited by blue collar blacks and Hispanics. It was into this community that Juan Cantu invested his hopes and dreams of a better life.

Juan first came to Elston from Monterrey years ago, working as a laborer at a landscape nursery a few miles west of town. He would leave his home and family in Mexico in the early spring, work long hours at two jobs, save as much money as possible, and then return to Mexico in the late fall as the landscaping season came to an end. After two years, he brought his family to live with him in a Mexican neighborhood in town. To save money, the family crowded into a two-bedroom apartment, the top flat of a run down, three-story, Victorian. Juan, Maria, and the baby slept in one bedroom. The two teenage girls shared the other, leaving the two boys to double up on a bed in the living room.

Because of the crowded conditions, Juan's dream was to own his own home. With Maria's help working part-time as a maid at the Holiday Inn, the couple had saved up for a down payment on a three-bedroom Victorian just a few blocks from their present apartment. The house was in need of repairs, but Juan was handy and so he made an offer. He was on the phone with the real estate agent as the family was sitting down to supper.

"Miguel! Javier! Come! ¡Pronto!" Maria Cantu shouted in Spanglish to her seven and nine-year-old sons as she placed a pan of chicken and rice on the table.

"Just a minute!" Miguel shouted back. The boys were playing a video game in the living room.

"¡Ahora!"

"Hold on! I'm about to set a new record!" Miguel protested.

Juanita and Lucita were just sitting down at the table. Ernesto, the eight-month-old, was strapped in his high chair and crying for his supper.

"Lucita! You should see the new guy who works at Sam's!" Juanita said.

"Oh, really! What's he look like?"

"He's kinda short but he—"

"Quiet!" Juan said, standing at the refrigerator, his hand over the phone.

Juanita lowered her voice but her animated description continued. Then Javier pranced into the kitchen with Miguel straggling behind, loudly bemoaning his near miss.

"I could've set a new record if you wouldn't have messed me up."

"What? I didn't do anything!"

"You did, too!"

Juan put his hand over the phone again. "Be quiet! I can't hear!" he said angrily. Then he returned the phone to his ear and plugged his other ear with his finger. The boys sat down exchanging dirty looks and muffled threats.

"¡Muchas Gracias! ¡Adiós!" Juan said finally and hung up the phone. "That was thee realtor," he said as he joined his family at the table.

Everyone drew silent and stared at Juan, anxiously awaiting the news. Juan heightened the suspense by slowly dishing himself a large helping of chicken and rice.

His wife asked impatiently, "Juan, what deed he say?"

Juan put down his fork. With a blank expression, he looked around at his wife and children. Then his face lit up with a wide grin. "They took our offer," he said.

The older children broke into cheers. Maria put her hands together in thanksgiving, flashing a big smile. She said exuberantly, "¡Bueno!"

"Awesome! We get our own bedroom!" Miguel said.

"Cool!" Javier added.

"Hold on!" Juan interrupted. "It's not ours yet. We still have to get our loan approved."

"But we will get the loan, won't we, Papa?" Lucita asked.

"I hope so. Say your prayers."

It was a restless night for Juan. Worries over the loan and the anticipation of owning his own home left him tossing and turning. At three-thirty, his alarm pierced the dark silence. He had fallen asleep only an hour before; but in half-an-hour, he had to be at the clinic for two hours of janitorial work before heading to his landscaping job. Juan reached for the clock. After a few seconds of fumbling, he found the button and silenced the shrill reveille. From force of habit, he rolled out of bed immediately and quietly pulled on a pair of old, faded jeans and a fresh, white T-shirt. Then he crept into the living room to check on his boys and discovered that Miguel had robbed Javier of his covers. Juan retraced his steps to the hallway linen closet and pulled out an extra blanket. He returned to the scene of the crime, covered up the victim, and gave Javier a kiss on the forehead before tiptoeing out to the kitchen. Forsaking breakfast, he pulled on his heavy boots, grabbed his lunch out of the refrigerator, slipped out the back door, and descended the black wrought iron stairwell. He trudged wearily around the building to the street where his rusty, wrinkled, 1984 Chevy sat tired and reluctant.

The door creaked as Juan grabbed the handle and gave it a sharp pull. He climbed into the front seat and shivered in the cool, pre-dawn air. When he turned the ignition, the grumpy engine refused to turn over. Juan gently prodded the stubborn mechanical mule with pedal and key and eventually coaxed it from its lethargic slumber.

The five-minute drive to work took him north along the East Side of the Wolf River for several blocks to a neighborhood where long-standing commercial, industrial, and residential properties merged together. The abortuary, a corner building on the main highway running through the northeast part of town, was kitty-corner from a century old firehouse that had been converted to a city warehouse. Just up the street from the clinic, Elston Paper Products churned out corrugated boxes. Two blocks down the street, the local middle school sat quietly enjoying its summer respite from the neighborhood teenagers. Across the street from the clinic sat a parking lot. Beyond that began a residential neighborhood, a mix of homes built in the first half of the century or earlier. A duplicate neighborhood began just one block behind the clinic.

The front of the one story clinic was demure, shunning attention. Its pale yellow brick exterior was broken up by two large picture windows, one on each side of a single glass door, with blinds concealing the interior. A small sign mounted next to the door read, "Women's Health Clinic of DuKane." The only clue exposing the real business conducted within was a frequent group of pickets across the street holding signs, "Abortion Kills," or "It's a Child, Not a Choice!"

It was four o'clock when Juan pulled into the empty parking lot behind the clinic. On most days, he immediately climbed out of his car to begin his duties, but this morning was different. He felt inclined to sit for a moment. He sensed an obscure presence although the street, like the parking lot, was deserted. When he pulled himself out of the car, he looked around for something the essence of which he was not sure. As he walked to the back door of the clinic, he passed the trash bin sitting just outside the rear entrance. All at once he was overcome by a vague, eerie feeling.

When he opened the door, he immediately recognized the previously nebulous presence of evil. He sensed in his soul the silent screams of the dead calling out to him from every brick, every tile, every cabinet, and every file. Behind those screams, a sinister laugh seemed to resonate, and the laugh wore on him heavily. He shivered as he felt the finger of death beckon him, also. For a moment, he was paralyzed. Finally and deliberately, he reached for the switch and turned on the hall light. Then he took one last look outside before he closed the door behind him. After a few moments, the tugging at his soul faded and he pushed his uneasy feelings to the back of his mind.

Juan worked quickly. He began by vacuuming the front lobby and waiting area. Next, he moved back to the small consultation and counseling offices for more vacuuming and dusting. Then he mopped the lab and "treatment" room floors, scrubbed the sinks, cleaned the bathrooms, and finally, hauled two large plastic garbage bags out to the trash bin in back of the building. By this time, the dawn's illuminating rays had filled the dark void of night. Juan threw open the lid of the trash bin and found a small paper package sitting on top of the other bags of garbage. A large red spot on the side of the package piqued his curiosity. He reached in and picked out the article. As he examined it closely, he realized there were several layers of paper drape concealing the contents. He set the package on the ground and carefully began to unwrap it. As he peeled away the last layer, he found the bloody remains of a premature baby with its head shrunken and crushed. The baby's blood had seeped through the paper overnight, leaving a red stain on the outside of the package. Juan turned his head to the side and averted his eyes. After taking a couple of deep breaths, he looked once again at the remains. A tidal wave of disgust and outrage washed over him. He ran inside the clinic to the supply room and rummaged for a small container. Finding a cardboard box with a few rubber gloves inside, he took the remaining gloves out of the box and set them on the shelf. Hastily, he returned to the trash bin with the box and carefully wrapped up the baby and put it into the makeshift coffin. After placing the box in the trunk of his car, he hurried back into the building to finish his chores.

• • •

Hours earlier, the tiny corpse had been alive and well, "safely" nested in its mother's womb. The baby's mother, Jan Coleman, had arrived early the previous evening at the request of the clinic staff.

"I'm nervous," she confessed to the nurse who led her from the waiting area to the back of the clinic.

"You'll be okay," the nurse said as she led Jan into the examining room. "Please take off your clothes and have a seat on the edge of the table."

The nurse covered Jan with a sheet. As she was leaving she said, "I'll tell the doctor you're ready."

Jan was ambivalent about the abortion. Her maternal instincts were crying out, "Don't do it!" Yet, at twenty-seven and single, with a high paying job and a rising star in the corporate world, she realized she couldn't have the dual responsibilities of motherhood and a career at the same time. She would have to give up one or the other. Besides, the father, her boss, was a man ten years older and already the father of two children. He was not interested in having another child, especially under the present circumstances. "With his divorce almost final," Jan had confided in a friend, "he's been under a lot of stress. I don't want to add any more." She relented and agreed to have the abortion.

Within minutes the doctor, Tom Morlon, entered the room. He was a short man with a slight build and golden hair. Jan guessed he was in his late thirties or early forties.

"Hello, Jan," he said with a smile.

"Hi," Jan replied nervously, forcing a taut smile.

"How are you?"

"Okay, I guess."

"Good. Let's see how you're doing. This won't hurt at all. Just relax."

Jan's "procedure" began two days before. When she first came in, the doctor determined she was twenty-six weeks LMP, or, "last menstrual period." This put the child at or past viability in most cases. Because of the size of the child, approximately eight inches long and weighing nearly a pound, and because of the toughness of the "fetal tissue," Dr. Morlon decided to try a new procedure he had learned recently at a seminar.

The procedure, a partial birth abortion, required three days to complete because the opening of Jan's cervix had to be greatly enlarged. The first two days were used to dilate her cervix through the use of laminaria, or cylindrical shaped devices. These were inserted into Jan's cervix and were expected to gradually increase in diameter as they absorbed water. Hence, it was necessary for Tom to re-examine Jan prior to the abortion to make sure she was sufficiently dilated.

When Tom finished his examination, he said, "It looks like you're ready. I believe you had decided on general anesthesia, is that correct?"

"Yes. My sister is waiting out front. She's going to give me a ride home."

"Good. You can get dressed and go back to the front desk and take care of the bill. We'll call you back in just a little while. When we're done, I'll give you a prescription for pain just in case."

Jan was led to the "treatment" room a short while later. She was put on the table and the anesthetist put her to sleep. When everything was ready, Tom came in to begin the procedure. He started by cleaning off Jan's cervix with Betadine. Next, a loud humming sound filled the room for a few seconds as he used the vacuum to break the bag of amniotic fluid surrounding the baby. Assisted by an ultra-sound machine, he probed for the child by inserting forceps through the vagina and cervical canal into the uterus.

In the standard procedure, the object was to dismember the child and remove it piece by piece. Because of its size, the head would have to be crushed with the forceps inside the uterus before it could be removed. However, following the partial birth technique, Tom proceeded by grasping one of the baby's legs with forceps and pulled the baby around inside the uterus to position the child so it was feet first and face down toward the floor. He then pulled one leg out at a time followed by the torso until he exposed the child to the outside world up to its neck. Half born and still alive, Jan's baby could not be removed any farther because the size of the head was still too large for the opening of the cervix. But even if it were possible to remove the child at this point, Dr. Morlon would not do it. If he did, he would be dealing with a live birth, which was not only contrary to the whole point of the procedure, but the laws of the state would protect the child. Sadly, in the case of this child, the long arm of the law was two inches too short!

The nurse, unfamiliar with the procedure, leaned over to see what was happening. Tom had slid his hand up the baby's back and hooked his index finger and ring finger over the baby's shoulders. He used his middle finger to hold Jan's cervix away from the baby's neck. The nurse could see the child's tiny legs kicking frantically as it struggled to return to its protective enclave.

"Scissors," he said.

The nurse looked at Tom curiously and handed him the scissors. Tom located the base of the skull and forcefully jammed the blunt instrument into the back of the baby's head. Then he spread the tips of the scissors to enlarge the hole. After removing the scissors, he inserted a suction catheter into the opening at the back of baby's head.

"What are you doing?" the nurse asked.

"Do you really want to know?"

"Yes."

"I'm sucking out the brains."

"Oh, my God!" she gasped as she suddenly felt sick to her stomach.

"There," he said as he finished the vacuum extraction.

With the skull collapsed, the child was dead. It was now safe, surgically and legally, to remove the rest of the child from the mother's birth canal.

Tom dumped the baby's lifeless remains into the disposal pan. He said with an air of callousness, "This one doesn't look like it's going to fit down the garbage disposal. You'd better wrap it up really well and bury it in the trash bin."

The seasoned nurse, who had been working at the clinic for nearly a week, had witnessed a lot in her career. She had assisted doctors in the emergency room for many years, helping victims of serious accidents. Some of those victims were badly disfigured or had severed limbs, stories too gruesome to tell. In each of those cases, she was able to cope with the gory reality because she was helping someone in need. But this was entirely different. As she looked at the ghastly remains of the child lying in the pan, her eyes welled up with tears. She said disgustedly, "I can't do this. I'm sorry but I quit." She walked briskly out of the room, never to return.

•••

After locking up the clinic, Juan hurried back to his car. He drove a few blocks to St. Agnes Catholic Church that had just opened for morning mass. He stepped inside the church and found himself alone in the lobby. Out of habit, he dipped his fingers into the bowl of holy water next to the door and made the sign of the cross. Then he took a small sponge from his pocket and soaked it with holy water. Repeating the sign of the cross on his way out, Juan quickly returned to his car and made the fifteen-minute drive to the nursery.

Juan arrived at work with half-an-hour to spare. He went into the barn and brought out a shovel, some string, and a four-foot piece of wooden lath. Then he went back to the car for the "coffin" and the sponge. He set the materials on the front seat of a nursery pickup and drove off to a remote part of the property. In a heavily wooded area of century-old oak trees and tall, thick brush, he dug a tiny grave three feet deep. Then he dropped to his knees, opened the box again, and loosened the paper. In an impromptu ceremony, he squeezed the holy water from the sponge onto the corpse as he made the sign of the cross over the dead child. He said, "I baptize you in the name of thee Father, and of thee Son, and of thee Holy Spirit. Amen." He was not sure if a posthumous baptism was acceptable by God or the Church, but he felt it ought to be done, just in case. After performing the sacrament, he wrapped up the corpse again and put it back in the box and lowered it into the grave. When the hole was filled, he took the lath and broke it into uneven pieces. Using the string, he put the pieces together to form a cross. Finally, he stuck the cross in the ground and said, "At least now you're with Him."

A Morning at the Clinic

The sun ascended accusingly over the posh suburb of South Burlington, some thirty miles west of the city. The radiant red orb rising out of the east was like a fresh wound inflicted on the morning sky, welling up blood from the heart of heaven. By the time the full sphere was visible over the horizon, its red rays had stained the entire sky a crimson hue. Large white clouds, which had marched in from the west under the cover of night, began soaking up the bloody rays of the sun like large cotton balls attempting to stop a massive hemorrhage. The effort was to no avail. The clouds had absorbed their fill, but the rays of the sun were as infinite as the power of the holy God who created them.

Tom Morlon was sleeping soundly when the sun's rays, now laser white, tried piercing their way through the heavy drapes guarding his bedroom window. But like a heart shrouded in self-deceit, he was untouched by the light. Instead, it was his alarm and a nudge by his wife, Beth, that stirred him. After several rings, he reached over and pressed the snooze. He repeated the act twice before giving in and rolling out of bed. The procrastination was brought on by a late "business meeting" with his clinic director, Lisa Slatkin, a voluptuous redhead, willing to mix business with pleasure.

"How about making me some bacon and eggs while I take a shower?" Tom said in a deceitfully endearing tone as rolled over and cuddled up to Beth.

"What time is it?" Beth mumbled, half asleep.

"Six-fifteen. Time to get up."

"I'm tired, Tom. There's a box of doughnuts in the refrigerator."

"Come on, Beth," he said. "You can always go back to bed."

"Oh, all right."

While Beth put on her bathrobe and trudged sleepily to the kitchen to make breakfast, Tom shaved and showered and stepped into the large walk-in closet off the bathroom. After dressing for work, he selected his "lucky" green pants for his afternoon golf match. Then he searched for his green and white short sleeve shirt.

"Where is it?" he said, annoyed. He decided to look in the hamper. After rummaging through the contents, he discovered the shirt near the bottom.

"I don't believe it! She can't even get the laundry done!"

He picked out his white shirt instead and put it together with his yellow pants on a hanger. Then he walked down the grand spiral staircase to the spacious kitchen of the five-bedroom English Tudor. He was greeted with the smell of sausage and eggs. His morning newspaper was set out on the breakfast table.

"Why are you making sausage? I thought I asked for bacon," he said.

"We ran out of bacon. I thought you'd like sausage with your eggs."

"No, not really. Just give me the eggs."

"What about the sausage?"

"You can eat it, or give it to Chester," he said.

The large Labrador retriever lying on the floor next to the stove perked his ears at the mention of his name, but he disappointedly dropped his jaw to the floor again after nothing came of it.

Tom began reading the front page of the *Journal*. Suddenly, he exclaimed, "They did it again!"

"What's that?"

"Some jerks sabotaged another clinic in Florida. They busted windows and spray painted the walls!" he said disgustedly. "This is getting out of hand. One day somebody is going to get killed at a clinic!"

"Here's your eggs, Dear," Beth said as she placed his eggs and orange juice in front of him.

Tom put down his paper and looked at his plate.

"These are sunny side up. I wanted scrambled eggs."

"But Tom, you almost always have your eggs sunny side up."

"Yeah, but I wanted them scrambled today. Why don't you ever check with me before you screw things up?"

"If you want scrambled eggs, I can do it in a jiffy."

"Nevermind. I've got to get going."

Tom grabbed the box of doughnuts from the refrigerator and stormed out of the kitchen. A tear escaped Beth's eye.

It was seven o'clock when Tom backed his silver Lexus out of the garage. Lisa Slatkin was already at the clinic when Tom called her from his cell phone.

"Good morning!" he said.

"Did you get enough sleep, Tom?"

"Yeah, enough," he said through a yawn. "How's our schedule today?"

"We've got a full slate."

"Great! I'll be there in about ten minutes. Oh! Before I forget, I wanted to remind you that Hope is starting today. She called yesterday and I told her to come in about nine after things got going a bit."

"That's fine. I'll get her started."

When Tom pulled into the parking lot, he passed the usual group of protesters parading across the street. Each demonstrator was armed with a sign reminding the reader, "Abortion Kills Children" or "It's a Baby, Not a Choice." The pickets recognized Tom's car and wildly waved their placards as he drove by. But the effort and energy was lost on the man. He paid little attention to the messages intended to prick his conscience. After parking in the rear lot, Tom entered the clinic through the back door. He went directly to Lisa's office. She was at her desk waiting for him with some bad news.

"Dr. Bernard just called," she said. "He can't come in this afternoon. His father died last night and he's flying to Florida to help his mother with the funeral arrangements."

"Oh, great! Is anyone else available?"

"I've already tried Dr. Patel but he has surgery at noon."

"What about Young?"

"He's busy, too. Besides, we have two second-trimesters and he won't do them. He's a little gun shy after the one he botched in March. He's worried about a lawsuit."

"Shoot! There goes my golf this afternoon!" Tom said. "Give Harry a call and let him know I won't be there."

"Sorry," Lisa said with a frown. "These things happen."

"I know," Tom said with a hint of a smile. "It's not your fault."

•••

The first patients arrived at quarter to eight. One young woman, Cheryl, had come in with her boyfriend, Jeff. She was sixteen with dark brown hair, brown eyes, and a full figure. He was tall and blonde and two years older. He remained in the waiting area in front while Cheryl was taken to the back.

Jeff was on edge as he waited for the news. At first, he paced back and forth with his eyes downcast, avoiding eye contact with the others in the room. Then he sat down and nervously leafed through a short pile of worn magazines. When Lisa finally appeared and asked for him, he knew it wasn't a good sign. If Cheryl had come out by herself, then he knew the test was negative and he was in the clear. Instead, Lisa led him back to her office where Cheryl was sitting teary-eyed. As soon as Jeff appeared in the doorway, Cheryl ran to him and wrapped her arms around him. Neither one said a word, but both understood that a critical decision had to be made. Lisa directed them to the two chairs in front of her desk. Then she sat down at her desk and organized Cheryl's file.

"Well, Jeff," Lisa said, "our tests have confirmed that Cheryl is pregnant. She's probably about six or seven weeks along."

Jeff nodded silently. He gently squeezed Cheryl's hand.

"How do you feel about that?" Lisa asked.

"I don't know," he said. He turned to Cheryl and asked, "How do you feel?"

Lisa interrupted, "Sorry, but Cheryl has already told me how she feels. I'd like to know how you feel."

Jeff paused for a moment. "I don't know. Scared, I guess."

"In what way?" Lisa asked.

"Well..." he said, hesitating, "I guess I'm scared about what will happen when our parents find out."

"Will they be angry?"

"Will they ever!"

"Why?"

"They don't know we've been having sex. If they did, her father would probably shoot me."

"Is that right, Cheryl?"

"Execution style," Cheryl said, looking at Jeff. "We probably wouldn't be able to see each other anymore."

"That would be a shame, wouldn't it?"

The young couple looked at each other and nodded their heads.

"Have you two thought about getting married?"

Jeff said, "Maybe some day. But we're too young right now."

"I see," Lisa said, making a note in her file. "Then it seems the best thing to do in this situation is to terminate the pregnancy."

"You mean have an abortion?" Cheryl asked.

"Yes."

"I wish I could, but I don't think my parents will let me."

"Why do your parents have to know?"

"Because they have to sign a consent form, right?" Cheryl asked.

"Not in this state," Lisa said. "Here, a pregnant woman under eighteen is considered to be an 'emancipated minor.' That means she has the rights of an adult, including the right to terminate a pregnancy. Your parents don't even have to know about your decision."

"Really?" Cheryl asked.

"Really."

"Boy, that makes things a lot easier!" Jeff said.

"The only possible problem I see is paying for the procedure," Lisa said.

"How much will it cost?" Cheryl asked.

"It depends on the anesthetic. With a local anesthetic, it's two hundred and seventy-five dollars cash or two hundred and eighty-five dollars if you use Visa or Mastercard. It's four hundred and fifty dollars if you have what we call the 'Twilight' package. That's a combination of local and general anesthesia. It's our most popular package and what we recommend in early pregnancies."

"I only brought three hundred with me," Jeff said. "I guess I could go to the bank and take out more."

"How bad will it hurt?" Cheryl asked.

"With a local anesthetic there will be some discomfort, but it won't be unbearable. And after the procedure, the doctor will give you a prescription for pain, just in case."

"I'll go with the local anesthetic," Cheryl said.

"Are you sure?" Jeff asked. "I'll get the money if you want."

"No. You need the money for college. I'll be all right."

"Okay, I guess that's settled," Lisa said. "Are you ready to have the procedure done today?"

"I guess the sooner the better," Cheryl said.

"Good, we'll get you started right away."

"Just a minute," Jeff said. "Before we do this, is there any risk involved?"

"You mean medically?" Lisa asked.

"Yeah. I don't want anything to happen to Cheryl."

A Morning at the Clinic

"Don't worry, Jeff. It's a safe, simple procedure. And when you leave here today, your worries will be over!"

•••

It was a busy morning when Hope arrived at the clinic a few minutes before nine. She parked her car in back and walked around the building to the front entrance. As she came around the front corner, another young woman intercepted her.

"Would you mind talking with me for just a minute before you go into the clinic?" the woman asked.

"Who, me?" Hope asked.

"Yes," the woman answered. "Before you have an abortion, you should know that there are organizations that will give you support and help pay the costs for you to have this baby. Someone will adopt your child."

Hope blushed. She said, "I'm not pregnant. I work here."

"I'm sorry. I didn't realize."

"It's okay, but excuse me. I have to go inside now."

As Hope opened the door, the young woman said, "We can help you find another job where children aren't being murdered."

"No, thanks."

Hope stood just inside the doorway and looked around. To the right was the waiting room where she noticed a dozen or more people, mostly women and teenage girls. Two women were sitting in one corner of the room crying quietly together; most, however, were sitting anxiously silent. She walked up to the receptionist's desk and announced, "Hi, I'm Hope Stuart. I'm Dr. Morlon's niece. I'm supposed to start working today."

"Oh, yes," the receptionist said with a smile. "I'll call Lisa. She was expecting you."

Lisa appeared a minute later. "Hello, Hope," she said. "I'm Lisa Slatkin, the clinic director. It's nice to meet you. Your uncle has told me so much about you! I'm glad you've come to work for us."

"I'm glad, too. A little nervous, but glad," Hope admitted.

"Well, let me just show you around and make you feel at home," Lisa said.

Hope was given the grand tour. She was shown the counseling office, the lab, the examination room, the supply room, and the recovery room where several women were lying in the wake of their abortions. In recovery, Hope noticed one woman crying, suffering intense pain. As they passed the operating room, Hope heard a loud hum, a suction abortion in progress.

"What's that?" she asked.

"The patient is having a routine procedure. That was the vacuum."

"Oh," Hope said. After a brief pause, she asked, "This may sound like a dumb question, but is that how it's done? With a vacuum?"

"Actually, that's a good question. It's something you should know if you're going to work here," Lisa said. "There are several kinds of treatments. The type of procedure used depends on the woman and how far along she is in her pregnancy. The vacuum procedure is common in the early stages of a pregnancy."

"Really? What does it involve?"

"The procedure?"

"Yes."

"Well, first, the patient is given a local anesthetic in her cervix," Lisa explained. "Then the cervical canal is dilated. After that, the doctor inserts a small plastic tube and vacuums up the tissue. To make sure all the tissue has been removed, the doctor gently scrapes the uterine wall with a spoon-shaped instrument called a curette. The whole process takes about ten minutes. It's a simple, painless operation actually."

"I guess that's not so bad," Hope said. "I always thought abortions were messier if you know what I mean."

"That's what a lot of people would want you to believe. It's really not a big deal."

Just then, Tom emerged from the operating room. He had a worried look.

"Hi, Hope," he said, forcing a smile. "Excuse us a minute. I have to speak to Lisa."

The two stepped into Lisa's office.

"We had a complication with that last girl," Tom said with an edge to his voice.

"With Cheryl? What happened?"

"She's got a small tear in her cervix. It'll require stitches. Right now she's bleeding badly. The nurses are applying pressure with pads, but the blood is pouring out. We've got to keep an eye on her blood pressure. You'd better keep her here a bit longer and make sure she's okay before you let her go. Who's here with her?"

"Her boyfriend," Lisa replied. "Her parents don't know she's here. He's out front waiting. He was worried that something might happen. I'd hate to tell him that there's been a complication. What am I supposed to tell him?"

"I don't know. That's your job. I just work in the back," Tom said with a smile as he was slipping out the door.

"Thanks," said Lisa.

"Hi, Hope! How's my favorite niece?" Tom said as he met her in the hallway again.

"Fine! I'm ready to start."

"Great! I can't talk to you now, but I'll catch you a little later. Lisa will get you all squared away."

As Tom disappeared into the operating room, Lisa led Hope into her office and handed her a list of guidelines for abortion counseling.

Lisa said, "Why don't you just read this for a few minutes while I take care of another matter? I'll answer any questions you have when I come back."

Lisa hurried out to the waiting area and intercepted Jeff in the middle of his paces. She gently took him by the arm and led him to the small counseling room immediately behind the receptionist area. She closed the door and said, "Why don't you sit down, Jeff? There's something I have to tell you."

"How is she? Is she all right?"

"She's fine."

Jeff gave a sigh of relief. "Will she be out soon?" he asked.

"Well, that's what I have to tell you."

"Oh, no! Something's wrong! Something happened! Didn't it?" he said, his worried eyes riveted on Lisa.

"Nothing's wrong. Be calm. Her procedure is finished," Lisa said. "Everything's fine. I just need to tell you that Cheryl did require a few stitches. It's nothing out of the ordinary. It happens all the time. It just means that she has to stay a little longer in the recovery room so we can make sure that the bleeding has stopped completely. It will be a little while. You might want to go to lunch and come back."

"No, that's okay. I'll wait."

"That's fine, but it may be a couple of hours. She has to take it easy for a bit before we can let her go."

By the time Lisa returned to her office, Hope had finished looking over the guidelines.

"I don't understand," Hope said. "I thought I was going to be a receptionist. These guidelines make it seem as though I'd be some kind of counselor."

"Your primary responsibilities will be as a receptionist. You'll refer calls to a counselor, a doctor, or me. But there are going to be times when everyone is busy and you'll have to make a sale," Lisa explained.

"A sale?"

"I'm sorry. I guess that did come across kind of crass," Lisa said. "Of course, our primary goal is to provide optimal health care for women and to help those who are facing an unwanted pregnancy. We feel that every woman who inquires about terminating a pregnancy must be presented with the facts in such a way that she feels she's making the right decision. Here at Women's Health Clinic of DuKane, we feel it is our responsibility to enlighten women concerning the reproductive aspect of their lives. Facing an unplanned pregnancy is such an emotional experience that we want to allay any fears they have concerning the termination of a pregnancy—whether they're physical, emotional, psychological, moral, or legal fears. There are so many misconceptions about our business. We're only here to help women. Sometimes your job will require you to help a woman think clearly about terminating a pregnancy."

"How would I do that?"

"We have standard replies for any concerns a customer might have."

Hope nodded as Lisa continued.

"For example, if a woman wants to terminate but doesn't think it's the right thing to do, then we have to talk her through her hang-ups. If she feels as if she's taking a life, we tell her that a fetus is not a person. It's only tissue that should be removed like you would remove a tumor. That's why we never refer to the fetus as 'the baby.' We always refer to it as 'tissue.' We also tell the client that she has a right to control her own body and can do whatever she wants with it. We also like to point out to the client that 'every child should be a wanted child.' Most importantly, she has to understand that she has the right to choose what's best for her in her present life situation."

"I guess that's not too hard. I can do that," Hope said. Then she blushed as she confessed, "I have to admit that I really don't know what happens in an abortion."

Lisa pounced on Hope's language. "The correct terms to use are 'procedure' or 'treatment,'" she said. "Try to avoid the word 'abortion.' Some clients react negatively to the word. 'Abortion' carries negative connotations for many women."

"Sorry."

"No, that's all right. I'm not criticizing. I'm just training you, that's all. But I interrupted you. What was it you were saying?"

"I said I don't know anything about how a 'treatment' is done. And if someone asked me how it's done, or if it's safe, I wouldn't know what to say."

"No problem. I'll give you a small packet of literature that explains all that. The important thing you have to convey to the clients is that terminating a pregnancy is simple, safe, legal, and most often, the best choice for everyone involved."

"Okay, I guess I'll give it a try. I'll do my best."

"You'll do fine!" Lisa said. "Why don't you take this reading material and look through it at the front desk. You can have a seat next to Sandy and listen to how she answers the phone. That will be the best way to learn. Then maybe you can start taking over for her in the afternoon. If you have any questions, don't be afraid to ask."

"Great!" Hope said with a smile.

Lisa extended her hand and said, "Welcome aboard!"

•••

It was after lunch when Lisa finally led Jeff to her office to see Cheryl who was waiting anxiously to be discharged.

"Are you okay?" he asked.

"I'm fine," Cheryl said with a wince. "I'm sore though. Really sore."

"She'll be all right. She'll have cramping sensations and she'll be bleeding more than a normal period, but she'll recover quickly. She just needs some rest," Lisa said. "But if anything happens, especially if the bleeding gets too heavy, give us a call. We'll take care of her."

"Okay," Jeff said.

He put his arm around Cheryl and slowly led her down the hallway to the front entrance. Tears of pain, physical and emotional, began to drip from her face. When they opened the door they were greeted with a heavy downpour. Thunder echoed across the heavens as lightning lit the sky; and all the angels in heaven were in mourning as they looked down on Uncle Tom's clinic.

Protest 10

It was Sunday noon and the Brandons had just arrived home from church when the phone rang.

"Hello," Faith said as she answered the phone.

"Hello, may I speak with Ryan, please?" the male voice asked.

"I'm sorry, but he just went out jogging. He'll probably be back in about an hour. Can I take a message?"

"Yeah, I'd appreciate it. This is Jason Warner. Have him give me a call as soon as he gets home."

"Okay, will do," Faith said as she began writing down the message. "I'll tell him you called."

Faith clipped the message on the refrigerator door. Then she walked into the family room where her parents were reading the Sunday paper.

"I'm going to Hope's house now," she said from the doorway.

"Okay, have fun. Don't forget your sun tan lotion," her mother said.

"I won't. By the way, there's a message for Ryan on the refrigerator."

"We'll make sure he gets it," her father said. "We love you. Stay out of trouble!"

"Oh, Dad! When was the last time I was in trouble?" she asked. Then it struck her. "If he only knew the trouble I was in!" she thought.

Hope was lying out by her small kidney shaped pool wearing her florescent green bikini and sunglasses when Faith arrived.

81

"I knew you'd be out here already," Faith said.

"Why not? Get changed and get out here!"

"I'll be right out."

Faith entered the house through the back door off the kitchen. Eliza, the live-in maid, a slight, middle-aged, black woman with gently graying hair, was cleaning up around the sink.

"Hello Faith! I thought I'd see you here on a hot day like today," Eliza said.

"Hello, Eliza. How are you?"

"I'm fine, just fine. Are you gettin' all excited about goin' off to college?"

"Well, I'm not really going away. I'll be living at home and going to Justin."

"Oh, that's right. I keep forgettin' your father is the President there. Of course, it wouldn't make sense to go anywhere else, now would it?"

"No, it wouldn't. It's nice to be able to go to college for free. On the other hand, I feel like I don't have a choice."

"Yeah, I guess you're right. You're kinda stuck. But be glad for what you got, child. My nephew, Harry, graduates next year and my sister has no idea where they're goin' to get the money for college. She's hopin' he can earn a basketball scholarship somewhere. She doesn't know how else she can pay for it. Just count your blessin's!"

"I guess you're right," Faith said. "I am fortunate."

"Run along now," Eliza said. "Don't let me keep you from the sun."

Faith used the bathroom off the kitchen to change into a modest, one-piece suit. She turned sideways and examined herself in the mirror, moving her hand up and down across her stomach to see if she could feel a difference. When she returned to the pool, she discovered that Hope had company. Kris Haas, a high school classmate, had joined them.

Kris had a slim figure, long, curly, black hair, and a pretty smile. She was already in her suit.

"Hi, Kris!" Faith said. Her friends were lying side-by-side facing the afternoon sun. She dragged a third chaise lounge chair along side the others.

"Hi, Faith," Kris said. "How's it going?"

"All right, I guess. How's it going for you?"

"I'm *so-o-o* depressed," Kris said dramatically.

"Why? What's wrong?"

"Her beautician is moving out of town. Isn't that terrible!" Hope said facetiously.

Faith and Hope laughed.

"Well, it is terrible!" Kris protested. "I have this naturally curly hair and not many beauticians know how to work with it."

Faith and Hope laughed again.

"Don't laugh!" Kris said.

"I'm sorry," Faith said.

"I can't help it," Hope said between laughs. "You make the littlest thing out to be a crisis."

"Well, it is a crisis," Kris said adamantly.

"No, it's not," Hope said. "Faith has a crisis. You have an inconvenience."

"Hope!"

"Oops! I'm sorry, Faith," Hope said as her laugh evaporated.

"Crisis? What crisis?" Kris asked. "You have a crisis and you haven't told me about it? What is it?"

"Hope!" Faith repeated as she stared sternly at her confidant.

"Sorry."

"Sorry about what? What's the matter?" Kris begged.

"It's nothing," Faith said.

"Come on! It can't be 'nothing.' Hope said it was a crisis. Tell me!"

"It's nothing. Really."

"Come on! Did you and Chris break up?"

"No! We're fine! It's no big deal."

"What is it then? Come on! You can trust me. I won't tell anyone. I swear!"

Faith looked to Hope to extricate her. Instead, Hope said, "Go on. Tell her. It's better to talk about it. If you don't do something about it soon, people are going to find out anyway."

"I know!" Faith snapped as a tear came to her eye. "I just want it to go away!"

"That's okay. It's none of my business," Kris said.

"No. Hope's right," Faith said, eyes downcast. "I just don't know what to do."

"Do you want me to tell her?" Hope asked.

Faith nodded as tears rolled down her cheeks.

"What's wrong?" Kris asked, her eyes begging for an answer.

"Faith is pregnant," Hope said.

Kris bolted up in her chair. She gasped, "Oh, my God! Does Chris know?"

"No, it's not his," Hope said.

"Then who?"

"She was raped," Hope said matter-of-factly.

"Oh, no! You're kidding!"

Kris moved next to Faith who was sitting sideways on her chaise lounge. She pulled Faith's head on to her shoulder and embraced her. Then she looked at Hope and asked, "How did it happen?"

"Our last night on spring break in Florida, we went to a party. She let a guy walk her home and while they were walking along the beach, he attacked her. It was my fault. I left her alone and went off with another guy," Hope confessed. Then she began crying, too. "I'm sorry, Faith," she said.

Now with a tear in her own eye, Kris asked, "What are you going to do, Faith? Have an abortion?"

"I don't know!" Faith said, the flow of tears subsiding. "Some days I think about having an abortion. But, I know that's not the right thing to do. I can't take this child's life!"

"Faith, you have to be sensible about this!" Hope said.

"That's easy for you to say!"

"Yeah, I know," Hope said. "But, at the clinic they tell the girls that every child should be a *wanted* child."

"What do you mean?"

"I mean this pregnancy is upsetting your life," Hope said. "You can't be raising a child and going to college at the same time. And be realistic, if you have this child, your relationship with Chris would be over. He's not going to be interested in you if you have a kid. A kid will get in the way of everything!"

"What do you think?" she asked Kris.

"I would definitely get an abortion."

"Why?"

"Because I'd be in big trouble with my parents. And because of what Hope said."

"So you guys think I should get an abortion?"

"I would," Hope said.

"Me, too," Kris added.

"Maybe you're right," Faith said. "But how do I get it done without anybody else finding out?"

"I'll help you," Hope said.

"But how am I going to pay for it? I can't ask my dad for a few hundred dollars for an abortion. It wouldn't go over very well."

"I can work things out with my uncle. It won't cost you a penny," Hope said.

"Are you sure you can do that?"

"Sure. It's no problem. He'd do anything for me."

"Well, okay," Faith said hesitantly. "But what if something goes wrong?"

"*Don't worry!* Girls have abortions all the time and nothing happens to them," Hope said. "Why don't you come to the clinic tomorrow and talk to my boss, Lisa."

"I don't know."

"Come on, Faith. You have to do something soon," Hope said.

"I know!" Faith said. She sat quietly for a moment, deep in thought. Finally, with a sigh she said, "Okay."

"Good. Let's meet tomorrow for lunch and we can go to the clinic together."

"That's fine, I guess."

•••

It was shortly after one in the afternoon when the phone rang in Jason Warner's dorm room.

"The Warner residence," Jason said, stretching his long, thin frame out on his bed.

"Jason. It's Ryan. You called?"

"Yeah. What are you doing tomorrow afternoon?" he asked as he combed his wavy black hair with his hand.

"I don't know yet. Why? What's up?"

Ryan was slouching in a chair at the kitchen table sipping on a big glass of ice water. His mother was at the sink peeling potatoes for dinner.

"There's a demonstration in front of the abortion mill here in Elston. Do you want to go?"

"You mean a protest demonstration?" Ryan asked, now sitting up, glancing at his mother.

"That's right."

"You're talking about carrying signs, walking up and down the sidewalks, singing and chanting slogans—that kind of thing?"

"You've got it!" Jason said.

Even over the phone, Ryan could sense Jason's energy.

"Gee, I'm pro-life, but I'm not sure I want to demonstrate."

"Why not? If guys like us don't do something, who will?"

"Well, yes, I know, but—"

"But what? Tomorrow we might change a girl's mind. A life would be saved! That life may turn out to be the next Abraham Lincoln."

"Well, I suppose I could come and check it out."

"That's right. And if you don't feel comfortable, I'll give you a ride home."

Ryan turned in his chair and peeked at his mother.

"We're not going to be lying down in the driveway, or blocking the door, or doing anything else that might get us arrested, are we?" he asked.

"No," Jason laughed. "I swear. All we'll be doing is holding signs and parading up and down the sidewalk across the street from the clinic. I promise."

"Okay, I think I can do that much."
"Great! I'll pick you up about noon."
"All right. I'll be here."
Ryan hung up the phone and glanced at his mother.
She said, "What was that all about?"
"I'm not sure. I think I'm becoming a radical."

•••

The next day was hot and humid. Jason arrived at Ryan's promptly at noon. He leaned on the horn twice as he pulled his blue Escort into the driveway. Ryan was in the garage putting the lawn mower and yard tools away. He walked out to Jason's car to greet him.

"Hi! I'll be out in just a second. I've got to change my shirt. Are shorts okay?"

"You can come naked if you want," Jason said with a smile.

"That's all right. I'd rather not be quite so conspicuous."

"Why not? That's why we'll be there. We want to be noticed."

"Not that way I don't," Ryan said.

"What's the difference? Don't you know the ends justify the means?"

"Not if it means my bare end."

"Oh! Bad pun! Hurry up!" Jason said.

On their way to the demonstration, Ryan asked, "You're really serious about this pro-life stuff, aren't you?"

"This thing has to be stopped, by whatever means," Jason said.

"What do you mean by that?"

"Sometimes you have to fight fire with fire."

"I hope you're not burning anything today," Ryan quipped.

"No, don't worry. It would be dumb to do something in broad daylight," Jason said with a smirk. "Nighttime is better."

Ryan smiled quietly, not sure if Jason was serious. As the boys arrived at the demonstration, a score of protesters were marching up and down the block on the sidewalk across the street from the clinic.

"Looks like a big crowd today," Jason said.

"Is that good?"

"You bet. It's more intimidating. Sometimes the girls turn around and get back in their cars when there's a big crowd," Jason explained proudly.

"Really?"

"Yeah. The trouble is, some come back later. Then they get escorted in by someone from the clinic."

Jason and Ryan parked the car down the block. As they approached the demonstration, Ryan surveyed the scene. A score of protesters were parading up one side of the sidewalk for half-a-block and then returned down the other side to complete the circuit. All the while, they carried signs and chanted pro-life slogans. One elderly man wore a set of placards displaying Deuteronomy 30:19. The front placard read, "I have set before you life and death…" The back read, "choose life, that you and your descendants may live."

The demonstrators were partially spared from the early afternoon heat by the shade of the large, century old, oak trees growing in the parkway. The sidewalk appeared to be at least as old as the trees. The cement was worn away in some places, slightly uplifted by the roots of the trees elsewhere, and cracked nearly everywhere. These irregularities, however, went virtually unnoticed by the pickets. They had become sure-footed on the rough surface by the endless repetition. When the boys joined the group, Jason received a hug from Claire Boudreau, a sprite, gray-haired lady.

"Thanks for coming, Jason. I knew we could count on you," she said with a smile. "Introduce me to your handsome friend."

Jason laughed. He said, "Claire, this is Ryan Brandon. His father is President of Justin College."

"So you're Ryle's son, are you?"

"Yes."

"I should have recognized you. You look just like him!" she said. "Good man, your father." Then pointing towards the lot, she said, "There are some signs in the back seat of my Dodge. Grab one that suits you and join the party."

Ryan picked up a sign from the top of the pile that read, "Honk if you're pro-life!" Jason's sign said simply, "Adoption—Abortion's Option." The boys slipped into the procession with Jason marching just ahead of Ryan. Ryan felt self-conscious at first, but the warm smiles and greetings from the other marchers soon made him feel at ease. Before long, he was enthusiastically waving his sign at the cars passing by and cheering every time a driver honked in response.

After more than twenty minutes of marching, Ryan asked, "How long do you do this?"

"Usually two or three hours," Jason said.

"You're kidding? That's a workout!"

"Good thing you're in shape, huh?"

Just then, a silver Lexus passed in front of the marchers and turned into the clinic driveway. A few in the crowd, including Jason, began to jeer and shout, "Murderer!" But Claire Beaumont raised her hand and assembled the protesters in a huddle.

"I know how some of you feel," she said. "But calling Dr. Morlon names and cursing him will not bring him to righteousness. Christ told us to pray for our enemies. So let's do that."

The group bowed their heads as Claire led them in prayer.

"Heavenly Father, we realize that all of Your children matter to You. So we come together in the name of Your Son, Jesus Christ, to ask You to pour Your love into the heart of each woman who is presently considering an abortion. Give her courage in the midst of her crisis, so that she may choose life for her unborn child. We ask that the Holy Spirit speak to the heart of every doctor who is destroying life. May the convicting power of Your Word bring about his or her repentance so that he or she will understand the sanctity of life and realize how precious each child is to You. We pray that You bring light to the eyes of state and national legislators and pro-abortion groups and individuals. As the Judge of the world, we pray that You show mercy to those justices whose decisions have rendered this great injustice in our land. We also pray that You serve a wake up call to all the faithful in our nation, that they may rise up out of their apathetic slumber, and confront, through love, the evil of abortion in our society. And finally, we pray for ourselves. Help us to remember that, ultimately, You, Lord, are in control in this crisis. Protect us from the evil one, that we may not be tempted to fight evil with evil. Let us always love our enemies and return evil with good, according to Your will. Amen."

"Amen!" the group echoed.

Ryan raised his head from prayer and glanced at Jason who was staring at two young women on their way from the clinic parking lot to the front door. Then Ryan recognized the girls.

"Hey, Faith!" he yelled.

"You know them?" Jason asked.

"Yeah. That's my sister and her best friend."

Faith looked over in the direction of the protesters to see her brother crossing the street with Jason a few steps behind.

"Oh, God!" Faith gasped. Her heart stopped as she and Hope paused in front of the clinic door.

"What are you doing here?" Faith asked.

"I've been across the street for half-an-hour. What are you doing here?" Ryan asked.

Jason was standing behind Ryan giving Hope the once over. She caught his glance and returned a smile.

Faith was at a loss. Hope jumped in and said, "I invited her to see where I work. My uncle owns the clinic."

"Dr. Morlon is your uncle?"

"Yes. Who are you?" Hoped asked defensively, looking over the shirtless and sexy, young man.

"I'm sorry," Ryan said. "This is my friend, Jason Warner. Jason, this is my sister, Faith, and her best friend, Hope."

"It's nice meeting you, but I have to get back to work," Hope said. "Come on, Faith. I'll give you a quick tour."

"Can I come, too?" Jason asked with a smile.

"Maybe another time," Hope said. "I don't think you'd be much appreciated inside carrying a sign like that."

"Just thought I'd ask," Jason said with a laugh.

The girls disappeared through the clinic door. On the way back to the picket line, Jason said to Ryan, "You were holding out on me."

"What do you mean?"

"You didn't tell me you had a cute sister, or that she had a gorgeous friend."

"My sister has a boyfriend. I'm not sure about Hope's status."

"I guess I'll just have to call later and find out if she's available."

Meanwhile, inside the clinic, the girls were assessing the damage.

"Do you think my brother suspects anything?"

"I don't think so."

"Whew! That was close!"

"Then why don't you just get this thing over with and you won't have to worry about it anymore," Hope said.

"Well, I certainly can't do it today. My brother is expecting me to leave here in just a few minutes."

"You're right. You'll have to come back another time. But don't worry. We'll work it out."

"Thanks, Hope. I owe you big time."

"Then find out about your brother's friend."

"What do you want to know?"

"Find out if he's available."

Discussions Over Dinner 1.1

"Women's Clinic of DuKane. How may I help you?" Hope said pleasantly as she answered the phone. It was nearly five o'clock, almost time to get off work.

"May I speak to Hope Stuart, please?"

"This is Hope," she said. The voice was vaguely familiar.

"Hope, this is Jason Warner, Ryan's friend. We met this afternoon."

"Oh, Jason! Sorry about this afternoon. I was a bit rude."

"Not really. But I was wondering if you were free tonight. I thought maybe we could go for a pizza or something."

"Boy, you don't waste time, do you?"

"Not if I can help it. What do you say?"

"Well," she said, hesitating.

"Don't worry, dinner's on me. Or, if you're the liberated type, I'll let you pay."

"I'm liberated, but I'm not a fool," Hope said with a laugh. "I'll let you pay."

"Great! I'll pick you up about six-thirty."

"That's fine. But, I've got a call on the other line. Hang on a second. I'll give you directions."

•••

"Hello, Chris," Joan said as Chris followed Faith into the kitchen. "I'm glad you could make it for dinner."

"Oh, Mom! He's here almost every night," Faith said. "Why do you make it such a big deal?"

"I'm not making it a big deal. I just want Chris to feel welcome, that's all."

Chris and Faith began dating after he asked her to prom their junior year. He was athletic and handsome, and Faith was crazy about him despite her parents' apprehensions. They would have preferred for their daughter a young man with lesser gifts and greater faith.

"What's for dinner?" Chris asked, combing his red hair with his hand.

"Liver and onions," Ryan said as he joined them in the kitchen.

"Quiet, Ryan! We're having roast chicken," Joan said.

"When are we eating?" Faith asked.

"Just as soon as your father gets home," Joan said.

"I hope he doesn't have another one of those long afternoon meetings," Faith said as she began probing the cabinets looking for a small tidbit to hold her over until dinner.

"Don't spoil your appetite, Dear."

"Mom! You know how it works," Faith protested. "If I don't eat something, Dad will be delayed for hours and I'll perish for lack of nourishment. If I do snack, he'll come right through that door in a matter of minutes. So for everyone's sake, I'll just find something to nibble on so we can all start dinner soon."

"Oh, be quiet!" her mother scolded. "You're just rationalizing."

"No, I'm not. Watch. I'll prove it!"

Faith stuffed her mouth with an Oreo, gave another one to Chris, and filled her hands with a half dozen others. Then the phone rang.

"Hello," Joan said as she picked up the phone. After a short pause, she said, "Okay. I love you."

"There. I told you," Faith said with a self-satisfied smile. "He's on his way home, isn't he? All I had to do was put this magic cookie in my mouth like I said."

"Is that right?" her mother asked. "Well, it just so happens that your father called to say he won't be home for a while and that we should start dinner without him."

Faith's smile evaporated.

"I guess you were wrong, huh, Sis?" Ryan said with a smirk.

"Not really. I only ate one cookie. It wasn't enough for Dad to come home, but it was enough for him to call and not make us wait. I'll just put the rest of these back like I intended."

"Oh, get out!" Ryan said.

"That's enough," Joan said. "Ryan, you carve the chicken, and Faith, you set the table."

"She never admits she's wrong," Ryan said to Chris as Faith carried the plates and utensils into the dining room.

"Yeah, I've noticed."

"Heh! Whose side are you on?" Faith yelled, as she was setting out the plates in the dining room. While returning to the kitchen, she asked, "Can we eat?"

"Of course," Joan said. "Ryan, put the chicken on the table. I'll bring the rest of the meal in."

Joan said the prayer and then opened the discussion over dinner.

"I meant to ask you, Ryan, how did things go at your demonstration today?"

"All right, I guess."

"There wasn't a counter demonstration, was there?" Joan asked.

"No. Just us."

"What were you protesting?" Chris asked.

"We were protesting in front of the abortion clinic," Ryan said.

"Oh, really."

"Yeah. You can join us next time if you'd like," Ryan said in jest.

"No, thanks."

"Why not? Faith was there today."

"You were?" Chris asked.

All eyes focused on Faith. She winced, saying inwardly, "Thanks for opening your big mouth, Ryan."

"Not as a demonstrator," she quickly explained.

"No. She was there for an abortion," Ryan teased, straight-faced.

"I was not! Don't even say that! I went there with Hope because she wanted me to see what her job was like!"

"Okay, okay! Take it easy. I was just kidding," Ryan said.

Faith's heart sank. She felt ashamed of her intentions. After a short, silent moment, Joan said, "I didn't know Hope was working at the clinic. Why is she working there?"

"Her uncle owns the clinic," Faith said, picking at her chicken.

Then Ryan asked, "Mom, what would you and Dad do if Faith was pregnant?"

"Ryan, why do you ask such *stupid* questions all the time?" Faith replied.

"It's not a stupid question. Why are you so sensitive about this?"

"I am not sensitive about it! I just don't see why we have to talk about this in front of Chris. It's embarrassing."

"Are you embarrassed, Chris?" Ryan asked.

"A bit."

"Why?"

"Because I'm Faith's boyfriend. Naturally, I would be the one assumed responsible," he said, blushing.

"Okay, let me rephrase the question," Ryan said. "Mom, suppose you had another daughter named Sally. What would you and Dad do if Sally got pregnant?"

Joan sipped her glass of water and gathered her thoughts.

"Of course, your father and I would be disappointed. We would have hoped to impress on Sally the merits of abstinence," she said taking a glance at Faith, a subtle way of saying, "Are you listening?"

"But what would you do?" Ryan insisted. "Would you tell Sally to have an abortion or what?"

"Obviously, an abortion would be out of the question."

"Why? A scandal like this would be embarrassing for Dad, don't you think?"

"A child's life is more important than anyone's reputation," Joan said.

"What would happen to the baby?" Ryan asked.

"I imagine the baby would be given up for adoption. It's possible Sally would keep the baby, but that's something we would have to pray about."

Faith was digesting her mother's comments as she contemplatively stirred her peas with her fork.

"What do you think Sally ought to do, Chris?" Ryan asked. He took a fiendish delight in putting Chris on the spot in front of his mother.

Chris took a moment to swallow before answering. Finally, he said, "I think the decision should always be left up to the woman to decide what's best for her."

"How politically correct!" Ryan quipped.

Chris glanced at Ryan, felt the sting of his scorn, and looked at Faith for support. Perceiving neither support nor opposition, he set out to defend his position.

"I think a woman has the right to control her own life, that's all. If she doesn't want to have a baby, then she shouldn't be forced to have one. People have a right to live their lives as they wish."

"Yes, but there's another life involved, Chris," Joan said. "That life has rights, too."

"Yes, but it's not a *real* life," Chris said.

"It's not? Then what is it? Just pretend?" Ryan quipped.

"Be quiet, Ryan! You're so obnoxious sometimes," Faith said.

"Ryan, just let Chris explain what he means," Joan said.

"What I mean is that an unborn baby isn't really aware that it's alive. In a way, an unborn baby is like a plant. In fact, if it's unwanted, it's like a weed. It's a living thing, obviously, but it doesn't think. Thinking develops after birth. And so, if it's like a weed, what harm is there in weeding it out?"

"Come on! A baby is like a weed? How absurd!" Ryan said.

"Calm down, Ryan," Joan said. Then she said to Chris, "It seems as though you've given this some thought."

"A little. I wrote a position paper on abortion for my English class."

"From what you've said, I assume you wrote in defense of abortion," Joan said.

"Well, yes. I read some articles on abortion and I even read about *Roe v. Wade*," Chris said proudly.

"I see," Joan said. After a moment's reflection, she asked, "Have you considered that even though an unborn child may not have self-awareness in the same way an adult or even a three-year-old child does, God *is* aware of the unborn child's existence? The Bible tells us that God knows each one of us even before conception. We matter to Him. And He wants a relationship with each and every person He creates, including the unborn child. Therefore, as our Creator, it is His prerogative, His choice, as to when we shall die. You see, the offense is not just against the child, it's an offense against God. It's just best if we obey God and choose life."

"You now have one minute for rebuttal," Ryan said to Chris.

"Well, if all life decisions should be left up to God, why are we eating this chicken, or these peas?" Chris asked.

"The Bible tells us that God has given man dominion over the Earth and all its creatures," Joan said. "Man is the centerpiece of His creation. We must respect all life, but the plant and animal world were created for man's benefit. It is only human life which is sacred."

•••

Hope was putting on the finishing touch, a pair of gold earrings, when the doorbell rang. "I'll get it!" she yelled. She grabbed her purse and made one last vanity check in the mirror before walking briskly down the stairs to the foyer. When she opened the door, Jason was waiting with a single yellow rose.

"Hi. This is for you."

"Hi, Jason! How sweet! Let me go put it in a vase. I'll be right back," she said with a smile. Eliza was cleaning up the kitchen when Hope walked in with her rose.

"Who's the gentleman that brought you a flower on your first date?" Eliza asked.

"His name is Jason. He's a friend of Faith's brother."

"Pretty handsome."

"You peeked out the kitchen door to check him out, didn't you?"

"Of course. I can't let my little girl go off with no stranger without checkin' him out first."

"So you think he's handsome, huh?"

"Yep. Very handsome."

"I think so, too."

"You be careful with these older men, now. Some of them are pretty slick and know just how to get what they want," Eliza said.

"How do you know he isn't the one who has to be careful?"

"Go on, girl. You best not be messin' around. What with all this AIDS and other things goin' around. Not to mention, girls that fool around get themselves pregnant."

"Don't worry, Eliza. I only take chances with the real cute ones," Hope said. "Don't wait up for me."

Eliza shook her head as Hope returned to her date in the foyer.

"You have a nice house," Jason said as they slipped out the door.

"Thank you. My mother's done very well for herself."

"And now she's running for Congress."

"Yeah, and she's doing well in the polls."

"Too well."

"You sound disappointed," Hope said.

"Well, it's just that," Jason said, pausing to find the right words.

"Just what?"

"Just that she's very liberal."

"Meaning what? That's she's pro-choice?"

"That's part of it."

"If you don't like my mother's politics, why'd you ask me out?"

"You want me to be brutally honest?"

"That would be a refreshing change."

"Okay. I asked you out because you're a sexy blonde."

"You don't care about personality or intelligence?"

"That's important. But I couldn't judge that till I went out with you."

"What about my mother's politics?"

"That's your mother, not you."

"My mother and I think alike."

"That's okay. You're young. There's still hope."

Hope smiled. "I see," she said.

"Why did you say 'yes' when I asked you out?" Jason asked.

"Because you're handsome and assertive. You seem like a guy who knows what he wants and goes after it. Am I right?"

"Yeah, I guess so. I like to get involved."

"So that's why you protest in front of health clinics?"

"Abortion mills," Jason corrected her with a smile.

"Health clinics," Hope reiterated with a smile. "Where are we going, anyway?"

"The Italian Garden."

"Oh, I know a waitress there. She won't card me," Hope said.

"What if I don't want you to have alcohol?"

"What's wrong? Don't *you* drink?"

"No, it's not that," he said.

"Then what?"

"You still want me to be honest?"

"Yes."

"Okay. I read an article today about a study on sex and first dates."

"Oh, yeah? What did it say?" Hope asked.

"It said that teenagers and young adults are more likely to have sex if the male drinks but the woman doesn't. I was going to check it out and see if it was true," Jason said with a devious smile.

"Oh, you were, were you? So I'm a guinea pig, huh?"

"Well, no. Let's just say that we're both volunteers in an important, sociological experiment."

"Since you put it that way, I guess I ought to be honored, I think," Hope said with a wry smile.

They were seated in a quiet corner of the restaurant. Before long, the waitress came to take their order.

"Hello, Hope. How's it going?" she said.

"Great."

"That's good. Can I get you guys something to drink?"

"I'll have a half carafe of your house wine. She'll have a Coke," Jason said.

"Make that a Diet Coke," Hope said. When the waitress left, Hope said, "I don't like the way this experiment is set up. Can't we change it to see what happens when we've both had some wine?"

"That would be unscientific. You don't want to be unscientific, do you?"

"Maybe. Tell me more about the article," Hope said.

"It said that women who drink on their first date are more defensive because they know their guard is down from the alcohol."

"So, what happens to males when they drink?"

"Males become less inhibited. They become more talkative, open, and vulnerable, which makes them more attractive to women, and makes women more open to sex."

"All right then," Hope said. "Since you're going to be open and vulnerable, tell me why you protest in front of abortion clinics. What does it matter to you?"

"I'm a male. I'm supposed to have alcohol before I answer questions like that."

"Come on. If I have to drink Diet Coke instead of wine, you can be prematurely vulnerable," Hope argued with a smile.

"I guess that's fair," he said and then paused as if reflecting. "I had a girlfriend in high school. Her name was Jenny. She got pregnant our senior year. I wanted to get married and raise the child. She didn't. I tried to talk her out of it but she had an abortion anyway. We stopped going together after that."

Hope gave a sympathetic nod. She said, "I always thought it was the other way around. I thought the girl wanted the baby and the guy wanted her to have an abortion."

"I think it happens more often that way. Guys don't want to be tied down."

"So why are you different?" Hope asked.

"I don't know. I just think life is important. I was awed by the idea that Jenny and I had created a life. When she told me afterwards that she had an abortion, I felt this huge loss. In a sense, it aborted our relationship."

"I'm sorry things didn't work out," Hope said.

"Well, I guess it happens, right?"

The waitress returned with their drinks. Hope took a straw and pensively stirred it around in the glass.

"You know what really surprises me?" she said.

"What?"

"That a good Christian boy like you would get yourself in a situation like that in the first place. I thought Christians wait until they get married to have sex."

"I suppose," Jason said. "But I'm not sure I believe in God."

"Really?"

"Yeah. Does that surprise you?"

"Well, yes, because you go to Justin College. Why would you go there if you didn't believe in God?"

"I'm going there because that's where my mom wanted me to go. She would only pay for my college education if I went to a Christian college."

"How come?"

"She thought I'd be less likely to turn out like my dad. When he divorced my mom to marry a younger woman, she blamed it on the fact that he wasn't a Christian."

"Is that what you think?"

"No. I think Dad left because Mom tried to shove religion down his throat."

"That's too bad."

"Yep," Jason said as he poured a second glass of wine. "I was twelve and my brother was ten at the time."

"Well, at least you know your father. My father left home when I was two."

"Really? Do you ever see him?"

"No. He just dropped out of sight and lives on the West Coast somewhere. I vaguely remember having a father, but I can't tell you what he was like. I was too little to remember anything," Hope said.

"Did your mother ever remarry?" Jason asked.

"No."

"Then it's like you've never had a father."

"No. Just my mother and Eliza. And to be honest about it, my mother hasn't been there much for me either. She was always busy with business. And now it's politics," Hope said with a forlorn look.

"And you don't have any brothers or sisters?"

"No. It's just me."

"That must be lonely," Jason said.

Hope shrugged and said, "I guess I'm used to it."

The waitress returned shortly and asked, "Are you ready to order yet?"

"Not really. But can you bring us another wine glass?" Jason asked.

"Sure thing. I'll be back in a minute."

After the waitress returned with a glass and took their order Hope asked, "Have you given up on your experiment?"

"Yeah. I'm going back to my old theory that this seduction business is more of an art than a science," he said with a smile.

When Jason filled her glass, Hope proposed a toast.

"Here's to fine art!"

Faith's Desire 12

Faith fell in love with Chris the first time they met as high school freshmen. He was broad-shouldered and muscular, like a Roman god, with blue eyes and a square chin. His loose, red curls seemed as radiant as the sun resting on the western horizon. Intelligent and self-assured, he had an aura about him, a charisma that made him the most popular boy in their class. Never thinking he would have an interest in her, Faith was speechless when, in the spring of their junior year, he asked her to prom. Classmates began to treat Faith differently and she picked up on it quickly. She had acquired an aura of her own. As Chris Walters's girlfriend, her self-esteem had blossomed. After fifteen months together, she could not imagine life without him. Yet, because of her pregnancy, she realized their relationship was in jeopardy.

After dinner, Faith and Chris were walking hand-in-hand along the sidewalk to an ice cream shop only a few blocks away. Faith summoned the courage to resurrect the conversation at the dinner table.

"You didn't agree with my mother, did you?" she asked.

"No."

"Then why didn't you say so?"

"There wasn't any sense in arguing about abortion when the real issue is something else."

"What do you mean?"

"Your mother is religious. You know I don't believe that stuff. It was better just to drop it. Besides, it's not that important."

"But it *is* important!" Faith said, surprising Chris with her emotion. Chris looked at her oddly.

"Why?"

"Because it is, that's all."

"Am I missing something here?"

"What if I *was* pregnant, what would you do?" she asked insistently.

"In case you've forgotten, we've been abstinent," Chris replied sarcastically. Then he asked, "What's with you tonight, Faith? You're acting so strange! What's wrong?"

"Nothing's wrong! I just want to know how you'd feel if I was pregnant, that's all!"

"Where did all this come from all of a sudden?" he wondered. Then he said, "I don't know. I guess we'd have to sit down and evaluate the situation."

"Evaluate the situation!" Faith cried out in a loud voice. She stopped, grabbed him by the arm, and squared off to look him directly in the eye. "What do you mean, 'evaluate the situation'? If we had a baby together, wouldn't you want it?"

Chris replied firmly, "I don't know what's bugging you tonight. But, if you were pregnant, we would really have to talk things over. I'm not going to lie to you and say that 'Sure, we'd have the baby,' because I'm not sure that's what I would want at this point in my life."

Tears welled up in Faith's eyes and she hurried away in a huff. Chris ran after her and grabbed her by the shoulder, turning her around.

"What's wrong with you?"

"What's wrong with me? What's wrong with you? How can you be so selfish?" Faith asked, wiping her eyes.

"How you can be so emotional over a hypothetical situation?"

"What does it matter if it's real or not? All you care about is yourself!" Faith said angrily.

"Wait a minute!" Chris said, his face turning red. He put his two hands on Faith's shoulders, looked her in the eye, and took a deep breath. "Tell me what this is all about."

"It's not about anything. I just don't understand how you can be so callous about abortion!"

"And I don't see how you can be so upset over something that doesn't even affect us!" Chris shouted back.

Faith noticed a gray-haired man sitting on his front porch listening in on their conversation. She lowered her voice as the man tucked his head behind the evening newspaper. She asked, "What if it does affect us?"

"That's impossible! We haven't done anything."

Chris breathed an exasperated sigh. Then he put his arm around Faith and began to escort her down the sidewalk once again, but she would have none of his embrace and pulled away. He raised his arms up and dropped them in frustration.

"What if I was raped by someone? How would you feel?" Faith asked as she walked briskly in the lead.

"Come on!" Chris moaned as he followed a few steps behind.

"No, really. How would you feel?"

"Angry. And I'd try to find the guy that did it and castrate him."

"And what if I was pregnant?" Faith asked as she stopped suddenly, turning toward Chris. "What would you tell me to do?"

Chris nearly ran her over, but he was now close enough to reach out to hold Faith's two hands in his. He said, "I suppose the only thing to do in that situation is have an abortion."

Faith's heart sank as she pulled her hands from his and put them on her stomach.

"Why?"

"Well, because it's something neither one of us would want," he said matter-of-factly.

"What about the baby?"

"It's not a baby."

"What is it then?"

"It's a problem, an inconvenience, that's all. And you shouldn't be so sentimental about it. You wouldn't want the child of someone who raped you. You would resent it. It would just be better to nip it in the bud."

"I see," Faith said. She became quiet for a moment. Finally, she asked, "What would you do if I was pregnant and wanted to have the baby?"

"To be honest with you, I'd be very annoyed, probably angry."

"Why?"

"Because you have the right to choose not to have a baby. You'd be messing up our relationship. And if our relationship isn't important to you, then that's your choice. I would have to move on."

"But what if I gave the baby up for adoption?"

"It would still mess things up. Who wants a pregnant girlfriend who has to lie around all day? What fun is that?"

"That's not fair!" Faith said angrily.

"What's not?"

"Your attitude!"

"Why not?"

"Because you don't care about my feelings. You just care about yourself."

"That's not true. I do care about your feelings. I just don't agree with your beliefs," he said.

"What beliefs?"

"About God."

"So we're back to that are we? How can you be so sure there isn't a God?"

"How can you be so sure there is? Maybe you ought to examine your own beliefs and not believe in fairy tales just because your parents do," Chris said.

"Why do you have to be so negative about everything!"

"Why do you have to be so emotional?"

Faith stormed away in a tizzy.

"Where are you going?" Chris asked.

"Somewhere to be alone!" Faith shouted without turning around.

Chris was speechless. "What was that all about?" he wondered.

•••

Faith couldn't sleep. Passing cars on the street below slipped past her bedroom window at brief intervals. Each heralded its approach with faint flashes of light on the bedroom ceiling and a rising crescendo of tires on pavement; then the sound faded away into the distant darkness. At one stretch, she heard the long, piercing whistle of a passing freight train and the rumbling of its cars on the tracks. She tried to shut out the noise but it was too intrusive on her senses. She tossed and turned. She was emotionally exhausted and desperately wanted to fall asleep and forget her dilemma. Yet, she knew that a decision had to be made. If she chose to have an abortion, it would have to be done soon. She could not go on hiding her pregnancy any longer.

Her heart was heavy. Her eyes stared blankly out the window at the moon shining brightly above. She was lying on her side stroking her stomach gently. Over the last several weeks, she had come to realize that a new soul had entered this world and its physical being was developing inside her womb. Many nights in recent weeks she had lain awake imagining what this new creation would be like if allowed to live. She also tried to imagine the consequences of her options.

If she decided to raise the child herself, she would be confronted with a legion of concerns. Would she live at home, and if so, what would her arrangement be with her parents? She was certain they would continue to support her. But would she be able to go to college? Or, would she have to find a job and day care for the child while she was at work? Or, was it possible to go to work and school and still be a good mother? She also wanted the child to have a father. And if Chris wasn't willing, who would be willing? She had no answers.

If she decided to place the child for adoption, an entirely different set of concerns surfaced. Would there be anyone interested in adopting her child? And if they did, would they be loving parents? And what about the child? When the child got older and understood what it meant to be adopted, would he or she feel abandoned or unwanted? Would she ever be able to see her child again? If so, would she be able to explain to the child that adoption was the best option? Again, she had no answer.

Finally, what if she decided to have an abortion? The very thought was deeply repugnant, in both the abstract sense and the intimate, personal reality. Yet, the alternatives were messy, too. And not only that, there was so much to lose. It was evident that the young man she treasured most in this world would leave her if she decided to choose life for the child.

Before this personally cataclysmic event transpired, her dreams had clearly mapped out her future. She and Chris would continue to date through college. It would be a long distance relationship since he would be out east and she would be at home. But they could make it work, she thought. After graduating from Justin, she would marry Chris, who would continue on to law school. She would work a couple of years supporting his ambition. Once he had established himself in his career, they would have children; she would stay home to take care of them. It was a simple dream, quite unlike Hope's dream. Hope wanted power, prestige, and wealth. But these or the other trappings of this world did not enamor Faith. Rather, she desired the security and joy of a faithful husband, a loving family, and a happy home. She was interested in intimate relationships and so the dream of having a family was absolutely fulfilling. In her mind, the foundation of this architecture was Chris. Hence, he was the primary object of her desire.

"Chris, how can you be so selfish? Why do I always have to be the one who gives?" she moaned softly.

As she sorted things out, her dilemma was sharply coming into focus. Being raised in a Christian home, it was very clear that she *ought not* to have an abortion. This child, though ill-conceived, still mattered to God. Yet giving birth, whether she kept the child or placed it for adoption, flew in the face of all her own dreams and desires. As she lay in bed, she opened her heart to God.

"God, why did you let this happen to me? It's not fair! Lots of girls, like Hope, who don't even know You, who have sex all the time, don't get pregnant. But I've obeyed You and I'm the one who gets raped and gets pregnant! Why? Don't You see it's going to mess up everything I have with Chris?"

•••

The next evening after dinner, Faith went to see Hope. The girls were in Hope's bedroom as she prepared for another date with Jason. Hope was standing in her walk-in closet while Faith sat on the edge of the bed.

"I thought you said you weren't going to get serious about anyone after breaking up with Chad," Faith said.

"Who's getting serious?"

"You are."

"Why do you say that?"

"You're going out with Jason two nights in a row. Week nights at that!"

"I'm not getting serious. There's just nothing else to do."

"Sure."

Hope smiled. After a quiet moment, Faith announced matter-of-factly, "I've decided to have an abortion."

"Are you sure? Without even talking to anyone at the clinic first?"

"Yes."

"How come?"

"Because I just want this to be over."

"Are you sure?"

"No. But whatever decision I make there are problems. At least, by having an abortion, it would be over with."

Hope was certain Faith was sure to have regrets. But overall, from her own perspective, this was the best option.

"When do you want to get it done?" Hope asked.

"As soon as possible."

"Tomorrow is a light day. I can get you in tomorrow morning."

"As long as my brother isn't there protesting again."

Conspirators 13

The moon reflected dimly off the Wolf River as it flowed past the Justin College soccer field just before midnight. Across the river to the north, the pale glow of street lamps from a trailer park stretched its way up to the scattered, wispy, white clouds passing quietly overhead. To the south, scant specks of light peeked out from scattered cottages hidden away in the thick brush lining the river. The chill air was still and the night was quiet except for the sound of tiny waves rippling along the shore. Two dark silhouettes sitting on the top row of bleachers overlooking the field jumped when a voice called from behind.

"Good evening, gentlemen," a third shadowy figure said as he stood looking up at the pair above.

Jason turned and looked through the railing to the shadows below.

"Oh, it's you!" he said. "Don't sneak up on us like that!"

"You asked for it," Ryan said.

"Why do you say that?"

"Because you were the one who wanted to meet at midnight in the middle of nowhere."

"So what's wrong with that? Some things are meant to be done in the dark...and in secrecy," Jason said mysteriously.

"What do you mean?"

"Oh, I don't know. That's what we have to talk about," Jason said as Ryan climbed the bleachers and sat down on the row just below the others.

"You're really strange sometimes, Jason," Ryan said. "Introduce me to your friend."

"Sorry. Ryan, this is Dan Crider."

"Nice meetin' ya," Dan said in a southern drawl as he unfolded a mammoth frame to a half-standing position. Ryan's hand was that of a small boy in the vice grip of Dan's handshake. Dan had long red hair, bushy eyebrows, and a full beard, but it was the look in his eyes that drew Ryan's attention. For in the large man's eyes, he saw pain and anger festering within.

"Dan's one of us," Jason said.

"What do you mean?" Ryan asked as he glanced at the imposing figure dressed in jeans and a black leather jacket.

Jason looked at Dan and said, "Why don't you tell him?"

Dan stared silently at Ryan for a moment. His eyes gripped Ryan with the same crushing power of his handshake. The big redhead then looked away toward the lights of the trailer park. Pain oozed from his eyes. He growled, "My kid sister died in a botched abortion two months ago."

"I'm sorry to hear that," Ryan said.

"Yeah, well, somebody's got to pay, that's all."

"Are your parents going to sue?" Ryan asked.

Dan grabbed his bleacher seat with both hands and leaned forward a bit.

"There's just me and Ma and my ma can't afford no lawyer. Besides, a lawsuit ain't justice enough. The doctor's got to hurt like me and Ma. Then we'll be even."

Ryan glanced at Jason and then back at Dan.

"Did this happen here in Elston?"

"Yep," he said with another far away look in his eye. "We came up here together about ten months ago lookin' for work. I got a job drivin' a cement truck. My sister was a waitress. She met a guy and got pregnant. One day she went for an abortion and never came home," Dan said, his face and eyes now showing little emotion. "I didn't even know she was pregnant until I got a call from Ma tellin' me she was dead."

"I'm sorry," Ryan said again. "I don't remember hearing anything about it."

"Yuh never do," Dan said with a huff.

"That's a shame. Something ought to be done about it," Ryan said.

"That's why we're here. It's time to strike back," Jason said.

"What are you thinking of doing?" Ryan asked.

"Cause a little trouble, that's all."

"What kind of trouble?"

"A pipe bomb oughtta do it," Dan said.

Ryan glanced back and forth between Jason and Dan. "You sound like you're serious," he said with a nervous grin.

"We are," Jason said.

Ryan squirmed on the bleacher seat.

"What's wrong with peaceful protest?" he asked.

Jason laughed. "Do you see any results?"

"Well, I don't know. Some, I guess."

"Oh, come on, man. Be honest," Jason said. "People have been protesting since *Roe v. Wade* and we still have a million-and-a-half abortions a year. That's forty million deaths while we're protesting peacefully. Maybe it's about time we try something else."

"What we really need to do is abort a few doctors," Dan said gruffly.

"You guys sound like a couple of terrorists," Ryan said.

"I'm afraid it's our only choice," Jason said, "especially now that we have Stanton as President."

"Why do you say that?" Ryan asked.

"Wake up and smell the coffee, Ryan. We're hamstrung politically," Jason said. "Before we had Stanton in office, any pro-abortion legislation was vetoed by conservative presidents. Under Stanton, pro-abortion lobbyists have pushed legislation through Congress to prevent people from demonstrating and using nonviolent direct action in front of clinics. Pro-lifers are being denied first amendment rights that other causes have always relied on. Before Stanton, we also had more conservative federal judges appointed. Now, the only way you can be appointed to a federal court is if you're in favor of abortion."

"That might be so, but things will change eventually. Stanton may only be in office one term," Ryan said. "You have to be patient and work within the system."

"And what happens in the meantime? Think about it. In the four years that Stanton is in office, six million lives will be lost. That's as bad as the Holocaust," Jason argued.

"But the President isn't the problem. It's the Supreme Court that's caused all the trouble."

"Well, you're right except that when a new justice has to be named to the Court, our pro-abortion president will pick a pro-abortion judge," Jason said. "And that influence is going to be there for a long time."

"Save your breath, Jason!" Dan said sharply as he stretched his long legs over the bleacher below. "Politics and protest ain't gonna end this thing. Either we gotta shoot the President, shoot half the Court, or shoot a few doctors like that one feller down in Florida. Nothin' else is gonna make a difference. And till things change, there's gonna be more women like my sister who's gonna die. As I see it, it might as well be the bad guys who die."

Dan broke out a new pack of cigarettes and lit up. There was a short silence.

"I understand how you guys feel," Ryan said. "But it's a question of the ends justifying the means. Besides, you're being hypocritical. You're talking about killing people in order to save lives. That just doesn't add up."

"Why not?" Jason asked. "This is a war, Ryan."

"War or terrorism?"

"Call it what you like. I don't care. The point is, this holocaust has to stop!"

"Still, I don't like it," Ryan said. "Everyone matters to God, even the abortionists. We shouldn't be attacking them. We ought to be praying for them."

Dan stood up with a grunt. He said, "You guys can sit around and pray all you want. I got better things to do. Catch yuh later, Jason."

"I'll give you a call," Jason replied.

"Don't bother," Dan said. "It'll be better if I just handle this myself."

Then he stomped down the bleachers and lumbered to the parking lot. In a moment, the rumble of a motorcycle ripped through the still night.

"He's a big guy," Ryan said with a shiver.

"And tough," Jason replied.

"Boy, I'll say. Was he serious about killing people?"

"I don't know. I wouldn't doubt it."

"You don't agree with him, do you?" Ryan asked.

"I wouldn't go out and shoot people. But I think a little vandalism might not be a bad idea. I wouldn't be opposed to breaking in and tearing a clinic apart, or just busting some windows."

"Don't expect me to help you with anything like that," Ryan said.

"Why not?"

"It just isn't right."

"How about a little graffiti? We could leave a message with spray paint."

Ryan sighed. "Where?"

"At the clinic here in Elston."

"That's still damaging property," Ryan said.

"Well, it wouldn't be anything permanent. All they have to do is paint over it. It would be a nuisance though. And who knows, it might affect the doctor's thinking."

"I kind of doubt it," Ryan said.

"Come on! You've got nothing else to do tonight," Jason said as he started down the bleachers.

"Except sleep," Ryan retorted.

"That's what mornings are for! Come on!"

"Right now?"

"Yeah."

"But where are you going to get paint this time of night?"

"I took care of that this afternoon," Jason said.

"You what?"

"Sure. Come on!"

"Geez, I must be nuts!" Ryan said in pursuit of Jason.

Shortly afterwards, the boys arrived at the clinic in separate cars. They parked along the curb across the street from the clinic. Jason jumped out of his car and scurried over to Ryan's window.

"Here's the plan," Jason said. "I'm going to park my car behind the clinic. You stay here. I'll be back in a minute with the paint. You be the lookout and give me a whistle if someone is coming. Okay?"

"Are you sure you want to do this? You could be in big trouble if you get caught."

"I won't."

"All right. But if you're caught, I don't know you," Ryan said.

"Fine. Just give me a whistle if anyone comes."

Jason jumped back in his car. He made a loud screech with his tires as he made a sharp U-turn. Then he disappeared down the side street next to the clinic.

Ryan shook his head. "Take it easy! Don't wake up the neighborhood for goodness sakes!" After a moment's reflection, he added, "I can't believe I'm doing this!"

Ryan noticed that the front of the clinic was particularly dark. He looked up and saw a broken street lamp on the corner. "I bet Jason took care of that," he said.

With a yawn, he looked down at his watch. It was half past midnight. When he looked up, his attention was drawn to two headlights looming down the street. He slumped down in his seat, just able to peek out over the dashboard. As the headlights grew closer, he recognized the distinct sound of Latino music blasting from the car stereo. Two Hispanic men wearing western hats were laughing loudly in the front seat as the car passed by. He sat up and peered up and down the street. The scene grew still once again.

"This is dumb. No, I'm dumb," he chided himself. The morning headlines flashed in his mind. "Son of Justin College President arrested for vandalism." Then he thought, "And what good is it going to do?"

At that moment, a silhouette emerged from the darkness into the dim moonlight. He was carrying a brown paper bag.

"Hurry up!" Ryan chastised under his breath.

Jason looked up and down the street and then pulled from the bag a can of red spray paint. He gave the can a couple of quick shakes and started his inscription on the pale yellow wall. Ryan tried but couldn't make out the message in the dim light. When Jason stepped back for a moment to admire his handiwork, Ryan whispered loudly from across the street.

"Come on! Let's go!"

"Just a minute!"

Jason began inscribing another message.

"That's enough!" Ryan yelled.

"Hold on!"

Suddenly, a siren blared in the distance. The boys gaped down the street and saw flashing red lights growing closer.

"Oh, great!" Ryan said. "Get going!"

Jason turned back to the wall to finish his message.

"Forget about it! Go!" Ryan shouted as the siren and flashing lights were now only two blocks away.

Jason paused to take one last look at his handiwork. Then he took off in a sprint around the corner. In his flight, he ditched the paint can in a hedge of lilac bushes lining the parking lot in back of the clinic.

"Why did I let him talk me into this!" Ryan fumed as he pounded the steering wheel with both fists. He quickly slumped down to the floor on the passenger's side and tucked himself into the fetal position.

"Why do I feel like I'm about to be aborted?" he quipped. "Lord, just get me out of this and I'll never do anything dumb like this ever again!"

Ryan closed his eyes; his heart was pounding. He waited for the screeching halt of tires on the pavement; but instead, the screaming siren passed by and the numbing noise grew fainter. Ryan climbed quickly off the floor onto the seat and peeked out the back window. The flashing lights and siren had belonged to an ambulance! He breathed a sigh of relief and hastily headed for home.

The Writing on the Wall

14

Faith was hurrying along the sidewalk, anxious to get to her appointment.
"I've got to get this over with before anyone finds out!"
Peering over her shoulder, she said again, "I've got to get there!" She tried to walk faster but her legs grew heavy as if walking knee-deep in mud.
"What's wrong with me?" she whined.
Out of sheer exhaustion, she sat down on a curb in front of a white, Queen Ann, Victorian.
"I can't go on. I need a rest," she sighed.
She lay back on the grass parkway and closed her eyes. When she opened them again a moment later, she discovered a funeral procession moving slowly down the block. The lead cars of the procession had already passed and were turning at the next corner.
"Who died?" she shouted. Then she realized that every other car was a hearse.
"What happened?" she cried. Then she saw her brother hanging out the window of the family sedan.
"Come on, Faith! You're gonna be late!" he yelled.
"Where are you going?" she yelled back.
"To the cemetery! She's being buried today!" he said as the car rolled slowly by. Then she saw her father behind the wheel with her mother sitting beside him. In the back seat next to her brother sat a blonde woman dressed in black with a veiled face.

121

"Who's being buried?" she shouted. Then she heard a cry from behind. She turned around and saw on the porch a young biracial girl struggling with a man dressed in a white robe.

"Let go of me!" the girl shouted, kicking wildly at the man who was trying to grab her by the legs. "Leave me alone!"

Faith shouted, "Leave that girl alone! Help! Somebody! Help!"

The man turned and stared menacingly at Faith as she walked towards him.

"This was your choice! So just stay away!" he shouted back angrily.

"Let go of her! I've changed my mind!" Faith screamed as she beat her fists on the man's back.

He turned to push her away. Then he saw that the procession had stopped and the people were watching from their cars. He pushed Faith aside and walked away angrily, growling something unintelligible. Faith's attention turned to the sobbing little girl.

"Are you okay?"

The girl nodded but the sobs continued.

"Here. Wipe your nose and eyes with this," Faith said as she handed the girl a tissue.

"What's your name?" Faith asked as she sat down and put her arm around the girl's shoulder.

"Hope," the girl said quietly.

"Your name is Hope?"

The girl nodded again.

"You're kidding? My best friend's name is Hope!"

The girl took a deep breath and replied, "I know."

"How do you know that?"

The girl shrugged her shoulders but said nothing. Finally, she whispered, "Thank you."

"For what?"

"For chasing the man away."

"I was glad to help," Faith said. "But who was that man? And what did he want?"

"He's a very bad man. He wanted to kill me."
"How do you know?"
"My mother told me about him. She said he tried to kill me before."
"He did? When?"
"When I was still in my birthmom's tummy. But my birthmom wouldn't let him."
At first, Faith was confused. Then she asked, "Are you adopted?"
"Yes."
Faith smiled and noticed the girl's light copper skin, long, golden brown, curly hair, and big brown eyes. The lovely features were oddly familiar. Then the girl's mother opened the front screen door and stepped out onto the porch.
"Thank you for saving my daughter," she said as she picked the little girl up in her arms and gave her a kiss.
"It was nothing. I just did what I had to do."
The mother and daughter smiled and stepped back into the house. As Faith turned toward the street, the cars in the procession began honking their horns loudly. A young man began yelling.
"Faith! Wake up!" he shouted.

•••

"Faith! Wake up!" Ryan said as he shook her gently. Faith was lying on her stomach with her head buried in her pillow. As the fog began to clear from her mind, she heard her alarm buzzing and her brother complaining, "Wake up and shut that thing off!"

Faith rose up suddenly as if doing a push-up. She turned on to her side and reached for the alarm. Ryan stumbled sleepily out of the room as Faith squinted to read the time: seven-fifteen. She lay dazed for a second. Then she remembered her appointment. She jumped out of bed and hustled to the shower. As the water sprayed her face, she recalled the dream which moments ago was a vivid reality. She tried to analyze it, but nothing made sense. She was sure she had never met the girl before, but the man seemed familiar.

"And who was it that died?" she thought.

Faith dressed in a hurry, fixed her make-up, and scurried downstairs. When she walked into the kitchen, her parents were sitting at the kitchen table.

"You're up early this morning," her father said.

"Yeah. Hope and I are going out for breakfast."

"Are you going to be gone long?" her mother asked.

"Well, I was planning on going back to Hope's house. I was gonna sit next to the pool and read. Why?"

"Oh, nothing. I was counting on a little help this morning with the housecleaning. But that's okay, you go ahead with your plans. I'll manage on my own."

It was a clever ploy, pushing her daughter's "guilt button," but Faith was not about to be manipulated. To Joan's surprise, she said, "Thanks, Mom."

Dr. Brandon was tuned into the subtle battle of wits and wills. He peeked over the newspaper and looked back and forth between his wife and daughter. Amused by his wife's stunned expression, he stuck his head back in the paper and smiled to himself.

"I had the strangest dream last night," Faith said as she poured a small glass of orange juice.

"Oh, what's that?" her father asked from behind his newspaper.

"I dreamt about this long funeral procession that went on and on. And the really strange thing was that every other car was a hearse. Can you think of anyone who died recently? It seems so strange to dream of someone dying, let alone about lots of people dying, when you can't think of a single person who died."

"I can't think of anyone," her father said.

Faith looked at her mother who frowned, shook her head, and said, "I can't either."

"Why does it have to be someone we know?" her father asked.

"Well, because you and Mom and Ryan were in one of the cars," Faith said.

"Maybe you're just worried about someone, Dear," Joan said.

"Yeah, maybe. But I don't understand why there were so many hearses in the procession. That was the really strange part."

"Maybe you're worried about a particular group, like the people dying of AIDS, or the kids in the cities dying in the gang wars," Joan suggested.

"Or maybe you're worried about the four thousand children dying daily in abortions," her father said. "Just imagine what a procession that would be! I'll bet that's what you dreamt about! With all this anti-abortion business Ryan's been getting into lately, you probably picked that up subconsciously and it manifested itself in a dream."

"Yeah, I guess so," Faith agreed quietly.

"It's such a shame this abortion business! I guess people just don't realize that they're going to be called into account for their actions," Dr. Brandon said as he folded his newspaper and reached for his Bible sitting on the kitchen table. "I was reflecting on this recently as I was preparing a talk on abortion and euthanasia. I had come across a passage from Proverbs 24. Let me read it to you."

Faith rolled her eyes as she turned to open the refrigerator for a refill on her orange juice. Her father read:

> Rescue those being led away to death;
> hold back those staggering toward slaughter.
> If you say, "But we knew nothing about this,"
> does not he who weighs the heart perceive it?
> Does not he who guards your life know it?
> Will he not repay each person according to what he has done?

Then he said, "Sounds like it applies to women contemplating abortion, doesn't it?"

Faith stared at her father. "Why does he always do this to me?" she thought. Just then Hope pulled into the driveway honking the horn.

"Gotta go!" Faith said as she quickly rinsed her juice glass and put it into the dishwasher. Then she hurried out the front door and hopped into Hope's car.

"Why couldn't you have been early for once?" Faith asked.

"Good morning to you, too!" Hope replied as she backed out of the driveway.

Faith sighed. "Oh, I'm sorry," she said. "It's just that I got a sermon on abortion from my father just before you got here."

"Oh, my God! You didn't tell him, did you?"

"No, of course not! It just seems that Dad has this intuitive sense of when I'm in need of a sermon. It's uncanny!"

"Do you still want to go through with it?"

"I don't know. I guess so. But why do things have to be so complicated?"

"Well, why don't you talk with Lisa when we get to the clinic? Then make a decision."

"No. That's okay. I'm gonna go through with this. I just shouldn't have opened my big mouth about my dream," Faith said.

"What did you dream about?"

Faith sighed.

"Oh, it was about this long funeral procession and every other car was a hearse. And, of course, Dad had to suggest that it represented all the babies that die from abortions."

"It's not a baby, Faith. It's just tissue, kind of like marmalade."

Faith wanted to believe her, but she couldn't. She said, "There was something else in the dream that was strange."

"What's that?"

"There was a biracial girl about seven or eight fighting with a doctor. She said he was trying to kill her. Her name was Hope. When I told her my best friend's name was Hope, she said she knew that already. It was really odd."

"That's not so odd," Hope said.

"Why's that?"

"Because going to the clinic was on your mind. And the fight represents the struggle you've gone through in making this decision."

Faith was impressed by the interpretation.

"Maybe you should forget about business and study psychology," she said.

"I've thought about it."

Faith reflected a moment on Hope's analysis. Then she said, "In the dream, I saved the girl from the doctor. Wouldn't that mean that I really don't want an abortion?"

"Maybe. Did you know you were saving the girl from an abortion when you helped her?"

"No, I guess not. I think I just saw the doctor bothering her and I instinctively went to help."

"Well, there you go," Hope said. "You're making too much out of this dream, probably because of your dad."

"I guess you're right."

"Of course, I'm right."

The restaurant was humming with busy chatter when the girls arrived. They were immediately seated in a corner booth.

"So how did things go with Jason last night?" Faith asked as she closed her menu.

"Oh, all right, I guess."

"You sound bummed. What happened?"

"Nothing! That's the problem!"

"What do you mean?"

"We had a nice time. The movie was good," Hope said. "But when he took me home, he kissed me good night right away and said he had to go. I asked him why he was in such a hurry and he said he had to meet with some guys. I thought, 'You can have me and you want to be with some guys?' I was like totally bummed."

"Such a shame!" Faith said in a mocking tone.

"Well, it was a shame! Especially after our first date!"

"You're kidding? You made love with him on your first date?"

Hope smiled.

"I think you're foolish, Hope Stuart."

"Why? I'm careful."

"But what if one time you're not? Or the condom fails? Then what?"

"Then I guess I'll have to have an abortion," Hope said matter-of-factly.

"It's not that easy. To tell you the truth, I'm really scared about this."

"Why?"

"Because women have been known to die in abortions you know."

"What are the odds of that happening? You have a better chance of dying in a car accident. But that's not going to keep you from driving, is it?"

"Still, it's been known to happen," Faith said. "Besides, I'm already regretting my decision, and I haven't even gone through with it yet."

Faith's eyes moistened with tears. Hope reached across the table and took hold of her hand. She said, "It's going to be all right."

Faith forced a smile. "Thanks for being here for me," she said.

"Sure. What are friends for?"

Then the waitress came to take their order. "Have you decided yet?" she asked.

Faith looked at the waitress with an ironic smile. "I think so," she replied.

•••

"Do most girls come in alone?" Faith asked on their way to the clinic.

"To the clinic?"

Faith nodded.

"Yeah, most do, I'd say. Some come in with their boyfriends."

"I wonder if they feel as alone as I do right now?"

"You won't be alone," Hope said. "I'll be there for you."

"What? At the front desk answering the phone?" Faith said sarcastically.

"Come on! Don't be that way! There's nothing you could've done to prevent this. You just gotta take it in stride."

"That's easy for you to say," Faith mumbled.

"I know," Hope said. "But just think, in a couple of hours this will all be over. And *I will* get somebody to cover the desk for me so I can be there with you."

"Thanks," Faith said.

As they approached the clinic, they spotted two police cars parked on the street with their lights flashing. Two officers were talking to Hope's uncle. Then they saw the writing on the wall. To the left was written, "Thou shalt not kill!" To the right, "Abortion is murder!" The messages were sprayed in red, slowly and heavily, to make it seem as if tiny rivers of blood were dripping from the letters.

"Oh, my God!" Hope said.

"I don't believe this!" Faith said, nearing tears.

"Don't worry! It'll be all right. It looks like everything is all right inside."

Hope parked the car in the back lot and the girls entered through the rear entrance. As they passed Lisa's office, Hope peeked in and saw Lisa sitting at her desk with the phone held to her shoulder. Her forehead was propped in her other hand.

"What's going on?" Hope asked.

"We were vandalized last night," Lisa said. "Juan saw it this morning when he came to work. Your uncle is in front with the officers filling out a police report. I'm trying to get somebody to clean up this mess. But everybody is busy and can't get here until tomorrow. If they ever catch the people who did this, they ought to throw them to the lions!"

Faith's head was spinning. She was irritated at the vandals for complicating the situation again just when things seemed settled. But she also felt convicted by the graffiti, as if the messages were meant for her in particular.

Then Lisa said, "This is going to back everything up today. Faith, would you mind coming back tomorrow? It would make things a lot easier."

With the other thoughts going through her mind, it took Faith a moment to process the request. Finally she said, "No. Of course! I understand. It's no problem."

"Lisa!" Hope exclaimed.

"No. It's okay. Really," Faith said with a growing sense of relief. The baby had a reprieve and she was glad.

"Come on. I'll walk you back to the car," Hope said, disappointedly. When they got to the car, Hope said, "I'm really sorry!"

"It's okay. Honest."

"No, it's not. I know how much you wanted to get this over with."

Hope gave Faith a hug. She said, "I think I'd better stay around to help. Take my car and I'll give you a call later. Sorry!"

An Open Window 15

The hand of God had been busy painting a portent of divine inspiration. A seemingly impenetrable, gloomy, overcast sky hung overhead as Robert drove to his weekly men's breakfast Bible study. Turning east, he was suddenly struck by an intensely bright light radiating from a heavenly aperture. He quickly reached for his sunglasses, but the dark lenses could not prevent the light from penetrating to the depths of his soul. He felt a stirring in his spirit. As he waited patiently for a green light, he felt these words wash over him: "Be still and know that I am God."

Robert arrived at the pancake house just before seven. He nodded to the hostess and walked directly to a semi-secluded section of the restaurant set apart for large gatherings. When he entered the room, there were already a dozen men seated at four small tables placed end-to-end in a straight line.

"Hello, Robert!"

"Good morning, gentlemen," he replied.

He shook hands with a few of the men before sitting down near the foot of the table. Almost at once, Earl Hansen, the group leader, a large, burly man with a deep voice, stood up and called the meeting to order with a prayer. Then he said, "We're going to do something different today. Rather than study a passage from the Good Book, I've invited John Spivek here to tell us about his ministry and give him a chance to tell us how we can help him. I think it will be of interest to many of you. But that's all I'll say. I'll let him tell you about his ministry, how he got started, and how we can help him."

Earl nodded to John.

"Good morning," John said in a quiet voice as he now stood before them. He was a slender man in his early forties, with thinning reddish-blonde hair and mustache, nicely, but casually dressed, and gentle in manner.

"Thank you for allowing me this opportunity to speak to you this morning. I am a social worker by profession. For the last ten years, I have been counseling young women facing unwanted pregnancies. Some of them had come from desperate situations. In many cases, one or both of their parents wanted nothing to do with them. A few of the girls were literally kicked out of their homes. They were told, 'You created the problem; you take care of it.' Many of them took the easy way out. They chose abortion over adoption or parenting because there was no other recourse in their eyes. In some of those cases, there was a lot of psychological damage after the fact. And to make a long story short, my wife and I began to talk about what we could do as a couple to help these young women. After much prayer and discussion, we felt called by the Holy Spirit to provide a safe haven for unwed mothers. We moved into an old Victorian with lots of space, and, with the help of people from our church, we fixed it up and began to take in unwed mothers. We made our home a place for them to live and carry their child to term while they made the decision of whether to place their child for adoption or parent the child themselves.

"To be honest with you, our ministry has been a real burden at times, especially financially. But through the generous giving of Christian brothers like you, God has been faithful and has provided the means to do His work. And that's why I'm here today. I would like you to prayerfully consider supporting our ministry in any way you can."

As John paused for a sip of water, one of the men raised his hand and asked, "Can you be a little more specific in how we can help? Do you expect us to write you a check, or is there something else we can do?"

"For anyone who is interested, the first thing I would do is give you my card," John said. "Then you can set up an appointment to come out to our home and see first hand what our needs are. You can also meet with the girls who are staying with us. Then it is up to you to decide the best way you can help. Many people write checks. Others have donated new and used maternity clothes, baby clothes, televisions, radios, furniture, and all sorts of things. Others have helped by lending a hand with remodeling. It's entirely up to you. We'd appreciate any help you can give us."

Another man asked, "How many girls do you usually have staying with you?"

"Generally, about three or four."

"Are you affiliated with any agencies or organizations?" another asked.

"Yes. We work closely with Rainbow Family Center, a non-profit Christian agency. It is through them that most of the girls, who decide to do so, place their child for adoption. I would encourage you to call them as a reference."

Robert asked, "What's the racial background of the girls you minister to?"

"It's very diverse," John said. "But since we're located in the western suburbs, it's predominantly white although we have had some black and some Hispanic. In many cases, there's a biracial factor. Many of the girls who come to us are white, but the birthfather is black."

"Is that right?" Robert said as the wheels began turning in his mind.

After taking a few more questions from the group, John closed his presentation by saying, "You know the Lord teaches us that whatever you do for the least, you do for Him. Well, certainly, there is no one in more need of compassion in our society than pregnant teens. There is no one in our society more powerless than an unborn child. When we help unwed mothers and when we defend the right to life of unborn children, we are doing this for Christ. I encourage you to consider some type of donation to our ministry and to use your vote to support pro-life candidates."

Earl Hansen stood up, shook John's hand, and said, "Bless you brother, and thank you for coming by."

Before leaving, John took a moment to personally hand each individual a card.

"Thank you," Robert said as he received a card. "Would you be able to give me the phone number of the Rainbow Family Center? My wife and I are interested in adopting a child."

"Certainly. I'll write it on the back of the card."

"Is there anyone in particular I should talk to?"

"Yes. Ask for Terri Moore. Tell her I referred you. Ask her about the transracial program."

"Will do," Robert said with a smile. "Bless you."

"Good luck. I hope your prayers are answered," John said.

•••

Robert entered the kitchen through the garage. "Kara!" he yelled, but there was no answer. He called again toward their bedroom and office. There was still no answer. "Maybe I'd better call Rainbow Family Center first," he thought.

He sat down at the kitchen table with the cordless phone and pulled John Spivek's business card out of his shirt pocket and started dialing the number written on the back. Robert knew better than to get his hopes up, but he intuitively sensed this was the miracle they had been praying for. When the receptionist answered, Robert asked, "May I speak with Terri Moore please?"

"Just a minute, please."

"Good morning," Terri said in a bubbly voice.

"Yes. My name is Robert Ellison. I'm calling in regard to the transracial adoption program. I just heard about it this morning from John Spivek. He told me to give you a call."

"Okay. Let me just tell you a little bit about our program and then you can tell me if you're still interested," Terri began. "At Rainbow, we place about sixty infants for adoption each year. There is no waiting list *per se*. All applicants develop a profile of themselves including personal backgrounds, their present family situation, and the type of adoption that they are interested in; that is, whether they want a traditional, confidential, adoption, an open adoption, or something somewhere in between. After reading through the profiles, the birthmothers select the adoptive parents.

"In our entire program, we have about six hundred couples who have completed profiles. And as I mentioned before, only sixty infants were placed last year. So, you can see that your odds of receiving an infant are slim even though there is no waiting list. That's the bad news if you're waiting for a white infant. The good news is that if you're applying into our transracial program, your odds are dramatically increased. Presently, we have about twelve couples who have applied into our transracial program. And as I said, last year we placed sixteen infants through that program. As a rule of thumb, no one has had to wait more than nine months to receive a child through the transracial program."

"That's encouraging," Robert said.

"Well, there's more good news," Terri said. "The cost of a transracial adoption is generally less than half the cost of a white adoption. Our fee for a white adoption is twelve thousand dollars. The fee for a transracial adoption is only five thousand."

"Why is that?"

"Supply and demand. We can ask for more for the white infants because there is more of a demand. Biracial children are often the hardest ones to place because, to be honest about it, whites prefer to adopt children who are all white, and blacks prefer to adopt children who are all black. That leaves many of the biracial children in limbo. Because we almost have to recruit parents into our transracial program, we lower the fee."

"Well, five thousand dollars sounds like something we can afford. It's a lot less than some of the numbers we've been hearing," Robert said. "What do we have to do to get started?"

"We have an orientation meeting for the transracial program coming up in a few weeks. If you're interested, we'll reserve a place for you. Then we'll give you some forms to fill out and you can start putting together your profile."

"Sounds great!"

"Good. Let me get your address and we'll notify you when we set the date for our next orientation meeting."

When Robert hung up the phone, he could hardly contain his elation. "Praise God!" he shouted just as Kara stepped through the sliding glass door.

"Praise God for what?" Kara asked.

"For opening a window!"

Vivian's Stand   16

The sun's powerful rays glared down on Elston in the early afternoon as a crowd gathered downtown for an Independence Day political rally. Several Democratic dignitaries were on hand as well as reporters and camera crews from two major networks.

The speakers were assembled on stage in a small plaza off the main mall. Flanked to the left of the stage were members of the American Women's League. To the right stood demonstrators from the Pro-Life Action League. Between the quarreling factions gathered curious onlookers observing the circus atmosphere as the two groups hurled slogans across the courtyard. In a few moments, the verbal artillery exchange abated as the mayor, a short, rotund man with a thinning scalp, local popularity, but little political consequence, stepped to the microphone and opened the ceremony. After a few brief remarks, he was followed by the lieutenant governor, who, in turn, reluctantly relinquished the microphone and made way for the featured guest, Vivian Stuart, the Democratic hopeful for the United States House of Representatives.

Vivian confidently stepped up to the lectern. The reception was loud and mixed. She waited for silence; but instead, the verbal battle escalated between the pro-life and pro-abortion factions. Finally, she held up her arms, signaling a truce. The commotion eventually subsided, fading to a faint murmur.

"I appreciate the opportunity to speak on such a special occasion in a city I've called home for many years," she said. "Let me begin by expressing my strong conviction that what we need in our nation today is more women in Washington making the decisions about the tough issues facing us now and in the years to come."

A hearty cheer rose up from the left and center of the audience.

"From the outset, I want to say, unequivocally, that for a state to force a woman to bear a child against her will is outrageous. Therefore, I believe that any law, forbidding a woman's right to choose, violates her right to control her own body, as well as her life, liberty, and happiness."

Cheers rising up from the left were answered by jeers from the right. Vivian waited once again for the crowd to quiet.

"Women should have the right to take their destiny into their own two hands and make a choice they can live with comfortably in the future."

A tall, lean man with a raspy voice from the pro-life contingent shouted, "Who can live comfortably knowing they've committed murder?"

A murmur rippled through the crowd.

"Let's be honest," Vivian said. "We live in a time of sexual freedom. The taboos, which once restrained us, have died. Accidents happen and they always will. Women must be given the opportunity to correct their mistakes."

"It's a child! Not a mistake!" shouted an elderly woman.

Vivian grimaced with contempt, but like a seasoned politician, she maintained her composure. She raised her hands again to quiet the crowd and said, "Let's not forget the social costs involved. I think America would be much better off if, rather than chastising women for their occasional sexual indiscretions, it would be more concerned about protecting itself from the consequences of an unwanted child. Why can't we be refreshingly honest for a change and acknowledge the threat to society that an unwanted child really is? The plain truth is that unwanted children tend to grow up in psychologically and emotionally unhealthy homes. That's not fair to them and it's not fair to society. Those of you who think abortion is evil ought to realize that it is the lesser of two evils. The advantages of abortion to parents and children in low-income groups, to women in general, and to society as a whole, clearly outweigh the negatives. Therefore, I will not waver in my support of a woman's right to choose. It is not only in her best interests, but it is also in the best interests of America."

Again, Vivian paused momentarily for the mixture of applause and groans to subside. Then she looked directly at the pro-life contingent and said, "I see some of you in the crowd today holding up signs saying, 'Abortionists are murderers!' I say to you, they are not murderers. They are great humanitarians doing society a great service. If the environment into which a child would be born promises to be harsh and a source of suffering, then an abortion is an act of love. It is an incomprehensible shame that these courageous doctors are now becoming the innocent victims of anti-choice terrorism. After all, they are the ones protecting unwanted children from living lives of rejection and poverty outside the womb. It's time we begin to acknowledge that abortionists are heroes guaranteeing a better quality of life for everyone and a more liberated America for women."

The crowd responded vociferously. The pro-life chant, "It's a child, not a choice!" battled to a standoff with, "A woman's right, keep it safe, keep it legal!" Vivian held her arms up but the shouting match continued for several minutes. Finally, the mayor walked up to the lectern and pleaded for silence. When the shouting faded to a murmur, the mayor said, "Please give the candidate the opportunity to speak her mind. That's what this country is all about, isn't it?"

Vivian returned to the microphone and said, "Critics of abortion claim that since *Roe v. Wade* over forty million children have died. Let me ask you this? What do you think our society would be like today if we had another forty million unwanted people in our midst? I'll tell you what it would be like. Our urban jungles would be much more overcrowded. If you think we have too much violence now, think of what it would be like under those circumstances. Moreover, our welfare rolls would be endless, and our national debt even greater. On the other hand, a woman's right to choose promises a future of peace, liberty, and freedom.

"I also would suggest that there is an economic benefit to a woman's right to choose. What Americans have to understand is that we will save money by funding all abortions under a comprehensive health care plan. Twenty-five percent of women who might have Medicaid-funded abortions have children instead. Then we end up paying for pre-natal care, childbirth, and even more public assistance. Why do you think the private health care insurance providers are willing to pay for abortions? Plain and simple, it just makes economic sense. It saves money.

"To sum up then, let me say that I regard myself as being pro-life and pro-choice. I am pro-life in the sense that I believe we must maintain a high standard in regard to the quality of life. I am pro-choice because a woman's decision about abortion is not a decision the government should be making. Although I know abortion is not the right choice for everyone, I strongly believe it should remain available as an option for all women. Abortion should always be considered as a last option, but the final decision must ultimately be left to each woman's individual conscience. Let me say, finally, that I have a seventeen-year-old daughter. As a parent, I want my daughter to be guaranteed the opportunity to make the choice that's right for her. As a voice for women everywhere, it is extremely important to me that we keep abortion safe and legal."

The candidate's concluding remarks on abortion drew another round of raucous cheers from her supporters. The pro-life group responded again with jeers and boos. When Vivian turned to other issues—the economy, foreign affairs, the increase in violence, and education—the crowd grew impatient. At long last, she completed her canned litany and opened the forum for questions. Many hands shot up in the pro-life contingent, but the candidate acknowledged several people on the left and center and answered their questions first. Finally, she pointed to the tall, lean man with the raspy voice on the pro-life side.

He asked, "First, I would like to know if you believe in God, and if so, aren't you being a hypocrite because of your stand on abortion?"

The questions drew enormous cheers and applause from the pro-life crowd. Finally, they thought, someone had pinned the candidate down.

"Let me tell you this," Vivian began. "I grew up in a Christian home but I am not Catholic. But even if I was Catholic, I would not follow the Pope's dictates on abortion. And even though I don't carry a Bible around with me as many people do, I do have some sense of what's in the Bible. And to my knowledge, the Bible never says that abortion is wrong. It does say 'Thou shalt not kill.' But in my mind, to kill someone, that person must first be born. A fetus is not yet a human life until it is born. I think the anti-choice groups have to realize that. They have to get over their love affair with fetuses. To answer your question, I think there are some gray areas in theology where there is legitimate dispute, and I think the issue of abortion is one of those gray areas. I think God understands a woman's choice when she avoids bringing an unwanted child into an undesirable life situation. After all, such a choice is an act of love." Then she abruptly closed her comments by saying, "I thank you for coming here today."

Vivian shook hands with the other politicians on stage and quickly made an exit to the right. As she descended the stairs, a short, stocky, bearded young man, wearing a pro-life T-shirt and cutoffs, moved to intercept her at the bottom of the steps.

"Mrs. Stuart, I have something for you," the man said nervously as he handed her something wrapped inside a brown wash cloth. As the young man turned and walked away briskly, Vivian unfolded the wash cloth and discovered a bloody, half-mutilated, aborted fetus. Despite her rhetoric to the contrary, what she held in her hands was more than just a foul sample of tissue. She clearly recognized a distinctly human form in its earliest stages. Her heart stood still. Shock turned into revulsion. Vivian gasped and averted her eyes. She felt faint as she realized she was holding in her hands the concrete reality of the abstraction she defended so staunchly. For the first time, she had encountered the fetid result of this violent act against human life. Her knees buckled. James quickly grabbed her by the arm and escorted her to his car.

"Come on. Let's go home," he said, taking the aborted fetus from her. He then turned and gave the dead child to Vivian's campaign manager.

"What do you want me to do with this?" Jack asked, his stomach turning at the sight of the tiny human remains.

•••

When Vivian arrived home, she jumped out of the car and slammed the door behind her. She stormed into the house, still visibly shaken, and marched directly to the family room. She tossed her purse onto a chair and collapsed onto the sofa. She sat quietly and stared blankly into space. James was but a few steps behind. He stood at the doorway between the kitchen and family room for a moment and said nothing. Then he turned and walked into the kitchen and pulled a beer out of the refrigerator. When he returned, Vivian suddenly exploded.

"I just don't believe those people! How could anybody do that?"

James was about to respond but he was cut off.

"They're so self-righteous! They think they can do anything to anybody to try to make a point. Ugh! That was so disgusting! It almost makes me vomit just thinking about that…that…fetus," she said, exasperated.

"Viv, you just have to be philosophical about this."

"Philosophical? They put a fetus in my hands and you expect me to be philosophical?"

"Yes. Just calm down a second and think about it," James said. "They got the exact reaction from you that they wanted. You have to remember who these people are. They're not rational people. They're ruled by emotion and sentimentality. And they're trying to get you to think like them."

"You mean *irrationally*," Vivian answered in a sarcastic tone.

"Yes."

Vivian shook her head. She got up from the sofa and walked across the room toward the television. With folded arms, she stood thinking for a moment, shaking her head in disapprobation of the appalling tactic. James continued with his analysis.

"To say that they're irrational is not to say they're stupid," he said. "They know you've been able to take the position you do because you've been able to separate your feelings from your beliefs. You're able to think abstractly about abortion. You're able to look at the big picture and see what's best overall for society and women. They have tunnel vision. Their view is narrowed by sentimentality. They're trying to get you away from the big picture and get you to reduce your focus. And they're doing it with emotional ploys like the incident this afternoon."

"Maybe you're right. But you'd think they'd have some compassion for the women who are in impossible situations and can't give birth to another child."

Then Vivian paused for a moment and added, "If women are ever going to be equal with men they have to have the right to control their reproductive life. Can't they see that? For God's sake, a fetus doesn't even know it's alive! What does it matter?"

"That's the point!" James said. "It doesn't matter. Nothing really does. We exist only by chance. All of nature is a freak accident. And for some reason, we were lucky enough to have evolved into thinking beings on the only inhabitable orb in the universe. It's not a nice story like the one that the Bible tells, but it's reality. There is no God. And any meaning that there is in life is what we add to it by our actions and decisions. Nature doesn't care one way or another about abortion. So why should we?"

"So how am I supposed to deal with the 'bleeding heart' religious right?"

"Ignore them as much as possible. You're not going to change their minds and they're not going to change yours. Just keep your answers simple. Don't go into detail like you did this afternoon. It just gives them more to shoot at. Stick with the platitudes like 'women ought to have the right to choose.' Then it comes down to your rational platitudes against their religious platitudes. The bottom line is that your platitudes are more popular than theirs. And besides, the issue of abortion is just not that important to most voters, so don't worry about it. You'll win the election as long as you stick with the platform you have. You're leading in the polls now and you'll win the election in November. That's all that counts. You're in a position to grasp a level of power that few women in American history have ever enjoyed. And who knows what else is in your future! It could be the White House. But to get there, you'll need a thick skin. You have to let the incidents like today roll off your back. Just focus on winning. That's what politics is all about. How do you think President Stanton got to be where he is today?"

"I guess you're right," Vivian said. Then she walked across the room to where James was standing at the door. "Thanks."

"For what?"

"For being here for me," Vivian said as she put her arms around him.

Still holding his beer in one hand, he wrapped his free arm around her waist. She rose up on her tiptoes and gave him a kiss.

"Do you want to see yourself on the news?" he asked.

"Only if I'm in charge of the remote," she said.

"You are a power hungry woman, aren't you?" he said with a smile.

The Innocent Condemned

17

Dr. Morlon arrived at the clinic early Tuesday morning for a special meeting with Lisa Slatkin. He found her in her office sitting in her chair pouring over the clinic's recent sales figures. He immediately made his way around her desk and began massaging her shoulders.

"Tom, we have to talk," Lisa said with a tense smile.

"So talk," Tom said as he brushed her long red hair out of the way and began kissing her neck.

"No, really," she said as she gently grabbed his arms and spun around in her chair. "It's time to talk business."

"Okay," he said with a smirk. "Talk to me."

"I would feel better if you sat down and treated this seriously."

The smirk on Tom's face faded. He sat down on a chair in front of Lisa's desk. Then he leaned forward laying his forearms on the desk with folded hands.

"What's up?" he said.

"It's time to talk about our partnership agreement."

"Okay. What do we need to discuss?"

"Last month we reached a new plateau," Lisa said. "My marketing ideas have generated a lot of business. Our ten percent discount coupons, our advertising program, the low potency pill prescriptions, the publicity we've received for offering free abortions to rape victims, and our presentations

145

in the high school health classes have all improved sales dramatically. Now, it's time for me to start receiving the bonuses we agreed on. Friday's paycheck did not include the bonus I earned."

Tom nodded.

"You're probably right," he said. "But maybe we ought to keep more cash in the business until we establish more of an upward trend. You know what they say about small businesses. The three major problems are cash flow, cash flow, and cash flow."

"Tom! You've made a lot of money off my business savvy. And a deal is a deal. I expect to be paid!"

"Okay, okay! Don't get upset," Tom said with a defensive chuckle. "If that's the way you want it, I'll call John this morning and tell him to cut you a bonus check."

"Good."

"Anything else?"

"No, that's all, except..." Lisa said, and then paused.

"Except what?"

"Except that the way business continues to increase, I think we should be looking for another doctor to help with the workload."

"You are so sexy when you talk business," Tom said. He stood up, leaned across the desk, and tried to pull Lisa close for a kiss.

Lisa put her hand up to his lips and said with a smile, "Tonight, after hours, after I get my bonus check."

"You're a tough woman to deal with."

"Just remember that," Lisa said. Then she pulled Tom close for a passionate kiss. "Remember that, too!"

"We'll continue this meeting at your place tonight," Tom said. As he turned to leave, there was a knock at the door.

"If I get my check," Lisa said coyly.

"Shrewd," Tom said whimsically.

"Hi, Uncle Tom!" Hope said as he opened the door.

"Good morning, Hope," he said with a smile. "How are things goin' so far? Everything okay?"

"Yeah! Great! In fact, I think I deserve a raise," she said jokingly.

"You women are all alike," he muttered facetiously on his way out the door. "Talk to Lisa about it. But good luck!"

"What can I do for you, Hope?" Lisa asked.

"I need to talk to you about my friend, Faith."

"Oh, that's right! She was supposed to come in last week, wasn't she?"

"Yes, but the graffiti incident ruined everything. I talked to her last night and now she knows she has to do something soon."

"Is she leaning toward an abortion?"

"That's just it. She doesn't know what to do. She comes from a really religious family and she's feeling guilty just thinking about abortion."

"How far along is she?"

"About fifteen weeks now, I think."

"What does her boyfriend want to do about it?"

"He doesn't know she's pregnant."

"Don't you think she should tell him?"

"That's part of the problem. It's not his fault."

"What do you mean?"

"She was raped. It happened in Florida over spring break."

"I see," Lisa said. After a brief pause, she added, "Can't she just explain that to her parents? Surely, they would understand."

"Well, she's feeling guilty about the circumstances. She was at a party that her parents wouldn't approve of."

"Do you think she'd have an abortion if someone gave her some counseling?"

"I hope so!"

"A second trimester abortion is expensive. Can she afford it?"

"She *was* raped. Our ads and brochures say we'll do the procedure for free."

Lisa paused for a moment. It was the first time anyone had actually taken the clinic up on the offer. She said, "Just have her bring in a copy of the police report and we'll take care of it."

"Police report? There is no police report. She didn't tell anybody about it, not even me, until more than a month after it happened."

"Oh, that's too bad!" Lisa said. "We really need verification."

"What? Don't you believe me? I'm not lying about this, Lisa! My girlfriend was raped! She needs help! Can't we help her?"

"I'm sorry. But that's against clinic policy. You see, if we start doing free procedures without proof of victimization, then pretty soon every girl coming into the clinic will say she was raped."

"You're kidding!"

"I'm sorry, Hope. We have to keep complete records just in case we're audited some time. You understand."

"I don't believe this!"

"I'm sorry. I wish we could help."

Hope sat quietly for a moment. Finally she said, "Well, I can't let her down. I'll pay for it if I have to."

"That's very generous of you, Hope."

"Well, you have to let me be there when you talk to her so that I can talk her into letting me pay for it."

"That's assuming she'll have the abortion."

"She'd better! I don't want her to wreck her whole life. Talk some sense into her!"

"I think we can convince her. Why don't you bring her in Thursday morning?"

•••

The weather was foggy Thursday morning, almost surreal, as in a dream, reflecting Faith's profound confusion. She parked in the back lot and began walking toward the clinic for her "counseling" session. It seemed odd that everything outside the clinic was still. There were no protesters, no sidewalk pro-life counselors, and no graffiti. It was almost too easy, but the real challenge lay ahead.

When Faith passed through the front door, there were a half dozen other teenage girls and a woman in her late twenties waiting in the reception area. Most had come with a friend, a boyfriend, or a relative—someone to give them support. Faith felt conspicuous in her solitude. Yet, just being there was even more upsetting. She was in an establishment that her parents held in total disdain. She felt utterly ashamed, almost as if she were a half-clad whore in a brothel awaiting her next trick. She scanned the room, but as far as she could tell, there was not a familiar face in the crowd. She was relieved. Then she heard a familiar voice. "Faith!" She looked over to the reception desk and saw Hope discreetly waving to her. She walked briskly up to the desk.

"Hi," Faith said sheepishly.

"I'm glad you came," Hope said. "I'll get you in right away. It'll only be a couple of minutes. Have a seat and I'll call you when the nurse is ready."

"Thanks," Faith said, attempting a smile.

"If you don't mind, I'll come into the counseling session with you."

"Thanks. I'd appreciate it."

"Good. It'll be just a second."

Faith found an empty seat and was praying for a clear sign from God when Hope approached.

"Are you ready?" she asked.

"As ready as I'll ever be," Faith said as she put the magazine on the table next to her chair. She followed Hope to a small examination office in the back.

"Here. Put this on," Hope said as she handed Faith a white hospital robe. "A nurse will be in here in just a minute to do an ultra-sound."

"An ultra-sound? How come?"

"We've got to make sure you're pregnant."

"What? You know I'm pregnant!" Faith said, irritated. "Why do we have to do this?"

"It's routine. You wouldn't believe how many girls come in here thinking they're pregnant when they're not."

"What happens if they're not pregnant?"

"We perform an abortion anyway. They don't know the difference," Hope said straight-faced.

"You're kidding!"

Hope laughed. "You're so gullible sometimes!" she said.

"Get out of here!" Faith said. But the real joke was on Hope. She was unaware that over the last few months Lisa and Tom conspired to do an increasing number of "phantom" abortions to maintain a steady workload.

The nurse came in to do the examination moments later. Hope said, "Let me know when you're finished. I'm going to join Faith in Lisa's office. I'll be up at the front desk."

"Will do," the nurse said. After Hope left, she said to Faith, "Okay. I need you to lie down on the table."

Faith followed orders but asked, "Will I be able to see the picture?"

"Well, I don't see why not," the nurse said as she applied a gel to Faith's stomach. "I'll see if I can adjust things when I'm done here."

When things were ready, the nurse began moving a roller wand, much like a deodorant dispenser, over Faith's stomach. Sound waves produced an x-ray image on the monitor. Faith was able to make out the outline of a child—its head, torso, legs, and arms—sitting Indian style with one arm cocked at a ninety degree angle and its hand held to its mouth as if sucking its thumb. Then she heard an unmistakable sound.

"Is that its heart beating?" she asked.

The nurse smiled. "Yes, it is," she said.

"Oh, my God!"

Faith's heart sank to her stomach as a shroud of sadness overwhelmed her. For the first time, she was confronted with the concrete reality of her child. Previously, she had acknowledged it only in an abstract sense. Now, that was no longer possible. With the sound of every heartbeat, and with the undeniable image of a tiny human form on the monitor, Faith began to experience the powerful bond that exists between mother and child. The baby in the picture was not just a child, it was *her* child, and she was its mother.

"Is it a boy or girl? Can you tell?" Faith asked.

"I'm sorry. But I really can't tell you."

"Why?"

"Clinic policy. You can get dressed now."

The ultra-sound took less than fifteen minutes. Minutes after the nurse left, Hope knocked on the door and peeked in.

"How'd it go?" she asked.

"Okay, I guess. I'm definitely pregnant. I saw the baby on the monitor."

"Really?" Hope said, wincing inwardly. She knew that was taboo. She once overheard Lisa chastise another nurse for making the same blunder.

"She wouldn't say but I think it's a girl."

"Oh, come on! It's just a blob of tissue. You can't tell yet," Hope said.

"Yes, you can! I could see its silhouette!"

"Well, let's go. I think Lisa is ready for us."

Lisa was not in her office as the girls stepped in and sat down in the two chairs in front of Lisa's desk. Faith's eyes skipped around the room examining the posters on the wall displaying the various abortion procedures. Then Hope picked up a large brochure from Lisa's desk and handed it to Faith.

"Here," she said. "Why don't you take a look at this while you're waiting?"

Faith began leafing through the brochure.

"Hope."

"Yeah."

"I don't know if I can do this."

"Sure you can! Why not?"

"I saw my baby! I don't want it to die."

"It's not a baby!" Hope said as Lisa suddenly slipped into her office.

"Good morning, Faith," she said, startling the girls.

Faith smiled apprehensively.

"I understand you're fifteen weeks along. Have you made a decision?" Lisa asked.

"Honestly," Faith said, "I wish someone could make the decision for me."

Lisa looked Faith in the eye and nodded sympathetically. She said, "This is not an easy thing for me to tell you, but you should know that we've looked at the printouts of your ultra-sound and it appears as though the fetus has a cyst on the brain."

"Oh, my God!" Faith gasped. She put her right hand on her stomach and reached out to Hope with her left hand. Hope grabbed her hand and squeezed it gently.

"I'm sorry," Lisa said.

"What does that mean?" Hope asked.

"It means the baby will likely be handicapped in some way, perhaps mentally retarded."

"My baby!"

Faith's eyes flooded with tears. Hope squeezed her hand and asked, "How do you know there's a cyst?"

"A trained eye can look at an ultra-sound and tell these things."

Faith began sobbing. Hope moved closer and put her arm around Faith.

"Are you sure there hasn't been some mistake?" Hope asked.

"I'm afraid not. I went over the printout with your uncle," Lisa said.

Faith continued to cry softly. Hope began stroking her back. She said, "Maybe this is for the best, Faith. Maybe it's a sign you shouldn't go through with birth."

Faith wiped her eyes and nose with a tissue. Then she took a deep breath and composed herself.

"Can I see the printout?" she asked.

"It really wouldn't help. You need a trained eye to interpret the pictures," Lisa said. "In light of the circumstances, I think we should schedule a procedure."

Faith looked at Hope who said, "I don't think you have a choice."

Faith nodded and the tears started again. Through her tears she asked, "What will it be like?"

"Since you're fifteen weeks along, the procedure is a little more involved," Lisa said. "The doctor will start by numbing a small area about two inches below your navel. Then he'll insert a long needle into the amniotic sac and withdraw about two ounces of fluid. After that, he'll inject about two hundred milligrams of saline solution. That will dry up the moisture in the sac. In about twenty-four hours your uterus will automatically contract and force the fetus out. You'll have to stay here in bed until the next day."

Faith sat up in her chair. "Stay here overnight! There's no way! What will I tell my parents?"

"You can tell them you're staying at my house for the night," Hope said.

Faith settled back. She asked, "What happens the next day?"

"The placenta has to be removed by a 'D and C,'" Lisa said as she glanced at her watch.

"What's that?" Faith asked.

"A 'D and C?'"

Faith nodded.

"The doctor dilates your cervical canal and then scrapes the inside of the uterus with a spoon-shaped curette," Lisa said.

Faith sighed deeply as she looked at Hope. She asked, "How much will it cost?"

"It's eleven hundred dollars."

"Oh, my God! Why so much?"

"An overnight stay means we have to pay a nurse to be here with you. Of course, there are other expenses as well."

Faith let out a dejected sigh. She said hopelessly, "I can't afford it."

"Don't worry, Faith. I'll take care of it," Hope said quickly.

"No way! I can't let you do that!"

"It's okay. I have that much cash sitting in my drawer at home. Really! It's no problem."

"I don't care. That's too much!"

Hope huffed impatiently. She said, "Faith, we've been best friends a long time. If the situation was reversed, I'm sure you'd do the same for me."

"I know. But eleven hundred dollars is too much to ask."

"Not to me it isn't."

Faith knew it was true. Hope had more money than she knew what to do with.

"Okay. But this is a loan, not a handout," Faith said adamantly. "I'll pay you back—not all at once and not right away. But I will pay you back eventually."

"That's fine," Hope said, forcing a little smile. Then she gave Faith a hug.

"Well, now that that's settled, when do you want to schedule this? Are Monday and Tuesday okay?" Lisa asked.

"I guess that will be fine. But we'll have to think of something to tell my parents," Faith said.

As the girls got up to leave, Faith felt like a judge who had just condemned an innocent man to death merely because justice demanded retribution and the guilty party was nowhere to be found. Moreover, the condemned was denied even a semblance of a defense. Even so, the highest court in the land would surely have looked on the proceedings with approbation. An even higher court, however, would just as certainly have handed down another verdict, going beyond justice and mercy. Even if the condemned child were guilty of a heinous crime against humanity, which of course it wasn't, there is nothing more certain on Earth or in Heaven than that the Supreme Judge of us all would have granted the child grace and life.

The Truth Comes Out 18

Faith returned home shortly after nine. She parked the car in the garage and sat quietly, thinking about all that had transpired. After a long moment, she dropped her head forward, butting the steering wheel.

"God!" she cried out quietly as tears dripped down her cheeks. "Please let me know I'm doing the right thing! My baby is so beautiful! I don't want her to die! But how can I let her be born handicapped?"

At last Faith composed herself. She could not give her mother the slightest clue about her crisis, especially now that she'd been to the clinic. She wiped her eyes with a tissue and took a deep breath. As she climbed out of the car, her mother opened the laundry room door leading to the garage.

"Where have you been, Faith!" Joan said angrily. "I had an appointment this morning and I had to cancel it! Why didn't you tell me you were going somewhere?"

Faith scurried through her mind for an excuse but was still too distraught to be evasive. Instead, the emotional dam suddenly burst open and she wept inconsolably as a mother who had just lost a child.

Joan's anger melted instantly. She sensed a crisis and her mind raced in search of possibilities. But she had no idea of her daughter's predicament. She hurried to Faith and wrapped her in her arms. Her emotional energy now flowed in new channels of motherly compassion and love.

"What's wrong, Faith?" she asked.

Faith replied only with tears, burying her face in her mother's shoulder. Joan gently led Faith into the family room. She sat next to her on the couch and held Faith in her arms.

"Take a deep breath. It'll be all right," she said. When Faith finally composed herself, Joan said, "Faith, you've got to tell me what this is all about."

"I can't," she said quietly.

"You have to."

Faith shook her head.

"Please!"

After a moment, when Faith realized that only the truth could explain her tears, she said, "Mom! I couldn't stop him! He raped me!"

The revelation pierced her mother's heart like a stiletto.

"Who raped you? Chris?"

"No! Chris doesn't even know what happened. Nobody does except for Hope. I'm sorry! I should have told you!"

"Faith, take a deep breath and tell me the whole story."

Joan was trembling. Her eyes were wet with tears. Faith paused, breathed deeply a couple of times, and began her tale.

"It was our last night in Florida. Hope and I were at a party. Hope went off with a guy and I was alone. As I was leaving, a black guy named Jimmy offered to walk me home. He seemed to be a nice guy and so I let him. We were walking along the beach and came to this vacant lot. Then he…"

Faith was too choked to finish. Her mother wept, too. After a moment of crying in each other's arms, Joan asked, "Faith, why didn't you tell us this right away?"

Faith shook her head with downcast eyes. "I couldn't," she said. "I was too ashamed!"

"About what? Being raped is not your fault."

"I had made such a big deal about being able to take care of myself so you'd let me go to Florida without Hope's mother there to chaperone us. I didn't want you to know."

"Honey, that's okay. You should've told us so that you could've had some counseling," Joan said. "We love you and we're always here to help you!"

After giving Faith another hug, Joan said, "Be honest with me. If you've held things in for so long, why did this come out now?"

Faith sighed and kept her teary eyes averted.

"Tell me."

Faith took another deep breath.

"I can't tell you. You're going to hate me!"

"Nothing you do will ever make me hate you! You know that!"

"No. You don't understand!"

"Understand what?"

With her eyes still averted Faith confessed, "I'm pregnant."

"Oh, Lord! Why didn't you tell us?"

"I couldn't! I didn't want to embarrass you and Dad."

"You don't have to worry about us, Dear. What's important is you!"

"That's easy to say," Faith said, wiping her eyes. "But think how it would look for the President of Justin College to have a daughter who's an unwed mother."

"There are things more important than our image. I wish you would have come to us for help."

"I guess I was just hoping that somehow the problem would just go away."

"Honey, you know problems don't just go away. You have to face them head on!"

"I know. That's why I finally listened to Hope."

"You went to Hope for help?"

Faith nodded.

"What did she tell you to do?"

Faith hung her head and confessed, "I went to see a counselor at the clinic."

"You went to the abortion clinic?"

Faith nodded.

"That's where you were this morning?"

Faith nodded again. The thought of Faith having an abortion made Joan sick to her stomach, but she knew her daughter needed understanding, not reproof. Gently, she lifted her daughter's head with her hand. She looked into Faith's eyes and said, "We love you! Your dad and I are always here for you, no matter what you've done or what the consequences might be for us! From now on, please understand that! And don't hide anything ever again."

"Okay," Faith said, giving her mother a hug.

"Now tell me what happened at the clinic," Joan said.

"They did an ultra-sound."

"And?"

"The baby has a cyst on the brain. They said it'd be born handicapped and that I should abort it," Faith said, teary-eyed. "I can't do anything right! I can't even have a healthy baby!"

"It's okay, Dear!" Joan said as she gave Faith a reassuring squeeze. She was skeptical of the diagnosis but thought, "There's nothing we can do about it now!"

Then Faith said, "I don't want to have the abortion! But what else can I do?"

"You mean you didn't have an abortion?"

"No, not yet. I'm supposed to go back on Monday."

"Oh! Thank God!" Joan sighed as her eyes quickly moistened with tears.

"Mom! Why are you crying? I'm the one who's supposed to be crying!"

Joan forced a smile as she wiped her tears. She said, "Where there's life, there's still hope!"

"Hope for what? The baby has a cyst on its brain!"

"I think we should have a second opinion."

"Why?"

"Because they may be lying."

"They wouldn't do that!"

"What makes you think so?"

"Well, because they're nice people. And Hope works there and she wouldn't let them lie to me," Faith said adamantly.

"Wake up! All they want is your money!"

"No, they don't!"

"Well, maybe they made a mistake. Did they show you the film?"

"No! But they can't be mistaken! Lisa looked things over with Hope's uncle."

Joan was still skeptical. "How much is the abortion going to cost?" she asked.

Faith rolled her eyes. She said, "Eleven hundred dollars."

"Oh my! That's a lot of money! There are a lot of people who would lie for a lot less than that," Joan said. "How were you going to pay for it?"

Faith took another deep breath.

"Hope was gonna loan me the money. I was gonna pay her back a little at a time."

"Before you do anything, let's get a second opinion," Joan said.

Faith nodded reluctantly. "Okay," she said.

"Good. Do you want to tell your Dad or do you want me to?"

"I'd rather you did. I need to lie down."

"You do that," Joan said and gave Faith a hug.

•••

Dr. Brandon's secretary was typing correspondence when the phone rang.

"Dr. Brandon's office. May I help you?" Patty said in a crackly voice.

"Patty, this is Joan. I need to speak to Ryle."

"Sorry, Joan. He's in an important meeting. He wanted me to hold his calls," Patty said with authority.

"This is important, too. Can you have him call me as soon as his meeting is over?"

"Will do!"

Joan hung up the phone and sat down at the kitchen table contemplating her next move. "Lord, give me some direction," she prayed.

She started by calling her gynecologist. With some persistence, she was able to persuade the receptionist to squeeze in an appointment that afternoon. Then she tried the yellow pages. She was not sure what she was looking for so she first looked under "abortion" and found a heading for "abortion alternatives." She surveyed the list of agencies and ads and discovered another heading which promised some possibility—"adoption." She started with the pro-life agency that had the biggest ad. As she dialed, she prayed, "Help, Lord!"

A pleasant female voice answered, "New Life Crisis Counseling. This is Sandy. May I help you?"

"I hope so," Joan said. "I just found out that my daughter is pregnant. I don't want her to have an abortion. Where do I go from here?"

"Can you give me some more background about your daughter and the baby's father?" Sandy asked.

"My daughter is seventeen. She just graduated from high school. She went on a trip to Florida in March and was raped. She became pregnant but was too ashamed to tell us about the rape or the pregnancy. A friend took her to an abortion clinic this morning for some counseling and they advised her to get an abortion. They said the child has a cyst on the brain. She came home all upset and that's when I found out."

"Are you certain that she was raped?" Sandy asked. "We have a lot of girls who use that story to cover up for their boyfriends."

"I believe my daughter. Besides, she says a black man raped her. If she does give birth, it'll be pretty obvious whether she was telling the truth or not."

"Okay. Then the next thing we have to determine is if the abortion clinic was telling the truth," Sandy said.

"How do we do that?"

"Well, for one, we have a doctor who works with our agency on a volunteer basis. He gets involved in cases like this and offers his opinion. I can give you his number and he will probably want to get a hold of your daughter's records. He should be able to tell by looking at the pictures whether the clinic was telling the truth. I assume she had an ultra-sound."

"Yes, she did."
"Good. Hang on just a minute and I'll give you his number."

•••

Dr. Petrone was out of the office. Joan left a message with the receptionist and went to her bedroom to pray. At eleven-thirty, after nearly two hours of prayer, he returned her call.

"Hello, Mrs. Brandon. I understand that you were referred by New Life. How can I help?"

Joan outlined the situation as she had done for the counselor.

"I'd really like to see the ultra-sound records," Dr. Petrone said. "I need you to be on the line to authorize the release of the records. We'll set up a conference call with the clinic now if that's all right with you."

"The sooner the better."

In a few minutes, Hope answered the phone at the clinic.

"Hello, this is Dr. Petrone. I'm calling in regard to one of my patients, Faith Brandon. I'd like to speak to the counselor who handled her case this morning."

"Oh, my God! Her mother knows!" Hope thought. She said, "Just a minute. I'll see if she's available."

Hope rang Lisa's office.

"Lisa. There's a doctor on line two who wants to talk to you about Faith. I think her mother must know what happened."

"Okay, I'll handle it," she said. Lisa took a deep breath and punched line two. "Hello. This is Lisa Slatkin. May I help you?"

"Yes. This is Dr. Petrone. I understand you counseled one of my patients this morning. Her name is Faith Brandon. I also understand that you took an ultra-sound and told her that the baby had a cyst on the brain. Is that right?"

"Well, I don't recall off hand. I've had several cases this morning and I'd have to check my records."

"That's all right. I'll wait. And while you have them out, I'd like you to send them to me," Dr. Petrone said.

"I'm sorry but we need authorization from the girl's parents to release any information."

"That's fine. Her mother is on the line and she'll give you authorization. In fact, I'm sure she'll be willing to pick up the file today. Won't you Mrs. Brandon?"

"I certainly will," Joan said.

Lisa was silent for a moment. Finally, she said, "Let me check the records. What did you say her name was?"

"Faith Brandon," Joan said.

"Just a minute," Lisa said. She set the phone on her desk and waited a couple of minutes. Then she picked up the phone and said, "I'm sorry, but I can't find her records. Are you sure she didn't go to another clinic?"

"Oh, come on!" Joan said. "You know perfectly well that she was at your clinic this morning! Her friend, Hope Stuart, invited her."

"I'm sorry. But you must be mistaken. We don't have any record of her attending the clinic," Lisa said.

"That's a lie!" Joan said sharply.

"It's all right, Mrs. Brandon," Dr. Petrone said. "We'll deal with them later. Give me a call back at my office when we hang up. Thank you, Ms. Slatkin."

In a moment, Joan and Dr. Petrone were back on the phone together.

"I'm sorry," Dr. Petrone said. "There isn't much we can do. But it's quite apparent that they didn't want us to see the records."

"So what do we do?"

"I suggest you get another ultra-sound from your gynecologist."

"We have an appointment for this afternoon," Joan said.

"Good. Then follow up with that. That's about all you can do."

•••

Joan had three hours to fill before the appointment. She tried to pass the time with household chores, but nothing could take her mind off her daughter's dilemma. The anxiety over Faith's physical and psychological health, the concern for her first grandchild, the anger over the rape in Florida, the deception at the clinic, the potential for personal embarrassment, and the uncertainty of her daughter's final decision, consumed her. Shortly after noon, Joan went to the kitchen and contemplated her options for lunch, but she had little appetite. As she closed the refrigerator door empty-handed, the phone rang.

"Hi, Honey! I got your message."

"Oh, Ryle! I don't know how to tell you," Joan said. "It's about Faith."

"What happened?"

"She's all right, don't worry! It's just that we've got a problem, a serious one. Do you think you can come home and talk?"

"Sure, I can. But what's the problem?"

"I don't want to tell you over the phone. Come home, please!"

"Okay. I'll be on my way home in a couple of minutes."

Dr. Brandon hung up the phone and sat back in his chair. At first, he was numb. Then his mind raced through several tragic possibilities. Finally, he told Patty on his way out the door, "Cancel my appointments for the rest of the day."

•••

When Ryle Brandon returned home, he found his wife waiting for him in the bedroom. Joan got up from the bed and embraced her husband.

"What's wrong?"

Joan turned and sat down on the bed.

"What's wrong?" Ryle asked again as he sat next to his wife.

Joan said with a sigh, "Faith is pregnant."

"What? Ugh! I knew that boy was trouble!"

"Stop jumping to conclusions. It's not Chris."

"It's not? Then who?"

"Faith was raped."

"Oh, no!" he moaned. The news was like a hard, sucker punch to the stomach. "How? When?"

"It happened in Florida, the night before she left."

"Oh, my God! Why didn't she tell us?"

"She was afraid to. She was too ashamed."

"Does she know who it was? How did you find out?"

"She just knows it was a young black man named Jimmy. I found out when I started yelling at her this morning and she fell to pieces. She had just returned from the abortion clinic."

"Oh! Not that!"

"It's okay. She didn't have an abortion. She just talked to someone there who advised her to have an abortion. They did an ultra-sound and told her the baby has a cyst on the brain. I think they're lying so I scheduled an appointment later this afternoon with our gynecologist."

"Good. Thank you," he said. Then he embraced his wife and they wept.

"How could this happen to our little girl?" Ryle asked through his tears.

"I don't know."

Then, for a moment, as random memories of his "little girl" came to mind, Dr. Brandon's sadness turned to anger, not only at Jimmy, but at a society which sowed the seeds of violence, sexual and otherwise. Finally, in another sudden emotional turn, his anger dissipated into despair.

"Lord, give me wisdom," he prayed silently. After a short moment, he asked, "Is she okay? Should I go see her?"

"Not right now. She's sleeping. That's probably the best thing for her."

"You're right," he said, nodding gently. "But what are we going to do?"

"I don't know. We just have to support her no matter what she decides."

"What do you mean? I didn't think there was a choice. She's going to have the baby and that's all there is to it!"

"Ryle! We have to be realistic. Faith has always been strong-willed in her own quiet way. You have to realize that she can just sneak out any morning and have an abortion and we won't be able to stop her. And if we use any pressure, she may resent it for the rest of her life."

Dr. Brandon fell back on the bed in exasperation. After a moment of silent reflection, he said, "You're right. We can't *make* her do anything.

It's got to be her decision. But I'll be sick if she decides to have an abortion."

"We both will," Joan said. "That's why we've got to make her see that she's got some options and that we're there to support her all the way. You realize don't you, if she does give birth to a child, she is going to have to raise it herself with lots of help from us, or, she's going to have to place the child for adoption?"

Dr. Brandon sighed and said, "There aren't any other options, are there?"

"I'm afraid not," Joan said. Then she added, "You know that if she chooses adoption, we may never see our grandchild again?"

Ryle sat up, put his arms around his wife, and said, "I know. But at least we'll know that he or she had a chance at life, and that's the most important thing right now."

•••

Faith woke up from her nap shortly before three. As she walked into the kitchen, she found her father sitting at the table. When their eyes met, her heart sank.

"I'm sorry, Daddy," she said and began to cry.

Her father rose up from the table and threw his arms around her. "It's all right, Faith. There's no need to be sorry. I love you. The important thing is, are you holding up okay?"

Faith looked up at her father and nodded. Then she sunk her head into his chest and absorbed his unconditional love. When Joan walked into the kitchen, she smiled at the warm embrace.

"Faith, we'd better get going," she said. "I had to do a lot of pleading to get this appointment today. We'd better not be late."

Faith peeked up at her father again who was now smiling tenderly. He said, "We'll talk things over tonight after dinner."

"Thanks, Dad," Faith said with a faint smile.

"I love you, Kiddo, no matter what. Always remember that."

•••

Dr. Benson's exam was brief. "I want you to have another ultra-sound done," he said.

"Right now?" Joan asked.

"Yes," the doctor replied. "I'm going to instruct the technician to do a thorough exam and to specifically look for an abnormality in the baby's brain."

Faith and Joan were led back to a small examination room. Faith put on a hospital gown and sat on the exam table. Joan sat in a chair, praying inwardly.

"Do you really think this is necessary?" Faith asked after several minutes of restless waiting. "I still can't believe they would lie to me."

"Why not? They lied about your exam this morning. That I do know."

"I can't believe that either. I'm sure Hope can explain it."

Joan smiled. She said, "Just be patient and humor me on this. It never hurts to have a second opinion."

When the technician arrived, she greeted the women cheerfully.

"Hi! I'm Sue. I'll be doing your exam today."

Sue was a tall woman in her early thirties with long, light brown hair.

"I talked with Dr. Benson and he gave me some specific things to look for. Let's hope none of it shows up," she said.

Sue positioned the monitor so Faith would be able to see the child during the ultra-sound. As she began applying the gel to Faith's stomach, Joan pulled her chair over to the right to get a better view of the monitor. Before long, a child's image appeared on the screen.

"Do you want to know the sex?" Sue asked.

Faith and Joan looked at each other and nodded.

"It's a girl!"

"Oh, my! She's beautiful!" Joan said with tears in her eyes.

"Look, Mom! It looks like she's praying!" Faith said excitedly.

"This is so amazing!" Joan said.

"Really!" Faith said.

"That's your daughter and my granddaughter," Joan said in an obvious plug for life.

"I know," Faith said quietly.

Then Sue shook her head in dismay.

"What is it?" Joan asked in a panicked voice.

"I just don't see anything wrong with this baby," Sue said.

Joan let out a sigh of relief. "Oh, thank God!" she said.

Faith looked at Sue, then at her mother, and again at the screen. "I don't believe it. Why would they tell me that the baby has a cyst if it didn't have one? Are you sure?"

"I'm going to keep exploring here to make sure, but I don't see anything wrong."

Faith looked at her mother.

"They only care about money," Joan said.

"That's awful!" Faith said.

"It's evil!" replied Joan.

"I have to call Hope and tell her about this!"

•••

Shortly after eight that evening, there was a knock at Faith's bedroom door. Faith had been sitting up in bed leafing through a magazine inattentively, mulling over the events of the day and the past few months.

"Come in!" she said, setting her magazine aside.

"Are you ready to talk?" her father asked, poking his head into the room.

"I guess so," she said. "I'm sorry, Dad."

"I told you there's nothing to be sorry about," he said as he sat down on the side of the bed. He reached out and took her hand in his, giving it a gentle squeeze. After a quiet moment, he said, "I just want to know why you didn't come to us right away."

Faith shook her head. She said, "I know I should've. I guess I was just scared."

"About what?"

"About a lot of things."

"Like what?"

Faith hung her head and said, "Like admitting what happened in Florida."

Ryle looked compassionately at his daughter. "Honey, everybody makes mistakes," he said. "Your mother and I do, too. We know you're not going to be perfect, just like we aren't perfect."

"Well, that's just part of it," Faith said. "I was worried about you, too."

"You mean you didn't want to embarrass me."

"Yes."

Her father shook his head sadly.

"Your mother told me that. It made me feel ashamed."

"Ashamed? Why?"

"Because I haven't made it clear to you that *you* are so much more important to me than my reputation."

"I know you feel that way," she said. "It's just that I wanted to fix things myself."

"It is a difficult situation, isn't it?"

"Oh, Dad! My life is all messed up now!"

Dr. Brandon looked compassionately into his daughter's eyes and said, "Tell me exactly how you feel right now."

Faith sighed, reflected for a moment, and said, "I guess I feel trapped."

"In what way?"

"Well, I have only three choices. And none of them are good ones. I could have the baby and raise it myself. That would be hard. I don't think I'm ready for that now, especially if I had to take care of it myself. Or, I could give the baby up for adoption. That would be hard, too. I know that would probably be the best thing to do, but how do I give up my baby? Or, I could have an abortion. But if I did that, you and Mom and Ryan wouldn't respect me anymore. And Mom would be really hurt knowing I didn't let this baby live. She's already talking about it being your first grandchild. And I know it's something I would always have to live with."

"But you were about to do it, weren't you?"

"Yes," Faith said sheepishly.

"Why?"

Faith shrugged her shoulders and shook her head sadly. Finally she said, "It just seemed like the easy way out. Having a baby would mess up college and a career. And I'm still worried about Chris. He doesn't know I'm pregnant. I'm afraid I'll lose him if I keep the baby."

Dr. Brandon leaned over, pulled his daughter close to him, and gave her a hug.

"You're right," he said. "It is messy. And no matter what you decide to do, there are going to be problems. But your mother and I want you to know that no matter what you had decided to do, or will decide to do, we will still love you."

"Do you mean you and Mom would let me have an abortion if I wanted one?"

"Well, let's say we would not disown you if you had one. But we would be very disappointed, more in ourselves than in you."

"What do you mean?" Faith asked.

"Well, your mother and I would feel like we've failed in getting you to understand the Christian perspective in all this."

"I know the Christian perspective, Dad. It's 'Thou Shalt Not Kill!' It's not that complicated."

"It's not quite as simple as that."

"What do you mean?"

"I mean Christianity is more than just a set of rules to follow. It is developing a relationship with Christ. You matter to Him, Faith, and He wants you to get to know Him and His ways."

Faith stared blankly at her father.

"God had a real problem when He created us," he continued. "He wanted to make us in His image as thinking and feeling beings who could return His love. That's why He gave us self-awareness and a free will. But being aware of ourselves naturally makes us selfish and we tend to make selfish choices. Those choices often times hurt others and offend God. But by the same token, our free will gives us a chance to love God and others, because love is a choice, not a feeling. It is choosing to do for others and to put others ahead of us. God took a risk in creating us with free will because there's always the chance we'll choose to sin. But He had to give us choice, or our love for Him wouldn't be authentic. It would be meaningless."

"So what's your point, Dad?"

Her father smiled.

"My point is this, Faith. You are in a uniquely challenging situation in which you must choose between what is best for the child or what seems best for you personally. And make no mistake about it; you matter to God just as much as this child does. But the crucial thing to remember is, for some reason beyond our limited understanding, God meant for this child to be conceived. Nothing happens apart from the will of God. And unless the life of this child is ended by God's own hand, He intends for it to be born. As a Christian, you are expected to submit to God's will, not because you have to, but because you want to. You must realize that just as He died for you and your salvation, you too must die to yourself for the sake of others. That is the test you are facing."

"Are you saying that God wanted me to be raped to test me *and* so I could give birth to this child?"

"No. Rape is one of the most evil acts on this earth and God is not the author of evil. Evil occurs because men choose to sin. But He has promised us 'that in all things God works for the good of those who love Him, who have been called according to his purpose.' It's right there in Romans 8:28. If you give birth to this child out of love for her and God, you will have turned evil into good. And God will honor you for that."

"Well, now I really don't feel like I have a choice," Faith said.

"Of course you do. You can choose to please God, or to please yourself, or to please others. That's what life is all about."

"But Dad, if I give birth to this baby, what am I supposed to do? I can't imagine raising the child all alone, and I can't imagine giving the child up for adoption. No matter what I do it's going to be hard!"

"You're right. And I don't want you to rush into a decision. I want you to take your time and think things through. I want you to pick up your Bible, read the Word of God, pray about it, and listen to the Holy Spirit. I'd also like you to see a Christian counselor."

"A counselor? Why?"

"Because I want you to fully understand the options you have. A Christian counselor who deals often with crisis pregnancies can really help you understand the options of parenting or adoption. But most of all, a Christian counselor will help you to understand how serious this decision is—that there is another life in the balance."

"Dad, I know that. When I saw the ultra-sounds today, it really hit me. I know I have a life here inside," Faith said as she gently patted her stomach. "It's just that when I think about myself and everyone else, it gets confusing again."

"That's because you're hearing two different messages. Some of the people around you, like Hope and Chris, are filling your mind with their own worldly perspective that is very selfish and focused on earthly desires. But as Christians, we are asked to be *in* this world but not *of* this world. It's an entirely different message."

"You're telling me?"

"That's why you have to pray a lot. If you do, God will give you the strength and wisdom to do what's right. Philippians 4:13 tells us we can do everything through Christ who gives us strength. And you know what else?"

"What?"

"If you honor God in everything you do, and especially in these life and death matters, He will bless your life in ways beyond your wildest dreams."

Faith smiled modestly. "I hope so," she said. "Thanks, Dad."

"Your mother and I will be praying for you," he said. "Now give me one more hug, Kiddo."

After her father had left, Faith switched off her lamp and lay back in the darkness.

"God," she prayed. "I know what you want me to do, but I'm not sure if I have the strength to do it."

Then she closed her eyes, rubbed her hands over her stomach, and drifted off to sleep.

Faith's Choice 19

Joan was loading the dishwasher after dinner on Friday when Faith stepped in to announce, "Chris and I are going out to a movie."
"Was that him on the phone just now?"
"Yeah."
Joan frowned as she nodded.
"What's that look all about?" Faith asked.
"What look?"
"Come on! What is it?"
"Nothing," Joan repeated. "I was just wondering if you've told Chris yet."
Faith sighed.
"No, not yet. I was thinking about telling him tonight."
"At a movie? That's not a good place to talk."
"I know. But—"
"But what?"
"Well, things haven't been very good between us lately. Now wouldn't be the best time."
Joan looked compassionately at her daughter and said, "I know it's hard. But you've got to be honest with him, Dear."
"But we only have a few weeks left together. I wanted to fix things up before he left."

"But eventually, he's going to find out. And the longer you hold the truth from him the more upset he'll be."

"I know, but I can't tell him now."

"Why?"

"Because."

"Because why?"

"Because the last time we talked about it hypothetically he said I should get an abortion. It's not fair!"

"I know it's not, Dear. But you've got to face reality."

"I'm afraid!"

Joan squeezed Faith tightly and then put her at arm's length. She looked her directly in the eye and said, "I know how much you adore Chris. *But*, if you're afraid of how he's going to react when you tell him, don't you have to wonder if he's worth the commitment?"

Before Faith could answer, the doorbell rang.

"That's him," Faith said.

"I think you should tell him."

Faith sighed and gave a reluctant nod.

Chris and Faith were quiet on the way to the theater. As they pulled into the parking lot, Faith said a silent prayer. Chris was about to unbuckle his seat belt when Faith said, "Wait, Chris. There's something I have to tell you."

"What?" he said impatiently. "Come on, we're going to be late."

"Please, this is really important."

"What's wrong?"

"I'm pregnant," she said and held her breath.

"What are you talking about?" he said sarcastically. "Don't bring up that hypothetical stuff again!"

"I'm not making it up! I'm pregnant, Chris!"

"That's impossible! We haven't done anything!"

"I was raped!" Faith shouted angrily and then burst into tears.

"What?" Chris said. He seemed surprised but indifferent. Then he said, "So that's why you've been acting so strange lately. Why didn't you tell me?"

"Because I was afraid!"

"Afraid of what?"

"Of you wanting to break up," Faith said, wiping away her tears with a tissue.

There was a short silence. Faith took a deep breath. She was hoping Chris would reassure her that nothing, not even her pregnancy, would come between them. Instead, he asked in an obligatory way, "When did this happen?"

"When Hope and I went to Florida. We went to a party. Hope took off with some guy and so I decided to go back to the condo. Then he offered to walk me home."

"Who did?"

"A guy named Jimmy. That's all I know about him."

Chris had been sitting forward, leaning on the steering wheel. He fell back into his seat and let out a sigh.

"I'm sorry. I wish you would have told me," he said.

Faith shrugged her shoulders.

"I guess you didn't report this to the police, huh?"

Faith shook her downcast head. She was waiting once more for Chris to reassure her. Instead he simply asked, "Does anyone else know?"

"I told Hope a long time ago. My parents found out yesterday."

"How did they find out? Did you just decide to tell them?"

"No. I started crying when I came home from the abortion clinic and my mom started asking questions. I had to tell her."

"Wait. I'm confused. Did you have an abortion, or are you still pregnant?"

"I'm pregnant. I just went in to the clinic to talk to them yesterday. They did an ultra-sound and told me the baby had a cyst on the brain. I believed them and went home and started crying. That's when my mom found out."

"What do you mean you 'believed them'?"

"We found out later that they were lying to me just to get me to have an abortion," Faith said as she dabbed at her tears. "Mom and I went for another ultra-sound and found out it wasn't true. There's nothing wrong with the baby. Can you believe it?"

"Maybe they were trying to do you a favor."

"What do you mean?"

"Maybe they were just trying to help you make the right decision."

"Chris!" Faith said in a flustered voice, "There's a living human being here inside me. I saw her in those ultra-sounds."

"You know it's a girl?"

"Yes."

They were silent for a moment. Then Chris asked, "Are you going to have the baby or are you going to have an abortion?"

"What do you want me to do?"

"It's your decision."

"Yes, but it's going to affect you, too."

Chris breathed a deep sigh. He buckled his seat belt and started the car.

"Where are we going?" Faith asked.

"I think we might as well go home. I'd just like to be by myself for a while if that's okay with you."

"I'm sorry I didn't tell you about this sooner."

"It's not that," Chris said.

"Then what is it?"

"Nothing."

"I don't believe you," Faith said.

Chris simply shrugged.

After a moment, Faith said, "I was thinking it might be good for us that you're going away to school. I mean, when you come back home at Christmas, this whole thing will be over—or almost over. I think I'm due Christmas day. You won't see me all fat and ugly and I'll have put the baby up for adoption. Then it will almost be like nothing happened. You know?"

Faith was again hoping for some kind of affirmation, yet none was forthcoming. Instead, Chris was quiet, apparently mulling over the situation.

Finally, Faith said, "You don't want me to have this baby, do you?"

"It's not that."

"Then what is it?"

As they came to a stop in Faith's driveway, Chris said, "There's something I have to tell you."

"What?"

"This isn't easy to say, especially after what you've told me tonight."

Faith stared blankly at Chris as he continued.

"I've been thinking for a while now that with me going away to college and us being separated so much, it would probably be best for both of us if we just agreed to part as friends and start dating other people. That way we could both go on with our lives and not waste our time waiting for each other."

Faith's blank expression suddenly caught fire.

"This has nothing to do with you being pregnant," he said.

Faith jumped out of the car, slammed the door, stuck her head in the open window and screamed, "I hate you!"

•••

Tears cascaded down Faith's cheeks as she unlocked the front door of the deserted house and stormed up the stairs to her bedroom.

"I hate you!" she screamed. "How could you do this to me?"

Faith collapsed on her bed and sobbed as she was tossed in a stormy sea of emotions. First came the waves of despair, then anger, then self-pity, and then despair again.

"God! How could you let this happen on top of everything else!"

When the emotional squall subsided, Faith took a deep breath and pulled the last piece of tissue out of the box. She blew her nose as she stood by the window and looked down on two squirrels playing tag in the yard and up the trunk of a large oak tree. At last, she decided to call Hope. She walked into her parents' bedroom and picked up the phone from the night stand. Rolling onto their bed, she lay on her side and dialed the number.

"Hello," Hope said.

"Hi. It's me."

"You sound congested."

"I've been crying."

"What happened? I've been waiting for you to call."

"I know, but last night wasn't a good night and I didn't want to call you at work. Then Chris and I were supposed to go out tonight," Faith said.

"Why didn't you go out?"

"Well, we did. But we changed our minds and he dropped me off early."

"How come?"

Faith sighed. She said, "I finally told him about being pregnant."

"What did he say?"

"He didn't seem to care. He just wanted to know what I was gonna do. When I told him I was thinking of adoption, he got really quiet. Then he said he wanted to go home and be by himself."

"Sounds like Chris, all right!" Hope said.

"Well, then he said we ought to start dating other people," Faith said with a sniffle. "I knew when I told him about the baby that he would want to break up. I just should've had an abortion a long time ago; then, at least, I'd still have Chris."

There was a brief silence.

"Faith, I don't think that's altogether true," Hope said finally.

"What do you mean?"

"Well, I probably should have told you about it before, but I didn't want to upset you with everything else you've had to worry about," Hope vaguely explained.

"Tell me what?"

"I heard through the grapevine that Chris has been going out with someone else."

"You're kidding! That jerk! Why didn't you tell me?" Faith shouted.

Hope pulled the receiver from her ear.

"Sorry," she said. "I guess I should've."

"It's okay," Faith said in disgust. "I should've known the way he's been acting lately. I'm such a fool!" After a sigh, she asked, "Who is she?"

"Her name is Jenny. You don't know her. She's a sophomore. She's cute, but I heard she's a slut."

"That figures."

"Sorry."

"You don't have to be sorry. It's not your fault. It's my fault. I should have given him what he wanted," Faith said, and then had second thoughts. "I take that back. I'm glad I never gave him anything. He's such a jerk!"

There was another silent moment as Hope wasn't sure how to respond. Finally, she drudged up the other bad news.

"I guess your parents know you're pregnant," she said.

"Yeah. When I got home yesterday, my mother came running into the garage screaming at me. I just started crying and I had to tell her. How did you know?"

"Lisa got mad at me because your mother called. Why was your mother mad at Lisa anyway? She didn't do anything. I was the one who talked you into coming."

"That wasn't the problem," Faith said.

"It wasn't? Then what was?"

"My mother and I went to our gynecologist and found out the baby is fine. There's no cyst."

"You're kidding!"

"No! Lisa was lying!"

"Why?"

"So I would have an abortion."

"No!"

"Yes. They did another ultra-sound and I got to see it. It's a girl!"

"You know it's a girl! Oh, my gosh! You're gonna have a girl!"

"Well, I'm not sure if I'm going to have the baby."

"What do you mean? If your parents know you're pregnant, you don't have a choice, do you?"

"Actually, I do," Faith said. "They said it's my decision. It's obvious they want me to have the baby but they're leaving it up to me."

"Oh, sure. And after you've had an abortion, they would only disown you," Hope said sarcastically.

"No, I don't think so. They'd be disappointed. I mean my mother would be really sick about it, but they wouldn't disown me."

"So, what are you waiting for?"

"What do you mean 'what am I waiting for?'"

"I mean, don't you want to get it over with?"

"Not after seeing the ultra-sound. I don't think I could do it."

"What would you do, keep the baby?"

"Well, that's the thing. The first decision is hard enough. But if I have the baby, then I've got to decide whether to keep her or put her up for adoption."

"If you ask me, I think I'd have an abortion just so I wouldn't have to make the other decision," Hope said. "I hate to say it but I'm really glad I'm not in your shoes."

"If you keep playing with fire, you may end up in my shoes," Faith warned.

"Not a chance! I'm careful," Hope said. Then her doorbell rang. She said, "I think Jason's here. Sorry, but I've got to go! Hang in there, Faith. I'll talk to you tomorrow, okay?"

"Sure. Bye."

Faith gently rubbed her stomach and said, "It's pretty much you and me now."

•••

Joan and Ryle Brandon arrived home at eight-thirty. They had gone out for an early dinner and then to the mall to look for baby books and magazines.

"How were you planning to give her the books?" Ryle asked.

"I thought I'd just leave them on her night stand tonight so she can see them when she gets home. Then we can talk about them at breakfast," Joan said.

"Well, just don't be *too* pushy. Your daughter can be very obstinate when she feels like she's being coerced into something."

"I know. But it's so hard to let go of something so important."

Joan carried her armful of baby literature up the stairs to Faith's room where she found her daughter sitting up in bed reading.

"Oh, hello," Joan said as she stood just inside the doorway. "I thought you'd still be out with Chris." She noticed Faith had her Bible open on her lap.

"Chris and I broke up. He wants to date other people," Faith said quite matter-of-factly as she was momentarily drained of emotion.

Joan sighed. "Did you tell him you were pregnant?"

"Yes."

"Do you think that had something to do with it?"

"No. Hope told me he had been dating someone else," she said with a sigh.

A pained expression spread across Joan's face. "Sorry," she said.

"Me, too."

Then Faith noticed her mother's armful of books.

"You plan on doin' a lot of reading tonight?" she asked teasingly.

"Actually, these are for you. They're baby books and magazines. I was going to leave them next to your bed so you'd see them when you got home."

Joan set them on the night stand and then sat down next to Faith on the bed.

"Thanks," Faith said with a quiet smile. "You really want me to have the baby, don't you?"

"She *is* my first grandchild."

Faith nodded. "I know," she said. She paused a second and then admitted, "I'm so afraid of the next decision. I don't feel I'm ready to take care of a child but I don't think I could give up my baby for adoption either. I'm afraid I'll never see her again."

"It's a tough decision. But your father and I will help any way we can."

Faith smiled as she reached for her mother's hand. "Thanks," she said.

Joan smiled and picked up one of the magazines. She opened it to an advertisement with a picture of a girl about two years old with a light brown complexion and golden brown, curly hair.

"Here. I saw this in the store and I thought you'd like to see this," Joan said. "Isn't she adorable!"

"She's beautiful!" Faith said as she studied the picture. "But do you think anyone would want to adopt a mixed-race baby? I mean, wouldn't you think that white parents would want a white baby and black parents would want a black baby?"

"I'm sure there would be someone who would love to adopt your child," Joan said. "We just have to look into it. I can start calling some adoption agencies on Monday if you'd like."

"Well, I'm not sure I'll be choosing adoption," Faith replied quickly.

"That's okay. No one is making you commit to anything. But it's better to have the facts before you make a decision."

"I guess so."

"Good. Well, I'll leave you alone now. Your father warned me not to be too pushy," Joan said.

Faith laughed.

"What's so funny?"

"Nothing," Faith said, still smiling.

"Oh, go on. There is, too."

"I was just thinking that this is like our family vacations."

"What is?"

"The books. Whenever we started to talk about places to go for our vacation, you'd suggest one thing and then Dad, Ryan and I would suggest others. Then a few weeks later, there would be a stack of literature from the place you wanted to go to sitting on the kitchen table. It was obviously intended for us to look at."

"That is, until Ryan figured out the system and sent away for all that literature from Disney World and beat your mother to the punch," Ryle interjected as he stepped into Faith's bedroom.

"Have you been snooping at the door?" Joan asked.

"No, just passing by when I heard Faith talking about vacations," he said, chuckling.

"Okay, you don't have to look at them if you don't want to," Joan said, referring to the magazines.

"I'll look at them, Mom."

"Good," Joan said with a smile.

Faith smiled, too. "Good night," she said.

•••

Joan spent the weekend totally pre-occupied with Faith's dilemma. By Sunday night, she was an emotional wreck. The worrying had taken a physical toll as well. She was exhausted and suffered from a throbbing headache. She slept little that night and the strain was evident in her eyes the next morning at Bible study.

"My family needs your prayers," she told the half dozen women present. "We just found out the other day that Faith is pregnant. She was raped. She had been hiding the fact from us for months and almost decided to have an abortion. Ryle and I are still leaving the decision up to her but we need your prayers. Pray that she chooses life and makes the right decision about raising the child."

Then she provided the others with all the facts, as she knew them, including Faith's incident at the clinic. The women prayed together and Joan sensed God's presence, as though He had given her a reassuring hug. She felt that for the first time, Faith's child truly had a chance at life. The powers of the dark world and the spiritual forces of evil were now being met head on by a prayerful petition to the Creator of the universe.

•••

That night, Faith was sitting in bed reading when there was a knock at the door.

"Come in," she said, without lifting her eyes from the print.

"Hi. How ya doing, Sis?" her brother asked as he stepped into the room. He was wearing a sweaty T-shirt and shorts.

"I'm okay. But you look disgusting."

"Yeah. We were playing hoops at Justin. I hope you don't mind," he said as he took the chair from her desk, turned it around to face the bed, and collapsed onto it in a sweaty heap.

"That's all right, I'll disinfect it tomorrow," she said and then smiled quietly.

"I hope I'm not interrupting," he said, glancing at the open Bible on her lap.

"No. I'm just flipping through, reading pieces here and there."

"So what have you decided about the baby? Ryan asked."

"I'm going to have it."

"Great! I'm glad. Are you going to keep it or go with adoption?"

"I don't know. For now, it's a relief to have chosen life. As I look back on it, I don't know how I could have even considered an abortion."

"That day in front of the clinic, you were going in for an abortion, weren't you?"

"Well," Faith said, hesitating, "it was a possibility."

"I guess it's a good thing I was there, huh?"

"Yeah," Faith said. "Actually, a couple of times, things got messed up. There was another morning where there was graffiti on the front of the clinic. It makes me think that this child was just meant to be!"

Ryan smiled sheepishly. He said, "Every child is meant to be."

Faith nodded.

"What made you consider an abortion?" Ryan asked. "Because you were raped?"

"Not really. Most of it had to do with Mom and Dad. I didn't want to embarrass Dad. And I listened to Hope. Abortion seemed like the easy way out. I don't know if I would have gone through with it, but I can understand why a lot of women have abortions. It's wrong, but that doesn't make it any less tempting. And if it's so easy to get one, why not?"

"Did Chris have anything to do with it?"

"I guess I was worried how he would react," Faith admitted, reluctantly.

Ryan smiled. "Forget him, Sis. He wasn't good enough for you anyway."

"I thought he was," she said, smiling at herself. "I was so foolish!"

"I guess it's a pretty difficult situation to be in, huh?" Ryan said.

"It's horrible!"

Ryan nodded sympathetically and said, "I'm glad you're choosing life. I really admire you for it."

"Thanks."

"Does Mom know what you've decided?"

"Not yet."

"If there's anything I can do, let me know," he said, getting up from his chair and walking to Faith's bedside.

"You can do me a favor right now," she said as he bent over to give her a hug.

"Anything."

"Take a shower before you touch me."

"Sure," he said with a smile.

•••

After Ryan left, Faith put her Bible to the side. She lay back in bed and closed her eyes. Suddenly, she sat up and jumped out of bed. She went to her desk to pick up her diary. Crawling back into bed, she opened to the first page and began to write:

July 11

Dear daughter,

You have been growing inside me now for over fourteen weeks. I want to confess to you that during that time, from the moment I knew you were there, I thought only of myself. You were not conceived by choice. I was the victim of rape. It was the most horrible experience of my life. I don't understand why it happened, but it did. I didn't think I deserved to have something like this mess up my life. You see, I just graduated from high school and I've been planning to go to college. Having a baby now was not a part of the plan. Sorry, but you just didn't fit in. And so I thought about the unthinkable—I thought about an abortion. But now, I understand, through the grace of God, how important you are to Him. I've also come to realize that life and love are the most important things. I could have died that night on the beach in Florida when I was attacked with a knife. But for some reason, God spared me and He wants me to spare you, too. Forgive me for even thinking about taking your life. I know God has a special plan for you. You matter very much to Him. And ever since I saw you the other day on the ultra-sound and heard your beating heart, you've come to matter very much to me. I love you!

Your Mom

Gray Skies 20

On a Wednesday morning in mid-July, Robert was standing by the sliding glass door off the kitchen staring at the gray skies overhead. Kara was emptying the dishwasher.
 "Do you still want to go on a picnic?" Robert asked.
 "What did the weatherman say?" Kara replied.
 "Warm and scattered showers."
 "That doesn't help us much, does it?"
 "No," Robert said as he continued to stare out to the west.
 "I was really looking forward to it. I haven't been on a picnic in years." Robert stepped over to the dinette table and sipped his coffee.
 "I was looking forward to it, too," he said. "But I don't want to go if it's raining."
 "Neither do I," Kara said. "The trouble is, this weather's been so unpredictable lately."
 "Well, why don't we wait an hour before we decide. It may be raining or it may clear up by then," Robert said.
 "Robert, it's going to take some time to get ready and then it takes about an hour-and-a-half to get there. By the time we find a spot, it will be getting late for lunch."
 "Well, let's wait until ten anyway. It's better to play it safe."

"But if it's scattered showers, waiting here isn't going to do us any good. Seventy-five miles from here, it may be totally different. Why don't we just go?"

"How about if we work on the adoption questionnaire until ten, and if it isn't raining, then we'll go?" Robert said.

"Fine. I'll get the picnic basket ready while you fill out the form."

"What if it rains?"

"Then we'll lay out our blanket in the family room and have our lunch there."

"All right," Robert said with a smile.

It had been almost a month since Robert discovered an open window through John Spivek and the Rainbow Family Center. The Ellisons began the initial steps of the adoption process immediately. They filled out the application form as soon as it arrived by mail but had to wait nearly four weeks to attend the next meeting of the transracial program. The protracted process seemed an eternity, and the long awaited meeting had been held just the night before. It was all Kara could do to keep Robert from staying up until midnight to complete the questionnaire. Although she was as anxious as Robert was to complete the survey, there were some issues raised by the questionnaire that the couple had not formally addressed. Kara was busy in the kitchen preparing their picnic lunch as Robert sat down at the kitchen table, pen in hand and paperwork in front of him.

"Are you ready for the first question?" he asked.

"I guess so."

"Okay, here it is. 'Are you still interested in pursuing the adoption of a black child? A biracial child?'"

"I wouldn't be opposed to adopting either," Kara said.

"Me too. But it seems to me that if anyone should adopt a biracial child, it should be us," Robert said.

Kara frowned. She said. "I'm afraid if we limit ourselves to a biracial child, we may miss out on our chance to adopt *any* child. I don't want to be *too* selective."

"I think if God wants us to have a child, there will be a biracial one available," Robert said.

"Well, I guess we can put down 'biracial' for now. We can always update our profile later."

"I can live with that," Robert said as he read the next question to himself.

"This next one might be tougher," he said.

"What is it?" Kara asked while spreading mayonnaise on a slice of wheat bread.

"'Would you consider a birthmother who has had little or no prenatal care?'"

"That's kind of risky. Don't you think?"

"Women have had babies for centuries without the kind of prenatal care they get nowadays," Robert said. "I'm more worried about the next question."

"What's that?"

"'Would you consider a birthmother who has used substances such as alcohol or other drugs?'" Then, after a short pause, he added, "The next question is similar. 'Would you consider prematurity or other medical problems? Please explain.'"

The couple looked at each other quietly for a moment. Kara finally said, "This is not at all what I thought it would be like. I was thinking of a perfectly healthy baby with no complications."

"Well, even if we could have our own child, there would be the possibility of complications. If that happened, we would have to accept it."

Robert paused for a sip of coffee. Then cocking his head, he said, "I have no idea how difficult it would be to raise a special needs child. But if we limit our preferences to a child that is perfectly healthy, isn't that being selfish and sinful? I think it would be showing a lack of faith. We just have to believe that if God puts us in a challenging situation, then He's going to provide us with what we need to make it through."

Kara sighed. She walked over and stood behind Robert and began massaging his shoulders. She said, "I'm afraid to commit to something like that. I don't know if I have the strength for it. I hear the horror stories of the other women at school. Working all day is hard enough. Then they go home and have to take care of their own kids after school. And those are healthy kids."

"What if you stayed home?"

"Robert," Kara sighed again. "You know we can't afford it. We can't pay the bills on one salary. And how would we save up for another adoption? Or what about saving for the kids' college fund?"

Then she laughed.

"Listen to me!" she said. "I sound like this adoption is a certain thing!"

"I think it is," Robert said. "Terri Moore said every couple in the transracial program received a child within nine months. I think it's only a matter of time."

"Not at the rate I'm cutting our chances. We're being too choosy for any birthmother to select us," Kara said dejectedly.

"Oh, stop being so gloomy! It's bad enough the weather is so gray!"

Robert got up from the table and walked to the sliding glass door for another look at the skies. "It looks a bit lighter up to the north. There's even a bit of blue out there," he said.

"That sounds like wishful thinking to me," Kara said. She picked up the questionnaire and read the next question aloud. "'Does your insurance cover an adopted baby? If so, from what point?'" Then she asked, "Did you ever check into your insurance?"

"Yes," he said, turning away from the window and returning to his chair at the table. "It's the same as yours. The baby is covered from the day of placement. It doesn't cover any pre-existing conditions."

"Isn't that awful!" Kara said. "It's like they want to discourage adoptions. It's so heartless!"

"Insurance companies will do anything to save a buck," Robert said. "That's why they'll pay for abortions. It's a heck of a lot cheaper than paying for a live birth and risk payments on any complications."

"That's just not right! They ought to have a law against it," Kara said disgustedly.

"They ought to, but they don't."

Robert swallowed his last sip of coffee and read aloud the next question, "'How do you plan to pay for this adoption?' VISA or Mastercard?"

"What!" Kara shrieked.

"Just kidding," Robert replied with a wry smile.

"Very funny."

"I put down that we'd take it out of savings," he said.

"Are there any more questions?" Kara asked.

"Two. The first one is, 'Do you feel you will be accepted and supported by your community?'"

The couple broke out in laughter. "Folks will still be staring at you and me. They won't even notice our kids," Robert said, still laughing. Then he said, "Here's the last one. 'How do you envision relating to your birthmother? Letters? Pictures? Gifts? Pre-placement meeting? Post-placement meeting?'"

"I don't know. How do you feel?" Kara asked.

"My first instinct is to have as little contact as possible," Robert admitted.

"That's how I feel," Kara said. "I think that the more a birthmother sees or hears about her child, the more she would want it back."

"I'd hate to go through a Baby Jessica or Baby Richard scenario," Robert said.

"That's in the back of my mind, too."

"It's all kind of like the weather today, isn't it?" Robert said.

"What do you mean?"

"I mean it's so hard to predict. From where we're at, it looks very threatening. You hate to jump in and do something because you don't know what's going to happen. But if you don't take chances in life, you might miss out on something great," he said.

"I guess this is what faith is all about, isn't it?" Kara said.

Robert nodded his head slowly.

"Do you want me to pack up the car?" he asked.

•••

"I knew we should've given ourselves more time. They'll be starting in five minutes," Kara said as she looked at the car's digital clock.

"Relax, Love. These things never start on time," Robert said. "The people who set up meetings know there are always people like us who are late."

The setting sun glared through the trees into Robert's eyes as he turned into the long gravel driveway at the adoption agency.

"See. We're not the only ones late," Robert said as they approached the parking lot in front of the barn.

The Rainbow campus was once the home of an investment banker from the city. The opulent estate, including a mansion, a small house for the servants, and a horse barn, had been built in the mid-twenties. It originally sat on twenty wooded acres. Later, all but five acres were parceled and sold separately when, in the late fifties, the estate was donated to a private foundation for homeless boys. Over the years, the foundation evolved into the present Rainbow Family Center. The mansion and servants' house were converted into offices and meeting rooms while the barn was remodeled into a meeting place for large gatherings.

Robert and Kara were invited to a panel discussion featuring two birthmothers who, in the past year, placed their babies for adoption through the agency. As they entered the large hall, ten other couples milled around three dozen folding chairs set up in a semi-circle facing two stools. Robert and Kara took seats in the front row along the outside. A moment later, Terri Moore, the program director, a short woman with brown but graying hair, introduced the two birthmothers seated on the stools behind her.

"We'll hear from Carrie first," she said at the end of her introductory remarks.

"Hi. My name is Carrie," the girl on the right began nervously. Carrie was tall with dishwater blonde hair and brown eyes hidden behind a pair of large brown-rimmed glasses. She spoke in a deep voice.

"I'm nineteen years old. I came to Rainbow a little over a year ago when I was five months pregnant. I'm from a nearby suburb. My father is the president of a consulting business. My mother stays home. I'm the oldest child. I have two brothers and one sister. We're Catholic. I guess we're a pretty average family.

"I met my daughter's birthfather, Darrell, through a mutual friend. Darrell is black. And my father is kind of prejudiced. He was upset when he found out I was dating a black guy. He almost went through the roof when he found out I was pregnant. He pretty much disowned me for a while. Because we're Catholic, he didn't want me to have an abortion.

"He made me feel pretty uncomfortable at home after I got pregnant. He said a lot of sarcastic things and he got mad at me pretty easily. So I moved into an apartment with a girlfriend the last few months of my pregnancy. I wasn't even allowed to come to Thanksgiving dinner unless I had given birth.

"My mother was okay about it. I mean she was upset about me being pregnant, but I could feel she still loved me. But she didn't want to go against Dad.

"My mother heard about Rainbow through a priest at church. So I started to come for counseling. Becky, my counselor, helped me realize that raising a child by myself would be really hard. I had one year of junior college when I got pregnant, and I wouldn't have been able to get a good job. Darrell and I didn't want to get married so I wouldn't have had another income to rely on. We talked about sharing responsibility for raising Alicia, but it didn't seem like a good situation for her. Already, she was going to be half-white and half-black. I'm Catholic and Darrell isn't religious at all. Alicia would have been going back and forth between two homes and two different cultures. I wanted her to have one home with two parents where there was one religion, preferably Catholic, although that really didn't matter. In fact, the adoptive parents I chose, Rick and Natalie, are Christian but not Catholic. I just wanted her to have a more normal life. And though there are times I miss her and think about her..."

Carried was suddenly overcome with emotion. She took out a tissue and dabbed at the corner of her eye. After a moment, she finished by saying, "I know she's in the best situation possible and that makes me glad."

There was a brief, silent moment. Robert and Kara glanced at each other, touched by Carrie's story.

Then Terri said, "Amy, why don't you tell us a little about your background?"

A petite figure, Amy weighed less than a hundred pounds. She had short red hair and a very fair complexion. She was generally quiet and serious, rarely smiling. It was obvious that she was uncomfortable speaking in front of a large group, especially about her private experiences. She took a deep breath and began.

"Well, here it goes," she said softly, as if speaking to herself. "As you can see, I'm pretty thin. And I didn't gain more than ten pounds during my whole pregnancy. When I found out I was pregnant, I started wearing loose clothes so my parents never found out until it was time to go to the hospital. I mean that literally. I started having contractions one evening. It was about eight o'clock. I realized then that I couldn't keep this a secret anymore so I went downstairs to tell my dad. My mom had gone to the store. I said to my dad, 'Dad, there's something I've got to tell you.'"

A chuckle spread through the audience. Amy smiled nervously, slightly embarrassed.

"I know. As I look back on it, it's kind of funny. You can imagine the shock on my dad's face when I told him. We didn't know what to do. He called the doctor's office and they sent us to the hospital. Well, we got into the car and started to drive. On the way, a few blocks from our house, we saw Mom coming home from the other direction. Dad flashed his lights and got her to stop. He told her the situation so Mom turned around and followed us. Then Dad finally had a chance to ask me how it happened. I admitted that Mike, my boyfriend, was the father. We had broken up three or four months before. Mike didn't even know I was pregnant. I didn't tell anyone.

"My parents were okay about it. They were disappointed once they got over the shock. But after the baby was born, we talked it over and decided I should come to Rainbow and place the baby for adoption. This happened about a year ago in August. The adoptive parents, Jeff and Cathy, named our son, Elliot. I like to say 'our' son because we have a very open adoption and it seems like we're partners in this. After placement day, I didn't see Elliot for six months. That's how long it took for the adoption to be finalized and for him to have a new birth certificate and everything. Jeff and Cathy wanted to wait until then. And I felt I needed the time to get over the separation. But then we met here at Rainbow, and I got to see how Elliot was doing. And he was doing fine. I was getting my life back in order and so it just confirmed to me that I did the right thing about placing Elliot for adoption. Jeff and Cathy are wonderful parents and our relationship has grown from a semi-open adoption to a totally open one. We've exchanged phone numbers and we know where each other lives and we see each other about once a month. That's been especially good for my mom. This is her first grandchild. She actually talks to Cathy more than I do, and they've become good friends. I think the whole situation has worked out well. I know I'll be able to keep up with Elliot and he will be able to know me. I think if we had a closed adoption, I would always have been wondering what's going on in Elliot's life. And I'm sure he would always be wondering what his birthmother and birthfather were like and why we placed him for adoption. Now, as he gets older, I'll be able to explain to him how I was too young and how he really wouldn't have had the nice family he has today."

Then Amy looked at Terri as if to indicate that she was finished. Terri stood up and said, "We have some time now for questions. You can direct them to either Carrie or Amy."

Several hands shot up at once. Terri called on a tall, blonde woman in the front row next to Robert. She asked, "Carrie, what kind of relationship do you have with your child's adoptive parents?"

Carrie paused to reflect for a moment. She pursed her lips. Finally, she remarked, "I'd say you'd have to label our relationship as semi-open. I got to see Alicia when she was six months old. Before then, I received pictures and letters. And I have received some since. But I don't have the type of relationship that Amy has with her adoptive parents. I think my child's adoptive parents might be a little fearful of me. But to be honest, I've felt like I've had to distance myself from Rick and Natalie and Alicia. Now, when I get pictures or letters from them, I feel like I'm getting an update on a friend's child. And I think that's better for me. I don't want to totally cut my ties with Alicia because I do care about her; one day I want to get together with her when she's old enough. I want to have a chance to explain what happened and that I do love her. But I need the distance right now to get on with my life. I have a new boyfriend now and things are getting serious, and so keeping a close relationship with Alicia and her parents might prevent me from getting on with my life."

Kara quickly raised her hand. She said, "Amy and Carrie, you seem to have very different situations and attitudes about adoption in terms of open adoption or more traditional relationships. How do you think most birthmothers feel about adoption? Would more birthmothers prefer traditional relationships, or open relationships, or somewhere in between?"

The girls looked at one another. Then Amy said to Carrie, "You go first."

"That's a tough question," Carrie said. "I guess it depends on the individual. But it's important. It was one thing I wanted to be very clear about when I selected Alicia's adoptive parents."

Amy added, "I agree. It's an individual thing. But I admit that when I selected Jeff and Cathy, their willingness to go beyond a traditional adoption to a more open adoption was very important. When I read their profile, that was one thing that influenced me. It was like they were validating me as a person. They made me feel like they truly cared about me, and not just about what I was able to give them."

The questions continued for another half-hour. When the meeting ended, Kara remarked to Robert, "I'm glad we were able to come. It's given me a whole different perspective."

"Me, too," Robert said. "It made me realize that birthmothers are real people. And one day soon we're going to be starting a relationship with one of these young women."

"And it may last a lifetime," Kara added. "If we have an open adoption, it will be like adding more than a child to our family."

"It will be like having more in-laws," Robert said with a smile.

"Oh, stop it! It won't be like that!" Kara said.

"Just kidding," Robert said. Then he asked, "Seriously, is that how you feel? Do you want an open adoption?"

"Well, I'm not sure. I wish we could know more about a birthmother before we commit to an open adoption. I would hate to commit to it and then discover that we don't get along."

"Maybe the best thing would be to start out with a semi-open adoption, and then open it up more as we get to know the birthmother a little better," Robert said. "We'll have to pray about it."

Kara nodded. "Start praying now," she said. "I'm going to start working on our file tonight."

•••

Kara worked on their profile late into the night. She got up early the next morning and sat down at the computer once again. She had already completed short biographies of Robert and herself. She also had written a description of their daily routine. Now the task became more challenging. She needed to express their views on adoption in a letter. She tapped lightly on the keyboard and prayed, "I need your help, Lord."

After a moment, the words began to flow. She wrote:

Dear Birthmother,

We view adoption as an exciting opportunity. It is a chance for us to have the child or children we could not have otherwise. We have a saying at our church, "You matter to God." We believe these words apply to everybody, especially to children who need a home. We know that somewhere there is, or will be, a child who matters to God and needs a home and would fit in well with our family. We would love to share our home with that child.

Last night, we met with two Rainbow birthmothers. After our meeting, we came to realize that birthmothers also matter to God. We now have a greater understanding of the feelings birthmothers face in placing their child for adoption. We also know how much of a personal sacrifice you are making. We know how deeply concerned you must be about your child and how you want to be reassured that the child you are placing for adoption will be happy and well taken care of. In short, our views on openness have broadened.

We admit that, at first, we wanted our communication or contact with the birthmother to be very limited. Our attitude was the product of a fear that any communication with the birthmother might jeopardize our adoption, or that it would undermine our relationship with our child. Now, we know that is not true. We realize that the birthmother, in most cases, simply wants to be reassured that she made the right decision about adoption and that the child is growing up happy.

We would like to begin with a semi-open adoption. We believe it would be a good thing if we only exchanged pictures, letters, and presents at the beginning. At some time in the future, if everyone feels comfortable with the situation, we can increase the openness of our relationship. Also, if any of us ever begin feeling uncomfortable with the arrangement, then we can allow the interaction to taper off.

We would like to close by saying that we know how difficult this decision is for you, the birthmother. We do not know what your particular situation is at this point in life. Hopefully, we will learn a lot about you in the future. What we do know is that your choice of adoption over abortion makes you special because you care more about your child than your own convenience or self-interest. It's obvious that you have his or her best interests at heart. On an emotional level, we know how agonizing it must be for you to place your child for adoption. On the other hand, we are sure you have given much thought to the practical side of raising a child. We are praying for you and your child and have prayed for you for a long time. You will be forever in our prayers.

Robert and Kara

The Wisdom of Solomon

"You know you didn't have to drive me," Faith said to her mother on the way to the adoption agency.

"I'm just doing what I can to help. I don't want you to feel alone in this."

"It's okay, Mom. I can handle it," Faith said, an edge to her voice.

"You seem irritable. Is something wrong?"

"No. Just tired."

Joan nodded. Then she said, "Justin begins in three weeks. Have you decided on school yet?"

"I was looking forward to starting in the fall. But that's out the window now."

"How come?"

"Mom! I can't go now! I'm starting to show! I don't want to be walking around campus with people talking behind my back. 'Look! There's the president's daughter. She's an unwed mother.'"

"If you'd just be honest with people, I'm sure most people would respect what you're doing."

"Yeah, right. I bet most people believe I made up the story of being raped," Faith replied, staring out the side window.

"Honey, you can't control what other people think. So forget about it. Besides, all that matters is what God thinks."

Faith turned to her mother and said, "Still, I don't want other people staring at me. I was worried *before* this happened. I was afraid of how kids would treat me because I'm the president's daughter. Now I can't even imagine what it'll be like."

"Well, if that's the way you feel, that's fine. You don't have to start until second semester," Joan said.

Arriving a few minutes early, Joan checked in with the receptionist and sat down next to Faith on one of three large couches surrounding a square glass coffee table. Adoption and baby magazines were lined up in two neat rows across the table. Faith picked up one of the magazines and thumbed through it for a few minutes until Maggie came down to greet her. Then she was led up to an office on the second floor while Joan waited in prayer downstairs.

Maggie's office, once one of five bedrooms in the house, each complete with its own bathroom, had heavy oak doors, floors, and woodwork. The plaster walls were painted white in stark contrast to the dark woodwork. At one end of the room, a dark brown, antique oak desk sat in front of the bay window which looked out over the back yard. Off to one side, along the wall, sat a large couch with a small antique cherry coffee table perched in front. As the women entered the room, Maggie directed Faith to the sitting area and Faith sat down on one end of the couch. Maggie sat in the wing back chair directly opposite.

Maggie was an attractive woman in her late twenties with brown eyes and brown bobbed hair. She was sharply dressed with a black skirt, black hose, a white blouse, and a little red bow tied at the neck. She was sitting with her legs crossed and a notepad on her lap.

"I'd like to begin by discussing what you got out of your meeting with the other birthmothers," Maggie said.

Faith shifted on the couch as she thought about her reply. "I don't know. I guess it was good. It was nice to meet others in my situation. And it was good to hear a balanced view."

"What do you mean?"

"Two girls placed their babies for adoption and one kept her baby. It was good to hear both sides. But it didn't make things any easier for me."

"Why is that?"

"Because I could see that there are advantages and disadvantages to both choices. But I think the girls did what was right for them."

Maggie made a few notes, uncrossed her legs, and shifted in her chair. "Are you leaning one way or the other yet?" she asked.

"I'm not sure. Some days I feel like going with an adoption, and other days I feel like I should try parenting."

"That's perfectly understandable," Maggie said. "But I'm wondering if you have really considered the practical side of parenting?"

"What do you mean?"

"Allow me to spell it out for you," Maggie said. "Your baby will have to be cared for twenty-four hours a day. She may sleep a lot at first, but someone must be there at all times. You also have to provide the basic necessities of life—food, clothing, and shelter. How do you plan to do it?"

"I guess I would be counting on my parents at first," Faith said sheepishly.

"Have they told you that they would help?"

"Well, sort of. I mean we haven't talked out the details, but I guess the baby and I would be living at home. My parents still want me to go to college."

"And your mother would watch the baby while you're at school?"

"I guess so. I'm assuming she would. She's being very supportive."

"I suggest you talk it over with your parents so there's no misunderstanding. You would be asking your mother to take on a big responsibility. This could be a very important factor in your decision."

Faith nodded.

"Perhaps the other important question is—how would you feel about living at home for the next four years while you go to college? Most people your age are anxious to get out on their own. You won't have that kind of freedom if you're responsible for a child."

"I know. My friend Hope keeps talking about going away to school and being on her own. It does make me jealous."

"It's something you should consider. I'm not trying to be negative about this. I'm just trying to get you to be realistic. If you did feel you needed your freedom, you would have to move out to your own apartment because you can't keep a baby in a dorm. To have an apartment, you would have to give up your college education and get a full-time job to support yourself and a child. While you were at work, you would still need your mother to baby-sit or you would have to pay for child-care. Without a college education, the type of income you would have would barely pay for child-care, let alone, the basic necessities of life. And don't forget, when you're just starting out, you have to buy furniture, dishes, other household items, an automobile, and so on. Of course, you could get married and have some help with expenses. But you don't want to feel pressured into doing that. Are you starting to get the picture?"

"Yeah," Faith said dejectedly. "It seems like I don't really have a choice. But I know I'm gonna feel guilty if I give my child up for adoption."

"Tell me why."

Faith sighed. She said sadly, "I would worry about what others would think. I'm sure that people would think, 'How could you give up your baby?' And I would feel like I betrayed my child. Years from now, I know she's going to ask, 'Why didn't my birthmother love me enough to keep me?'"

"Would you mind if I read you a story?"

"No. Go ahead."

Maggie reached for her Bible and pulled it from a stack of books on the corner of the desk. She began reading from 1st Kings.

> Now two prostitutes came to the king and stood before him. One of them said, "My lord, this woman and I live in the same house. I had a baby while she was there with me. The third day after my child was born, this woman also had a baby. We were alone; there was no one in the house but the two of us. During the

night this woman's son died because she lay on him. So she got up in the middle of the night and took my son from my side while I your servant was asleep. She put him by her breast and put her dead son by my breast. The next morning, I got up to nurse my son—and he was dead! But when I looked at him closely in the morning light, I saw that it wasn't the son I had borne."

The other woman said, "No! The living one is my son; the dead one is yours." But the first one insisted, "No! The dead one is yours; the living one is mine." And so they argued before the king.

The king said, "Bring me a sword." So they brought a sword for the king. He then gave an order: "Cut the living child in two and give half to one and half to the other."

The woman whose son was alive was filled with compassion for her son and said to the king, "Please, my lord, give her the living baby! Don't kill him!" But the other said, "Neither I nor you shall have him. Cut him in two!"

Then the king gave his ruling: "Give the living baby to the first woman. Do not kill him; she is his mother."

When all Israel heard the verdict the king had given, they held the king in awe, because they saw that he had wisdom from God to administer justice.

Maggie closed the Bible and said, "I think the point I'm trying to make is that *real* love for your child means doing what is best for the child even if it means placing the child for adoption. It's a fallacy to assume that because a woman places a child for adoption, she doesn't love her child. Placing a child for adoption is most often an act of sacrificial love."

Faith nodded and asked, "But how will I know that my child understands that?"

"There's no guarantee she will. But if you have an open or semi-open adoption, you have a much better chance that she will."

"I would hope so."

The discussion continued for a while. At the end, Maggie said, "I have another assignment for you."

"Not more reading, I hope."

Maggie laughed.

"No," she said. "This is a hands-on activity. I would like you to baby-sit an infant, and then a two-year-old, a four-year-old, a six-year-old, *etc*. Then imagine yourself as the child's mother, doing this full-time. Then ask yourself, 'Am I ready for this?'"

Faith raised her eyebrows and smiled. "Okay," she said.

On the way home from the session, Joan asked, "How did it go?"

"Good, I think."

"That's good."

"Mom."

"Yes?"

"What do you think I should do?"

"Do what your heart tells you."

•••

That evening Faith wrote in her diary:

August 15

Dearest child,

I am so fearful of making the decision for your life. I guess the most important thing is that you do have life. Unfortunately, I need to make the decision of whether I should be your mother or to let someone else be your mother. I feel so inadequate. I know what I want for you, but can I give it to you?

Please remember that being a mother is so much more than giving birth. It is a lot of hard work to love and see to your needs 24 hours a day. No matter who your mother is (birthmother or not) love her, honor her, and respect her. She is your mother. I will have carried you for nine months, but she will love you and has loved you for years.

I pray that no matter what I decide that you will always be healthy and happy. I want you to know always that God loved you, even from the moment you were conceived. And once I realized that you were growing inside me, I began loving you, too.

Because I haven't come to a decision as to whether I am keeping you, it's hard for me to write about your future. I just want to love you enough to give you the best. I know what I want for you. If I can give it to you, I will keep you. But if I can't, I realize that I have to love you enough to give you up.

Love,
Your Mom

•••

"Why do I always wait till the last minute?" Hope asked as she stood looking down on the half-filled suitcases and boxes on her bed.

"Don't complain! At least you *are* going away to school!" Faith said.

Hope smiled. "It's too bad we're not going to college together. We should have planned better."

"I've kind of discovered that things don't always work out as planned," Faith said wryly.

Hope smiled compassionately. "No, I guess not," she said.

The last week of August had arrived. Hope was spending her last day at home packing for college. Faith was sitting uncomfortably on Hope's oak desk chair. She had turned it around to face the bed that was piled high with clothes, shoes, and accessories.

"I don't think you'll have enough space in your dorm room for all this stuff. I doubt that you'll have a walk-in closet."

"I know," Hope said, perplexed. "I think I'll just pack my fall stuff. At Thanksgiving I can switch over to my winter stuff."

"You're gonna have to do something."

Hope smiled. "I know," she said. "But how about you? What are you going to do?"

"What do you mean?"

"Have you made a decision yet about the baby?"

"Oh! I don't know!" Faith said with a loud sigh. "I'm leaning toward adoption but it's just so hard to give up control. I'm afraid for her. But then I wonder if I would be any better as a parent, especially parenting by myself. I think I'm going to end up tossing a coin. It's so hard to decide!"

"So the counseling hasn't helped much, huh?"

"I wouldn't say that. Maggie made me realize one thing."

"What's that?"

"That a birthmother who places her baby for adoption may be showing more love for her child than one who decides to keep her baby."

"Why is that?"

"She says some birthmothers keep their child just to meet their own emotional needs instead of thinking about what would be best for the child."

"Still, a woman has a right to keep her child no matter what," Hope said. "You can't always think about others, Faith. You have a right to think about yourself sometimes. What if everybody was so unselfish that they always did things for others instead of themselves? You'd have a whole world full of people who were frustrated and unhappy."

Hope sat down on a corner of her bed, the only available square foot of space. She started looking around the room and let out a sigh.

"I'm going to miss this place," she said. "My own bed, my desk—"

"Your walk-in closet," Faith said with a laugh.

"I'll miss Eliza and Mom, too, even though I haven't seen Mom much these days. And, of course, I'll miss you," Hope said with a tear in her eye. Then she walked over to Faith sitting in the chair, and leaned over to give her a hug.

"I'll miss you, too," Faith said. Then after a quiet moment, she asked, "What about Jason? Aren't you going to miss him?"

Hope straightened up, dramatically hitting her head with both fists. "Right now I just want to forget about Jason!" she fumed.

"Why? What did he do?"

"It wasn't him," Hope said. "It was me! I promised myself I would never do it!"

"Do what?"

"We had unprotected sex last night. Things just got a little out of hand. I don't know what happened!"

"I warned you not to play with fire," Faith said with a smile. But she could see Hope was not amused.

"Don't worry!" Faith added. "The timing all has to be right to get pregnant. One time isn't going to matter."

"Look who's talking!" Hope said. "The trouble is the timing was right!"

Faith frowned. Then her face lit up and she said with a smile, "Look at the bright side! We'll have kids the same age. They could play together and go to school together."

"I can wait ten years for that, thank you," Hope said. Then she looked at the piles of clothes on her bed and said, "That's what I'll do. I'm close enough to home to pack just my late summer and fall stuff. Then I'll rotate things for each season."

"Don't change the subject!" Faith said. "Are you going to miss him?"

"Maybe," Hope said, "until I meet another big man on campus."

"Be careful about burning the candle at both ends!"

"Look at you! You sound like Eliza, or my mom!" Hope shot back laughing.

Faith laughed too but her laugh quickly dwindled. Tears moistened her eyes.

"I'm going to miss you!" she said.

"I'm going to miss you, too!"

An Emotional Roller Coaster

22

Kara arrived home from school exhausted. She spent the last two days in meetings and in the classroom preparing for the new school year. In years past, she found this time to be exciting. But this year was different. Instead of recharging her batteries, the summer break left her despondent. For six weeks, she put her life on hold as she waited for the phone to ring with the news that she would soon be a mother. But the call never came.

By normal standards they had not been waiting long. Some couples wait for years before they successfully adopt. Robert and Kara had been waiting only a matter of weeks. Nonetheless, Kara had been secretly praying for a miracle. She had hoped that a baby would be delivered to them before the start of school. But the call never came.

What Kara found particularly difficult was facing her friends at school without the good news. And invariably, they had all asked about the adoption quest. At times, she had to fight back tears and swallow the lump in her throat. She was hoping her new students would lift her spirits.

Robert was sitting at the kitchen table attending to paperwork for school when Kara stepped in from the garage.

"Hi, Love," he greeted her with a smile.

"Hello," she said wearily and gave him a kiss. "I'm going to lie down for a bit before I start supper."

Kara trudged to the bedroom, kicked off her shoes, and had just stretched out on the bed when the phone rang. Robert answered. Seconds later, Kara heard him calling, "Honey! Pick up the phone! It's Terri Moore!"

Kara's heart leapt. She sat up in bed and picked up the phone.

"Hello, Terri," she said anxiously.

"Hello, Kara. I've got some potentially good news for you. A birthmother liked your profile. Her name is Amanda. She especially likes the idea that you're a mixed race couple because she is pregnant with a biracial child."

"That's great!" Kara said excitedly.

"That's wonderful news!" Robert echoed.

"I thought you would be thrilled," Terri said. "But I have to warn you up front not to get too excited. Amanda is not one hundred percent sure she wants to place the child. And I don't think she'll really know until after the baby is born."

"We understand," Robert said.

"When is she due?" Kara asked.

"In about two or three weeks."

"Oh, my! That's not much time to get ready!" Kara said.

"Amanda would like to meet with you as soon as possible, " Terri said.

"Yes, of course," Robert said.

"Would you be able to make it for a meeting tomorrow?" Terri asked.

"Ugh! Tomorrow is the first day of school. I shouldn't take tomorrow off. Can we do it after school?" Kara asked.

"I think that can be arranged," Terri said.

"That would be great! What time?" Kara asked.

"Four-thirty."

"Great! You don't have anything going on, do you Robert?" Kara asked.

"No. Four-thirty should be fine," he said.

"Good. We'll meet here in my office. See you tomorrow," Terri said.

Robert and Kara ran to each other. They met on the stairs with a hug.

"Oh! I can't believe it. And she's due in two weeks!" Kara said.

"Let's be careful. Let's not get too excited," Robert said.
"I know. But I can't help it. I'm going to call Mom."

•••

When Kara rushed home from school the next afternoon, she found Robert waiting anxiously.
"Did your meeting end early?" she asked.
"I couldn't concentrate so I bowed out," he said. "Are you ready to go?"
"We'll be fifteen minutes early if we leave now."
"That's okay. I would just as soon wait there as here," Robert said.
It was a forty-five minute drive to the agency. The first fifteen minutes languished in small talk as Robert and Kara recounted their day for each other. But the conversation dissipated of its own superficiality allowing a silence to settle in. The significance of the upcoming meeting weighed heavily on their minds. Robert prayed inwardly. Kara fretted the outcome.
"What if she doesn't like us, Robert? Do you think she'd change her mind?"
"We can't worry about that. Just try to be yourself."
"I'm not sure if I want to be myself. I feel like I have to be perfect or Amanda might change her mind," Kara confessed. "I just wish I knew how to act!"
"Do you have any idea what Amanda considers to be 'perfect'?"
"No."
"Then since you don't know how to act, just be yourself."
There were times when Robert's logic annoyed Kara. This was one of them.
"This girl has our lives in the palm of her hand," Kara complained.
"You have to trust God, Love, that's all."
Kara put her head back on the headrest, closed her eyes, and let out a big sigh. Before long, Robert turned into the agency's gravel driveway. He parked the car and then looked at his wife as he shut off the engine.
"Are you ready?" he asked.
"No," Kara replied with her eyes shut and her head cocked back on the seat. "But I guess we'd better go anyway."

They checked in at the front desk and sat down in the reception area. In a few minutes, Terri Moore came down the stairs wearing a warm smile.

"Hello, Robert. Hello, Kara," she said. "We'll be meeting in an office upstairs. Amanda is looking forward to meeting you. Shall we go up?"

Amanda was seated in one of the two wing chairs arranged opposite the couch. She turned and looked around the back of the chair as Kara and Robert entered.

"Hi!" she said with a nervous smile. Then she labored to get up from her chair.

"That's okay! Don't get up!" Kara said as she took Amanda's hand.

"It's nice to meet you, finally! Ever since reading your profile, I've wanted to meet you in person," Amanda said.

Robert and Kara smiled and sat down on the couch while Amanda returned to her seat. Terri settled into the other wing chair.

Amanda was a young woman with a large frame, long blonde hair, blue eyes, and fair skin. She had on a light blue maternity dress. On her lap she held a small, brown, leather photo album.

"Well, Amanda," Terri began, "you have an advantage over Robert and Kara. You've had the opportunity to read their profile. They know almost nothing about you. Why don't you go ahead and tell them a little bit about yourself?"

Amanda nodded. She said, "My family is Catholic. My dad is an electrical contractor and my mother works as a secretary. I have two older brothers and two younger sisters. We live in a nearby town. In high school, I played sports—basketball, softball, and track. My grades were mostly Bs and Cs. I started going to the local junior college last year but I quit after the first semester. I don't think I'm cut out for college. So I decided to enroll at beautician school and I went through that and everything and now I have a job as a beautician."

Amanda paused. She added, "I consider myself a good Christian, although obviously, I've made some mistakes. After a lot of prayer, I decided to dedicate this baby to Jesus. My family has been very supportive. My younger sisters are getting excited about the baby."

Amanda shifted in her chair. She said, "I could raise the child myself, but I want more for him than what I can give him. I want Tyler to have two parents. And I know Darius and I will never get married. In fact, I don't see myself getting married for a few years. That's why I've chosen adoption. We talked about sharing custody, but I don't want Tyler growing up confused about who he is. I didn't want him going back and forth between a black home and a white one or between a Catholic family and a Baptist family. Having one family with one religious background would be best. I really liked the idea of having Tyler raised by you guys so that he could have both a black and white heritage in one family."

Kara smiled. "Thank you," she said. "You don't know how much this child means to us."

"Can you tell us a bit more about the birthfather?" Robert asked.

Amanda tilted her head and stared up into space. Finally she said, "I met Darius at junior college. He's on the football team. He plays on defense, a safety or something. He is tall, about six-two, and thin. He has very dark skin. He's a nice guy and he likes to dance."

"Does he plan on going on to a four-year college?" Robert asked.

"Sure, if he can get a scholarship. He wants to keep playing football."

"Has he decided on a major?" Robert asked.

"I don't think he really knows. Deep down, I think he realizes that playing professional football is just a dream. He expects to end up in a sales job. He's a real smooth talker. That's probably what got me into trouble!"

Robert and Kara smiled. Then Robert said, "I hope he finishes college. He'll be better off in the long run."

"Well, he hasn't had any role models in that way," Amanda said. "Neither of his parents went to college and neither did mine. That's one of the reasons I picked you guys. You've gone to college and maybe that will be a good influence on Tyler."

"We'll certainly encourage him," Kara said.

For a short moment, no one knew what to say next. Finally, Terri suggested, "Amanda, why don't you show Robert and Kara your photo album?"

"Okay. How do you want to do it? Do you want me to sit on the couch between Robert and Kara?"

"That would probably work best," Terri said.

Amanda struggled up out of her chair and waddled around the coffee table and sat down heavily between Robert and Kara. Their eyes followed her closely as she moved from the chair to the couch. She looked like she might give birth any day.

As they came to the last picture, Amanda said, "I'll be adding more to the album until…" She paused briefly as her voice cracked. Then she added, "Until you take him home."

"That would be wonderful! We think it's important for him to know his roots," Kara said.

"Thanks. That's important to me," Amanda said with teary eyes.

Kara put her arm around Amanda who pulled a tissue out of her pocket.

"I'm sorry," Amanda said. "I don't mean to be such a baby. It's just that when I think of saying 'good-bye' I get a little sad. That's why I really want to keep in touch after placement."

"Don't worry! We'll let you know how he's doing," Kara said.

"That's right," Robert added.

"Thanks," Amanda said, straining to smile.

"And we can get together with the baby sometime after placement so you can see how well he is doing," Kara promised.

"That would be wonderful!" Amanda said, wiping her tears.

"Generally, couples wait six months after placement for a visit like that," Terri interjected. "The legal process is usually finished by then and the birthmother has had some time for her emotional wounds to heal. And Amanda and I have talked about this. She will certainly be feeling a sense of loss for a while. But that feeling will fade, although not completely, as she gets on with her life. I think after six months, she'll be ready to see the baby again. And it's generally a good experience for any birth-mother to see that her child is doing well."

Amanda returned to her chair and shared more of her background for nearly half an hour. When the meeting drew to a close, she exchanged hugs with Robert and Kara. Then Terri escorted the Ellisons down the stairs to the front door.

"I think it went pretty well," Terri said.

"Yes, I think so," Robert said.

Kara nodded reservedly.

"Now it's a matter of waiting, which can be difficult. Again, there's no guarantee that Amanda won't change her mind once the baby is born. In fact, it wouldn't surprise me if she did. But I'll give you a call when the baby is born and give you some of the details. Then I'll let you know when she's signed the relinquishment papers. Remember, she can't legally sign the papers until seventy-two hours after the baby is born."

Kara let out a sigh.

"I'm sure I'll be holding my breath the whole time, too," she said.

"I wouldn't advise that," Terri said with a laugh. "Besides, my gut feeling on this is that it's fifty-fifty that she'll choose to parent. I don't want to discourage you. I just want you to be realistic. And if this adoption doesn't go through, I'm sure there will be another one soon."

"Yes, I know," Kara said. "My mind wants to think that way, but my heart doesn't understand."

"That's perfectly natural," Terri said. "But sooner or later, you *will* get the child you've always wanted."

On the way home, Kara asked, "So how do you think it went?"

"I think it went well," Robert said. "If she does decide to keep the baby, I don't think it's because we weren't good enough."

"So you think she's going to keep the baby, don't you?"

"Now I didn't say that, did I?"

"No. But that's what you're thinking."

"I think Amanda is much like you. In her head, she knows that adoption is probably best for the child. But, in her heart, I think she can't part with him."

Kara slipped into a despondent silence.

"It won't be the end of the world, Love," Robert said. "Besides, we just have to wait and see. We really don't know what she'll decide."

Kara pouted and said, "It's not going to happen this time. I just know it."

•••

Everyday for nearly two weeks Kara would wake up in the morning thinking, "This is going to be the day." But everyday turned out the same. On school days, she would try to keep her mind on her work; but all the time, she was waiting for the call from Terri Moore. The most difficult part was being stopped by fellow teachers. They would see Kara in the hallway before school or in the lounge at lunch. Everyday they would ask, "Have you heard anything yet?" Each time Kara would have to admit that they hadn't. When she did, it was like her soul was siphoned a little more until she had become a hollow, brittle eggshell.

The weekends were even more difficult. With the exception of going to church, Robert and Kara stayed home waiting for the phone to ring. They decided not to make plans in anticipation that they may be bringing home a baby any day.

It was a Tuesday afternoon in mid-September, nearly two weeks after the meeting with Amanda, when the call finally came. Robert and Kara were in the back yard enjoying one of the most glorious sunny days of the waning summer season. Kara was sitting at the patio table reading a magazine while Robert was busily attending to his yardwork. Kara picked up the cordless phone from the patio table.

"Hello, Kara. This is Terri Moore. I've got some good news. Amanda gave birth to a healthy boy yesterday. He is eight pounds, seven ounces, and cute as a button!"

"That's wonderful!" Kara exclaimed, drawing Robert's attention. "How is Amanda doing?"

"She had a difficult delivery but she's doing all right now."

"How is she doing emotionally?"

"Fine, I think," Terri said. "I just finished talking to her on the phone and it sounds like she's still planning on going through with the adoption. She was talking about the outfit she received from her parents that the baby would wear on placement day."

"Really?"

"Yes. She sounded more positive about adoption today than ever before."

"That's great!" Kara said, radiating a smile.

By now, Robert was standing next to his wife, trying to assess the state of affairs by listening to one end of the conversation.

"But remember," Terri cautioned again, "Amanda has to wait until Thursday morning before she can sign the papers."

"Yes. Yes, I know," Kara said. "I'm still holding my breath and I guess I'll keep holding it until I'm holding the baby in my arms."

"I'm sorry I can't make it any easier for you," Terri said. "I would have called yesterday with the news, but I wanted to wait to see how Amanda was doing and what her state of mind was before getting your hopes up."

"I understand. Give our love to Amanda and the baby," Kara said.

"Will do."

Kara turned off the phone and set it on the table. Then she stood up and gave Robert a hug.

"I think we'd better get serious about deciding on a name," Kara said with her head resting on Robert's shoulder and a tear in her eye.

"Maybe we'd better get started fixing up the baby's room," Robert said.

"Do you really think it's going to happen? Is this our baby?" Kara asked.

"God only knows."

•••

Kara spent a sleepless night tossing and turning in bed. Try as she might, she could not get her mind off the baby. She went through a cycle of concerns over and over again. First, she thought about names for the baby. Then she thought about how to decorate the baby's room. Next, she worried about whether Amanda would follow through with the adoption. Finally, she even succumbed to thoughts of jealousy. Even though she knew she had no right to do so, she was upset thinking about Amanda holding the child. And then the cycle would begin again as she came up with a new name for the baby. It was almost dawn before she finally fell asleep from sheer exhaustion.

"Ugh!" Kara groaned when the alarm went off. She had less than an hour of sleep. She climbed wearily out of bed. While shuffling her way toward the shower, she peeked in the mirror through half closed eyes and groaned again, "Ugh!"

Kara reached in and turned on the shower. She leaned against the wall with her eyes closed and waited for the water to heat up. Sluggishly, she stepped into the shower, but within seconds the invigorating spray began to take effect. She thought, "Tomorrow could be the day! I've got to get things ready at school in case I need to take off a couple of days."

The very idea of bringing home the baby gave her the spark she needed. When she walked down to the kitchen the aroma of fresh brewed coffee gave her another lift. Robert had already left for work. But, on the counter, next to the coffee cup he had set out for her, Kara found a note from her husband. It said, "Remember Love—whatever comes our way is the Lord's will. If this adoption does not work out, another one will. I love you, Robert."

Kara smiled and knew he was right. She felt foolish for not getting enough sleep the night before. Once at school, she went immediately to the teacher's lounge to check her mailbox.

"Good morning," Kara said to Sharon Huxtable in front of the mailboxes.

"Are you sure?" Sharon replied.

"Excuse me," Kara said.

"Are you sure it's a good morning? You look like you didn't get any sleep last night."

"It shows that much?"

"Yes."

"Well, you're right. I didn't sleep at all."

"What happened? Did the adoption fall through?" Sharon asked.

"No, it's not that. We got the call yesterday that the baby was born. I was so excited, *and worried*, I couldn't sleep at all," Kara said.

"That's wonderful!" Sharon said with a big smile. "But what are you worried about? Are you afraid the birthmother is going to parent the child?"

"Exactly."

"Well, there's nothing you can do about that. And, who knows? It may turn out to be a blessing in disguise."

"I know. Robert keeps telling me that," Kara said before being cut off by Angela Portillo, a sprite elderly woman sitting at a nearby table.

"Did you say the baby was born?" she asked.

"Yes," Kara said, turning red and dismayed that the whole lounge was buzzing with the news.

"When will you receive the baby?" one woman asked.

"I don't know. It's not a sure thing yet. The birthmother can still change her mind," Kara tried to explain.

"Is it a boy or girl?" another asked.

"It's a boy," Kara replied.

"Oh! How about that! A boy! Have you picked out a name yet?" Angela asked.

"Well, no. Not yet," Kara said.

"I think Kevin is a good name for a boy," Angela said.

"Well, it's not a done deal," Kara tried to explain again.

Then she heard Angela and the other women talking quietly among themselves about a baby shower. The scene was exactly what she wanted to avoid. She turned and began walking toward the lounge door. Sharon followed and caught up with Kara a few steps down the hallway.

"I'm sorry I started such a fuss in there," Sharon said.

"That's okay."

Sharon smiled as she gently grabbed Kara by the elbow and pulled her to a halt. She said, "Don't worry if it doesn't work out this time. I've been through the same thing. There are lots of highs and lows; but in the end, it'll work out. Just have faith."

At day's end, Kara was physically and emotionally exhausted. When she arrived home, Robert was on the back patio, sitting at the table with a large glass of lemonade, grading tests. Kara set her purse and briefcase on the kitchen table and opened the sliding glass doors leading to the patio.

"Hello," she said wearily as she sat opposite him at the patio table.

"Hi, Love. How was your day?"

"Horrible. I didn't sleep at all last night. I was wiped out. And then the ladies in the lounge heard about the baby and so now everyone is excited. I tried to tell them that it's not for certain yet, but I overheard some women talking about a shower. Robert, I'm going to be so disappointed and embarrassed if we don't get this baby."

Then the phone rang. Robert picked up the cordless phone that was resting on the tests as a paperweight.

"Hello," he said.

"Hello, Robert. This is Terri Moore."

"Hello, Terri. Just a minute. Kara is going to pick up the other phone," he said.

Kara quickly got up from her seat and rushed to the kitchen. Her heart was pounding. She knew this was the moment of truth. She also knew that a call coming this quickly, before Thursday, was not likely to be good news.

"Hello, Terri," Kara said anxiously as she picked up the phone with a trembling hand.

"Hi, Kara," Terri said. "I'm afraid I have some bad news for you. Amanda has decided to parent her baby."

Terri continued explaining and tried to encourage Kara to look forward to the next opportunity, but the encouragement could not penetrate

Kara's profound disappointment. From the start, her mind feared the worst, but her heart held out hope for the best. After hanging up, Kara sat down at the kitchen table with a dazed look and a tear in her eye.

Robert came in, stood behind his wife, and began massaging her shoulders. Finally, Kara burst out in tears. Robert wept, too. After a moment, Kara got up from her chair to embrace him. The couple stood holding each other tightly amidst their sorrow. There was nothing for them to do but mourn the loss of the child they desired so dearly.

Moonlight in the Darkness

23

It was a late Friday afternoon in mid-October, but the weather was made for December. A cold front had moved in at noon and the sky was overcast and misty. It seemed as though the dark gray clouds, which hung heavy overhead, longed to open up and pour out their burden on the earth below. Only a sprinkle escaped intermittently, however, out of the vast, pent up reservoir above. Something held the rain inside, denying the clouds the expression of their nature and the wonder of their purpose. Perhaps it was pride that would not allow them to let go of their encumbrance—the kind of pride that won't accept comfort and sympathy, or advice and counsel. After all, clouds are much like people. And these particular clouds, like many clouds before them, had been deceived by their perspective from above, fooled by the worldly winds that blew them freely about, and deluded by the vain admiration of their own reflection in the surface waters below. They were clouds who knew not their Creator and hence misunderstood themselves. They were a lot like Hope.

Faith was sitting in her bed reading a magazine when the doorbell rang.

"I'm coming!" Faith mumbled as she gingerly climbed out of bed and walked slowly toward the stairs.

The doorbell rang again.

"I'm coming!" Faith shouted. Then she said to herself, "Just give me a minute."

The bell rang a third time as she reached for the doorknob.

"Just a minute!"

When the door swung open, Hope was standing outside with a bouquet of red carnations, smiling.

"Hi!" she said with a big smile.

"Hope! You're home!"

Hope stepped into the entry and gave Faith a hug.

"I thought you weren't going to be home until this evening," Faith said excitedly.

"I decided to skip my afternoon classes," Hope said matter-of-factly. Then she stepped back and said, "Boy! You look—"

"Pregnant?" Faith said. "I'm almost seven months now, the longest seven months of my life. Let's go into the kitchen and sit down and you can tell me about college."

"Where's your family?" Hope asked.

"Dad and Ryan are still at school, I suppose. Mom went shopping," Faith said as they entered the kitchen. "Can I get you something to drink?"

"A Diet Coke would be great."

Faith went to the refrigerator, pulled out a can for each of them, and sat down next to Hope at the table.

"You're really getting big," Hope said.

"I know," Faith said with a smile. "You can touch it if you want."

Hope smiled, hesitated, and then gently put her hand on Faith's stomach.

"Oh, my! I think she's kicking!" Hope said with a laugh as she quickly pulled her hand back.

"Yeah, she does that a lot. I think she wants to get out," Faith said with a smile. Then she grew serious. "So tell me about college," she said.

Hope shrugged and said, "It's great! You have so much freedom!"

"*You've always had freedom,*" Faith said caustically.

"Yeah, but it's different when you're away from home. It's like you're really on your own."

"I'd give anything for that right now!" Faith said. "I feel like a prisoner here. And carrying this baby is like having a ball and chain!"

"It was your choice," Hope said.

Faith smiled and replied softly, "I know. And I'm glad I made it."

Hope's eyes suddenly grew misty. Faith reached for a tissue on the counter and handed it to Hope.

"What's wrong?" she asked.

Hope shook her head and mopped her eyes as Faith inwardly reviewed her last few comments.

"I'm sorry," Faith said. "It's not your fault. Besides, I think God has been teaching me a lot through this experience."

Hope shook her head dramatically this time and stood up. "It's not what you think!" Hope blurted out, almost in an angry tone. "It's..." she began and then shook her head again.

"It's what?" Faith asked.

Hope took a deep breath. She said quietly, "I'm pregnant."

"No!"

"Yes," Hope said, dabbing her eyes with a new tissue. "I think it happened the last night with Jason. Remember I complained about it that day I was leaving?"

Faith's heart sank.

"Do you know for sure?" she asked.

Hope sighed.

"I took a home pregnancy test because my period was late. The test came out positive," she said.

"What are you going to do?"

"I'm going to the clinic tomorrow morning to have a test done to make sure."

"Then what?"

Hope shrugged.

"I'll do what I have to."

"Meaning?"

"I guess I'll have to have an abortion."

Faith's heart nearly burst as she felt movement in her stomach and a great sense of sorrow for the child her friend was carrying. She wanted to shake Hope and make her realize the truth. But she knew that for the moment Hope needed compassion, not correction. She asked, "What about Jason? Does he know?"

"No. But I'll be seeing him later tonight."

•••

By evening, the intermittent mist that fell earlier in the day had grown into steady drizzle. Jason pulled his jacket collar up around his neck and kept his shoulders shrugged to protect himself from the elements as he walked from his car to Hope's front door. The bell rang twice before Hope appeared. He quickly stepped into the entry to escape the cold, wet weather.

"Hi," he said with a smile as he moved toward Hope to greet her with a kiss.

"Hi, Jason," Hope replied as she turned her head to accept his kiss on the cheek.

Jason felt the sting of rejection and it confirmed his fears.

"I missed you," he said.

"Did you?"

"Yes," he said as he held her hands and tried to look her in the eye.

But Hope averted his eyes, smiled, and said, "Shall we go?"

"You haven't been returning my calls lately," Jason said as he pulled out of Hope's driveway.

"I know. I've been busy. You know how it is."

"Is that all it is?"

"No," Hope said softly as she looked out the side window.

"Then what? You seem distant. You've been that way the last few weeks. You haven't been calling me back; and when you do, you cut me off because you always have something else to do," Jason said.

Hope shook her head slowly. She turned to Jason, put her hand on his leg, and peered into his eyes. She asked, "Will you be mad at me if I tell you the truth?"

"Boy! That's a loaded question!" he said sarcastically. His stomach turned as the bad news he had feared was materializing. The pain was evident in his face.

"I don't want to hurt you, Jason," Hope said quickly.

"But?"

Hope sighed.

"But I've been thinking about our situation, and I've decided that being separated and trying to work out a long distance relationship isn't good for either of us."

"That's what I thought!" Jason said, his pain now turning to anger. "I thought it was coming to this!"

"Come on, Jason! Don't be like that. Why can't we just be glad for the time we had together and be friends?"

Jason scoffed. "I thought we were more than that. I thought we had something special," he said, now biting his lip.

"Well, we did," Hope said. "We were good lovers," she said with a smile.

Jason nodded with a half-hearted smile.

"That's what I thought made us special," he said with misty eyes.

"Come on, Jason! We're too young to be tied down to one another! Our only chance to be together is on weekends here and there. We should be seeing other people, not wasting our lives waiting for each other!"

"Is that what you want? To see other people?"

"Well, yeah. I mean it's not that I'm rejecting you or anything. It's just that I think we both ought to be free at this point in our lives. Don't you think?"

He followed her reasoning but his heart disagreed. "Okay. If that's what you want," he said, not wanting to appear weak.

"I think it's best," Hope said. Satisfied that she got her way, she tried to change the mood. She asked, "So what have you been doing lately besides going to class?"

"Do you really want to know?" he asked in a sardonic tone.

"Yeah," she said with a curious smile.

"I've been working at Bill Johnson's campaign headquarters," he said caustically.

"You've been working for that conservative, chauvinist jerk? He's completely out of touch!" Hope said brusquely.

"He's pro-life!"

"So."

"So that's important! If we don't elect a pro-life Congress, in the next two years, another three million babies will be killed!"

"And what about the rights of millions of women?"

"How does the right to kill innocent children compare with the right to life? Which is more important?"

"Oh, come on, Jason! Stop being so sentimental. They aren't innocent children."

"They're not? Then what are they?"

"They're just mistakes! That's all!"

"Mistakes? How can you say that? What if we had conceived a child? Are you telling me that our flesh and blood would be a mistake?" Jason asked scornfully.

"Yes! And that's why I'm getting an abortion!"

Suddenly, silence reigned. Hope immediately regretted her admission. As her words sank in, Jason looked for a place to pull over. He turned into a strip mall lot and parked the car. He was speechless and stared at Hope in horror. His worst nightmare had happened again. He had fathered another child he would never know. Hope turned away with red, watery eyes. Her few tears were filled with anger, frustration, and repressed guilt. They sat silently for a long moment.

Finally, Jason asked, "Are you really pregnant?"

"Yes," Hope answered quietly.

"Am I the father?"

"You're the one who got me pregnant if that's what you mean."

"So, I am the father."

"You can't be a father unless there's a child. And there's not going to be a child!"

"You can't make that decision by yourself!"

"Yes, I can. The courts say I can and I'm going to!"

"That's not right! This is *our* child—*my* child!"

"It's my body and my life! I don't want to be pregnant. I don't want to give birth. And I don't want to be raising a child when I'm eighteen!"

"You don't have to raise the child. I will," Jason said.

"Oh, sure! You want to be a single parent!" Hope scoffed. "I've seen what my mother's gone through. It's not easy!"

"I don't care. I'll do what I have to. Besides, we could get married and raise the child together," Jason said.

"Jason, I'm not ready to get married."

"Why not?"

"I'm too young. I still want to enjoy life before I settle down. It's nothing against you. I'm just not ready to be married."

Jason put his head in his hands for a moment. On the verge of tears, he looked up at Hope and pleaded, "Please! I will assume full responsibility for the child. Let it live!"

"I'm sorry. But I have to do what I have to do."

"Then I'll have to do what I have to do."

"Is that some kind of threat?"

"Take it any way you want. It seems to me that you've always gotten things your own way," Jason said bitterly.

"Take me home!"

•••

The next morning, Hope felt nauseous as she climbed out of bed and made her way down to the kitchen. It was seven-thirty and Eliza was sitting at the table drinking coffee and studying her Bible.

"What are you doing up? It's Saturday," Hope said.

"Good mornin' to you, too," Eliza returned with a smile.

"I'm sorry. Good morning, Eliza. It's good to see you," Hope said with a hug.

"It's nice to have you home," Eliza said. "It's been lonely around here with you away at college and your mother out campaignin'."

"I can imagine," Hope said as she sat in the chair opposite Eliza.

"Are you all right?" Eliza asked. "You don't look so well. You must have had a late night with that good lookin' boy, Jason," she teased.

Hope put her head in her hands.

When she didn't respond, Eliza asked, "Where did you go to eat?"

"We didn't."

"Why not? Your mother said you were going out to dinner."

"We got in a fight. We're not going to see each other anymore."

"Oh, that's too bad. He seemed like such a nice boy."

"Yeah, I guess so."

"So what did you do?"

"He drove me home and then I called Kris and we went out."

"Did Faith go with you?"

"No. She was feeling about as bad as I do now," Hope said, then realized that she may have said too much.

"Are you sick?" Eliza asked.

"No. I'm all right. Just tired."

"So, how is Faith?" Eliza asked. "I haven't seen her since summer."

"She's really big now!"

"When is she due?"

"Right around Christmas. What a way to spend your holidays, huh?"

"Well, she's doing the right thing. That's what counts," Eliza said.

Hope felt uneasy with the direction of the conversation.

"Where's my mom?" she asked.

"Oh, she had a campaign breakfast this morning. That's why she asked me to be up early this morning."

"Is she feeling guilty about never seeing me anymore?"

"I don't know. She left this for you," Eliza said as she pushed a note across the table. Hope picked it up and began reading.

Hope,

Welcome home! Sorry I couldn't be home last night or this morning. My campaign schedule has become unbelievably hectic this last month. Today is going to be just as hectic. I'll see you late tonight if you're still up. Let's go out for breakfast tomorrow morning. I don't have anything scheduled until noon.

Love,
Mom

Hope crumpled the note and said with a bitter smile, "I guess nothing's changed around here. Mom's busy."

"Don't be upset with her, child. This is what politics is about. She's got a lot of commitments to keep."

"What about her commitment to me? What if I was going through a crisis and really needed her?"

"Are you in a crisis?"

Hope looked her in the eye, thought briefly about disclosing her secret, but then changed her mind.

"No," she said.

Eliza took a sip from her cup, then asked, "What can I make you for breakfast?"

"Nothing. I'm not hungry."

"But Hope, you should have somethin'," Eliza scolded gently.

"I'll just have a little bowl of cereal then," Hope said, avoiding an argument.

"What kind would you like?" Eliza asked as she began getting up from the table.

"That's okay, I'll get it myself."

"No," Eliza said firmly. "It's my job. Now what do you want?"

"Special K."

As Eliza pulled a milk carton out of the refrigerator and gathered a bowl, a spoon, and the cereal, she asked, "What do you have planned for today?"

"Not too much. I'm going to the clinic to say hello to everyone this morning."

Eliza raised an eyebrow and asked, "Then what?"

"Then I think Kris and I are going to the Elston football game."

"What about Faith? Isn't she going with you?"

"I think she'd like to if she wasn't pregnant."

"That's too bad," Eliza said. "She ain't got nothin' to be ashamed of."

Hope smiled. "Thanks," she said as Eliza set the cereal in front of her.

"You don't have to thank me. It's my job."

"Well, somehow I think you'd do it for me even if it wasn't your job," Hope said.

"Maybe," Eliza said with a smile.

•••

Hope arrived at the clinic after nine. The usual small band of pickets was parading across the street when she turned onto the side street along the north end of the clinic. After parking in the back lot, she sat behind the wheel quietly thinking about Jason's plea and the comments made by Faith and Eliza. Then she thought about her new life at college. She drew a deep breath, exhaled, and climbed out of the car. She walked briskly into the rear entrance of the clinic. "This is embarrassing," she thought, "but it's better than the alternative."

As she slipped through the rear door of the clinic, she found her uncle standing with Lisa in the hall outside Lisa's office. They were talking in animated whispers. Her entrance interrupted the conversation to the apparent relief of her uncle.

"Well, look who's home from college!" Tom said with a smile.

"Hi, Uncle Tom!" Hope said as she gave him a hug. "Hi, Lisa," she added.

"Hello, Hope," Lisa replied with a strained smile. Then she said to Tom, "We'll talk later."

"Fine."

Tom then led his niece down the hall to his office.

"I hope I didn't interrupt anything important," Hope said.

"Oh, it was nothing. Just an administrative disagreement, that's all," Tom said. In truth, the small rift was personal, not administrative, having to do with Lisa's growing impatience over Tom's procrastination to file for divorce.

"So, how's college life?"

"It's really great. I've got some new friends. My classes are interesting. *And* I like being on my own," she said.

Tom smiled. "Yeah, I remember those days. I had a good time, too," he said as he sat down behind his desk.

Hope picked up the picture of Tom's family and asked, "How is everyone?"

"Everyone's fine. Things couldn't be better," he said.

Hope smiled as she placed the picture back on his desk. Then she turned and walked to the door and closed it quietly. She turned around again and quickly sat down in one of the chairs in front of the desk. Tom looked at Hope quizzically.

"Uncle Tom, this isn't just a social visit. I've got a little problem."

"Well, I'll certainly help you if I can. You know that."

Hope blushed. "Well, you've got to promise not to tell Mom."

"Okay," he said slowly, as if hesitant to limit his options.

"Okay," Hope repeated and then breathed a heavy sigh. She said nervously, "I'm pregnant. At least, I think so. I took a home test and it came out positive."

Tom leaned forward in his chair.

"I see," he said. "Who's the father?"

"Jason. The guy I was dating this summer."

"Does he know?"

"Yes. I wasn't going to tell him, but it accidentally came out last night. He wants me to have the baby. What do you think I should do?"

"Well, frankly, it's your life. There's no reason why you should disrupt your plans just because of one little mistake. Why don't you take another test here to confirm your condition and then we'll schedule a convenient time."

"What about today?"

"Sorry, Hope, but we're overbooked as it is. Are you going to be around Monday?"

"No. I have to get back to school. Are you sure you can't take me today?"

"I'd like to, but Dr. Bernard just called and said he would be a couple of hours late because of a delivery."

"You're kidding!" Hope said, holding back a tear.

"When are you planning to come home again?" Tom asked.

"In about three weeks on Election Day. I wanted to be here with Mom."

"How about the day after the election? You can stop in here in the morning before you head back to school."

"That would be okay, I guess. It's just that I would like to get this over with."

"I understand your anxiety. But, to tell you the truth, it really doesn't matter if the procedure is done today or three weeks from now."

"Okay," Hope said, still disappointed. "It can wait until after the election."

"Don't worry! We'll take care of you."

"Thanks, Uncle Tom."

"No problem," Tom said with a smile. "But I think your mother would understand if you told her."

"I know she would. I just don't want her to think I can't take care of myself."

"Okay. If that's how you feel, then your secret is safe with me."

•••

That night Hope invited Faith over to her house. The girls took a walk in the back yard beyond the pool where months before Faith had revealed her secret to Hope. The darkness was pervasive. The lights around the back patio reached only to the edge of the pool while the half-moon's glow was partially blocked by the surrounding trees and scattered clouds that moved in at sundown. In spite of the dim moonlight and the shadows of night, the girls found their way to the small wrought iron bench in the tiny clearing by following the crushed gravel pathway.

"Everyone was asking about you at the game today," Hope said as they sat down on the bench.

"What did you tell them? That I was as big as a house?" Faith said with a laugh.

"No. I told them you looked good."

"That's not true, but thanks anyway," Faith said as she leaned back on the bench.

"They were all wondering what you were going to do with the baby. I said I didn't know."

Faith sighed. "I've decided to place the baby for adoption. I know it'll be hard, but I love this little girl inside me. And I want what's best for her," she said. "Besides, I'm not ready to be a mother yet. And there are so many couples who want kids but can't have them."

Hope looked intently at her friend as she reached over and grasped her hand.

"I really admire you, Faith."

"Me? Why?"

"Because you're so unselfish."

"No, I'm not."

"Yes, you are. You had every reason to have an abortion and you decided not to. And now you're ready to give the baby away, not because you want to, but for her sake, and because it will make someone else happy."

Faith looked down at her lap and shook her head in shame.

"You know I was thinking of an abortion at first," she said. "I even secretly prayed for a miscarriage. And I still may change my mind about adoption. The truth is, I think about myself all the time. And I'm not nearly as unselfish as I ought to be."

"Still, in the end, you always do what's right."

Faith blushed. She said, "You really don't know me, Hope. You don't know how much I've always wanted to be like you, to be uninhibited and free to do what I want. I really struggle with my faith."

"And you don't know me," Hope said. "You don't know how much I've wished to be like you. You seem so secure. I often wish I had your faith."

The girls smiled at one another. Then Faith leaned her head way back. "It's so pretty," she said, gazing at the moonlight filtering through the trees.

Hope also leaned back to take in the natural beauty.

Faith said, "This reminds me of something my dad told me once when we were lying down on the grass together in the front yard and looking up at the moon."

"What did he say?"

"Dad? He's always so theological!"

"Why? What did he say?"

"Oh, he just started talking about how our time here on Earth is like the night and how there's mostly darkness in this world and evil all around. And God is like the sun and there's only going to be goodness and the light of day when we get to heaven. But he said until then, as Christians, we've got to be like the moon. And our faith has to be like moonlight because the only light and goodness we'll find here on Earth is what we reflect of Christ. And it's hard to be a Christian because darkness hates the light. And I've thought about that a lot, especially when I've been tempted. Lots of times I've just wanted to be a part of the darkness. I've just wanted to fit in with everyone else."

Then Faith blushed again and added, "I'm sorry. I guess what I just said was really corny."

"Oh, no! Not at all! I think you're right! Absolutely!" Hope said.

"No, it's all right. You don't have to humor me."

"I'm not. In fact, I wish I had a dad who would tell me things like that. That's probably what I've missed most in life."

The two girls were silent for a moment as they looked up at the moon again. Then Faith chuckled softly.

"What's so funny?" Hope asked as she sat forward.

"Oh, nothing. I was just thinking how I wanted to be more like you and you wanted to be more like me, and here we are, a little more like each other," Faith said.

"How's that?"

Faith chuckled again and said, "We're both pregnant."

Hope smiled painfully. She said, "But that's how we're different."

"What do you mean?"

"I mean I'm going to have an abortion. I'm sorry, but I can't do what you're doing. It would be too hard!"

Faith sat up and became animated as she replied, "No, it's not! You can do it! I didn't think I could. But now I know I can! Christ has given me strength and He can do the same for you!"

Hope sighed and said, "I'm sorry, Faith. I can't. It would spoil things. I'm really enjoying life at college," she said. "No, I couldn't do it."

"But think about the baby! If you don't want to raise it yourself, you could place it for adoption like I am. It would be such a gift!"

Hope leaned back again and looked up at the moon. But the moon slipped behind a cloud and the night grew darker.

"I can't, Faith. I'm sorry," she said.

A Match Made in Heaven

24

The following Monday afternoon the air was cool but the sky was filled with golden sunshine. There was only a trace of a breeze. The fall colors were magnificent, having reached their peak just days before. The reflection of the blue sky and the resplendent red, yellow, and orange leaves on the slow moving water of the Wolf River magnified the glory of the Lord. The scene would surely inspire the most vainglorious artist to praise the Creator and to cause the staunchest agnostic to question his doubts. The ceaseless beauty of creation was enough to brighten anyone's day—anyone, that is, except Kara.

Robert and Kara had decided to go for a walk before dinner on the bike path that ran along the river. The stillness of the air and the peaceful, patient flow of the water were in stark contrast to Kara's gloomy, gray, turbulent emotions. Robert had been cheered by the natural splendor, but he could see it had little effect on his wife.

"What's wrong?" he finally asked.

Kara shook her head. "Nothing," she said.

"Come on! Tell me!"

"Why? It won't do any good."

"You're still upset about the adoption that fell through, aren't you?"

"Well, why shouldn't I be?" Kara asked. "It just isn't fair! First, it's my infertility. Now, I can't even adopt a child!"

"You just have to be patient, Love."

"I'm trying. But it's hard! Do you think we'll ever be chosen? I mean *for real?*"

"You have to have faith," Robert said, as he was careful to step over a stream of tiny red ants crawling across the bike path. "Who knows? There may already be a match made in heaven for us."

Kara flashed a cynical smile. "You're always so optimistic," she said.

"I try to be."

"I'm sorry but I just can't be so optimistic."

"You can't? Why not?"

"Because."

"Because why?"

"Because I know I'm being punished! That's why!"

"Punished? How?"

"I think God aborted our adoption just like I aborted my child."

"God isn't like that. He treats us better than we deserve. The problem isn't that God hasn't forgiven you; it's that you haven't forgiven yourself."

"I don't deserve to be forgiven."

"Of course, you don't! None of us do! But God grants us grace. Now stop beating up on yourself!"

"What am I supposed to do?" Kara asked, exasperated.

"Try praising God for all that He *has* given you instead of wallowing around in self-pity."

"That's easy for you to say!" she said angrily. Then she turned and walked briskly back to the car.

Robert stood for a moment watching his wife retreat. He said quietly, "Lord, whatever you have in store for us, we can use it now!"

•••

The last Friday in October was chilly and the skies were gray. Faith had driven to Justin in the late afternoon to pick up her father. His car was in the shop and wouldn't be ready until the next afternoon. As she drove through the campus set on scenic, rolling, wooded hills along the river, Faith observed a cluster of students hanging out in front of the library. Seeing others living the life she had long imagined for herself evoked a twinge of regret and sadness. She understood all too well that her college experience was delayed because of her choice to carry her child to term.

Faith pulled into a parking slip in front of the administration building and spotted her father, briefcase in hand, talking to a small group of students. When Dr. Brandon saw his daughter, he immediately broke off his chat and began walking toward the car. As Faith waited, a young couple, obviously in love, walked by hand-in-hand on the sidewalk in front of her. They were laughing, talking, and carrying on, oblivious to the rest of the world. The joy and connectedness they shared painfully reminded Faith of her own broken relationship with Chris. This, in turn, engendered contradictory impulses. On the one hand, she blamed the baby for her break up with Chris and felt a strong resentment toward it. On the other hand, she felt a deeper bond with her child. The baby had replaced Chris as the primary object of her love.

"Hi, Kiddo," Dr. Brandon said affectionately as he climbed into the car. He was in high spirits. He kissed Faith on the cheek and asked, "Where's your mother? I was expecting her to pick me up."

"She had a late start making dinner and so I volunteered."

"Why was she late?"

"She went to Rainbow to pick up profiles so we can start looking through them."

Dr. Brandon nodded and asked, "Faith, is there something wrong?"

Faith shrugged and said, "Not really. It's no big deal."

"I know something's bothering you. What is it?"

Faith shrugged again. "Nothing," she said sadly. After reflecting for a second, she added sardonically, "Just my whole life."

Her father patted her gently on the thigh and said, "I know how difficult this has been. I'm very proud of the decisions you've made and how you're handling all of this."

Faith felt like crying and jumping into his arms like she did as a little girl. Instead, she put on a brave smile and said quietly, "Thanks, Dad."

After supper, after the table had been cleared off and the kitchen cleaned up, the Brandons sat down at the kitchen table with three profiles that Joan had brought home from the agency.

Dr. Brandon said, "I think before we start looking at the profiles, we should establish some criteria."

Faith and Ryan nodded. Then Joan said, "I think we should start with a prayer before we do anything."

"You're absolutely right! I'll lead," Dr. Brandon said as he bowed his head. "Dear, Lord, we have an awesome responsibility before us tonight as we help Faith search for the right parents to adopt her child. We pray that You would bless our efforts and guide us toward the family that You would have us choose. You know it is our hope, Lord, that we place this child into hands that will love her and care for her and raise her to be the godly woman You want her to be. Give us wisdom and discernment as we make this critical decision. We pray this in Your name, amen."

Dr. Brandon raised his head and opened his eyes to find his wife and daughter dabbing at tears. The pain that the process was bringing out in his family now brought a tear to his eye.

Ryan came to the rescue by saying, "I'll get some paper and a pen."

He jumped up from his chair and took a couple of steps to the drawer where the articles were kept. He returned to the table seconds later and said, "I'll take notes."

"Thank you, Dear," his mother said.

Dr. Brandon started off. He said, "I think we're all in agreement that the couple should be Christian and have Christian values."

"Can they be Catholic or Lutheran? Or do they have to be Baptist?" Ryan asked.

"I don't think it's that important as long as we know they have a good relationship with the Lord," Joan said.

"Okay. What else?" Ryan asked as he noted the first criterion.

"Wait!" Faith said. "How can we tell?"

"Tell what?" Ryan asked.

"Tell if they're good Christians," Faith replied.

"We'll just have to go by what's in their profile," her father said. "But we'll be meeting them before you make a final decision. We should be able to get a good idea by talking to them."

The others nodded quietly. Then Ryan said, "Next criterion."

"I think they have to have a stable marriage," Joan said.

"Yeah. You don't want anyone who's going to be divorced in a couple years," Ryan added.

"How are we going to know if they're stable?" Faith asked.

"Good question again," Ryan said.

"There really isn't any guarantee of that either," Dr. Brandon said. "We just have to proceed on faith."

As Ryan added the second criterion to the list, his mother said, "I think a mother who stays at home instead of working full-time is very important."

"I think you're right," Dr. Brandon said. "That's very important in the child's early development."

"Again. How do you know if someone isn't just *saying* she's going to stay at home? How do you know she won't put the baby in day care and work full-time?" Ryan asked.

"This is horrible! How can you know for sure about anything?" Faith asked. "Maybe I should just keep the baby and raise it myself!"

"I don't think we have to overreact here," her father said. "I'm sure that of all the couples who want to adopt a child, we'll find one couple whom we can trust. In fact, we'll probably find a couple who'll turn out to be better parents than your mother and I."

"Impossible!" Ryan objected playfully.

Everyone smiled. Then Faith said, "I'd like her to have a brother or sister."

"Yes. That's important, too," Joan said. "If they don't have other children already, they should be planning on adopting at least one more."

"Hopefully, a sister," Faith remarked teasingly to her brother.

Ryan smiled. "A brother would be better," he replied as he added to his notes.

After a short pause, Joan said, "You know, there's one important factor we seem to be neglecting."

"What's that, Dear?" Dr. Brandon asked.

"This child is going to be half black," Joan said. "We can't deny her that aspect of her identity. I think we ought to be open to black or white parents, preferably living in an ethnically diverse community. We don't want this little girl growing up in an all white community where she'll stick out like a sore thumb."

"I never really considered the baby being raised in a black family," Faith said.

"I think you should consider it, Dear," Joan said. "By traditional perspectives, a half-black baby is considered black."

"That's not right!" Ryan protested. "She's just as much white as she is black!"

"I'm not saying it's right," Joan said. "I'm saying that's how it's been. Most people in our society will perceive her as black. If there's a suitable black family, it might be in the best interests of the child to be raised where she may feel like she fits in."

"It seems to me that other things are more important," Ryan said. "What do you think, Faith?"

"I don't know. I guess you're both right. I'm more worried about whether I'll ever get to see her again. At some point I'd like to be able to tell her how much I love her. And I'd also like to be able to explain to her why I placed her for adoption."

Suddenly, tears flooded Faith's eyes and she began to weep. Joan put her arms around her daughter and wept with her. Dr. Brandon fought back his own tears as looked at his daughter with compassion. Even Ryan had a hard time swallowing the lump in his throat.

"I'm sorry," Faith said finally.

"There's nothing to be sorry about," Joan said. "I think it just shows that a semi-open adoption or an open adoption is a real important consideration."

"Are there any more criteria?" Ryan asked.

Blank stares crisscrossed the table.

"Then I guess we're done with that," Ryan said.

"How about if we start passing around the profiles?" Dr. Brandon said. "We'll keep our own notes, but let's not comment on any of the profiles until we're all done looking at them. Then we'll take a vote and see if there's a consensus. If not, we can debate the pros and cons of each couple. Of course, Faith has the final say. This is her decision after all."

"Sounds good," Ryan said.

Faith nodded in agreement.

Then Joan said, "Remember, we're not limited to these three couples. If we don't feel comfortable with any of them, we can ask to see more profiles."

They got down to work immediately. After an hour of careful study, they were ready to make a decision.

"Do any of these couples look good?" Dr. Brandon asked. "Faith, why don't you tell us your opinion first?"

"I like Robert and Kara," she said.

"Me, too!" Ryan seconded.

"How about you, Hon?" Dr. Brandon asked.

"I liked Robert and Kara."

"I thought that they were the clear choice," Dr. Brandon added.

"It's unanimous!" Ryan beamed.

"Can we call Maggie tonight and tell her we want Robert and Kara?" Faith asked. "I don't want anyone sneaking in ahead of us!"

"I think it can wait until the morning," Joan said. "Besides, Maggie may not be in the office again until Monday."

"Are you sure you don't want to see any other profiles?" Dr. Brandon asked.

"I'm sure," Faith said. "They're the ones. I just know it."

•••

Kara was standing in the living room looking out of the large picture window at the surrounding neighborhood. She had just arrived home from school and was waiting for the onslaught to begin. Her wary eye spotted a small band of sinister characters forming across the street. They were making their way up and down the block in a systematic foray. No doubt they would soon be knocking at her door making threats and demanding tribute. Before long, the menacing marauders were next door adding to their sacks of plunder. As the band of ghosts, devils, witches, and other creatures of the underworld turned their sights on the Ellison's front door and began their assault across the lawn, Kara called out to Robert, "Brace yourself! Here they come!"

She opened the door just as the first of eight looters stormed the castle.

"Trick or treat!" they shouted.

Kara picked up a large bowl of miniature candy bars from the kitchen chair she had placed near the front door.

"I have treats. Keep your tricks to yourself!" she said with a smile as she doled out the candy.

Robert walked to the door and stood behind Kara. After she passed out a treat to the last child, Robert said, "Trick or treat!"

Kara jumped. "Don't do that! You scared me!" she scolded.

"Sorry. It's just that those treats look pretty good!" he said with a smile.

"That's too bad! You'll have to wait until the trick-or-treaters are done for the night."

"What if I put on a costume and come to the front door?" he asked playfully.

"Only if it's a nice costume. I don't like all these ghosts and witches," Kara said. "If we ever have a child, he or she is going to be a princess, or an angel, something that isn't satanic."

"You're right," Robert said. "There's no sense in glorifying the occult."

Just then the phone rang.

"I'll get it," Robert said.

He walked to the kitchen and picked up the cordless phone.

"Hello," he said.

"Hello, Robert. This is Terri Moore. I've got some good news for you!"

"Just a minute. I'll get Kara on the phone."

Robert walked quickly out to the living room and gave Kara the cordless. "It's Terri Moore," he said.

He ran quickly to the bedroom to pick up the other phone. Then he heard Terri say, "Her name is Faith. I can't guarantee anything, but she appears to be more committed to adoption than Amanda."

"That's encouraging!" Kara said.

"But there is one thing you should know, and you have a right to pass on this situation if you'd like," Terri said.

"What's that?" Kara asked, her heart skipping a beat.

"You'll never have signed surrender papers from the birthfather."

"Why is that?"

"Faith doesn't know who he is or where he's from. She was raped."

"Oh! Poor girl!" Kara said. "That's awful!"

"I know. It's a shame. But she's making the best of a bad situation."

"That's good."

"It is," Terri said. "But to get back to your situation, you have to realize that there's an upside and a downside to this adoption. The upside is that even though the birthfather did not sign surrender papers and would have the right to contest the adoption, he'll never do it because if he did come forward, he would be facing rape charges. Also, he has no idea that the child even exists. The downside is that you won't have any personal or medical history of the birthfather."

"Well, I guess we'll have to live with that," Kara said. "Is the child black or biracial?"

"I'm sorry. I should have mentioned that right away. She's biracial. Faith is white. The birthfather is black."

"It's a girl?"

"Yes. I guess I should have mentioned that, too," Terri said. "And Faith is seven months pregnant."

"Well, that gives us a little time anyway," Kara said.

"So you're interested?" Terri asked.

"Yes! Of course!"

"Good. Can you make a meeting with Faith and her parents on Wednesday? Let's say about four-thirty."

"Yes!" Kara said.

"We'll be there!" Robert added.

"Good. You'll be meeting with Maggie, Faith's social worker," Terri said.

After hanging up the phone, Robert rushed down the stairs to the living room to find his wife sitting quietly on the couch staring out the picture window.

"What's wrong? That was great news! I thought you'd be happy," he said.

"Well, it is good news. It's just that I'm worried that the same thing will happen again—that the birthmother will change her mind after birth."

"That's a possibility. But you can't be holding your breath for two months. Just put it in God's hands," he said.

"I don't know if I can," Kara said. "I want to know *now* if this is a trick or a treat!"

•••

The Brandons arrived at the agency nearly fifteen minutes before Robert and Kara. Maggie led them to her office on the second floor. Faith and Joan immediately sat down on the couch and began talking to Maggie about the bagful of emotions they were feeling as they awaited the meeting. They were nervous, self-conscious, and yet anxious to meet the possible parents of their child and grandchild.

Meanwhile, Dr. Brandon's curiosity led him to the large bay window overlooking the property in back. Two tall oak trees, still clinging to a few brown curled leaves rustling in the wind, stood between the house and the renovated horse barn. Beyond the barn lay the woods. Just over the trees in the clear blue sky glared the bright orange sun setting quickly over the horizon.

As he turned his attention back to the room, Dr. Brandon heard his daughter ask, "What are they like?"

"I haven't met them yet," Maggie said. "All I know is what I've read in their profile."

"I hope they're as nice as they sound," Faith said.

When the office phone rang, Maggie picked it up and said to the receptionist, "I'll be right down." Then she announced to the Brandons, "They're here. I'll go down and greet them and we'll be up in a couple of minutes."

Faith flashed a nervous smile.

"Everything will be fine," her father said.

Maggie was smiling as she rounded the bend of the grand oak staircase. "Hello," she called out as she descended the last few steps. "You must be Robert and Kara. I'm Maggie, Faith's social worker."

They greeted each other with a handshake. Then Maggie said, "Faith and her parents are waiting upstairs. Is there anything you would like to ask me privately before we go up?"

Robert and Kara looked blankly at one another and shook their heads.

"Okay then, if you're ready, we'll go up," Maggie said.

Robert reached over and grabbed his wife's hand and gave her a reassuring wink and smile. Kara returned a nervous smile.

When Maggie led them into the office, the Brandons stood to greet the Ellisons. Kara and Faith immediately focused on each other. Kara felt a strong urge to give Faith a hug, but she held back. The Brandons then settled back on the couch while Kara and Robert sat in the two opposing wing chairs. Maggie rolled her chair from behind the desk to the sitting area. In doing so, she formed a U-shaped forum with the Brandons on her left and the Ellisons to her right.

"Why don't we start with Faith telling Robert and Kara a little bit about herself?" Maggie suggested.

Faith looked at her parents and then at Maggie and asked, "How much can I say?"

"As much as you feel comfortable with," Maggie said.

"Okay," Faith said and then let out a nervous sigh. "I'm eighteen. I've graduated from high school. I would've started college this fall if it wasn't for my...condition. I decided to wait until second semester to start school. I have a brother who is a senior in college." Then she shrugged and asked, "What else do you want to know?"

"What are you going to major in?" Robert asked quickly.

"Education. Either elementary or music."

"Really?" Kara said. "I'm an elementary teacher. And I love music!"

"We know," Faith said with a smile. "That's kind of why we picked you."

Kara smiled, but before she could say thanks, Joan interjected. "Actually, there are several things we liked about you and Robert."

"Such as?" Robert asked with an embarrassed grin.

"I think the most important thing was that you are Christians and have the right values," Joan said. "We also thought that having a mixed-race couple was a perfect situation for the child since she is biracial. We felt she would have a chance to experience both a black and a white heritage directly from her parents. We thought that would be more ideal than having two white parents or two black parents."

Robert and Kara looked at each other and smiled. Then Dr. Brandon asked, "How difficult is it to be a mixed-race couple?"

Robert smiled and said, "We get a lot of second glances, but it's becoming more common to see people of different races together. Once people get to know us, then it seems as though they're able to get beyond the race thing and start to accept us for who we really are. They begin to see us as Robert and Kara and not just 'that black man' and 'that white woman,' if you know what I mean."

Dr. Brandon nodded. He said, "We also thought it was good that you live in an ethnically diverse community. We didn't want the child to have to grow up in an all white community where she might feel more self-conscious."

"We live in a neighborhood that is mostly white," Kara said. "But the elementary school has some black kids and the junior high has a large minority of blacks and Hispanics so we think she'll fit in."

After a brief lull, Robert asked, "What do you folks do for a living?"

"I'm a college administrator," Ryle said. "Joan has always stayed at home. We felt it was important for her to be there for the kids, even after they started school."

"I hope to stay home some day," Kara said. "But right now, we're trying to build up our savings for another adoption."

"We understand that," Joan said. "Society is much different now than when we started raising our kids. Do you have a day care provider picked out?"

"I have a friend right on our block who used to be a teacher but now stays home with her two kids," Kara said. "She's already told me that she'd be willing to take care of our child if we needed someone. She's done some child-care before and so I feel a lot better about her than leaving a child with a large commercial day care center. Even so, I know it's going to be really hard to go to work and leave my child with someone else."

After another quiet moment, Kara asked, "Faith, what sort of hobbies and interests do you have?"

"I like music. I played the flute in my junior high and high school orchestras. I also play piano a bit," she said.

"Faith's too modest," Joan interjected. "She's an excellent musician. If she wanted to, she could become a professional."

"Is that right?" Kara said with a gleam in her eye. "I always wanted to be a professional musician. I played violin. I just wasn't that good."

"Mom is exaggerating," Faith said with a blush.

"I am not. You're very good, Dear," Joan said.

"She's exaggerating," Faith said again. "I also like to read a lot."

"Really? So do I," Kara said.

"I know. I saw that in your profile. We have a lot in common," Faith said.

The conversation continued for another half-hour. At the end of the meeting, Kara wrapped her arms around Faith and whispered softly, "Thank you." Faith smiled. Then they looked each other in the eye and felt the same unspoken conviction that the crossing of their paths was meant to be. The incompleteness of one was being redeemed through the sacrifice of the other. It was a minor variation on the central theme of God's creation.

Election Day! 25

When Election Day arrived, the Stuart camp was excited and optimistic. The hard work over the long campaign had apparently been fruitful. Two independent polls conducted the day before showed Vivian leading by three-to-five percent over the Republican incumbent. Hope looked forward to the evening with great anticipation. She arrived at the hotel shortly before seven and slipped her Miata into a space near the front entrance. She quickly hopped out of the car and ran to the passenger's side to help Faith out of her seat.

"The person who designed this car obviously wasn't pregnant," Faith said.

Hope smiled. "Come on! Let's go!" she said. Then she spotted a television truck at the far end of the parking lot. "Look! NBC is here! Do you think they're here to cover Mom's election?"

"I don't know. Maybe."

As they walked to the hotel entrance, a handful of pro-life demonstrators caught Faith's attention. They were parading on the sidewalk in front of the hotel to protest Vivian's stand on abortion. One placard in particular captured Faith's sympathies. It read, "Equal Rights for Unborn Women." She reflexively put her hand on her stomach as if to say, "Don't worry! I'll protect you."

When the girls entered the lobby, Hope's eyes brightened. She said excitedly, "Look! There's John Sutton, the political reporter for Channel Five News!"

Then Faith spotted a large sign in the lobby that read, "Stuart Reception." An arrow above the name pointed past the front desk and down a long hallway to a large banquet room.

"Do you want to see what it looks like?" Faith asked.

"No. We can go there later when Mom gives her victory speech," Hope said. "Let's go up to her room and see what's going on."

The girls boarded the elevator and heard a man ask a woman, "Have we gotten anything back from the exit polls?"

"Yes," the woman answered. "Vivian appears to be winning."

Hope looked at Faith with gleaming eyes and a smile that lit her face. Faith squeezed Hope's hand and returned the smile. When the door opened, they followed the man and woman off the elevator onto the fifth floor.

"What's the room number?" Faith asked.

"Five-ten."

A security guard was standing sentry at the door of the private suite, checking the guests as they arrived. Hope said to the man proudly, "I'm Vivian Stuart's daughter and this is my friend."

As they entered the suite, they found Hope's mother near the door, greeting the special guests that made up her inner circle. The girls waited patiently as Vivian chatted with the couple from the elevator.

Faith scanned the crowded suite until her eyes settled on a group sitting in front of the television. Jack Ruland was manning the remote, changing channels in rapid fire. At the same time, the other half of his attention was occupied with the telephone. Milling about the suite were many friends and supporters engaged in animated political discussions. The room was crackling with electricity. At last, Hope greeted her mother.

"Hi!" she said with a big smile.

"Hi, Honey!" her mother replied with a hug. "Hi, Faith. How are you?"

"We're fine," Faith said smiling.

"We?" Vivian said with a puzzled grin. Then she saw Faith gently rub her stomach. "Oh, yes! Of course!" she said with a laugh. "When is the due date?"

"Right around Christmas."

"Well, I hope everything goes well. Hope told me you've selected adoptive parents."

"Yes. They're very nice people."

"Good. I can see that this was definitely the right choice for you," Vivian said. "But, I'm really sorry about this! If I had not accepted this crazy challenge, I would have been with you in Florida and maybe none of this would have happened."

"It's not *your* fault," Faith said.

"Well, if there's anything I can do to help, just let me know."

Then Vivian looked at Hope again and smiled.

"How does it look?" Hope asked.

"So far, so good! Jack is already calling me Congresswoman Stuart. It has a nice ring to it, don't you think?"

"I'm very proud of you, Mom," Hope said. "Or should I call you Congresswoman Stuart?"

Just then Jack Ruland interrupted. "Excuse me, Vivian," he said, "but I think we should take a few minutes to polish up your victory speech."

"Don't you think that's kind of premature?" Vivian asked.

"Believe me," Jack responded. "Based on yesterday's polls and today's exit polls, this election is in the bag."

"All right. If you say so. Excuse us, girls."

The girls smiled at one another. Then Hope looked around and said, "Come on. Let's get something to drink."

The girls stood in line at a small makeshift bar. The bartender was a handsome young man in his early twenties with an athletic build, blue eyes, and short brown hair. Hope was attracted by his smile. Faith felt slightly jealous as Hope turned on her charm and flirted casually with the young man. Then they grabbed their Cokes and found a private corner of the suite.

"How can you be flirting while you're pregnant with another guy's child?"

"It's only a temporary condition," Hope said with a shrug. "It'll all be over tomorrow."

Faith suddenly grew despondent as she thought of Hope's child.

"Are you sure you want to go through with it. You know you can still change your mind. Think of the baby!" Faith pleaded.

Hope smiled and sighed. Then she looked around the room at all of the excitement and said, "This is what I want. And I don't want anything to get in my way!"

"But it would only inconvenience you for another seven months if you placed it for adoption."

"Sorry. I can't do it. Come on! Let's go watch the results on TV."

For the next three hours, the returns kept coming in regularly. A man got up from the couch and offered Faith his seat while Hope sat on the floor in front of her. Every time a new count came in showing Vivian in the lead, a roar rose from the partisan gathering. When the first major network projected Vivian as the winner, Pandemonium broke loose. The guests cheered, hugged one another, and offered Vivian their congratulations.

Then came a second projection by another network. Vivian was again declared the winner and another round of cheers went up. Shortly afterward, Bill Johnson, Vivian's opponent, appeared on the local channel to make his concession speech, the first in his career. At one point in his uncharacteristically short statement he said, "My biggest concern right now is not for my own political fortunes. I feel that I've let down millions of unborn children who can hear the pounding of another nail in their coffins."

The verity of the statement gripped Faith and made her realize that Vivian's election was nothing to celebrate. At the same time, a large man standing behind Faith gave out a loud snort of a laugh. He said sarcastically, "Yeah, right, Johnson! You're just ticked off that the religious right didn't come through for you this time!" Then he bellowed another loud laugh. Several of the others laughed with him. Faith felt strangely alone in the room. Even Hope, who was also laughing, now seemed oddly foreign to her.

Then the station cut back to its chief political analyst. He commented, "Vivian Stuart's political future seems very bright tonight. An upset victory over a powerful, long-time incumbent is something of an achievement in itself. Add to that, that she did it in a year in which it looks like her own political party is going to lose both houses of Congress, you truly realize how remarkable her victory is here tonight. This could be the birth of a new political star."

Hope was giddy with pride. But the highlight of the evening was yet to come. Just as Vivian was about to lead her entourage to the banquet hall to give her victory speech, a call came in from Washington. Jack Ruland tried to quiet the crowd as he called Vivian to the phone. Then he announced in a loud whisper, "It's the President!"

The room was humming with excitement. James Ashton, standing next to Vivian, tried to hush the crowd. Vivian held the phone to one ear and held her hand over her other ear to filter out the chatter going on around her. After a moment, a silence settled in as everyone listened intently to Vivian's side of the conversation.

They heard her say, "Thank you, Mr. President…Yes, of course. From now on I'll call you 'George'…Yes, I can see that we have our work cut out for us…No matter what the numbers are on the Hill, I'm not going to back down on women's rights…Well, thank you for your support…Yes, I'll do that…Good-bye."

Then she switched off the phone and announced, "That was President Stanton."

Hope looked at Faith with sparkling eyes. Faith returned a polite smile.

"He congratulated me and said we had a lot of work to do. He wants me to meet with him as soon as I arrive in Washington."

The President's call was like uncorking a bottle of champagne. The emotional energy bottled up in the suite now bubbled up and spilled out into the hallway. Vivian, James Ashton, and Jack Ruland led the way down to the banquet hall to meet the larger crowd of supporters on hand to celebrate the biggest story of the election.

Hope and Faith trailed Vivian as she entered the room. A large ovation broke out as Vivian triumphantly marched up the short set of stairs to the top of the platform and then to the lectern at center stage. Faith waited in the wings and watched as Hope followed her mother onto the platform and stood with Vivian's other core supporters. Hope could not contain her glee. She was bouncing up and down, clapping and smiling, while looking out on the enthusiastic crowd below. Several times Vivian put her hand up to quiet the crowd, but each time they cheered louder. She took a moment to give Jack and James a big hug and then turned to her daughter. Their eyes connected and they moved toward each other with open arms for a warm embrace. Then Hope pulled away to wipe the tears of joy from her eyes. Finally, the crowd began to settle as Vivian again stepped to the microphone.

"Thank you," she said. "Thank you for your hard work and support! This victory is because of you!"

Vivian applauded her supporters. Another roar rose from the crowd. The pattern of brief statements followed by short, loud cheers continued as Vivian worked through her list of obligatory acknowledgments. At last, she moved on to the substance of her campaign.

"This victory is a victory not just for the Democratic Party or for Vivian Stuart," she said. "It's a victory for women everywhere! That's been the crux of my campaign. When I take my seat on Capitol Hill, I promise you that I will not only be the voice of my constituents, I will be the voice of women everywhere. We are in the midst of a continuing struggle for political equality between the sexes. And the forces now amassing themselves against us, the radical religious right, are fighting to take away from women the fundamental freedom that is at the core of our movement. That freedom is, of course, the right to reproductive choice. And I will do what one woman can to protect that right for my daughter and for all women in America."

As Hope was relishing the spotlight near her mother, Faith was struggling with the dissonance in her spirit. She had difficulty reconciling the sign carried by the protester outside the hotel with the message being delivered inside. Her intuition told her that Hope's child was a girl. If that was the case, then there was, in fact, a very young woman in the crowd whose voice would never be heard and whose rights would not be protected because her mother was choosing to silence her forever. The problem was distinct and disturbing. Vivian's position on abortion was not really about women's rights at all; rather, it was about a conflict of rights. There were the mother's reproductive rights versus her daughter's right to life. Since the conflict was between two females, it could not possibly be a "gender equity" issue. The situation came down to nothing more than a power grab by the stronger of the two females.

As Faith witnessed the hoax being played out before her eyes, the hypocrisy became even more evident; she recalled Hope telling her how Jason had pleaded with her to grant the child life. Where, she thought, is the gender equity for the father of Hope's child?

When Vivian had finished her speech, there was one final cheer for the victor. After a few final congratulatory hugs on stage, Hope joined Faith once again and said, "I know it's getting late, but I'd like to stay around for a while. Why don't you take my car? You can pick me up in the morning about seven-thirty. I'll get a ride home with someone else tonight."

Haman's Gallows 26

Eliza was sitting at the kitchen table the next morning drinking coffee and reading her Bible when Hope walked in fully dressed, ready for her appointment.

"What are you doin' up so early?" Eliza asked. "I thought you'd be sleepin' in after all that celebratin' last night."

"Faith and I have plans for breakfast."

"Is that the truth?" Eliza asked, peering up over her reading glasses.

"Of course, it's the truth! Why would I lie?"

"Because I get the feelin' you're hidin' somethin'."

"What would I be hiding?"

Eliza sat back in her chair. With piercing eyes she asked, "You're pregnant, aren't you?"

"No, of course not!"

Eliza stared Hope down in silence. Hope rolled her eyes and let out a sigh. She said, "You're right. I'm pregnant."

"I thought so. Sit down."

Hope followed orders and took a seat across the table from Eliza.

"You're gonna have an abortion, aren't you?"

"Yes," Hope said, squirming in her chair, avoiding Eliza's eyes.

"Your mother doesn't know, does she?"

"No. And you can't tell her!"

263

"Don't you think she should know?"

"It's none of her business!" Hope said. "Besides, she's pro-choice! She wouldn't stop me anyway."

"Even when it's her own grandchild?"

"I don't know. What's the difference?"

Eliza took a sip from her coffee mug. "Do you know what you're gettin' yourself into?" she asked.

"Yes. I've thought it all through. I don't have a choice!"

"Why do you say that?"

Hope shrugged. She said, "A baby would mess things up, that's all."

Eliza nodded thoughtfully. Then she asked, "Have you ever heard the story of Haman? It's in the Bible."

"No."

"Well, let me tell it to you," Eliza said.

"Faith will be here any minute."

"This won't take long," Eliza said with a smile.

Hope let out a sigh. "Go ahead," she said, obviously annoyed.

Eliza smiled gently again and then began her tale.

"Haman was an important noble in the land of King Xerxes. He didn't like the Jews. In fact, there was one Jew in particular that he hated most because this Jew would not bow down to him. His name was Mordecai. Haman asked the king for permission to get rid of the Jews once and for all.

"Now Haman really felt he had to do somethin' about Mordecai. The people around him, includin' his wife, advised him to build a gallows where Mordecai could be hanged. Well, to make a long story short, the plan backfired. Mordecai had found favor with King Xerxes and the king had Haman executed on the gallows that Haman had built for Mordecai."

Eliza sat back and took another sip of coffee, apparently finished with her story. After a silent moment, Hope asked, "Is that it?"

"Yes."

"So, what's the point?"

"I think there's a parallel here, girl. Can't you see it?"

"No. Not really."

Eliza was obliged to explain. "It's simple," she said. "Havin' an abortion is like buildin' a gallows. And if you're not careful, the gallows you're buildin' for your child may do *you* in."

"Don't be silly. Women don't die in abortions," Hope said.

"Maybe there aren't many who die physically, but emotionally, a lot do after they realize what they've done."

"Well, thanks for your concern. But I really think I'm doing the right thing," Hope said as the doorbell rang. "That's Faith. I've got to go. Please don't tell Mom."

She got up from the table and walked around to the other side to give Eliza a hug.

"I'll be prayin' for you," Eliza said.

"I'll be back before noon."

As Eliza turned back to her Bible and coffee, a teardrop dampened the seventh chapter of the book of Esther.

•••

When Hope stepped out the front door, Faith was waiting in the passenger's seat of Hope's Miata.

"Hi!" Faith said as Hope climbed into the driver's seat.

"Hi," Hope said, obviously tired and distracted.

"How late did you celebrate?"

"Until about three," Hope said with a yawn as she backed out of the driveway.

"How'd you get home?"

"Mike gave me a ride."

"Who's Mike?"

"The bartender in Mom's suite."

Faith just shook her head. She said in a playfully sarcastic tone, "You're just the Energizer Rabbit of promiscuity, aren't you?"

"It isn't what you think," Hope said, annoyed by the remark.

"Okay. I'm sorry," Faith said. After a quiet moment, she added, "You know you can still change your mind."

"I'm not changing my mind! And I don't care what you or Eliza think! It's my life!" Hope said testily.

"Okay, okay!"

Hope sighed. "I'm sorry," she said. "I'm just tired."

Hope parked in the rear lot of the clinic. They entered through the back door and found Hope's uncle coming out of Lisa's office.

"Well, look who's here!" Tom said with a broad smile. "How does it feel to be the daughter of a Congresswoman-elect?"

"How does it feel to be the brother of a Congresswoman-elect?" Hope replied.

"Hello, Hope," Lisa said, putting on an insincere smile. She ignored Faith.

"Hi, Lisa," Hope said coolly.

"I'm sorry I can't chat right now," Tom said. "I have to get to work. It looks like we're going to have a busy day today, and I'm starting out short-handed. Dr. Lesniak is going to be late."

"Uncle Tom," Hope said. "Would you mind if Faith and I waited in your office?"

"Sure. Go ahead."

"Thanks."

Once inside her uncle's office, Hope closed the door behind them. As they sat down, Hope asked, "Did you see the dirty look Lisa gave you?"

"Yeah, I saw it."

"She's still mad at me for bringing you here. She didn't like getting caught in her lie about the cyst."

"I wouldn't trust her about anything," Faith said. Then she asked, "Did you see the paper this morning?"

"No. What did it say?"

"There was a front page article about your mother. It said her victory was the only bright spot the Democrats had in the whole election."

"Really?"

"Yeah."

"Well, when we get done here, would you mind stopping with me to get some copies? I've been keeping a secret scrapbook for Mom."

"How nice! I bet she'll really appreciate that," Faith said.

"I hope so."

"Just save some pages in the scrapbook for the next election."

"Why? What do you mean?"

"Well, the paper said that Yates is planning to retire from the Senate in two years, and your mom could be a leading candidate to replace him."

"Really!"

"It's just speculation."

"Still, if she was elected to the Senate, I could work for her in Washington after I graduate. Wouldn't that be exciting!"

"I guess."

"What's wrong? Wouldn't you want to go to Washington?"

"Not really. I'm not interested in politics."

"Well, I like being where the action is!" Hope said.

Then a nurse knocked at the door and entered with a hospital gown draped over her arm. She looked, first at Faith, and then at Hope and appeared to be puzzled.

"That's for me," Hope said in reference to the gown.

The nurse smiled and said, "I thought so. Otherwise, I was thinking your friend sure took her time to decide."

The girls laughed. But as the nurse left, Hope noticed a change in Faith's countenance.

"What's wrong?" she asked. "You look almost sad."

Faith strained to put on a smile. "It's nothing," she said quietly.

"Come on! There's something bothering you. What is it?"

Faith sighed. "I was just thinking," she said.

"About what?"

"Nothing."

"Come on! Tell me."

"It's nothing. Really!"

"Come on! It's got to be something. And I bet I can tell what it is!"

Faith shrugged. Finally she said, "I was just thinking how, because of a few twists of fate, my child still has hope. Your baby isn't going to be so lucky."

"Don't talk like that!" Hope said. Her mood had now taken its own sullen turn. "This isn't easy for me you know. I have some regrets. And I really do feel bad for Jason. But, you know, I've been thinking; if everyone acted unselfishly, no one would ever be happy. Sometimes, if you're going to be happy, you've got to do things for yourself and not worry about others. I think if everyone took responsibility for his or her own happiness, then we wouldn't have so many miserable people in the world."

"I think the opposite is true," Faith said. "I think if everyone tried to make others happy, then everyone *would be* happy."

A moment later the nurse returned. She said, "We're ready if you are."

Hope took a deep breath. She said, "Wish me good luck."

"I'll be praying for you," Faith said. She reached out and squeezed Hope's hand as she passed by on her way out of the office. "And I'll be praying for the baby," she added in a despondent whisper.

The office door was left ajar but Faith lacked the energy to close it. It made her uneasy, especially when she heard a patient sobbing on her way to the recovery room. She sat back in her chair, closed her eyes, and prayed that by some miracle, Hope would change her mind and the child's life would be saved. But in the midst of her prayer, Faith succumbed to weariness from the late night before and dozed off. She had been asleep for only a short while when she was awakened by the nurse.

"Hope is in the recovery room. She would like to see you," she said.

Faith followed the nurse to the recovery room. With help from the nurse, she pulled a chair next to Hope's cot. As she sat down, Faith noticed two other women in recovery.

"How do you feel?" Faith asked.

"All right," Hope said. "I feel a little uncomfortable."

Faith gazed compassionately at her friend and nodded.

"You think I'm going to hell for this, don't you?" Hope asked.

The question caught Faith off guard. She said simply, "I don't know."

"Come on!" Hope said. "Tell me what you really think."

Faith hesitated. Finally she said, "God will forgive you if you're truly sorry."

"Well, I am sorry in a way," Hope said. "But, I'm relieved, too." After a short moment of reflection, she added, "I wouldn't have done it if the circumstances were different, you know."

"I know," Faith said.

The girls were quiet for a moment. Then Hope sighed and said, "I think the baby is better off not being born into this crazy world."

Faith wanted to protest, but an argument now would be fruitless; she let the matter go with a gentle nod. Then the nurse came by to take Hope's blood pressure. She was casually familiar with Hope from her summer employment at the clinic.

"Your blood pressure is ninety-four over sixty. That's a little bit low, Hope."

"I have low blood pressure all the time."

"Well, we'll keep an eye on it," the nurse said and left.

"I wonder how Mom's feeling right now?" Hope said. "I wonder if she's recovered from the celebration? She's supposed to have some TV interviews today."

"I'm sure she's doing fine," Faith said.

Hope nodded. She said, "I'd like to see what the newspapers are saying."

"Do you want me to go buy the *Journal*?"

"It can wait."

"It's no problem," Faith insisted. "You rest while I go get it."

While Faith was on her errand, the nurse returned to check Hope's blood pressure.

"You're ninety-two over fifty-eight. Your pulse is ninety," she said.

The numbers meant nothing to Hope, but the nurse decided to check again soon. Faith walked in just as the nurse was leaving.

"Hi! You're still here," she said jokingly to Hope.

"Yeah. Actually, I had fallen asleep. I woke up again when the nurse came in."

Then Tom appeared. "How's it going?" he asked.

"Okay," Hope said with a weak smile.

"Great! I just came in to check. You had a little more bleeding than normal but it's nothing to worry about. I'll be back in a little while," he said. Then he disappeared as quickly as he came.

"Well, your mother made the front page!" Faith said excitedly as she showed Hope the paper. "There's a picture of her giving her speech."

"Cool!" Hope said. "I'm sure James arranged this."

Faith read the article aloud. Then she opened the paper and found another article on Vivian. Hope's eyes lit up when the article mentioned her name.

"It looks like you're something of a celebrity, too," Faith teased.

"Get out!" Hope said with a laugh. Then she said, "If you don't mind, I'm going to close my eyes. I didn't get much sleep last night."

"Go ahead. I'll read the paper."

The nurse returned half-an-hour later to check Hope's vital signs. Tom came in just as she finished. The nurse said to him, "Her blood pressure is ninety over fifty-six and her pulse is ninety-six."

"Make sure she's stable before you let her go," he replied.

When they were alone again, Faith asked, "Are you planning anything special for your birthday?"

"Yeah. I'm going to register to vote."

"That sounds like fun," Faith said with a laugh.

Hope laughed too and said, "I know it sounds dumb but I was disappointed that my birthday is so late. I think it would have been neat to see my mother's name on the ballot. I would have liked to have voted for her."

Faith nodded. "So what are your real plans?" she asked.

"Mom is taking me to Washington for the weekend."

"Oh really? So you won't be coming home?"

"No."

"Then I'd better give this to you now," Faith said as she handed Hope a card.

"Thank you!" Hope said. "I wish you could come to Washington with us."

Faith smiled. "In my condition, I'd better stay close to home," she said.

Hope smiled and said, "I guess you're right."

Faith leaned over and gave her friend a hug. Then Hope closed her eyes and nodded off to sleep again. It wasn't long before the nurse came by to check on her.

"Let's see how we're doing," she said. After taking Hope's blood pressure, she added, "It looks like you're still low but at least you're stable."

"Does that mean I can go home now? I've been here two hours already."

The nurse hesitated. Finally she said, "Your vital signs aren't the greatest and your uncle wanted me to keep an eye on you."

"Oh, come on, Joyce!" she said. "I'm missing all the excitement at home!"

"Well, why don't you sit up for a few minutes and we'll see how you're doing?"

The nurse gave Hope a hand as she struggled to sit up on the edge of the cot.

"My stomach hurts," she said with a grimace.

"Cramping is a normal side effect. You're bound to have some discomfort," the nurse said.

Hope slid off the edge of the bed and stood up. "Where are my clothes?" she asked.

But before she could get an answer, she swooned. The nurse caught her and sat her on the cot again.

"I'm so dizzy!" Hope said.

"You'd better sit here a couple of minutes first before you try that again."

"Is anything wrong?" Faith asked. "She doesn't look so good."

"A lot of women get lightheaded after a procedure," the nurse said. "It's like giving blood."

Faith had never given blood before but nodded as if she understood.

"Just sit here for five minutes and I'll be back to check on you," the nurse said.

A moment later Hope complained, "My stomach really hurts."

"Just sit and take it easy. You'll be okay," Faith said.

"I can't! Hand me my clothes," Hope said as she stood up on her own. She was still lightheaded. Then she felt something wet running down her leg. She looked down and saw a puddle of blood forming at her feet. Her knees buckled. Faith tried to catch her but couldn't reach her in time. Hope collapsed in a pile in a pool of her own blood.

"Hope!" Faith cried.

The nurse, who had been attending to the other women in recovery, turned around and saw Hope lying on the floor. Faith leaned over her friend and shouted hysterically, "Hope! Hope!"

Lisa heard the commotion from down the hall. She ran to the recovery room and saw Hope lying in a sea of red. "I'll get Dr. Morlon!" she exclaimed.

Tom had just finished another "procedure" when Lisa shouted from the door, "Tom! Come to recovery! Quickly!"

"What's wrong?" he asked as he raced down the hall.

"It's Hope! I don't know what happened!"

As they hurried into the room, the nurse said, "I think she's unconscious!"

"Move out of the way!" Tom said as he pulled Faith away from her friend's side. Faith watched in horror as several members of the clinic staff scurried to help.

"Help me move her back on the cot!" Tom said to the nurse.

"I don't know what happened," the nurse said anxiously. "I was with another patient, and I heard a scream and looked around and saw her lying on the floor."

Blood was everywhere. Tom felt Hope's stomach. It was firm.

"Her stomach is distended! I think she's been bleeding internally!" he said to Lisa in a loud, agitated tone. "You'd better call an ambulance right away!"

"Can't we just take her in the car?" Lisa asked. "It doesn't look good to have an ambulance pull up to the clinic."

"Call an ambulance!" Tom shouted. "My niece is in danger here!"

"Oh, great! Another botched abortion!" Lisa thought as she stormed out.

Tom was perspiring profusely as he worked feverishly to slow the massive bleeding. He said anxiously to the nurse, "Keep the pressure on right there!"

Tom hurried toward his office. Lisa met him in the hallway and said, "The ambulance is on its way!"

Tom said, "I have to go to the hospital on this! Call Hershowitz and tell him we're coming! Have Lesniak do what he can here. Then call the other doctors and see if anyone can fill in. Otherwise, cancel!"

Faith was in shock. She stared down through teary eyes at her friend lying helplessly on the cot. Suddenly, Lisa grabbed her from behind and said, "You can't be in here! You have to wait out front."

Faith was distraught. Tears flowed down her cheeks as Lisa led her out of the room. She looked back at Hope but couldn't see her through the attending nurses.

She asked Lisa, "Which hospital are you taking her to?"

"Elston."

"Well, I'm going there!" Faith cried as she broke away from Lisa and ran down the hall toward the back exit.

Tom was hurrying out of his office as Faith passed by.

"Is she going to be all right?" Faith asked.

"I don't know!" he said as he ran down the hallway toward recovery.

Faith's heart sank. "Oh, God! Please help! Don't let her die!" she prayed. Hurrying to Tom's office, she frantically grabbed Hope's purse and rushed to the back exit. By now, her eyes were thick with tears and her hands were trembling. When she opened the door, she heard the siren of the approaching ambulance. By the time she crossed the parking lot to Hope's Miata, the ambulance had pulled up to the back door of the clinic. She saw two men jump out of the vehicle and race to the back to open the rear doors. At the same time, Tom and two nurses wheeled Hope outside on a stretcher. The men quickly transferred Hope into the ambulance with

Tom jumping in with her. Immediately the sirens were blaring and they were off to the hospital. Faith was in hot pursuit.

Inside the ambulance, the paramedics worked feverishly. The driver was on the telemetry phone communicating with the emergency room base station while the other began taking Hope's blood pressure and pulse.

"What happened?" asked the paramedic taking the vital signs.

"A 'D and C' complication. I think she's bleeding internally. Her stomach's distended," Tom said.

"How old is she?"

"Eighteen. No, seventeen. Her birthday's next week."

The driver began reporting back to the station.

"We've got a seventeen-year-old female in the rig. She had a 'D and C' in the clinic. Possible internal bleeding in the abdomen. She's unconscious."

The other paramedic shouted, "B.P. is seventy over palp!"

Tom put his head in his hands. The driver continued his report.

"Blood pressure is very low. We've got a line of saline started and it's wide open. She's on oxygen!"

"Hurry in! And keep the fluids running," came the reply.

While fighting back the lump in his throat, Tom whispered in Hope's ear, "Come on, Hope! Stay alive! You can do it!"

Within minutes the ambulance pulled up to the emergency room entrance. A team was waiting to take Hope directly to the trauma room. As the paramedics and hospital staff pulled Hope out of the vehicle and began wheeling her into the building, Dr. Hershowitz, a long-time friend and contemporary, pulled Tom aside and asked, "What happened this time?"

"I don't know! She was in recovery and doing all right," Tom said, shaking his head. "She tried standing up and then collapsed. She's hemorrhaging really bad and I can't stop the bleeding! I think I might have severed an artery."

"You've got to get out of this business, Tom! I'm not going to cover up for you anymore!" Hershowitz said.

"Just pull her out of this! The girl is my niece!"

"Vivian's daughter?"

"Yes."

"Oh, God! The media's going to be swarming all over this one!"

Meanwhile, Faith arrived at the hospital in time to see the ambulance parked in front of the emergency room door.

"Lord! Please don't let Hope die!" she cried.

She parked Hope's Miata in the lot and ran into the emergency room. By the time she got inside, Hope had been wheeled to the trauma room. Faith ran up to the reception desk and asked urgently, "Hope Stuart! Where did they take her?"

The round, middle-aged, black woman looked up over her glasses and asked quietly, "Who?"

"The girl they just brought in on the stretcher. Where is she?"

The woman answered calmly, "They took her back to trauma. You can wait here," she said, pointing to the waiting area.

"How can I know what's happening to her?" Faith whined.

"A doctor will come out and let you know," the woman said.

Back in the trauma room, the crew began cutting away the bloody hospital gown while Dr. Hershowitz barked out orders in rapid fire.

"We need an abdominal needle aspiration! Quickly!"

He was given a large syringe that he injected immediately into Hope's stomach. As he drew back on the syringe, it turned red with blood.

"She's definitely bleeding in there. What are her vitals?"

"Sixty over palp. Her pulse is one-sixty," the nurse answered.

"Did anyone call the blood bank? Get 'O'!" he shouted. "As soon as it comes, dump in six units right away! She's lost a lot of blood!"

The emergency room clerk peeked through the door and asked, "Has anybody contacted her parents?"

"I'm her uncle. I'll sign," Tom said. As he exited with the clerk, she said, "We really need for you to call her parents."

"Where's the phone?" he said. Then he thought, "How am I going to explain this to Vivian?"

The clerk pointed him toward the phone on her desk. Eliza answered. "Sorry. She's busy, Tom. There are people here from Channel Six taping an interview."

"This is an emergency, Eliza! I'm at the hospital with Hope. It's serious!"

"Oh, Lord! I'll get her right away!"

When Tom returned to the trauma room, there were tears in his eyes. He asked, "How's she doing?"

Dr. Hershowitz replied, "Not well. She may have lost too much blood!"

Then a nurse reported, "She's dropped to fifty-two over palp!"

Tom shook his head and said, "I don't believe this is happening!"

Meanwhile, Vivian fought back tears as she hung up the phone. She grabbed her purse off the kitchen counter and said to Eliza, "Tell them I had to leave!" She hurried to the garage and was soon on her way.

Eliza was in tears as she shuffled into the living room to inform the television crew of Vivian's hasty departure to the hospital.

"What about our interview?" the reporter asked.

Eliza just shook her head.

The reporter said to his cameraman, "Let's go to the hospital! There may be a story in this!"

Back at the emergency room, Dr. Hershowitz shouted, "Where's that blood?"

"Here it comes!" somebody said.

"Start pouring it in!"

"She's down to forty-five over palp!" the nurse said.

"She's going into cardiac arrest! Administer CPR!"

Tom bit his lower lip and combed his hands through his hair.

"Start zapping her and push the drugs!" Dr. Hershowitz barked.

The crew tried to revive Hope half a dozen times with electric stimulation, but it was no use. There was no blood pressure and no pulse.

"Okay. That's it!" Dr. Hershowitz said reluctantly.

Tom shouted angrily, "No! Keep trying!"

"Sorry, Tom. She's gone," Dr. Hershowitz said.

Tom pounded his fist into his hand and stared up at the ceiling for a long moment. Finally, he drew a deep breath and walked slowly out of the trauma room toward the waiting area to meet his sister. He had lost patients before, but he had never dealt with death personally as he had to now.

Vivian had just burst through the door into the waiting area as Tom appeared from the trauma room. Faith, who had been praying fervently, stood up as she saw Vivian rush to the reception desk. At the same time, the two women spotted Tom as he walked slowly toward Vivian. There was a tear in his eye. His lower lip trembled. Faith looked on as Tom put his arms around Vivian.

"She's gone!" he said in a whisper.

"No!" Vivian screamed as she pushed away from his embrace. With tightly closed fists, she began beating her brother on the chest. As Tom struggled to control his sister, Faith fell faint to the floor.

Esther's Choice 27

The high pressure system that brought sunshine, clear skies, and mild weather to the Midwest on Tuesday had moved on to the east by Wednesday afternoon; a low pressure system that brought in a line of thunder showers, overcast skies, and cool temperatures had taken its place. Those close to Hope went through a similar transition upon her death.

Jason was deeply asleep in his dorm room when there was a knock at the door. A few seconds later, the light tapping ascended into heavy blows and he was jarred awake. He sat up in bed, groggy and irritable. When the pounding continued, he yelled, "Just a minute! I'm coming!"

Jason trudged to the door with a big yawn.

"Oh, it's you!" he said as he opened the door. He left it ajar and shuffled back to his bed and sat down. Then he put his face in his hands and rubbed his eyes. "What time is it?" he asked.

"It's just after four," Ryan said as he closed the door behind him.

"What brings you here?" Jason asked through another yawn.

"I've got some bad news, man."

"What happened?"

"Hope had an abortion this morning. Faith was there with her."

Jason returned his face to his hands, shook his head, and said angrily, "I begged her not to do it. That was my child! I feel like strangling her! "

"You don't have to."

"What do you mean?" Jason asked, his anger burning away his sleepy fog. "She had complications. They took her to the emergency room."

"No! You're kidding?"

Ryan took a deep breath and sighed. He said, "She died of a massive internal hemorrhage."

Jason jumped up from his bed.

"You're lying!"

Ryan shook his head. "I'm sorry," he said.

"Oh, man!"

Tears welled up in Jason's eyes. His knees buckled and he grabbed the dresser for support. Then, in a sudden violent eruption, he pounded his fist on top of the dresser.

"I told her not to do it!" he shouted angrily.

"Sorry, man," Ryan said meekly.

Jason sat down heavily on the bed. Shaking his head, he exclaimed bitterly, "Somebody's going to pay for this!"

•••

Juan Cantu was rained out of work Thursday afternoon. He went home early and started in on the bathroom, installing a new countertop, sink, and faucet. Shortly before six, Maria was in the kitchen watching the evening news while preparing dinner. Suddenly, she cried out to her husband, "Juan! Come here! ¡Pronto!"

Juan dropped his tools and ran to the kitchen.

"What's the matter?"

"¡Mira! The clinic is on TV!"

"How come?"

"Listen!"

A reporter was standing in front of the clinic with a microphone in hand. Then the picture shifted abruptly to a group of pro-life protesters across the street, marching back and forth, carrying signs, and chanting slogans. Maria turned the volume up as the camera focused again on the reporter.

"Early indications from the coroner's office suggest that Hope Stuart's death was the result of massive internal bleeding stemming from an abortion performed here at Women's Health Clinic of DuKane," the reporter said. "The young woman's uterine artery had been severed and had bled into her abdomen. By the time she arrived at the emergency room at Elston Hospital, her blood pressure was critically low. Soon after being admitted, she went into full cardiac arrest. After several attempts to resuscitate her, she was pronounced dead yesterday morning, just hours after her mother, Vivian Stuart, was elected to the House of Representatives. Sources close to the Congresswoman-elect say she is in seclusion with her friends and advisers. She will have a public statement sometime after the funeral, which is set for Saturday.

"An ironic twist to this story is that the doctor who allegedly performed the abortion, Dr. Thomas Morlon, is the young woman's uncle. Dr. Morlon has not been available for comment. Jim Wallace reporting live from the Women's Health Clinic of DuKane. Back to you, Steve."

Maria turned down the volume and looked at her husband. She said, "I don't like it that you work there. It's an evil place."

Juan nodded. "I'll look for another job," he said. "I'll tell Dr. Morlon I'll work one more week. I'll leave him a note tomorrow."

•••

Tom had also seen the television reports that evening, and they infuriated him. But he turned the anger inward and shut himself up like a clam. It mattered little, however. Beth was angry, too, and would not talk to him. His three teenage girls were afraid to raise the topic and so nobody talked through dinner. The tension in the house was suffocating. Tom went to his study and closed the door. He called Lisa and said, "I'm coming over!"

When Tom arrived, Lisa opened the door but immediately turned and walked to the kitchen where she had been watching television. Tom followed and the two sat down at the dinette table.

Lisa said, "The reports on TV are going to be bad for business!"

"I know. I saw them."

"We'll probably have some cancellations tomorrow. I still don't understand what happened. She was looking normal in the recovery room."

"I told you what happened," Tom said. "It was an accident. When I perforated the uterus, I must have also nicked the uterine artery."

"Then why didn't she start hemorrhaging right away?"

"The artery must have clotted itself—kind of a natural tamponade. But there was enough leakage that as she was lying in recovery, it distended her abdomen. When she stood up, the clot broke open. It's one of those things you can't tell is happening until—" he said, his voice trailing off at the end.

"Until it's too late," Lisa said.

Tom nodded. Suddenly he pounded his fist on the table and burst out angrily. "Why did this have to happen to Hope of all people?"

"It's a shame," Lisa said. "Hope had a lot going for her."

Tom shifted in his chair, leaned way back, and stared at the ceiling. Then he lowered his gaze and looked at Lisa. He said, "You know, I was thinking today how, if any one of a number of things had been different, Hope would still be alive."

"Like what?"

"Well, if Hope hadn't been so careless for one. Or, if she hadn't met that guy in the first place."

"Kids are going to experiment with sex, Tom," Lisa said. "We can't stop them. All we can do is encourage them to use condoms. Still, mistakes are going to happen. That's why we're in business."

"But we shouldn't be compounding their mistakes," he said.

"Don't blame yourself for Hope's death."

"I'm not," Tom said. "If anyone is to blame, it's that nurse who moved her along too quickly. I told her to keep a close eye on Hope."

"Well, in her defense, Hope seemed to be doing all right."

"Yes, but her blood pressure was low, and I gave the nurse specific instructions to watch her closely," Tom said. "And Lesniak coming in late didn't help either. I felt like I had to rush to get things done. It's a miracle we didn't have more complications!"

"I've been telling you for a month now that we ought to be recruiting some more help."

"Lisa, we've gone over this before!" Tom said. "It's not that easy to recruit. Doctors are worried about the stigma. And others are afraid some lunatic will take a shot at them. In fact, I've been thinking about closing down the clinic for a couple of days to let things cool off."

"We can't do that!" Lisa protested. "We'd be losing a heck of a lot of business!"

"I feel like I ought to do something," Tom said. "Maybe it would pacify Beth and the kids. They won't even talk to me. Neither will my sister."

"Do you really care?" Lisa scoffed. "Beth isn't making you happy. And you and Vivian weren't that close anyway."

Then Lisa got up from her chair, walked around the table, and stood behind Tom. As she began massaging his neck and shoulders, she whispered in his ear, "You know who can make you happy, Tom."

Lisa leaned over to Tom's right and tilted his head toward her. She seduced him with a long, wet kiss. Taking his hand, she coaxed him from his chair and led him to the bedroom.

•••

By Friday morning, Thursday's heavy rain had dissipated to a light mist with lingering overcast skies. It gave Vivian even less desire to get out of bed, something that had never been difficult for her before Hope's death. Like the lingering skies, Vivian was emotionally spent and her life was now gloomy and gray. All she had worked to accomplish in her life, including her election to Congress, no longer mattered now that Hope was lost forever.

Just two days before, Vivian had been enjoying the greatest high in her life. Her possibilities seemed endless. Her skies were clear and blue for as far as she could see. Then the botched abortion happened and the storms began without warning. And she hadn't even a clue that her daughter was pregnant! In spite of all her other achievements, she now felt a failure because she had failed as a parent.

After suffering another sleepless night, Vivian reluctantly sat up on the edge of her bed. She knew the next two days would be the most difficult days of her life. Today would be the wake, tomorrow the funeral. And along with having to share her grief with her close friends and acquaintances, she would have to do it under the watchful eye of the media. She put her face in her hands and asked in quiet desperation, "God! Why?"

Eliza was in her customary chair pouring over her Bible when Vivian came down to breakfast.

"What can I get you this mornin'?" Eliza asked.

Vivian dismissed breakfast with the wave of her hand.

"But you've got to have somethin'," Eliza said. "You haven't eaten a morsel of food for the past two days."

"I'll have some coffee."

"Comin' right up."

"Don't get up," Vivian said. "I'll get it."

"Nonsense! It's my job," Eliza said. "You just sit down!"

Vivian relented. Eliza returned with the coffee forthwith and sat down across the table from Vivian.

"Did you get any sleep last night?" Eliza asked.

"None. I've haven't had more than a couple hours of sleep since Monday night. This whole thing is wearing me out. I really don't know if I can go on."

"I'm sorry," Eliza said.

"Why? It's not your fault. I'm the one who should be sorry. If I were a better parent, none of this would have happened."

"Don't blame yourself," Eliza said.

Vivian smiled as if to say, "That's absurd. Of course, it's my fault." Instead, she said, "I don't think it's really sunk in yet. It's so hard for me to sit here and think that Hope is never going to join us again for one of those early morning talks over coffee. I'm going to miss her so much!"

Suddenly she broke down into tears. Eliza got up to console her, but Vivian put her hand up as if to say, "Sit down. I'm okay." Then she began to mop her eyes with a damp tissue she pulled out of her robe.

"Perhaps this isn't the time to bring this up," Eliza said, "but you know, you lost a grandchild the other day, too."

"I don't even want to think about that!" Vivian said tersely.

Eliza sipped her coffee. She admitted, "All of this may be my fault."

"How could that be?" Vivian asked scornfully.

"Well, the truth is, I've been prayin' for you for a long time. I've been praying that you just might see enough trouble in your life that you'd turn to the Lord Jesus. I was praying for a little godly sorrow for you. Only I didn't think it would be anythin' like this!"

"Godly sorrow? What are you talking about?" Vivian asked.

"Second Corinthians 7:10 says, 'Godly sorrow brings repentance that leads to salvation and leaves no regret, but worldly sorrow brings death.'"

"How do you remember that?" Vivian asked. "All those Bible verses I mean."

"I memorize one verse a week. Besides, this is a special one. It's one I've had in mind all along as I've been prayin' for you."

"I'm sure your prayers had nothing to do with it."

"Don't underestimate prayer," Eliza warned. "It can do amazin' things!"

"Will it bring Hope back?" Vivian scoffed.

"No. But maybe it'll let you see the purpose in all this."

"What are you talking about?" Vivian asked. Then she combed her blonde hair with her hand and took her first sip of coffee.

"I'm talkin' about you bein' elected to Congress and the death of your daughter and granddaughter."

"What?"

"Sure. Let me put it to you this way. Have you ever heard the story of Esther?"

"No."

"Let me tell you then."

Vivian smiled sadly. "Somehow I knew you would," she said.

Eliza smiled and began her tale.

"King Xerxes of Persia was mad at his wife, Queen Vashti, for not obeyin' him," she said. "He was so mad, in fact, that he dumped her. Then he searched for a young virgin to replace her. His search led to a beautiful Jewish girl known as Esther.

"Now, Esther's father and mother had died when she was young and she was raised by an older cousin named Mordecai. He raised her as though she were his own daughter. When Esther was brought before the king, she did not reveal that she was a Jew because Mordecai had forbidden her to do so. Well, to make a long story short, Esther had won the king's approval and he made her queen in place of Vashti.

"Not long after, Mordecai had found out about a plot to assassinate King Xerxes. He told Queen Esther who reported it to the king. Esther gave the credit to Mordecai. So, the king felt he owed his life to Mordecai.

"Then along comes a noble named Haman. Haman had it in for the Jews and had persuaded the king to allow him to destroy them. When Mordecai learned of the king's edict to annihilate the Jews, he asked Esther to help.

"At first, she hesitated because by law, if anyone approached the king in his inner court without bein' summoned, he would be put to death unless the king decided to spare his life. When Mordecai heard of Esther's hesitation, he replied somethin' to the effect, 'Don't think that because you're the queen, you will escape the destruction of your people. And who knows but that you have come to royal position for such a time as this?'"

"What did she do?"

"She said, 'I will go to the king, even though it is against the law. And if I perish, I perish.'"

"And then what happened?"

"She went to the king and saved her people."

Vivian looked at Eliza curiously, pretending not to understand, and asked, "So what's your point? What has this to do with me?"

"You are Queen Esther," Eliza replied. "Your people are the thousands of babies who die each day of abortions. And who knows? You may have been sent to Washington for such a time as this! God may have led you to this place in your life so you would feel the need to know Him and that you would be willin' to be used for His glory. After all, your daughter and grandchild died as a result of an abortion. Who better to serve the Lord in this way than you?"

"Are you crazy?" Vivian said. "I'm the one who was elected to fight *for* abortion! Even if I was so inclined, that would be political suicide! I'd never get re-elected!"

Eliza looked directly into Vivian's eyes and repeated the end of her story, "And Esther said, 'I will go to the king. And if I perish, I perish.'"

Vivian frowned and shook her head. Then she said with an ironic smile, "That's a nice story, Eliza. But really, I can't imagine God calling on me!"

"Why not?" Eliza said. "Some of the biggest sinners turned out to be the greatest saints. He called on Paul to spread the Gospel, even though Paul persecuted Christians before he was converted on the road to Damascus."

"Well, I don't want to end up a martyr like Paul," Vivian said.

"That's your choice," Eliza said. "But as Mordecai told Esther, God can always find someone else to accomplish his purposes. It just seems sad that Hope's death will have been in vain."

Vivian sighed. She quietly stared into her cup of coffee, her sad eyes betraying her worldly sorrow.

The Hope of Heaven 28

The sky was a dark gray misty veil when Faith and her family arrived at the funeral home for Hope's wake late Friday afternoon. In the midst of the gloom, the setting sun quietly appeared through the mist as a faint white sphere, a portent of divine inspiration. It was as though the Creator had painted the heavens with a subtle reminder of His omnipresence, love, and power to those in mourning who had lost hope in the midst of tragedy.

As the Brandons turned into the funeral home parking lot, a small band of demonstrators was assembling in the park across the street. Before entering the home, Faith and her parents paused at the front entrance and watched the activity across the street with earnest interest. They soon recognized the demonstration as a mock wake. Resting on a card table under a large oak tree was a miniature coffin with the lid propped open. The sign-carrying demonstrators marched back and forth in front of the casket. Faith noticed that as each demonstrator passed the casket, he or she made some gesture as if paying last respects to the deceased. Then she caught a glimpse of a sign that read, "Abortion Kills Mothers Too!"

"Don't those jerks have any sensitivity!" she fumed. "I hope Hope's mother didn't see this!"

"Just ignore them, Dear," her mother said.

Joan put her arm around Faith's shoulder and escorted her through the front door into the lobby. Hope's body was resting in the parlor to the right. Having hardly set foot in the room, Faith was reduced to tears. Her father took her into his arms and led her to a folding chair in the last row near the door. For the next few moments, the Brandons huddled around Faith to grieve together.

Ryan, wiping his eyes with a handkerchief, was the first to break the huddle. For a moment he stood looking around the room surveying the throng of visitors who came to pay their respects. Many of those in attendance he knew as Faith's high school classmates and casual friends. They were gathered together in sorrowful, teary-eyed, groups of three or four. But there were many others whom Ryan did not know. These included Vivian's business and political acquaintances. They were also gathered into solemn and somber pockets of quiet conversation.

The open casket rested in the front of the room. To the left stood Vivian, alone, receiving guests with such a deep melancholy in her eyes that Ryan could feel her profound sense of loss from across the room. It was too much for him to bear. He turned and walked outside. Immediately, his eyes were drawn to the demonstration across the street and he felt pulled toward the other wake in progress. Taking a closer look, he recognized Jason. He shook his head in dismay and crossed the street. He waited at the end of the line farthest from the miniature casket. As Jason drew nearer, Ryan was able to detect the burning bitterness in Jason's soul by the flames in his eyes.

"Hello," Ryan said as they were now face to face.

"What are you doing here?" Jason responded coolly. "Did you come to join us?"

Ryan gently took Jason by the arm and led him a short distance away from the rest of the demonstrators.

"No," Ryan said. "I thought I'd see you in there," he said with a nod toward the parlor.

"Why? To curse the woman who killed my child?"

"Come on! Don't be like that! You loved Hope!"

"I also loved my child! It was a selfish, stupid decision she made! She deserves what she got!"

Ryan was about to object when Claire Boudreau, the petite, gray-haired leader of the demonstration, gathered the demonstrators in front of the small coffin and began to speak. Ryan listened from a distance.

"We have come here to mourn the death of one whom this world chooses to forget. It is only by self-deceit that we can deny the tragic loss of this unborn child. For this child's life is every bit as real and significant as the life of the mother who chose to abort it. But we mourn not only for this child and for the millions of other precious children whom this child represents, we mourn for ourselves and for our nation, for we are a lost people separated from our God. And while our sins are as infinite as the grains of sand, there is none as damning as the evil of abortion. The wrath of God will surely consume us if we do not repent and put an end to this abhorrent evil that stains our land. It is only then that our nation will be redeemed. Listen to these words from Isaiah, Chapter 59:

> 'Surely the arm of the Lord is not too short to save,
> nor his ear too dull to hear.
> But your iniquities have separated you from your God;
> your sins have hidden his face from you…
> For your hands are stained with blood,
> your fingers with guilt…
> they are swift to shed innocent blood…
> According to what they have done, so he will repay
> wrath to his enemies and retribution to his foes…

Then Claire looked up at her audience and said, "Abortion is a symptom of our divine deafness as a nation. It is also symbolic of our loss of hope. At some point, we must overcome our indifference to the shedding of innocent blood. Until we begin to grieve as much for this unborn child as we do for her mother, we are a nation without hope."

•••

Inside the funeral home, Faith had composed herself. Accompanied by her mother and father, she slowly crept up to the casket. Standing before the open coffin, Faith let out a sigh and raised her gaze from the floor to the lifeless form on display.

"It doesn't even look like her," she said quietly to her parents.

"You're right," Joan said. "Hope was always so full of life."

"I'm going to miss you so much!" Faith whispered as the tears began to flow. Faith's parents put their arms around her but it was no use. Human comfort could not salve her wounded heart. Then Vivian, witnessing the grief, joined in and gave Faith a consoling embrace.

"We're all going to miss her," Vivian said through her own tears. She wrapped her arms around Faith and the two women clung to each other and wept openly, drawing sympathy from those present. Finally, Vivian broke away from Faith's embrace and said to her parents, "Thank you for coming."

Joan and Ryle gave Vivian consoling hugs. Ryle said, "We're very sorry. We can't imagine how difficult this must be."

Vivian nodded as she wiped tears away with a tissue.

"Things were going great and then—wham!—this happens," Vivian explained through sniffles.

"It's a terrible loss," Joan said.

Ryle added, "It sure puts things into perspective."

Then Vivian looked deeply into Ryle's eyes and asked simply, "Why?"

Ryle shook his head. "No one knows but the Lord," he said.

Vivian nodded gently. Then she asked, "Ryle, would you mind saying a few words tomorrow? There will be a short service before we take Hope to the cemetery. The funeral director wanted to know if I had someone in mind to give the eulogy."

"Yes, of course. I would be glad to."

"Thank you," she said. Then she added with an embarrassed smile, "He had asked me if I had a clergyman in mind. I had to admit I didn't know any. You're the closest thing to a clergyman that I know."

Ryle nodded with a polite smile and said, "I understand. It will be an honor."

"Thanks," Vivian said quietly.

There was a short pause. Then Joan asked, "I don't see your brother here. How is he taking this? It must be very hard on him."

A bitter smile creased Vivian's face. "He won't be coming," she said. "He called earlier today. He said Beth and the kids would be here, but he didn't think he could handle it."

•••

It was shortly after six when Tom arrived home from the clinic. As he entered the kitchen, his wife greeted him.

"Hi, Honey. The girls and I have already eaten. I've got your supper in the microwave. We can go to the funeral home as soon as you finish supper."

Tom said coldly, "I'm not going. I called Vivian and told her I wasn't coming."

"But Tom!" Beth said. "This is your niece! Your sister needs your support!"

"Vivian would be happy if she never saw me again!" Tom said, raising his voice. "You know she blames me for this!"

Beth sighed. She said, "That's not true! She wants you there. You're the only family she has left."

Tom had a mean look in his eyes. "Just take the kids and go!" he shouted.

"But Tom!"

"Shut up!" he snapped. Then he turned coldly apathetic. He said matter-of-factly, "I called a lawyer today. I'm getting a divorce."

Without another word, he marched off to the bedroom to pack his clothes.

•••

The clouds opened up again overnight and another steady rain fell on Elston. By Saturday morning, the rain dissipated but the skies were still overcast. In spite of the threat of more rain, a large crowd gathered for the service, with the overflow standing along the sides and in the back of the room. Outside, television reporters and cameramen were ready to capture on tape the grief and agony of the congresswoman-elect. There was much interest in how the staunch women's rights advocate would react to her own daughter's death as a result of a botched abortion, especially since the accident was at the hands of her own physician brother.

The proceedings began promptly at ten-thirty. The funeral director, a tall man with a short cropped salt and pepper beard, placed a wooden lectern in front of Hope's casket. He said, "Before we take Hope to her final resting place, we will hear a few words from Dr. Ryle Brandon."

Dr. Brandon rose from his seat in the front row where he was sitting with Vivian and his family. He stepped quietly to the lectern and looked solemnly at the mourners. There were many in attendance who were choking back tears.

"This is a very sad and difficult occasion," he began. "Hope's passing away came about abruptly and took us by surprise, as is often the case with youth. We don't expect life to be so brief. The question haunting us at this moment is simply, 'Why?' How could such a thing happen to one who had so much promise, so much zest for life, and so much to live for? It is a very difficult question to answer."

Dr. Brandon looked directly at Vivian and saw the agony in her eyes. Then he looked at Faith and saw the same tears. He sighed deeply before continuing.

He said, "The question of the meaning of life is addressed in the book of Ecclesiastes. But even there, we find no real answer. At best, we hear the author say in Chapter 9, verse 12:

> 'Moreover, no man knows when his hour will come:
> As fish are caught in a cruel net,

or birds are taken in a snare,
so men are trapped by evil times
that fall unexpectedly upon them.'

"And so where is the meaning of life to be found? Is it to be found in wealth, power, education, work, pleasure, human relationships? Or, are all of these things meaningless as the author of Ecclesiastes suggests? Is that all there is to life? Or, can we expect something more beyond this life on Earth? In a kind of sad irony, the question might be, 'Where is our hope?'

"In another part of Scripture, we find the answer. Our hope is in Christ. John 3:16-17 says, 'For God so loved the world that he gave his one and only Son, that whoever believes in him shall not perish but have eternal life. For God did not send his Son into the world to condemn the world, but to save the world through him.' Those who believe in Christ have the hope of heaven. They can look forward to eternal life with the Father. It is our prayer that the young woman we loved so dearly and whom we mourn today, realized the ultimate hope, and that we will see her again someday in heaven."

After a few kind words about Hope, Dr. Brandon ended in prayer. Then those present were allowed one final pass in front of the open casket. Faith broke into tears again and was gently escorted to the car by her parents.

Vivian was the last to say good-bye. When the director closed the coffin, she received a glimpse of the eternal darkness which fell upon her daughter and realized that for the rest of her life, she would be walking in the shadow of death, a silhouette cast in the form of her lost child.

In a few moments, the coffin was loaded into the hearse and a long parade of cars followed in the procession to the cemetery. In the Brandon's car, Faith broke the morbid silence. With her heart wrung dry of emotion, she said dispassionately to her father, "You know she's not going to heaven."

Dr. Brandon looked at his daughter in the rear view mirror. He said, "We don't know for sure. Only God knows Hope's heart and He will be the final judge."

"No, Dad. I know," Faith replied solemnly. "She was not saved."

A somber silence set in. It was a difficult fact to deny. But no one wanted to admit it publicly or even to think about it. Once again, Faith interrupted the deathly quiet. This time she asked her father, "Do you think God punished Hope for having an abortion?"

"God doesn't go out of His way to punish us for our sins. He simply allows us to reap the natural consequences of our actions."

"Yes, but not that many women die from an abortion," Faith said. "It seems like God picked on Hope for some reason."

"You can't blame God. Hope was taking her chances."

Before long, the procession reached the cemetery at the south end of town. The string of cars wound through the wooded hills on a narrow black top road to the graveside. Umbrellas opened as people filed from their cars and gathered around the grave. A light rain persisted as Dr. Brandon said a final prayer. When it was all over and Hope's body was lowered into the grave, the crowd dispersed quickly to escape the wet weather. Faith and her parents gave Vivian farewell hugs. They realized they would be seeing little of each other in the future. The connection that brought them together was now irrevocably severed. Faith found one last reservoir of emotion and the tears came forth again. Before climbing into the car, she looked back at Hope's grave. She sighed and shook her head in despair.

•••

James and Vivian drove home together from the cemetery. Since learning of the tragedy on Wednesday, James had taken on the responsibility of Vivian's well being. Eliza was there to take care of Vivian's daily needs, but he knew she needed his emotional support. Vivian's parents had passed away years before, her daughter was now gone, and her brother had, in effect, disappeared. James was the only one left.

The house was empty when they arrived. Eliza had not yet returned from the funeral. Vivian hung her coat in the front closet and walked into the living room and sat down on one end of the couch in front of the picture window. She sat sideways with her feet up on the couch and looked out at the falling rain. James followed her into the room and sat at the other end of the couch.

"What do you think?" Vivian asked.

"About what?"

"About God. And heaven."

James was about to reply when Vivian added, "I've never really thought that much about death before, even when my parents died. But when I think of Hope, I wonder, 'Is that it?' Maybe those people are right about God and heaven. It would be nice if they were."

James sighed. "I would like to tell you it's so," he said. "It would be very comforting. But I'm afraid it's little more than fairy tales. It's man who made God to comfort himself in times like these," he said stoically.

"So what is there beyond this life?" Vivian asked.

"Nothing," he said.

"Nothing?"

James shrugged.

"Then what's the point?" Vivian asked.

"That *is* the point," he said. "There is no meaning to life except what we make of it."

"I don't know. All of a sudden it seems like a pretty empty existence to me. And I've been pretty successful."

James shrugged again. "I'm sorry," he said. "But that's all there is. What you see is what you get."

"It's not enough."

"It was enough for you before this happened."

"I know. But now, it's definitely not enough," Vivian said. "There has to be more."

Vengeance! 29

Late Sunday night, on a pedestrian bridge just a quarter-mile north of the Justin campus, a lone silhouette stood waiting amidst the midnight shadows and icy winds whistling through the river valley. The rippling river waters below were intermittently drowned out by the pulsing roar of sixteen-wheelers on the tollway bridge high above. As the cold, damp air chilled Jason's bones, vengeful thoughts over the tragic deaths numbed the young man's heart. But the undulating thunder of a motorcycle and the piercing flash of its headlight abruptly interrupted these thoughts. Shortly, the bike came to a halt in a little gravel turnoff adjacent to the bridge. A large shadowy figure dismounted and lumbered down the blacktop path and halfway across the long bridge.

"Isn't it a bit late in the year to be riding a motorcycle?" Jason asked the approaching figure.

"It ain't snowin' yet," replied the dark figure in a hoarse but booming voice.

"I guess not, but it won't be long," Jason said. "How's it going?"

"Better for me than you," Dan Crider said gruffly as he leaned his massive frame against the railing next to Jason. "Sorry to hear about your girlfriend, man," he added and then spit on the waters below.

Jason shrugged as if it was nothing, but Dan knew better.

"I ain't seen you since summer, that night at Justin," he said.

"I know. That was the night Ryan and I sprayed the clinic."

"Yeah, I figured that was you. I was gonna do more than that, but after what you'd done, I thought I'd wait a bit. Then I never got around to takin' care of business. But don't worry! That river scum has seen his last day. I'm just tryin' to decide what would be most fittin'. Do we tear him apart limb from limb, or do we stick a pair of scissors into the back of his head like he does to those babies?"

The thought was devilishly entertaining and Jason smiled with satisfaction as he toyed with it in his own imagination. Then he said, "It's too hot to do something like that now. They'd suspect one of us for sure."

Dan nodded. "Maybe you're right," he said. "There's no sense endin' up in jail. Heck, he kills twenty people a day and gets away with it. Why should we be punished for doin' what's right? Besides, it'll feel better if we get away with it like he does."

"What bothers me is what'll happen in the meantime," Jason said. "Maybe there'll be another girl like Hope."

"Yeah, you're right," Dan said. "We ought to do somethin' to put him out of commission for awhile."

"Like what?"

"I don't know. Maybe a pipe bomb will do the trick," Dan said.

"You mean bomb the clinic?"

"Yeah."

Jason shrugged.

"If we did it at night, then no one would get hurt," he thought out loud.

"Yeah. That's what I was thinkin'."

"Do you know how to make one?" Jason asked.

"A pipe bomb? Yeah. No sweat!"

"When do you want to do it?"

"Maybe tomorrow night."

"Don't you think that's too soon?"

"Not if I do it alone," Dan said. "You make sure you have an alibi. I'll see my boss tomorrow mornin' and tell him I'm goin' home to Texas to take care of my ailin' mother. Then I'll cut out right after the job's done."

"Are you sure you don't want any help?"

"Nah! It'll only complicate things," Dan said. Then he warned, "And don't try to contact me. We gotta have nothin' to do with each other just in case they do suspect us."

"Sounds reasonable," Jason said.

"We'll make him sweat out the next few months," Dan said with a satisfied look. "He'll be lookin' over his shoulder everywhere he goes."

"God knows he deserves to be dragged through hell!" Jason said.

Dan nodded. Then he cautioned again, "Remember! Get an alibi and no contact. We'll meet here one year from tonight."

"Okay," Jason said. "If that's the way you want it."

"That's the way I want it."

Without saying another word, Dan turned and disappeared into the shadows. In a moment, Jason heard the rumble of an engine and the sound of loose gravel being kicked up by a spinning tire. Finally, he saw a single taillight fade into the distance. He waited for a moment and then, unaided by a flashlight, began his walk back to campus. His vision, like his afflicted heart, was growing accustomed to the darkness.

•••

Early Tuesday morning, Juan rolled out of bed comforted with the consolation that this was his last day at the clinic. He quietly tiptoed out to the newly remodeled second floor bathroom and squinted as he turned on the bright vanity lights. He quickly splashed his face with cold water and brushed his teeth. Then he took a moment to admire his recent handiwork—a new vanity and sink, a new shower and tile floor, and new wallpaper. After returning to the bedroom, he quietly slipped on his work clothes by the dim light of his alarm clock. Before leaving, he leaned over and kissed his wife. She smiled without opening her eyes. As he crept quietly from the room, he stopped at the foot of the bed and gazed upon his precious thirteen-month-old son, Ernesto, sleeping soundly in his crib. With a warm smile, he carefully rearranged the blankets to cover his son's exposed shoulders and said a quick prayer of protection for his wife and children.

Juan's nephew, Lupe, was finishing a cup of hot coffee when Juan stepped into the kitchen. Like his uncle, Lupe was short and slim. He was renting the basement bedroom from Juan for himself and his pregnant wife.

"Ready?" Juan asked as he grabbed his lunch out of the refrigerator.

"Ready!" Lupe answered.

They had decided to drive together. Lupe worked with Juan at the nursery and was now taking over for him at the clinic. Today, Juan would show Lupe the ropes and explain all that he needed to do in the two hours he allowed himself each morning at the clinic.

"I still don't understand why you're giving up this job," Lupe said as they drove off to work.

"I told you, I don't feel right about being there. All this killing of babies is wrong!" Juan said.

"But don't you need the money?"

"I'll find something else to do. Besides, I'm a landlord now. I can afford to work only one job," Juan replied with a smile and a wink.

"Well, I need the money. The rent is too high! And pretty soon I'm gonna have another hungry mouth to feed," Lupe returned with a laugh.

When the men entered through the back door of the clinic, Juan switched on the hall light and said, "I'll just show you around the place first and then we'll get started."

As Juan was leading Lupe to the front area, he heard the sound of a motorcycle idling in front of the clinic. Then came the sound of breaking glass followed by a thunderous explosion. It was the last sound Juan and his nephew would hear this side of the grave.

•••

Jason was asleep on the family room couch when he was shaken awake early Tuesday morning.

"Wake up!" Ryan said in a commanding tone.

Jason had been lying on his stomach. He did a half push-up as he tried to shake the sleep out of his head.

"What time is it?" he asked with a yawn.

"Never mind! Come look at the TV! The clinic in Elston was bombed! They think it was a pipe bomb."

"What?" Jason said in a sleepy stupor. Then it hit him. Dan carried out the plan.

"Come and look!" Ryan repeated.

It was half-past six. Ryan's parents were sitting at the kitchen table watching the story with great interest.

"When did it happen?" Jason asked as he shuffled behind Ryan into the kitchen.

"Early this morning! About four o'clock."

"Really?" Jason said innocently.

"Good morning, Jason!" Joan said to her unexpected guest. "You should have told me you were staying and I would have gotten the guest room ready for you."

"That's okay, Mrs. Brandon. I didn't know myself. I guess I just fell asleep on the couch going over my notes for the test," Jason said. Then he turned his eyes to the television.

"Was there much damage?" he asked. Adrenaline was now surging through his body.

"Yeah," Ryan said. "The bomb blew away the reception area and a fire started."

"Two men were killed!" Joan added.

"Killed? Who were they?"

"Two janitors," Joan said. "They were Mexicans."

"Oh, my God!" Jason said. His eyes were now riveted to the television as the reporter gave the sad details.

"Police sources here have confirmed that the two men who died in the blast were part-time janitors. According to one spokesman for the clinic, one of the men was working today for the last time and was training the other. For the second man, it was his first day on the job. Both men had families. Juan Cantu was the father of five children. Lupe Martinez, Juan's nephew, has a wife who is expecting their first child. All of this, of course, comes in the wake of the tragic death of Hope Stuart, the daughter of Vivian Stuart, who died here several days ago as a result of surgical complications stemming from an abortion. Police speculate that this bombing is somehow related to that incident and are looking for suspects now. This is John Lacy reporting live in Elston from the Women's Health Clinic of DuKane. Back to you, Cheryl."

"Turn it off. It's making me sick," Dr. Brandon said.

Ryan reached over and pressed the power button.

"Looks like they'll be coming after you," Ryan said to Jason teasingly.

Jason strained to put on a smile, doing his best to mask his anxiety.

"I was here! You're all my witnesses!" he said with a nervous chuckle.

"What's it worth to ya?" Ryan teased.

"This is no laughing matter," Joan said to Ryan.

"I was just giving Jason a hard time, that's all!" Ryan said with a smirk.

"The whole thing makes me sick!" Dr. Brandon repeated. "This will set the pro-life movement back a few years. The idiot who did this just swung the tide of public opinion back to the pro-abortion side. What little momentum we gained by the negative publicity over Hope's death is now wiped out by this incident. This gives the pro-abortionists another reason to ask for more legislation to stifle protests."

After a quiet moment, Ryan said, "I know that two innocent people were killed last night, but I can kind of understand how someone could do this."

"How can you possibly condone such a reprehensible act?" his father replied.

"I don't know," Ryan said. "I guess it's kind of like war. Sometimes it takes violence to stop violence. Just think of what would have happened if no one stood up to Hitler in World War Two? It's the same thing. If an abortionist is taking innocent lives, aren't you morally justified in taking his life or at least preventing him from taking any more innocent lives by bombing his clinic? I think killing an abortionist could be considered justifiable homicide."

Dr. Brandon sighed as he leaned back in his chair.

"On the surface, what you say sounds reasonable," he said. "However, your argument fails because your premise is distorted."

"What do you mean?" Ryan asked.

"The fight against abortion is not a war in the traditional sense of an international conflict requiring military measures to defend our nation or an allied nation," Dr. Brandon said. "Nor is it a case of anarchy requiring vigilantism. It is a spiritual war requiring Christ-like responses."

"What do you mean?" Ryan asked again.

"The problem we're facing is that most Americans refuse to face up to the moral issue. Our ultimate task is to change hearts. This battle has to be fought with love, not hate; with gentle and kind persuasion, not violence. We have to act as Christ would act and we have to love our 'enemies' as He would love them. There is nothing that Satan would like more than for us to reject the lessons of Christ and fight evil with evil. As it says in Zechariah 4:6, 'Not by might, nor by power, but by my Spirit, says the Lord.'"

Dr. Brandon could see the Spirit of the Lord working on his son who, when confronted with the Truth, pulled a chair out from the kitchen table and plopped himself down in exasperation. Jason, who was now standing by the sink and leaning against the counter, looked on with growing remorse.

Then Ryan offered another objection. He said, "Okay, I can see what you're saying. And I would never resort to violence myself. But still, I would understand it if Jason, for example, decided to go out and shoot Dr. Morlon after what happened to Hope."

Jason nervously shifted his weight and looked at Dr. Brandon for a reply.

"Just because you can understand how a human can be blinded by passion or can be coldly dispassionate and seek vengeance does not justify a vengeful act," Dr. Brandon said. "On the Day of Judgment when you stand before the Lord, He's not going to buy it. Romans 12:19 says, 'Do not take revenge, my friends, but leave room for God's wrath, for it is written: 'It is mine to avenge; I will repay,' says the Lord.'"

True Tests of Faith

Six long, cold, wintry weeks had passed since Hope was buried. They had been the most difficult weeks in Faith's life. She had endured the physical and emotional strain of the last weeks of pregnancy and was now due any day, or hour. She was also suffering the lingering effects of depression having lost her boyfriend first, and then, even more tragically, her best friend, forever. Faith wrote in her journal:

Dear Hope,

I must admit that it feels a little strange using your first name. I'm so used to calling you "child." I decided to name you "Hope" in honor of my best friend whom I lost recently in a tragic accident. I hope that in some ways you are very much like her. She was always so fun and full of life. We shared everything together as only best friends can do. Perhaps one day you and I can be as close as I feel we are now. Only time will tell, I guess.

I hope you like the name I've selected for you—Hope Joan. It really doesn't matter too much though since your adoptive parents will be selecting their own name for you. Whatever it is, I'm sure it will be very nice. I picked "Joan" as a middle name because that's my mother's name. She is also a very wonderful person, and I hope that someday you are also very much like her. She is a woman of great faith and wisdom.

At this point, I want you to know that I am still struggling with my decision of whether or not to go through with the adoption. Several weeks ago, adoption clearly seemed to be the best option for everyone involved, including you. However, the closer we come to your birth, the more reluctant I am to let you go. I just pray that God gives me the strength and wisdom to do what's best.

Love always,
Your birthmother

Faith slept in late on the morning of Christmas Eve. When she finally rolled out of bed, she felt miserable. Her back ached more than usual; she was also suffering from indigestion. She was desperate for her physical ordeal to end. The only thing keeping her from being too anxious was the fear of delivery. "How much is this going to hurt?" she asked her mother several times as the due date was drawing near. But now that it was almost Christmas, the expected day of arrival, she hoped the baby would wait until after the holiday to make her entrance into the "outside" world.

It was nearly ten o'clock by the time Faith showered, dressed, and made it down to the kitchen. There she found her mother standing at the sink busily preparing the relish tray for the early afternoon dinner.

"Good morning!" Joan said cheerfully. "How are you feeling this morning?"

"Pregnant. Very pregnant. Is this ever going to end?"

"Probably sooner than you think. The most inopportune time is when it usually happens."

"Gee, that's comforting," Faith said, looking over her mother's shoulder and reaching for a few sliced carrots to nibble on. "Is that turkey I smell?"

"Yes, it's in the oven."

"Good, I'm starved."

"Well, you'd better find something else to eat because we're not eating until one."

"These carrots are pretty good," Faith said as she reached for another handful. Suddenly, she felt a stinging slap on the back of her hand.

"Ouch!" she cried.

"Leave them alone! Those are for dinner!"

"Okay, sorry! I just thought that in my condition..." Faith said with a wry smile.

"That what? That you'd get special privileges? You just get that thought out of your head! You might as well have that child because you're not getting any more pampering around here!" her mother said playfully.

"Believe me! I would if I could," Faith said as she pulled a chair out from the dinette table and sat down awkwardly. After shifting about in the chair for a moment, Faith breathed a heavy sigh.

"What's wrong?" Joan asked, looking Faith in the eye.

"Nothing."

"Are you sure? Yesterday you seemed a little blue."

"Yeah, I guess I was a bit bummed yesterday."

"How come?"

"Oh, I don't know. I guess I'm still not sure about my decision."

Joan began arranging the black olives on the relish tray. She said, "Do what you think is best for the child. Don't be sentimental. Base your decision on love."

"What about me?" Faith asked. "Everything's been happening to me lately! Now, everyone expects me to give up my child, too! It's not fair! You don't know what it is to give up a child!"

Joan was surprised by the comment. She said, "No one is expecting anything from you, Faith. This is your decision. We'll support you one hundred percent on whatever you decide."

Faith dabbed at her eyes with a tissue.

"It's too late! I can't back out now! Robert and Kara would hate me!"

"It's not too late," Joan said. "You still have the right to change your mind. And there will always be another child for Robert and Kara."

•••

The guests began arriving shortly before noon and the house was soon crowded with aunts, uncles, and cousins from both sides of the family. Faith had drawn considerable unwanted attention because of her pregnancy. Everyone was curious about her plans for the baby, and she labored to answer the same questions over and over again as the various family members came to greet her. Shortly before the main meal was served, Faith was sitting on the living room sofa when her mother's younger sister joined her.

"Hello, Faith. How are you?" Kate asked pleasantly as she sat down next to her.

"I'm fine, Aunt Kate. How are you?" Faith said. Then with a grimace she howled, "Ow!"

"Are you okay?" Kate asked.

"Yes," Faith said. She took a deep breath and exhaled slowly. "I've just had a couple of sharp cramps while sitting here."

"Abdominal cramps?"

Faith nodded with another grimace. "Long ones," she said.

"Are you sure they're not contractions?" Kate asked.

"I don't know. How do you tell?"

"You just know, that's all," Kate said with a smile.

"Great! Just what I was afraid of—going into labor on Christmas!"

"When's the due date?"

"Christmas," Faith said.

"Oh, dear!" Kate said with a surprised smile. "You're right on schedule!"

"Just my luck!" Faith replied with a sardonic smile.

"Is anyone going to be with you in the delivery room?"

"Just Mom. Dad says he can't bear to watch."

"What about me?" Ryan interrupted as he overheard the last bit of conversation.

"Yeah, right! Like you'd really be there!" Faith said.

"No, really! I want to be there for you," Ryan said with an embarrassed smile. "And I want to be there when my niece comes into the world."

"Really?" Faith said with a lump in her throat.

"Yeah. I wouldn't miss it for the world!"

"Thanks," Faith said, a tear coming to her eye.

Then Joan announced, "Dinner is ready! Everyone take your seats!"

The family gathered at the dining room table and at two long folding tables set up in the living room. After Dr. Brandon said grace, the two adjacent rooms were humming with lively chatter and a flurry of passing dishes. In the midst of the excitement, Joan noticed Faith grimace.

"Is something wrong, Dear?" she asked.

"No. Just a little cramp," Faith said.

"I think she's started her contractions," Kate said.

"Really? When did they start?" Joan asked.

"I've only had a couple," Faith replied, hoping to avoid further attention.

"The last one was about twenty minutes ago," Kate said.

"Do you want me to go upstairs and get her bag?" Ryan asked.

"Relax, Dear. It's not time yet," Joan said.

"When will it be time?" Ryan asked excitedly.

"When her contractions are five minutes apart," Joan said.

"When will that be?" Ryan asked.

"It could be another ten or twelve hours or more," Joan replied.

"Awesome! The baby is coming on Christmas!" Ryan said.

The word spread quickly to the other table. The tables were buzzing with the news.

"There's no turning back now!" Faith heard her Uncle Vince say with a chuckle.

"Shh! Leave the poor girl alone!" Kate scolded her husband.

Then, sincerely hoping to redeem himself, Uncle Vince said to Faith, "Don't worry! Just a few hours of labor and it'll be all over."

Kate gave him a sharp elbow and suggested, "Have some more stuffing, Dear!"

•••

By ten o'clock, the guests were gone. Faith's contractions were growing stronger and were now just five minutes apart. Dr. Brandon and Ryan had just put away the folding tables when Joan announced, "Okay, guys! It's time to go!"

Joan helped Faith up from the living room sofa as Ryan picked up his sister's bag.

"Let's say a prayer before we go," Dr. Brandon said.

Faith let out a sigh to show her displeasure. She just wanted to get it over with so even the shortest delay seemed a major hurdle. Grudgingly, she bowed her head and held hands in a circle as her father prayed, "Dear Lord, we praise You for the gift of life which You have given to us, and we thank You for helping Faith choose life in a culture that has become hostile to life itself. And so, we come before You to ask Your blessing this night. Please protect Faith and her child from all complications and provide a safe delivery. Amen."

"Amen! Let's go!" Ryan said anxiously.

"Since you're in such a hurry, why don't you do the hard part?" Faith asked sarcastically.

"Sorry! It's too late for a transplant! Otherwise, I probably would," Ryan replied with a wry smile.

"Yeah, right!" Faith said.

"Come on! Let's get in the car," Dr. Brandon said. "The baby's not going to wait for you two to finish your verbal sparring."

"She waited nine months. She can wait a few more minutes," Ryan quipped.

"Let's put it this way, son. You're sitting in the back seat with your sister. If the baby comes out before we get to the hospital, then you're in charge of delivery."

"Let's go!" Ryan said.

By three in the morning, the baby was ready to make its grand entrance. Dr. Brandon sat out in the waiting room praying. Joan and Ryan were in the birthing room standing beside Faith. Ryan held his sister's hand through the last stages of labor. He winced with every shriek of pain. Only when he heard his tiny niece cry for the first time did he breathe a sigh of relief. Joan's eyes were wet with tears when Hope announced her own arrival. Within minutes, the baby was wrapped up and placed next to Faith. The family prayer was answered. Mother and daughter were fine.

"She's beautiful!" Faith said.

"What a blessing!" Joan said.

Ryan gently touched Hope's tiny fingers and said, "Way to go, Sis!"

Faith smiled and said, "Will somebody tell Dad that he's a grandfather?"

•••

Faith and the baby were released from the hospital late Sunday evening, Christmas day. They arrived home shortly before ten. Joan had the crib set up in Faith's bedroom. Faith laid her sleeping child in the crib and sat down on the bed with her mother. The room was dark except for the light from the hall peeking through the half-open doorway. The two mothers began a whispered conversation.

"She's precious, isn't she?" Faith said.

"Yes, she is. She's got your nose."

"Do you think so?"

"Yes. And your chin."

Faith smiled quietly. "I can't believe I even considered an abortion," she said. Joan put her arm around her daughter and gave a gentle squeeze.

"Why don't you lie down for a little while and get some rest. You'll need it."

Joan stood over the crib while Faith quietly changed into her pajamas.

"Thank you, Lord," she said as she gazed at her first grandchild. Then a tear escaped her eye. "Will I ever get to know you?" she wondered.

Faith gingerly crawled under the covers. Her mother returned and kissed her on the forehead.

"I'll go down and make some bottles," Joan whispered. "I'm sure you'll be needing one soon."

"Thanks."

"Well, don't get used to it. I'll help you some for a day or two; but after that, you're on your own."

"I guess I won't be needing much help after that."

Joan nodded and smiled bravely as she stroked Faith's forehead. When her mother left the room, Faith rolled on to her side and stared in amazement at her child.

"If only I could keep you!" she whispered.

Suddenly, the baby began crying. Faith was startled and quickly went to the crib. As she was picking up her daughter, Ryan peeked in and asked, "What's wrong?"

"I don't know. Why don't you ask her?"

"Very funny."

Faith held Hope in her arms, rocking her back and forth. Then Joan arrived with a bottle and said, "Okay, who wants to feed her?"

"I will," said Faith. She sat in the wooden rocker that was moved into her room for the baby's short stay. Joan handed Faith the bottle and she popped the nipple into the baby's mouth.

"There you go!" Faith said with a smile. The quiet was quickly restored as Hope sucked hungrily.

"How come you're not breast feeding her?" Ryan asked.

"Her adoptive mother won't be able to breast-feed her," Joan said. "So it's better that she starts off with formula. Then there won't be any problems adjusting when she goes to her new home."

"That makes sense," Ryan said.

Faith was wounded by the thought of another home for her child. She complained inwardly, "This is my baby! It's not fair!"

•••

The next day, Monday, the precipitation vacillated between freezing rain and wet snow. Kara had gifts to exchange, but she refused to go out into the inclement weather. Instead, she spent the morning in the living room sitting on the couch, reading one of the books she had received for Christmas. From time to time, she would take a break from her reading and stare out the picture window at the mix of sleet and snow. Robert had been passing the time in the study working at the computer. Late that morning, he went to the living room to visit his wife. When he entered the room, he caught Kara gazing out the window, apparently deep in thought.

"What are you thinking about, Love?" he asked.

Kara was startled. She said with an embarrassed smile, "Nothing really. I was just thinking how Faith's due date was supposed to be around Christmas. For all we know, the baby might already be born."

"That's possible," Robert said and then gave a big yawn as he stretched his arms to the side.

"Doesn't it bother you?" Kara asked sharply.

"I don't know. Should it?"

"Of course, it should! We're the baby's parents! But, we don't even know if the baby's okay!" Kara said, now agitated.

"Well, all we can do is leave it up to the Lord."

Kara shook her head. She said, "Sometimes I wonder if you even care."

"Of course, I care," Robert said. "It's just that I know God has a plan for us, and we just have to be patient and see what happens."

"Well, I'm tired of waiting!" Kara said. "Why won't He let me have children?"

"He will. In His own time."

"I'm sorry. But I just don't have your patience, or faith."

"Maybe that's what he's waiting for."

Kara looked at her husband quizzically. The thought had never occurred to her. Then she said in a huff, "It's not right! He shouldn't do that!"

Kara turned back to the window and pouted. Robert sighed gently as he left the room. When he returned to his chair in front of the computer, he bowed his head.

"Lord," he prayed, "please give Kara the patience and faith she needs. But, if it's all the same to You, please give us the good news soon!"

Early that afternoon, the call came from Faith's social worker.

"Hello, Kara. This is Maggie. I've got some good news for you! The baby was born yesterday on Christmas, about three A.M."

"Oh! That's wonderful!" Kara said. "Did everything go all right?"

"Yes. Everything went well. Faith and the baby are dong fine. She weighs seven pounds, two ounces and had a good Apgar score. And everybody thinks Hope's adorable."

"Hope?"

"Yes. Faith named her after her best friend who died tragically about six weeks ago," Maggie explained.

After a short pause, Kara asked, "How is Faith feeling about her decision?"

"I was getting to that," Maggie said. "I want to warn you not to get your hopes up too much because you can never tell what might happen. I think her mind is telling her to place. But, her heart may have a hard time letting go."

"Yes, I understand," Kara said. "But do you know which way she's leaning? Do you think she's going to keep the baby?"

Maggie sighed. "I can't guarantee anything," she said. "My gut feeling is she'll place the child. But, like I said, you never can tell."

"Okay," Kara said with a sigh. "Will you let us know as soon as you have some news?"

"Of course! I'll let you know right away. I promise."

Robert walked into the kitchen just as Kara was hanging up the phone.

"Who was that?" he asked.

"It was Maggie. The baby was born yesterday on Christmas."

"That's great!" Robert said.
"Yeah," Kara replied with a brave smile.
"What's wrong?"
Kara shrugged and said, "I'm afraid Faith is going to keep the baby."

•••

"Good morning," Faith mumbled as she shuffled wearily into the kitchen for breakfast Wednesday morning.

"Where's Hope?" Ryan asked from his seat at the dinette table.

"I sent her out to 'The Donut Hole' to get breakfast," Faith replied as she sat down at the table.

Ryan shook his head and returned to his cereal and sports page.

"What's wrong, Dear?" her mother asked.

"Nothing. I'm just so tired!"

"How come? All the baby does is sleep all the time," Ryan said.

"You can say that again," Faith quipped.

"So why don't you sleep when she sleeps?" Ryan asked, thinking he'd found the obvious solution.

"Because she only sleeps two hours at a time!" Faith whined. "Once I get her to sleep, it takes me a while to fall asleep myself. Then as soon as I get to sleep, she wakes me up again and wants to be fed or changed. It's horrible!"

"That's what taking care of a newborn is all about," her mother said.

"It's almost over," her father interjected. "Pretty soon you'll be able to get back to life as usual."

"Ohhh! I know!" Faith said with a long whining sigh. "But it's so soon! Maggie's going to be here this morning to sign papers and I don't think I'm ready!"

"But I thought you were convinced that adoption was the best choice," Ryan said.

"I am!" Faith said, "It's just that now that it's so close to happening, I'm afraid."

"Afraid of what?" Joan asked.

"Of losing control after I sign the papers," she said. "I just want to make sure Hope has a good and happy life, that's all."

"Well, I think you picked out a great set of parents in Robert and Kara. I don't think you can ask for any more assurance than that," Joan said.

"You just have to put your faith in the Lord and trust Him to protect her," her father added.

"I know!" Faith whined again. "It just seems so rushed! And I'm afraid to say good-bye knowing I'll probably never see her again!"

The thought triggered another outpouring of tears. With a lump in his throat, Dr. Brandon suggested, "Why don't you just tell Maggie that you'd like another day with Hope? I'm sure she'd understand."

Joan did not like the idea but she bit her tongue.

Faith looked at her father with hopeful eyes and asked, "Can I do that?"

"I don't see why not?" he said. "She's still your daughter."

•••

Later that morning, Robert and Kara were sitting at the kitchen table going through names for the baby when the phone rang. Robert answered.

"Hello, Maggie," he said.

Kara's ears perked up. She stared intently at her husband as he listened to Maggie's news. There was little expression in his face, giving her little indication of the substance of the report. Finally, he said, "Well, we'll just have to be patient. Thanks for calling."

"What happened?" Kara asked.

Robert hesitated. He knew Kara would not take the news well.

"Maggie said Faith would like to keep the baby another day. She wasn't ready to sign the papers yet."

The news was devastating. Kara's hopes were like an untied, inflated balloon and the person holding it had just let go.

"She's going to keep the baby! I knew it! Why is God doing this to me?"

"Things will work out."

"Just leave me alone!"

Robert gave Kara an annoyed look. "I'm going for a walk," he said quietly.

He put on his coat and gloves and slipped out the door. The sun was shining brightly in the clear blue sky. As he stepped off the front porch, he shivered in the cold, wintry air. His breath formed a cloud in front of his face as he walked gingerly on the crusted snow covering the driveway and sidewalk. Robert felt the combined burden of his own disappointment and Kara's crushed hopes as well. In spite of his heavy heart, he prayed simply, "Thy will be done, Lord."

When he returned home from his walk, he found Kara in bed, depressed, with the television turned on. Her thoughts were only remotely tuned into the program. He sat down on the bed beside her, but she only looked past him and stared blankly at the screen.

"Let's pray," he said.

"Why?"

"Because we need to."

"It doesn't do any good," she said. "I've tried."

Robert attempted to hold her hand but she pulled away. He said sternly, "Kara! You just have to let go and let God's will be done!"

Kara looked at Robert and said softly, "Just leave me alone, please."

•••

Joan realized there would be a huge hole in her heart after placement day. But she felt adoption would be the best choice for Hope and Faith, and so her plan all along had been to give Faith as little help as possible with the baby. In that way, Faith would begin to discover for herself the awesome responsibility of parenting and, consequently, would stick to her adoption plans. Her strategy was evident Faith's first day home with the child. When Faith complained, "I can't do this myself!" Joan simply answered, "That's why God intended children to have two parents!" But by Wednesday morning, Joan's heart had softened after a discussion with her husband.

"I'm not sure that keeping Hope another day is such a good idea," she said.

"What's the harm?" he said. "Faith knows what's best for the child. She'll go through with the adoption. But you have to realize that this is a very difficult time for her. She's been through a lot already. Of course, she's going to have doubts. Anyone in her position would. Just have a little faith in her."

"I guess you're right," Joan said with a sigh. "I just know that she's had some second thoughts and it makes me nervous."

After a hug, Joan marched off to relieve Faith of her duties. "Why don't you go to sleep in our room?" she said. "When the baby wakes up, I'll take care of her."

Faith slept until two in the afternoon. When she got up from her nap, she found her mother rocking the baby.

"How do you feel?" Joan asked as Faith sat down on the bed.

"Better. Much better!"

"That's good! A little rest will do wonders."

Hope suddenly injected a loud burp into the conversation. The women laughed and Faith added, "I bet she feels better, too!"

Joan held the baby face to face and began cooing and singing softly.

Faith smiled. She said, "I had a dream while I was sleeping."

"About what?"

"Well, I was talking to Hope. Hope Stuart that is."

Her mother nodded as if to say, "Go on!"

"It was odd in a way," Faith said. "We were just sitting next to the pool, talking like we always talked. We weren't emotional, or sad, or anything, even though we were both aware that she was dead."

"What did you talk about?"

"A few things," Faith said. "One was that she admitted she had made a bad decision. And I said, 'Yeah, really bad!' and we both laughed. Then she asked me if I changed my mind about the baby. And I said that I hadn't made up my mind yet. So she said, 'I'm not the one to ask for advice,' and we both laughed again, 'but,' she said, 'I think you ought to go through with the adoption.' When I asked her why, she said, 'I never had a father and I really needed one.' Then she said, 'Your baby needs a father.' And then I said, 'I think you're right. But I'm afraid to let her go.' And she asked me why, and I don't remember what I said exactly, but it was something like, 'I'm afraid of not being there to protect her.' But I remember what she said because it was so unlike her. She said, 'That's what faith is all about. Going out on a limb where you don't feel safe, and trusting God to take care of things.' And then we hugged each other."

Faith choked up and cried quietly for a moment. Joan stood up from the rocking chair and sat down on the bed next to Faith. She held the baby in one arm and wrapped her other arm around her daughter.

"There, there. It's okay!"

Faith said, "I know it's only a dream, but it was sure wonderful to see Hope again." Faith fought back her tears and wiped a few away with her hands. A few quiet moments passed before Joan asked, "How do you feel about Hope's advice?"

"I think she's right. I just have to trust God. But it's going to be hard handing Hope over to Kara—not that I don't trust her. I think she's going to be a great mother."

"Of course, it will be difficult," her mother said. "And you'll have many more times in your life where you have to stop clutching things so tightly and just open your hands to God and say, 'I'm willing to let You take over.' That's a true test of faith."

Faith looked down at Hope who was now fussing in her grandmother's arms. She said, "Some day I hope you understand that I'm giving you to Robert and Kara because I want what's best for you."

"I'm sure she'll know that," Joan said.

Faith looked at her mother as if to say, "How can I be assured of that?" Then she suggested, "Let's go shopping and splurge on Hope!"

"Are you sure you're up to that?"

"Sure. I can last for an hour anyway. I want to spoil Hope while I still have the chance!" she said with a smile.

"What about Hope? We can't take her with us," Joan said.

"Ryan will baby-sit."

"Do you trust her with him?" Joan said with a laugh.

"Sure. We won't be gone that long."

"Okay! Then I'd like to spoil my granddaughter, too!"

•••

Robert and Kara left the house before noon on Thursday. They were driving to the mall to exchange Christmas presents when Kara said, "I have a confession to make."

"About what?"

"About the way I've been behaving lately. You know, about not trusting God about this adoption."

Robert just smiled politely and nodded.

Kara said, "You were right when you yelled at me yesterday for not leaving things up to God."

"I don't think I was *yelling*, was I?"

"Well, maybe not, but you should have yelled," Kara said. "After I told you to leave me alone, I felt convicted about my lack of faith. So I went to the Bible and read about Abraham and Sarah. Do you realize that they waited twenty-four years for God to give them a son? I think I'm ready to trust God and leave it up to Him."

"I'm glad to hear you say that," Robert said.

The Ellisons returned home from their errands by mid-afternoon. As they entered the kitchen, Robert set their packages on the counter and pushed the "play" button on the answering machine.

"Hello. This is Maggie. I'm calling to let you know that Faith signed the surrender papers this morning. Can you meet at Rainbow tomorrow for placement? Give me a call back as soon as possible. Thank you."

Kara's jaw nearly dropped off her face. She looked at Robert. He flashed a broad smile. Then Kara shrieked, "Yeow!" and began jumping up and down until Robert grabbed her and gave her a bear hug. After a joyous laugh, he released his tight clutch and held his wife gently by the shoulders at arm's length.

"Why are you crying?" he asked.

Kara shook her head and said, "I have never been so happy in my whole life!"

Robert gathered Kara up in his arms gently this time and whispered, "Thank you, Lord!"

Faith's Gift   31

After Maggie's call, the Ellisons were bustling. There were many things to be done and less than a day to do them. Robert dismantled the bed in the guest room and hauled the mattress, box spring, and frame down to the basement. Then he set up the crib and changing table Kara borrowed from Sharon Huxtable. After that, he went to the family room and confiscated the antique wooden rocking chair and placed it in a corner of the baby's room. When he finished putting everything in order, he went to the kitchen and found his wife talking excitedly to her mother on the phone.

"Can you think of anything else we'll need?" Robert heard Kara ask her mother. After a quiet moment, she said, "No. We have a car seat. I got that from Sharon, too. Which reminds me, I ought to call her. She'll be excited to hear the news!"

After another quiet moment, Kara said, "I think we should be home tomorrow between twelve and one." Finally, a quick, "Okay. See ya!" and Kara was off the phone.

"Are you ready to go to the store?" she said to Robert.

"Am I ready?" he said with a smile. "The question is, are you ready? You look out of breath."

"I can't help it! I can't believe this is actually happening!" Kara said, her eyes sparkling.

Robert smiled and said, "I've got the baby's room set up."

Then he noticed a far away look in Kara's eyes. Suddenly she exclaimed, "We have to buy a gift for Faith!"

"Did you have anything in mind?"

"Some kind of jewelry would be nice. Or a nice frame for the baby's picture."

"Well, we'd better get going. It looks like you've got quite a list there."

On their way to the store, Robert said, "There's an important detail we haven't settled yet."

"What's that?"

"The baby's name."

"I know," Kara said with a sigh. "But it's so hard to decide!"

"Well, I've got a name that came to me as I was reading James."

"What is it?"

"Well, I think it fits the occasion."

"What is it?"

"Joy!" Robert said. "'Consider it pure joy, the verse says, whenever you face trials of many kinds.' Waiting for this child has been a trial. But now, it's all joy!"

Kara sat quietly for a moment. Robert shifted his eyes back and forth between the road and his wife, waiting for her response. Each time he looked at Kara, he could see her lips move ever so slightly. It was like she was tasting the name, playing with it on her palate, taking time to explore the flavor and to compare it with the other names under consideration. Finally, she said, "How about Joy Elizabeth? Joy Elizabeth Ellison!"

"It sounds nice, doesn't it?" Robert said with a smile.

•••

The Brandons were struggling late Thursday afternoon and evening. The joy over Hope's birth was countered by a quiet sadness, the kind of sadness that comes with the death of a friend or with saying a final goodbye to a loved one. And everyone who came to the house that afternoon and evening—Faith's grandparents, Aunt Kate and Uncle Vince, and a few friends, including Kris—-shared the same mixed emotions. But no one felt these emotions as deeply as Faith herself. Beneath the smiles, beyond the flashes of a thousand photographs, and behind all the cooing and fussing in front of the baby, resided the pain of the family and the woman soon to make a sacrificial gift.

There was some solace in knowing her gift would bring joy to a couple who had long suffered the pain of infertility. But most importantly, Faith realized that adoption would also be a generous gift to her child. Although there was the ever-present concern of how Hope would react when she would one day understand adoption, there was still the comfort of knowing that in her early life, she would have two parents, not one, lavishing love on her and caring for her needs.

That night, after rocking Hope to sleep, Faith sat on the edge of her bed and watched the peaceful rise and fall of the child's tiny chest as she lay in her crib. It reminded Faith of a summer evening years ago when she and her father sat quietly in a secluded setting on the shores of Lake Superior, watching the sunset and the ebb and flow of the waves washing up on the sandy shore. Her father's softly spoken words still echoed in her memory. He said, "It's an amazing creation, isn't it? I'm so thankful the Lord gave us life and was willing to share it with us."

Not long after the memory warmed Faith's heart, her father peeked in through the small crack in the doorway.

"Can I come in?" he whispered.

Faith nodded with a soft smile. Her father sat down on the bed and put his arm around her shoulder.

"She's beautiful, isn't she?" he whispered.

"Yes," Faith said as she leaned her head against his shoulder.

"You know I'm very proud of how you've handled this," he said.

Faith sighed. "It's not over yet. Tomorrow I'm going to be a basket case."

"You'll be fine," he said. "You just have to keep reminding yourself that you're making the best of a difficult situation. And it will hurt for a while, but you'll heal with time."

"I know. I'm more worried about Hope," Faith said as she looked down on her sleeping child.

"She'll be fine, too. You just have to trust the Lord. Do you remember what Jesus said about the sparrows?"

"Vaguely," Faith said sheepishly.

Her father smiled and said, "In Matthew 10:29, Jesus says, 'Are not two sparrows sold for a penny? Yet, not one of them will fall to the ground apart from the will of your Father.' If He watches over them, you can be sure He'll be watching over Hope."

Faith gazed up at her father and smiled. After a quiet moment, he kissed her good night and said, "Get some rest."

Faith tried to do as her father said, but she was too emotional to sleep. After an hour of tossing back and forth, she decided to make a final entry in her journal, which was sitting on top of her dresser. She quietly slipped out of bed and tiptoed to get it. When she discovered she had misplaced her pen, she groped through the top drawer of the dresser to find it. In her search, her fingers came across the rough edge of something small. She pulled the object out and examined it closely in the dim light filtering in from the hallway. She recognized it as part of the broken seashell she brought home from the Florida beach.

The horrifying memory of the knife being waved menacingly in her face sent a shiver up her spine. A wave of nausea swept over Faith as she relived the terror and helplessness of that dreadful night when the salty, humid air was thick with evil. Trembling, with tears running down her cheeks, Faith reached back into the drawer and found the other half of the broken shell. She lay down on the bed clutching the two broken pieces in her hands. Her haunting thoughts were ended a moment later by the baby's stirring in the crib. Faith jumped up, stood over her child, and gently caressed her back. Before long, Hope returned to a sound sleep.

Faith took the two broken shell pieces and held them up to the hall light. The pieces fit together beautifully. Despite its brokenness, the shell was reparable, just like Faith.

•••

Faith had a restless night, having to endure the interruption of two feedings as well as her high-pitched emotion. When she woke up Friday morning, she saw her mother standing at the changing table applying powder to the baby's bottom.

"Good morning!" Joan said as she was putting a new diaper on the baby. "How did you sleep?"

"Don't ask," Faith mumbled, exhausted.

"Well, just be thankful that last night was the last for that sort of thing." Faith grimaced in reply. She was still groggy and struggled to sit up in bed.

"Why don't you rest?" her mother said. "I'll take care of things."

Faith rubbed her eyes and then ran her fingers through her hair.

"No. I can sleep tomorrow," she said. "Or later today. I want to be there for Hope's last bottle, her last bath—"

"Her last diaper," her mother interjected.

Faith managed a smile. "No, that's okay. I'll leave that privilege to her grandmother."

"Thanks," Joan said, now feeding Hope a bottle. "What I'm going to miss is her first step, her first word, the first time she says grandma."

"Her prom night and her wedding day," Faith added. Then a river of tears started flowing, welling up from the torn hearts of the two women.

"What's going on?" Ryan asked as he poked his head in the room.

The women could only respond with an outpouring of grief over the imminent separation, now only hours away. On most occasions, a clever, teasing remark would have quickly popped off the top of Ryan's head. But today, even his heart was too heavy for sarcastic wit. As it was, he simply nodded sympathetically and headed down to the kitchen for breakfast.

When Joan regained her composure, she said to Faith, "Why don't you take a shower and then we can give Hope a bath. It would be nice to take a few more family pictures before we go."

The baby's bath and photo session devoured two rolls of film. There were solo shots, pictures of Hope with grandma and then grandpa, pictures of Hope with Ryan and then Faith, and finally, family shots. Compounding the madness was the necessity of recording every precious moment on videotape as well.

In the last moments before departing for the agency, Faith inserted photos of the family and a few of her own early childhood pictures into her journal. She planned to give the journal to Kara so that one day, at an appropriate age, Kara would share it with Hope.

Faith placed the journal in the bottom of a large shopping bag. On top of the journal, she packed the many gifts they bought at the mall the day before. Finally, she put one last special gift into the bag. The gift was wrapped in a small box with a card attached.

By nine-thirty, the car was packed and everyone was wrapped up in winter coats, ready to leave. It was moments like these that Dr. Brandon would bring the family together and lead it in prayer. But this time, after the family gathered in a semi-circle around the kitchen table with Hope bundled up in her tiny snowsuit and blanket and set in a little wicker basket in the middle of the table, Faith said, "I'll pray."

Her father smiled as the family joined hands. After taking a deep breath, Faith prayed in a trembling voice, "Dear Lord, I know Hope matters very much to You. So please take care of her and watch over her all the days of her life. Bless her and her new family. Most of all help her to know You and love You so that some day we may be reunited in heaven. We pray this in Your name. Amen."

"Amen," replied the others.

After a round of hugs mixed with tears, Dr. Brandon said, "It's time to go."

•••

"Okay! Do we have everything?" Robert asked before turning the ignition.
"I think so," Kara said. "Do we have the camera?"
"Yes."
"The camcorder?"
"Yes."
"The baby's car seat and diaper bag?"
"Yes."
"Faith's gift?"
Robert hesitated. Then he said, "I don't remember handling it."
Kara frowned and then laughed at herself. "Duh!" she said in a self-mocking tone. "I put it in the diaper bag."
Robert smiled. "Okay! I think we're ready."
Just as they were beginning their drive, Kara confessed, "I had another one of my dreams last night."
"What dreams?"
"The ones about my son."
"I'm sorry, Love."
"No, it was all right this time. It was different."
"In what way?"
Kara smiled sadly. She said, "The whole mood was different. I was sitting at the dinette table watching over Joy. It was summer time. It was a warm day and as I looked outside through the patio doors, I noticed a nice little sun shower going on. Then I noticed my son playing in the yard and I was worried he was going to get wet. I stuck my head out the door and yelled, 'You'd better come in now!'"

Kara smiled sadly again as she paused reflectively. Finally, she said, "He came toward me but he stopped at the edge of the patio. Then he said, 'I heard I have a sister.' And I said, 'Yes! Would you like to come in and see her?' He seemed to be disappointed and said, 'I can't. But I'll see her another day.' 'When?' I asked. And he said, 'Someday we'll all be together again.' I looked at him, probably very oddly, because I was confused. I asked him, 'How do you know that?' He said, 'Because I asked Him.'

Then he turned and began walking away and I shouted, 'Where are you going?' And he said, 'Back home.' That's when Jesus appeared. They were standing next to each other in the back yard in the middle of this sun shower, but neither one of them was getting wet. Jesus put His arms around my son and hugged him. Then He looked at me with these compassionate eyes and said, 'Be at peace. Your sins are forgiven.'"

Kara smiled sadly again. She had a far away look in her eyes.

"Then what happened?" Robert asked.

Kara looked at Robert with an embarrassed smile. She said, "They just walked away together. I called after them. I wanted them to come back, but they just kept walking. Then the alarm went off."

Robert reached over and stroked his wife gently on the thigh.

"Now do you feel forgiven?"

"Yes," she said. And Robert could see by the look in her eyes that, for the first time, she really believed it.

•••

The Brandons arrived at Rainbow Family Center at ten-fifteen. They met Maggie in the lobby and were led directly to the placement room. There they chatted quietly, waiting for the Ellisons to arrive.

"I guess this is it," Faith sighed as she held Hope in her arms and looked around the room. Opposite the door, a large bay window looked out over the front of the estate. Along one wall sat a large couch where Faith, holding the baby, took a seat next to her mother. Across the room stood a large oak desk. Four identical navy blue wing chairs were arranged in a semi-circle in the middle of the room in front of the couch. Dr. Brandon, Ryan, and Maggie sat on the wing chairs facing Faith and Joan.

The most significant piece of furniture, a white wicker bassinet, stood directly in front of the bay window. In most cases, the bassinet was merely symbolic. Only on rare occasions, when the birthmother was absent at placement, was the child actually placed in it to await its adoptive parents. But that would not be the case today.

Robert and Kara arrived promptly at ten-thirty. They were greeted by Terri Moore who had emerged from her office on the main floor just off the entry. She led them into her office and closed the door. The Ellisons sat in the two chairs in front of Terri's desk.

"You must be pretty excited," Terri said with a smile as she scooted her swivel chair closer to the desk.

"I've been on pins and needles," Kara admitted with a nervous smile.

"Me, too," Robert said.

"Good," Terri said. "This is the best part of adoption. Seeing the joy and anticipation on the faces of the adoptive parents."

"I hope it doesn't come across too strongly," Robert said. "This has to be really difficult for Faith and her family."

"You don't have to feel self-conscious about your happiness," Terri said.

"But we're the ones causing the pain," Kara said.

"It's not you; it's the situation that's causing the pain," Terri said. "But seeing your joy will be good for Faith."

"Why is that?" Robert asked.

"It will confirm to Faith how special her child is to you," Terri explained. "She'll feel confident that you're going to take special care her child. It will help her feel good about her decision."

Robert and Kara nodded. Then Terri said, "I know you're anxious to get upstairs, but first we have some last minute paperwork to do and papers to sign."

The formalities dragged on for fifteen minutes as Terri went over the remaining fees and explained each document before it was signed. It made Kara anxious to the point of distraction. She would have signed anything without examination just to get the paperwork over with. But Robert, in his meticulous way, listened intently and asked a few clarifying questions, much to the consternation of his wife.

At long last, Terri said, "That's it. I'll call Maggie and tell her you're ready."

The ringing phone awoke the baby from her nap. She frowned as if ready to cry. Faith gently rocked her back to sleep as Maggie got up from her chair and answered the phone. The Brandons heard Maggie say, "I'll be right down." She hung up the phone and announced, "Robert and Kara are ready. I'll go down and bring them up."

Faith nodded as she subconsciously tightened the embrace of her child. In a moment, Maggie returned with the Ellisons. Dr. Brandon and Ryan stood up to greet them, but Kara's eyes immediately turned to Faith and the baby.

Maggie said, "I think everyone has met, except for Ryan."

After Ryan stepped forward and shook hands with Robert and Kara, there was an awkward moment deciding what to do next. Then Joan took command. She stood up and said, "Here! I'll move over to this chair. Kara, why don't you and Robert sit on the couch next to Faith?"

When they were seated, Faith looked into Kara's eyes and offered, "Why don't you hold the baby?"

Kara's eyes welled up with tears as she accepted her child.

"Thank you," she said, barely able to whisper. "She's so beautiful!"

Prior to placement, Faith had imagined this moment as an emotional storm. But to her surprise, it was like being in the eye of a hurricane, and she felt the warmth and love of the Lord's presence. Kara, holding the baby in one arm, leaned over and hugged Faith with her free arm. Faith returned the hug.

"Thank you so much!" Kara whispered in Faith's ear, choking back her tears.

When the mothers loosened their embrace, they looked one another in the eye. Tears fell, even among the men, and a box of tissue was passed about.

As the emotion subsided, Joan asked, "What name did you choose for the baby?"

Kara wiped her eyes with her free hand and said, "Joy! Joy Elizabeth."

"How lovely!" Joan said.

"And fitting!" Dr. Brandon added.

Faith was offended by the new name. It was her child, named in honor of her best friend. To hear "Joy," instead of "Hope," was like hearing the screech of fingernails dragging down a chalkboard. But as the conversation grew around her, and the baby's new name was freely bandied about, Faith began to understand the beauty, significance, and appropriateness of her daughter's new name. And it began to warm her heart.

The two families talked for nearly forty-five minutes. The Brandons began by recounting the details of Christmas Eve, Faith's labor, and the experience in the birthing room. And everyone laughed at Dr. Brandon's reluctance to be in on the delivery. Then the conversation went round and round with more laughs and a few tears. When the time came to open gifts, Kara had the pleasure of opening Joy's presents. As she tried to undo the wrapping on the first package, the task proved to be too difficult while holding Joy.

"I'll hold the baby!" Joan said.

Joy received clothes and toys. There was also a children's Bible with an inscription inside the front cover. It read, "To Hope—get an early start on this book. Love, Grandpa Ryle and Grandma Joan."

Kara smiled at the inscription and promised, "I'll read her a little bit from this book every night."

When all but one of Joy's presents had been opened, examined, and graciously accepted by Kara, Faith held up the last gift—the small box with the card attached. She said quietly to Robert and Kara, "You can open this one later."

Then Kara reached into the diaper bag and offered a gift to Faith.

"Here," she said. "It's nothing compared to what you've done for us, but I hope it reminds you from time to time of the gift you've given us."

"Thank you," Faith said as she pulled a small, gold, heart-shaped locket and chain from its box. "It's beautiful!"

Kara quickly explained, "If you open it up, you can see there's a place to put Joy's picture."

"Thank you!" Faith said again. Then she leaned over to give Kara a hug.

At last, everyone sensed their time together was up. Dr. Brandon suggested, "Why don't we huddle around Joy for a family prayer?"

Joan gave Joy a kiss and, with a painful smile, handed the precious bundle to Kara. Kara received the baby from Joan but quickly turned and offered to Faith, "Would you like to hold her again?"

Faith was too choked up for words. She nodded and smiled bravely. She realized this would be the last time she would hold her daughter in her arms.

Robert said, "I'll pray."

They all joined hands except for Faith who was holding the baby. Instead of grasping Faith's hand, Kara wrapped her arm around Faith's waist. Joan did the same on the other side. They all bowed their heads as Robert began to pray.

"Lord, we thank You for this moment and for the special gift of life. We pray that You continue to bless Joy throughout her life. Please help us to be the kind of parents You want us to be. We also pray for Faith and her family that the pain of separation will heal quickly. Please give Faith the comfort she needs from You. We ask this in Your name. Amen."

With tears streaming down her cheeks, Faith raised Joy to her lips and gave her a last kiss.

"Good-bye. I love you!" she quietly uttered over the lump in her throat.

The other members of the family followed suit kissing Joy good-bye. With a final sigh, Faith handed Joy over to Kara who, like the others, was deeply moved and reduced to tears. Then Joan put her arm around her daughter, and with the help of her husband and son, escorted Faith from the room. Robert sighed deeply as he watched the Brandons leave.

"Wow!" he said after they disappeared through the doorway. "That was tough!"

Even Maggie had tears to wipe from her eyes. "It's always tough at first," she said. "But over time, Faith will heal."

"I hope so," Robert said.

Then Joy began to cry.

"What's wrong, little one?" Robert said as he tried to soothe his daughter by caressing her forehead.

"She probably needs her diaper changed," Kara said. "Do you want the honors of doing the first one?"

"Me? No! I'd better watch you do it first!"

Maggie laughed and said, "Don't worry, Robert. Before long, you'll be an expert!"

Then Kara said to Robert, "Here. You hold Joy while I get out a diaper."

"How?"

The women laughed. "It's easy!" Kara said. "Just hold out your arms and make sure you support her head."

"What if I drop her?" Robert asked with a nervous chuckle.

"Don't worry! You won't!" Kara said with a smile.

While Kara was changing Joy's diaper, Maggie said, "I'll give you a call in a couple of days to schedule a home visit. The nurse will also call to schedule a visit."

"Great!" Kara said.

Robert and Kara were soon in the parking lot securing their precious cargo into her car seat. Kara climbed into the back seat and began feeding Joy a bottle. As they drove home, Robert kept his eye on the rear view mirror to see what was happening in the back seat.

"I can't believe we're taking her home and that she's actually ours!" Kara said. Then reflecting on the placement meeting, she sighed and said, "I just can't imagine how difficult that was for Faith."

"It's a very selfless thing to do," Robert said. "It's 'love of another kind.'"

"What do you mean?"

"I mean this is no ordinary kind of love," he said. "You could see how much she loved Joy. Imagine going through a pregnancy and the pain of birth just to give your child to adoptive parents because you know it's best for the child. It's too heroic to be human. She had to be filled with the Lord's strength."

Kara looked down on her daughter who was busy sucking the last ounce of her bottle. She said, "Your birthmother is a very special person."

When the Ellisons arrived home, they were greeted by both sets of grandparents. After giving the grandparents a chance to fuss over the baby, Robert and Kara described the heart-wrenching placement. Then they showed off the gifts Joy received from Faith and her family. When they came to the last gift, Robert pulled the small box with the attached card out of the bag. He asked Kara, "Should we open this now?"

"I don't see why not."

Robert opened the box. "It's a seashell," he said as he held it up to the light. "And it looks like it's been broken and glued back together."

He handed the shell to his father and opened the card to find a separate note inside. First, he read the card out loud. It said:

Dear Hope,

Keep this shell with you always. When things get messed up and life is difficult, take out this shell and say a prayer. Have faith and always remember that God can fix anything. He can make even the worst situation turn out for the good. I will always be thinking of you and praying for you. I know God has a beautiful plan for your life.

It is painful to let you go, but I know that your life and happiness was/is worth my pain. I trust God will always protect you. I know that He loves you! May you always desire to stay close to Him!

I Love You,
Faith

Robert smiled at the card, dismissing it as a maudlin attempt by Faith to provide meaning to her ordeal. Then he said, "Here's a little note to go with it."

As he read the note aloud, the card's excessive sentimentality blossomed into a deeply touching message. It said:

To Robert and Kara—

Just so you know and can explain it to Hope later—I found this shell on the beach the night I was raped. When I found it, it was beautiful and unbroken. Then Hope's birthfather attacked me; the shell, which I had put in my pocket, was broken somehow. I came across it again last night as I was looking through one of my drawers. I don't know why I saved it, but I'm glad I did. Please keep it in a safe place until she's old enough to take care of it herself. Thanks!

Although I'm writing this ahead of time, I know I'll be a basket case at placement. I'm hurting now, but I want you to know that with God's grace, I'll be okay. If you think of me from time to time, give Hope a hug and a kiss for me and tell her that I love her. I know you'll be wonderful parents. May God bless you and our daughter!

—Faith

Results 32

When the Brandons arrived home from placement, Faith went directly to her room, closing the door behind her. She changed into sweats and lay down on the bed. She stared blankly at the ceiling thinking of all that had transpired in the nine months since her trip to Florida.

In one sense, her ordeal was over. But in another very real sense, it had only just begun. In a relatively short time span, she had lost three of the most important relationships in her life—Hope, Chris, and Joy. It was like coming home one day to discover your house burned to the ground. The foundation, God and family, would still be there, but there was an enormous amount of charred ruins that had to be cleaned up first before the rebuilding process could begin. And it was not going to be easy.

When Faith eventually turned on to her side and looked across the room, the empty crib brought tears to her eyes and she sobbed openly. The sorrow echoed through the house, disrupting the somber silence pervading the home since the baby's departure hours earlier. Dr. Brandon was sitting at the dinette table with his wife.

"I'll go up and comfort her," he said.

"No. Stay here," Joan said. "She needs to release her pain."

"Are you sure?"

"Yes. Don't worry. She'll fall asleep soon and that's what she needs most."

True to her mother's prediction, Faith soon cried herself to sleep. She woke up a few times during the night, but she did not leave her room until coming down for breakfast the next morning.

"Good morning," her father said.

"Hi," Faith mumbled as she shuffled to the table.

"How did you sleep?"

"All right."

Dr. Brandon forced a smile. Despite the long rest, Faith looked sapped of energy. Throughout the next few weeks, it would be the most glaring symptom of her lingering depression.

Her family was very understanding and tried to accommodate her in every way they could. At breakfast that first morning, for instance, Faith complained about the "awful reminders," referring to the crib, changing table, and rocking chair still in her room. Fortunately, it was the type of problem that could be solved easily.

"Your brother will go upstairs right away and take care of that for you," Joan said.

Ryan was sitting across the table from Faith. He was eating a bowl of cereal and watching the morning news. When his mother volunteered his services, he raised his eyes toward his mother and said, "I will?"

When his mother gave a reproving cough, he immediately caught the point and modified his tone. He said, "Of course, I will! As soon as I'm finished with breakfast."

But there were other problems that could not be solved so easily. Faith had bouts of depression and loneliness. She had relied so much on Hope and Chris for companionship that she had no other significant relationships to fall back on besides her own family. Who was she to turn to?

Her parents were sensitive to her dilemma. They were hoping the new term at school would get her back into a social flow, meeting new people and building new friendships. But to their chagrin, Faith began expressing doubts about school. Although they were tempted to rebuke her for "moping around the house," they turned their requests to heaven in prayer.

Then the first letter arrived from Kara. It had come through the agency since the adoption was only semi-open. Faith began by thumbing through the dozens of pictures of Joy and her new home and family. Then she eagerly poured over the enclosed letter:

Dear Faith,

We hope everything is going well with you and your family. We have been praying for your physical and emotional recovery. Robert and I want to thank you again for giving Joy the gift of life and for selecting us to be her parents. We feel very fortunate to have Joy as a part of our family. Rest assured that we are going to be the best parents we can possibly be.

She has been here a little over a week now and she's beginning to fit right in. Joy is getting used to us, and we are getting used to getting up in the middle of the night to feed her. She is going three to three-and-a-half hours between feedings. She wakes up twice during the night. I usually get up for the first feeding and Robert gets up for the second.

Joy has been a very good baby and seems healthy. She did have a little problem with constipation, but the doctor said to put a little Karo syrup in some of her bottles and that seems to have done the trick. She will be seeing the doctor on Friday for her check-up.

We have been receiving many visitors and going on many visits. Everyone thinks Joy is adorable!

I started back to school yesterday and I already hate it. I wish I could stay home, but it would be a real financial burden for us right now. Maybe in a year or two it will be different. I'm already looking forward to weekends, spring break, and summer vacation. It's just so hard leaving Joy at the sitter even though I know she's receiving great care.

The only thing that made the first day away from her bearable was the surprise shower put on by the gals at school. Robert was in on the whole thing and never said a word. He picked up Joy from the sitter and brought her to school. After the kids left for the day, one of the other teachers kept me occupied in my room for about fifteen minutes until they had everything decorated in the lounge and Robert had arrived. When they were ready, another teacher literally dragged me down to the lounge where everyone was waiting for the big surprise. I kind of suspected a shower was coming sometime, but I never imagined that they'd do it the first day back after vacation. Needless to say, I was very touched! For so long, I thought I'd never experience the joy of a baby shower thrown for me! Thank you again! This has happened for me all because of you!

May God truly bless you! Give our regards to your family.

With love,
Kara, Robert & Joy

P.S. Enclosed are some pictures for you to keep. Also, you should see all the nice gifts Joy received at the shower!

The letter and pictures warmed Faith's heart and helped put her mind at ease. When her mother finished reading the letter, Faith smiled and said, "I guess she's doing all right."

"It certainly sounds like it. But I expected as much. Joy is in good hands," Joan said.

Over the next two months, Faith received letters regularly from Kara and Robert. They arrived every week to ten days. Half the time, the letters included a new set of pictures, but they always included an update on Joy's health and progress along with another sincere thank you for the gift of life. In return, Faith would send a "thank you" for the pictures and a brief note on how she was doing. On the anniversary of the attack in Florida, Faith wrote this letter:

Dear Kara, Robert & Joy—

How is everyone doing? I trust this letter will reach you during your spring break. I hope the extra time together has been special. I think of you often & it gives me peace to imagine the love you have for Joy & she has for both of you.

God has really been blessing me. As I told you earlier in one of my cards, I have started back at school and I've had some really interesting classes and experiences. It has been a lot of work and it has given me a new focus. I need to be careful though so that I don't keep too busy that it keeps my mind off feelings. Balance is so hard.

I am sorry that I have not written sooner. Please do not think that the pictures don't mean a lot to me; they do. As a matter of fact, they mean everything to me! I really see over & over again that the decision I made was the right one. I see Joy so happy in the pictures and it is confirmed. I show them to everyone at school & in my family. I carry some around with me. Everyone watches her grow. And *everyone* comments on how beautiful & happy she is. I agree with them. I'm sure she makes you as proud of her as I am. Thank you so much for the pictures. I hope it isn't too much trouble for you to send them.

God has really been blessing me. He is faithful. He has brought special Christian people into my life to walk with me during this time. He has also taught me tremendous lessons in the last year. Although painful at times, they are lifetime lessons a lot of people will never learn. One thing I have learned is that God doesn't give us anything we can't handle without showing us a way out. Thanks God! He is really showing me ways out of all my weaknesses.

I dream a lot of what my family would be like some day, & I hope it will be like yours. Through you and through my parents and others, I am really beginning to see how important it is to have a spouse who shares your faith. I guess my first task is to find a good Christian man. Although I'm not in a rush to find one and have not really been looking, I seem to have met an "interesting" guy at school. We have been dating a couple of weeks now and I still hesitate to call him a boyfriend. But, I'm beginning to like him more and more. His name is Don and he's really cute. He's a sophomore and a wrestler. Like me, he wants to be a teacher (or a missionary—God forbid!). I was afraid that when I told him about Joy, he would lose interest in me. But, he said he already knew about it and that it didn't matter. (It's true what they say about small towns and small colleges. Everybody does know everybody else's business!) Actually, he said he really respected me for the decision I made. Why didn't somebody tell me there were guys like Don when I was making my decision? It would have made things a whole lot easier!

Please tell your bundle of joy (excuse the pun) how much I love her.

Love you all—
Faith

•••

The last day of school in early June fell on a Monday. The sun was shining brightly and there was hardly a wisp of a cloud in the sky when the loaded buses pulled away for the last time. Kara waved her final good-bye from the sidewalk. As she turned to walk back into the building, Kara ran into Sharon Huxtable once again, exactly as she had the year before.

"Well, can you believe it? Another year has come and gone!" Sharon said.
"It is hard to imagine, isn't it?" Kara said.

"Of course, things are different now than they were a year ago," Sharon said.

"What do you mean?"

"How quickly we forget!" Sharon said with a laugh. "Don't you remember our little talk last June about adoption?"

"Oh, yes! Of course!" Kara said smiling.

"Didn't I tell you things would work out?"

"I guess they have, haven't they?"

"Ye of little faith!" Sharon teased. "How's the little one doing?"

"She's doing great! And this afternoon, we have our first post-placement meeting with the birthmother!"

"Really? That's wonderful! I bet she's looking forward to it."

"I'm sure," Kara said.

"Doesn't it bother you, though? I mean, don't you worry about having contact with the birthmother?" Sharon asked.

"No. Why should it? It's the least we can do."

"Well, you know. There's been so much in the news about Baby Jessica and Baby Richard. Doesn't it make you nervous?"

"Not really," Kara said. "Those are isolated cases."

"Yes, but still. Any kind of openness would be unsettling to me."

"I felt that way at first," Kara said. "But the more communication we've had with Faith, the more secure Robert and I have felt about our relationship with her. We feel it's possible that one day we'll have a totally open relationship."

"Wow! That would be great! But I'd still be worried."

"Well, we're still praying about it. Maybe after our meeting today, we'll have a better idea of where we'll want to go from here," Kara said.

"Good luck with it. Give me a call sometime and let me know how it went."

"All right, I'll do that."

•••

The post-placement meeting went well from the start. The two families pulled into the parking lot at the same time and met as they were getting out of their cars. The lively discussion gradually moved indoors to the placement room where Joy, as expected, was the center of attention. The Brandons each took turns holding Joy and having their picture taken with her. When they finally set Joy on the carpet, she continued to hog the spotlight. At one point, she pulled herself up on the furniture and smiled as if to say, "Am I not the cutest child you've ever seen?" To her biased audience, it was a fact.

As Kara opened Joy's presents, she said to Faith, "Thank you for the Mother's Day card."

"Thank you for the flowers!" Faith replied. "Which reminds me," Faith added as she reached into her purse. "Here is a card for you, Robert!"

"My first Father's Day card. Thank you very much!" he said.

"You're welcome," Faith said with a smile. "Have you discussed adopting another child?"

"Yes, we have," Kara said. "We thought we'd submit our application when Joy is fifteen months. That way she'd be between eighteen months and two years old when her sibling arrived."

"If we're that fortunate," Robert added with a smile.

"Are you going to adopt through Rainbow again?" Joan asked.

"Yes. We'll be applying through the same program," Robert said.

"That's great! We'll be praying for you," Dr. Brandon said.

"Request a girl," Faith advised as she stole a glance at her brother to make sure he was listening. "Brothers can be a pain!"

Ryan smiled wryly and retorted, "That sounds rather odd coming from a sister who worships the ground I walk on."

"Yeah, right," Faith replied sarcastically. Then she picked up Joy and, with a smile, advised her, "If you ever have a brother, let him know who's in charge. I did and it worked for me."

Everyone laughed. After nearly two hours, the reunion came to a close. The two families, now joined together by a common link, gathered together in prayer. Unlike placement day, this meeting ended not with a sense of abandonment, guilt, regret, anxiety, bitterness, despair, or sorrow. Rather, there was a sense of connectedness, fulfillment, optimism, hope, and love.

On the drive home, Kara said to Robert, "I think things went well, don't you?"

Robert smiled and said, "Yes, very well."

The Liberated 33

The months passed quickly for Faith. College life kept her busy, even during the summer when she took classes to make up for her "lost semester." Throughout the summer and fall, Faith kept up her correspondence with Kara. They even arranged another meeting, a picnic away from the agency. The contact with Joy and her adoptive parents freed Faith of the guilt and anxiety that had plagued her throughout her ordeal. Faith's relationship with Don also grew, and it lifted the romantic fog surrounding her feelings for Chris. In the liberating perspective of retrospect, Faith could now see Chris for what he was—vain, self-centered, and spiritually lost. However, there was still one very significant relationship she sorely missed.

In early November on the anniversary of Hope's death, Faith went to the cemetery with a bouquet of flowers. The sky was an ominous gray. The wind was the blustery bone-chilling kind; yet only an occasional mist escaped the clouds. Faith knelt down next to Hope's gravestone and read the name and dates, sighing at the sad irony. With teary eyes, she looked up at a tall oak tree standing nearby. The few remaining rusty brown leaves rustled in the howling wind. The leaves were clinging desperately to the limbs that had supported them in greener times and fairer weather. The stubbornness of the leaves made Faith reflect on how people can be much the same way. Even at the end of their days, the dried up, weather beaten leaves would not let go and allow themselves the freedom to test the wind and the faith to trust in the Author of nature.

All of a sudden, Faith was startled by a familiar voice from behind. It said, "I wondered if I would find you here today."

Faith turned quickly to find Vivian approaching with her own small bouquet.

"Hi, Faith," she said warmly. "It's so good to see you again."

Vivian knelt down next to Faith who sighed again and said with a half-hearted smile, "Hi, Mrs. Stuart."

"How are things going for you these days?" Vivian asked.

"Pretty well, I guess."

"That's good," Vivian said with a sad smile. Then she admitted sheepishly, "I got your birth announcement. I was really touched to see that you named your child after Hope. I wanted to call you or even write a note and thank you, but it was such a difficult thing to bring myself to do. You two were so close. Then I just got busy in Washington. I'm sorry. I should have made a better effort. I hope you understand."

Faith looked deeply into Vivian's eyes and saw the reflection of her own pain.

"I understand," she said.

Vivian looked down at Hope's grave and smiled with a deep sadness in her eyes. She said, "I never imagined anything like this would ever happen. This sort of thing is only supposed to happen to other people."

Faith nodded sadly. After a long, silent moment Vivian said, "I've tried to figure this thing out—life and death, that is. You know I've never been a religious person. But, I keep reflecting on what your father said at Hope's funeral. And the conclusion I keep coming to is that unless there is a God, there's no meaning to any of this. That really bothers me."

Vivian paused for a moment. Finally, she said, "I've been thinking about God lately. I've been asking myself, 'Is God real? And if He is real, how do you know?'"

Vivian stared down in silence at Hope's grave. Faith knew the silence was prompting her for a response, but she was at a loss. Then suddenly, a strong spiritual impulse gripped her. She said, "I never have gotten into all of the theological stuff my brother and father seem to enjoy. I just accept what Dad says. He says that you can't prove or disprove the existence of God—not with any philosophical arguments or any scientific evidence. God is kind of like the wind. You can't see it, but you can feel it, and you can see its effects. Faith is a spiritual thing. When I sit down and read the Bible, I can *feel* its truth. I feel like God is speaking directly to me. Maybe if you just let go of your doubts and start reading the gospel with an open mind and an open heart, God will speak to you like I've felt He's spoken to me."

Vivian looked longingly into Faith's eyes and truly desired the spiritual riches Faith had stored away in her heart. Vivian nodded silently. Then she smiled, as if embarrassed, and confessed, "I'm not sure that I have a Bible."

Faith smiled gently and said, "There's one in our car. I think it's one of my mother's. But I'm sure she'd be glad to let you have it."

"Thanks," Vivian said. "I would appreciate that."

•••

Just days after Vivian met Faith in the cemetery, an attempt was made on her brother's life. A sniper had taken a shot at him from long range as he was walking from his car to the clinic's back entrance. The wound in his shoulder was not serious, but the shot was meant to kill. When Vivian first heard of the shooting, she called Tom and talked to him for the first time since Hope's death.

"Why don't you get out of the abortion business, Tom?" she pleaded.

"I can't," he replied.

"Why not?"

"Because I can't afford to go back to general practice after the way Beth screwed me in the settlement."

"Is the money that great that you'd risk your life over it?"

"Yes," he replied tersely.

Vivian had not talked to her brother since.

Over the next several months, she found herself gently guided toward the light of Christ through scripture and Christian relationships. The spiritual awakening produced a personal political dissonance. Up till then, her stand on each issue had been the result of a secular humanist viewpoint combined with the practical politics of public opinion polls. But now, a developing Christian perspective provoked a series of inner struggles. Many of the great moral and social debates going on in the halls of Congress were raging in her own heart and soul. And the foremost issue tugging at her spirit involved her stand on abortion. Unfortunately, her growing sympathy for the pro-life movement came at a time when her re-election campaign was just getting underway.

The spiritual and moral challenge was clear, and she did not relish it. It was time for her to stand up to evil and reverse her stand on abortion. Her opportunity came at a women's rights convention in Washington. She was invited to speak at the opening breakfast meeting.

Vivian hardly touched her plate that morning. She prayed inwardly, instead, while going over notes prepared the night before. Her anxiety, however, did not escape the notice of the woman sitting beside her at the head table. The woman remarked, "Are you all right, Vivian? You seem quite ill at ease."

Vivian flashed an embarrassed smile. She said, "Let's just say I know what Esther felt like when she was waiting for her audience with the king."

"I don't understand," the woman said with a puzzled look.

"Never mind. It's a long story."

A few minutes later, her time had come. Vivian was given a flattering introduction as a champion of women's rights, making matters all the more difficult. She rose from her chair and approached the lectern. While accepting the applause, she whispered to herself, "Well, here it goes! If I perish, I perish."

"Good morning," she said. "I have to begin my talk today with a confession."

The opening line captivated the audience. Her solemn tone and grave countenance signaled a significant announcement in the offing. Those who were eating stopped suddenly and quietly put down their utensils. The hum of small talk faded and silence filled the room. Vivian had their undivided attention.

"I've come here this morning under false pretenses although my intentions were quite honorable when I accepted your invitation to speak several months ago.

"I have always considered myself to be a liberated woman, as I know many of you consider yourselves to be liberated. In the past, I have staunchly defended those rights which I understood to be critical in the lives of women. And, to be honest with you, I still feel that way. I believe we must carefully protect and defend those rights that are truly ours. However, I am taking this opportunity this morning to tell you, and to announce to the whole world, that my perspectives on life have radically changed in the last few months."

Vivian smiled. Her opening remarks had her audience riveted to every word, and the subtle body language fastened their attention ever more securely.

"In recent years," she continued, "we have heard about a lot of people and groups, 'coming out of the closet,' so to speak. Well, today it's my turn to come out of the closet. Over the last several months, I have had a dramatic life change. I have been 'born again.'"

Vivian's speech had come out easily at first. But these last words had given her more difficulty than she had imagined. Saying the words "born again" in front of hundreds of peers and followers reminded her of her own past feelings of derision for the speaker whenever the phrase was invoked. From her present perspective, she understood the truly liberating effect of the grace and love of Christ. But she realized, far too well, that the Christian perspective was no longer common in many of the circles in which she found herself in Washington. Hence, she felt like she was out on a dogmatic limb. For the blink of an eye, her spiritual strength faltered as she realized that most of the women in her audience understood liberation only in the worldly political sense. Then the passage from Matthew 5:18-20 came to mind. "On my account, you will be brought before governors and kings as witnesses to them and to the Gentiles. But when they arrest you, do not worry about what to say or how to say it. At that time, you will be given what to say, for it will not be you speaking, but the Spirit of your Father speaking through you." And the words gave Vivian the strength to continue boldly.

"Yes, you heard me correctly. I said I've been born again. I have become a follower of Jesus Christ. In the past, I had always considered myself a liberated woman. I now know the truth. That is, I know I can only be liberated if I am liberated in Christ and follow where He leads. Some of you women here today know what that means. Many of you, however, do not know. So let me explain it to you as best I know how.

"Being liberated in Christ not only means I'm free from the bondage of sin, it means I understand that my value or worth as a human being does not correlate to my power, or wealth, or vocation, or social position. My value is always priceless, no matter what, from the womb to the grave and for all eternity, just because I matter to God and He loves me and values me.

"Our mistake, as politically active women, as I see it, is that we have been overzealous in our defense of women's rights. Now, don't misunderstand me. I still strongly believe that women deserve, and must fight to protect, the same political and economic rights and opportunities that men have always enjoyed. On the other hand, I also believe that we cannot ruthlessly chase equality by denying the gift God gave us as women.

"Ladies! This may come as a shock to some of you although it is something quite obvious. But I feel I have to say it. It is simply this. *We are not men.* We should not aspire to be men or to be just like men. We are neither above nor beneath men. We are partners with men in God's creation. And we have been made special. God has given us a wonderful privilege and commission. He has given us the power to create life—to create others in His image. It is a very significant part of the wonder of His creation."

Vivian paused and took a moment to look into the eyes of several of the women present. After a big sigh, she continued.

"I say this to you today because I believe in recent decades, we, as women, and we, as a nation have been misled. We have come to view the gift of motherhood as something of a burden, or obstacle."

After another short pause, she came to the most difficult part of her speech. She said, "As a mother who has lost a child…"

As soon as these last words passed her lips, Vivian became choked with emotion. Bravely holding back tears, she reached for a glass of water and took a sip as she regained her composure.

"As a mother who has lost a child and a grandchild, I know how precious life is. It is God's supreme gift. Not only has He given all of us the gift of life, He has given us the power to multiply that gift and share it with our children.

"And so I want to address an issue that we in the women's movement have held to be a *necessary* part of our quest for power and equality. That issue, of course, is abortion. And as you know, it is an issue that is beginning to tear at the seams of our society.

"We must begin to understand that abortion is not a women's issue," she said. Then she added with emphasis, "Let me repeat that. *Abortion is not about women's rights.* How can it be when half of those who are aborted are women? The truth is, *abortion is a moral issue.* It is an issue of good versus evil. It is an issue in which our judgment has been befuddled by deceit. In our lust for power, we have embraced abortion in a way that transcends a just quest for equality between the sexes. In our society, fathers cannot choose to end a life by abortion; only mothers can. In that way, we have made ourselves superior to men. And, since decisions of life and death belong in the hands of God alone, we have to be honest enough to admit that *we have not been striving to be equal with men, but rather, we have been striving to be equal with God.*"

Vivian took another short moment to reflect. She bowed her head and folded her hands on the lectern, almost as if in prayer. Then she said, "Let me tell you a story I read the other day. It's a story we're all familiar with. But allow me to read a few short excerpts from the original text to refresh your memory. The story is found in the Book of Genesis."

Vivian read from her notes:

> And the Lord God commanded the man, "You are free to eat from any tree in the garden; but you must not eat from the tree of knowledge of good and evil, for when you eat of it you will surely die."
> Now the serpent was more crafty than any of the wild animals the Lord God had made. He said to the woman, "Did God really say, 'You must not eat from any tree in the garden?'"
> The woman said to the serpent, "We may eat from the trees in the garden, but God did say, 'You must not eat fruit from the tree that is in the middle of the garden, and you must not touch it, or you will die.'"
> "You will not surely die," the serpent said to the woman. "For God knows that when you eat of it, your eyes will be opened, and you will be like God, knowing good and evil."
> When the woman saw that the fruit of the tree was good for food and pleasing to the eye, and also desirable for gaining wisdom, she took some and ate it. She also gave some to her husband and he ate it.

Vivian looked up from her notes, nodded with a confident smile, and said, "This is an old story but it has some modern parallels. Here in America in recent decades, we have been offered an apple. Foolishly, we fell for the deception and ate it. Why? Because, on the issue of abortion, we wanted to be like God, knowing good and evil. We bought into the big lie that it was our right to choose between life and death for the unborn, even though God clearly commands, 'Thou shalt not kill.' And we continue to cling to the lie that abortion is not murder, that it is simply our 'right to choose.' But we are only fooling ourselves. Like Adam and Eve, we have been judged and banished from Paradise.

"As you look around our nation today, you can see how we are experiencing the fallout from our choice to permit abortion. Because we do not value life, we have not only killed untold millions in abortion clinics, but we are seeing more and more episodes of senseless violence in our homes, in our schools, and in our streets. Why? Because life is cheap—cheap enough that we callously sacrifice thousands of innocent lives every day on the altars of greed, feminism, and self-centeredness. As a result, a generation of Americans has grown up and become desensitized to the value of life. After all, if a mother can kill her own child, life must not be a dear thing or a thing to be respected."

Then with fire in her eyes, Vivian admonished the crowd saying, "Don't you realize what we're doing? By advocating abortion on demand, we mock God's precious gift! Yet Galatians 6:7-8 says, 'Do not be deceived: God cannot be mocked. A man reaps what he sows. The one who sows to please his sinful nature, from that nature will reap destruction.'"

Vivian took a moment to search the eyes of her listeners. Although many in the audience were not sympathetic to her views, there were just as many that felt the reproof of her message and the sting of her glance. She had, in effect, made them open their own eyes and, like Eve, realize they were naked before God.

With melancholy in her eyes and voice, she asked, "Women! What are we afraid of in protecting the lives of the unborn and valuing the lives of all of our children? Don't you see that it is not inconsistent to be pro-woman and pro-life? In fact, *choosing life is the truly liberated choice!* We should continue to press for equal rights and equal opportunities. But we should not demand the right to take the life of the unborn child. God did not abdicate that right to men, and neither did He surrender that right to women. The right to take human life is a right that God gives to no one."

Vivian searched the faces of her audience one last time. Finally, she stepped down from the podium and marched silently out of the deathly still room. She did not know the effect her message had on those listening, but she felt a burden lifted from her shoulders. She had at last faced the Truth about herself and about God, and the Truth had set her free.